Andrzej Stasiuk, born in 1960, is one of the most interesting writers to have emerged in post-communist Poland. As poet, playwright literary critic and publisher, Stasiuk is both versatile and prolific. Born in Warsaw into a working-class family, he was expelled from his vocational school. Conscripted for his national service during martial law, he deserted the army. Caught, he spent the next year and a half in prison, later detailing the experience in *The Walls of Hebron*, a collection of stunning short stories about life inside.

Feeling always an outsider, Stasiuk moved into an abandoned house in a remote mountain village on the Ukrainian border in south-eastern Poland, where he continued to write away from the literary establishment, supporting himself and his family by breeding llamas. His next book was a collection of poetry, *Poems About Love and Not*, followed by *White Raven* which won him the prestigious Kultura and Koscielski literary prizes. The novel, later turned into a feature film, made Stasiuk into a writer of national status. The success of *White Raven* was followed quickly by *Galician Tales*, an unusual portrait of the neglected rural community, told as a series of evocative prose ballads.

With nine books – stories, plays, poetry and novels – to his credit and his own publishing house, Stasiuk has become a fixture in the Polish literary firmament. He also writes regularly for Poland's leading papers and literary magazines. *White Raven* has been translated into Dutch, Finnish, German, as well as English.

White Raven

Andrzej Stasiuk

Translated by Wiesiek Powaga

The publishers have received support for this publication from
the Ariane programme (1999) of the European Community

Library of Congress Catalog Card Number: 00-102182

A complete catalogue record for this book can be
obtained from the British Library on request

First published by Obserwator, Poznań, 1995 as *Biaty Kruk*

First published in 2000 by Serpent's Tail,
4 Blackstock Mews,
London N4 2BT

Website: www.serpentstail.com

Typeset in 10.5 Ehrhardt by
Avon DataSet Ltd, Bidford on Avon, B50 4JH
www.avondataset.com

Printed in Great Britain by
Mackays of Chatham plc, Chatham, Kent

10 9 8 7 6 5 4 3 2 1

Chapter 1

"What a fucking mess," said Bandurko, stuck to his waist in slushy snow. All he could do was to start digging himself out.

It was early February and we got a bloody thaw. We'd been wading in snow for hours, getting soaked to the balls. It wouldn't be so bad if the snow were a bit firmer, but it wasn't. The south-westerly wind blew hard, and every step meant a knee-deep hole with water sloshing underneath. The woods boomed above our heads without let-up, and this alone could drive anyone mad. We were halfway up the third mountain. Bandurko said it was a good short cut: even stray dogs didn't stray here. He was right about that. But not about the short cut. I was keeping my mouth shut but I was sure we were lost. That thaw was making a hell of a noise. To the boom above was added the sound of streams gushing through even the smallest valleys. The water was turbid, freezing cold, and the same everywhere.

When everything is frozen still, when it's quiet, the brain works better. I observed Bandurko as his head turned nervously in every direction. He claimed he knew the area well, so he should be pushing ahead like a blinkered horse. But we seemed to have got inside some kind of a massive mill, or a nightmare city of thousands of crossroads, each a wrong turn. Yes, that beech wood boomed like a mill. Roared and crashed. I wasn't hungry or thirsty; all I wanted was to go deaf, at least for a moment. Not a flake of snow on branches, everything bent in a motionless tension, giving to the southerly wind.

My eyes rested on Bandurko's buttocks, working rhythmically in tight, green drill trousers – an element of stability in the surrounding chaos – and pushing forward. We didn't fancy a night in the woods. With no food, no dry clothes to change into. We had three hours before it got dark.

When we reached the top of the ridge I said:

"All right, let's take five and have a smoke."

Bandurko looked around as if the view could have offered anything new. Then he pushed the snow off the trunk of a fallen tree and sat down.

"I don't know. I've done this route twice, but it was summer. One could see paths, trails, something."

I took out a packet of cigarettes. It was soaked through, hard to say whether with water or sweat. I thought of a cigarette case. Having a bit of metal about the person helps to face the world. Bandurko took a cigarette, but the moment he put it in his mouth the paper disintegrated and he was left with a little white fan fluttering at his lips. I dug out from the packet another, healthier-looking cigarette. The third match struck lucky.

"Not a ray of sunshine. We can't tell which way is north, south or whatever."

"Moss," I said.

"What moss?"

"On the tree trunks."

But we didn't even feel like laughing. We were cold. Bandurko took off his black woolly hat and scratched his head. His yellow hair was stuck flat to his skull. With a pink round face he looked like Piglet, a very bothered Piglet. He had bags under his eyes like pools of shadow, though the light was milky and dispersed, like during those white nights in Petersburg.

"Czetwiertne should be somewhere there," he said and nodded towards the nearest trees.

"It should be. Unless we're going in circles or coming to it from the other side. It should be left of the mountain-top, on the north side."

"What mountain?"

"This mountain."

"But we've already climbed several mountains."

"Those were just smaller crowns of the same mountain. We've been walking along the ridge."

I thought I'd better keep quiet. It was his idea. I had none. Apparently there was no other way. We even got off the bus two stops earlier, at the hostel. The bus went on, but at the end of the line, in the village, where the old state farm used to be, everyone knew everyone and we didn't want to make ourselves conspicuous. So we got off at the hostel, just as any bunch of tourists would, and having passed the old wooden building with a rusting roof we entered the wall of forest. The road was well used by the sleighs, but after a few hundred metres Bandurko told us to turn right.

"Well, we could carry on along this road, but a few kilometres later there's a village, and we would have to march right through it. And you know these villages – five houses and five heads in every window. We can't risk it."

So we turned into a clearing. In the wet snow there were footsteps of rubber boots. That must have been the way lumberjacks took to work. But then the clearing disappeared and the forest barred our way. The last open vista was that of the hostel, far away in the valley. A tiny house against the vast expanse of white. A thread of smoke rose from the chimney; someone was filling red buckets with water from a nearby stream. We hoped that from now on we wouldn't see a soul.

The forest climbed up the mountain and we raced it, overtaking firs and beech trees. Bandurko walked fast and with confidence, as if guided by a path or an instinct. I could hardly keep up. We called the first stop after an hour, when the slope changed into a top and the wind became twice as loud. We didn't feel like sitting down. We didn't feel like smoking either, but we did. The cigarettes had a weird, kind of windy flavour, and they burned unevenly, sending off sparks and glowing flakes of paper.

"Did you hear that?" said Bandurko, and in a nonsensical gesture put his finger to his lips.

"No."

"The Czetwiertne dogs."

In an equally nonsensical gesture I put my hand to my ear and maybe even heard something, but it could have been a falling branch, a figment of my imagination or fear of the empty forest, so empty even dogs wouldn't live in it. Bandurko threw his cigarette into the snow and got up.

"Let's go." And he walked off as if he'd just got up from a park bench.

After a while the old beech wood grew thinner, then smaller, and then it disappeared completely. The flat top was covered by puny willows and birch trees. A few gnarled and stunted pine trees were clawing at the air with the same tenacity as their roots at the ground. Here and there stood huge rotting firs, like pillars of a nonexistent nave. Their trunks had holes whistling with the wind. It must have been a woodpeckers' paradise, I thought.

"They really went for it," said Bandurko. "Shame they didn't know how to finish it properly."

The trees on the ground were not felled by the wind. From under the thawing snow protruded neatly cut trunks. It looked a bit like one of those morgues in the movies: bodies heaped higgledy-piggledy one over the other, intertwined, still, with worm-eaten innards and rotten, flaking skin. It took us ages to get over them. The slash looked like a great amphitheatre. The warm wind revealed stumps; one could climb to the top of the auditorium, sit down and watch the changing landscape: stretches of white replaced by the emerging black and grey. Bloody slow spectacle.

The forest disappeared and we finally felt we were in the mountains. On the left and on the right the horizon bordered with the sky – grey, angry and hurried.

"It could be the top of Ickowa," said Vasyl Bandurko.

"Ickowa. I remember it was shaven on the top like this. On a good day you could see Pisany Vrh."

"What?"

"*Vrh*. It's 'mountain' in Slovakian, and it's a Slovakian mountain."

Bandurko slowed down as if trying to find this *vrh*. But then he said, "Either way, we don't know where we are."

"I didn't know from the beginning."

"All right, then. Let's say this is Ickowa. As soon as we've passed the logging we turn left and go all the way down into the valley. There should be a stream, a big stream. We'll follow it. We should make it before night."

Chapter 2

I was staring at the black face of the watch. The reflection of red flames flickered on it, giving an impression of motion. But the golden hands stood still. Only the seconds were struggling in an effort to deal with the night. It was nearly twelve. From time to time I would fall into a kind of slumber, but it wasn't proper sleep. Thoughts didn't have enough weight to gel into images. I couldn't go with their flow and put my faith in them, the way one does with dreams. Bandurko lay on the other side of the bonfire, probably asleep. Head resting on a log, hands on his stomach, he breathed slowly and rhythmically. His face was still and peaceful. His steaming trousers must have been getting too hot for him for now and again he moved his legs.

I lay on my side and moved my knees closer to the fire. The idea was to get dry and stop shaking.

It was no Ickowa. Bandurko had to have something to hold on to, so he came up with this name. After all, one needs to use names even when lost. We passed the clearing, went down the slope covered with young pines and then we saw the stream. But Bandurko was not sure.

"Looks small. And flows the wrong way. It should flow to the right. But it flows to the left . . ."

Yellow, turbid water rushed at our feet and we stared into the current, which insisted on flowing up itself. At the bottom of the ravine the darkness thickened so much that our faces lost all their features. We looked like clay podges, mud creatures, brittle as everything around us, like that precipitous bank from which now and again tumbled down big lumps of earth.

"We should cross the stream and climb the slope."

"Fine," I said and slid down on my ass straight into the murky water. It was just above knee level, a bit deeper in the middle.

Before we could get out of it we had to follow the stream for a good fifty metres as the opposite bank turned out to be a wall of clay.

Half an hour later we were on top of it.

"Fucking winter," mumbled Bandurko. "It will be dark soon."

The wood began to grow thin. We no longer tripped over felled or windfallen trees. Fields of blackberries were replaced by smooth sheets of snow, broken here and there by a solitary juniper bush, as if waiting for us. And then the blackness and the greyness disappeared. We entered whiteness in 3-D. Even if it wasn't pure whiteness it was material, tactile. The slope rolled away gently as we waded through a milky suspension, a giant candyfloss, an icy sauna.

When I was ten, steam engines were all black and only their big sprocket wheels were red. We lived near the railway tracks. Passing freight trains made our house shake, sending clouds of flour-like dust from the ceiling. The noise wasn't too bad, as we were fenced from the tracks by a line of birch wood. If I wanted to see a train, I had to go for a walk. Best was a walk to the station – two brown gravel platforms and a little wooden hut painted green. The brown of the gravel, the green of the paint, the black and red of the locomotives . . . Come to think of it, some of them weren't black but dark olive-grey . . .

On that little station, the last in the chain of musty little stations called Warsaw-this or Warsaw-that, only slow trains stopped. Yes, it was their trains that had olive locomotives. Freight and fast trains had black ones. The thing to do was to go to the end of the platform, stand on its very edge and wait for the great cloud of steam to emerge from under the machine's greasy belly and swallow me up. I felt its warm, furry touch on my face. It smelled of oil, coal, smoke, hot metal and of something else, probably the stuff they treat railway sleepers with. I imagined that's how it must have been in heaven, up in the clouds, that's what it must have been like for the angels, which I saw on the blue ceiling in the church one station down the line. The devil-like driver looked on my ascension from his little window, and if he happened to be waiting for a semaphore and in a good mood he would send out more clouds.

But what we were going through on that slope was more like

purgatory, a mean, northern, Slavic Elysium, a rarefied solution of cold, damp and twilight.

With dusk came frost. The surface snow hardened into a crackly glaze, and we rolled down the slope with a dry, insect-like crunch. Bandurko crushed through first, and I tried to follow his trail.

"Down there! I can see something!" he shouted against the wind, his words barely audible as they flew past.

Out of grey darkness emerged a wall and a tall steep roof.

"It's a hut."

"A hut? Would that be an African hut, Vasyl? Or an Indian pueblo?"

"A *kolkhoz* hut. They had sheep pastures around here. I know where we are. More or less."

The door hung on one hinge. Inside was filled with a rank smell of rotting rags. But it was windproof. The wind banged on the walls and the roof but failed to get inside except for an occasional high-pitched whistle. Bandurko squatted by the hearth, raked in some rubbish and an old box and kindled the fire. He spotted a plank in the corner, leaned it against the wall and broke it with a kick. Then we found remnants of an old bench, some branches, and finally pulled down a few loose rafters from the roof. Soon the fire lit the room. The little demolition job warmed us up. We propped up the fallen door, and there was nothing else left to do but to sit down, take our sodden boots off and start getting dry. The smoke billowed, desperately looking for an escape, but we didn't give a damn. We lay down on the ground. At least this way we could breathe.

"I know where we are. It could be worse. Two kilometres from here is a road, but it's no use in winter. We'll sit it out here until the morning and then it's all easy-peasy. I got it figured. Do you know how far we've covered today?"

"Haven't got a clue."

"Some twenty kilometres. About ten too many. We wanted to steer clear of the village and got blown off course. By fear or excessive caution. Maybe just as well. The only house in the area is five kilometres from here. A forester's lodge. Lumberjacks never pass this way. We'll check anyway. About that road. It was proper prewar tarmac. Two years ago there was a flood here. That stream we crossed flushed it clean away. Germans, Russians, even Poles couldn't destroy it, but that stream did. It's undrivable now. A vertical wall on one side, sheer drop into the river on the other. You can't squeeze through even on a bicycle. If there's no fog in the morning we'll check it out. And then – two hours and we're there. I'm hungry."

But we had nothing to eat. Only cigarettes. And the fire. The warmth, like vodka, made him talkative.

"It's a fucking desert. There's a house nearby but it's been abandoned. A whole farm. The owner's name was Voron–Raven in Russian. Hanged himself. People say he went mad. He was always mad, but in the end he went completely off his head. He had two sons. His wife died some time ago. People say he made his boys pull the plough. They were a bit slow up here. Maybe they couldn't tell the difference between men and beasts? If there is any. Look at Voron. Later he bought himself a new wife. A fifteen-year-old girl, bought her with money, from some greedy beggars. First he kept her to help him around the farm. When she was sixteen he married her. The new Mrs Voron pulled the plough too. People say he sometimes made her bark like a dog. Honest. And then he hanged himself, Mr Voron did. Have you ever seen those scarecrows in gardens? Dead crows hung on a pole? The sons and the girls have disappeared since."

The wind made a racket with loose asbestos roof tiles. It was getting in through a triangular gap above the door. We had to close our eyes and cover our faces with our hands when it spread the smoke low on the ground. Bandurko shut up and waited until the air cleared, wiped the tears with his dirty thumbs and started again.

"When the *kolkhoz* was here, they even had a regular bus line. Some three kilometres from here there is a proper road. These here were sheep and cattle pastures. Quite wild. They would go into the mountains for half a year and let the herds loose. They ate, slept and fucked here, whatever they could. Probably sheep. When someone spends all his life with animals he domesticates them in more than one way. It was a prison *kolkhoz*. When they did their time they stayed on. Daughters of screws married thieves, office screws fell in love with bandits. New mutation, new nation. Freedom? The clever ones figured there was not much difference. And they were right. Even when they closed down, the bars were left in the windows for several years. Barbed-wire fences too. Just think – bars, barbed wire and in the middle of it all kids and nappies. And now there's nothing left. Ruins. How they must have cursed and cried when they learned they could – and had to – leave the place. And no one knows where to."

He carried on talking but I stopped listening. I didn't think he wanted me to anyway. Staring at the fire, squinting his smoke-red eyes, he carried on telling those stories probably only because he wanted to convince himself the place he was in was real. Space betrayed him, led him astray, so he turned to memory. A good move. He fell asleep with a cigarette end between his fingers. I delicately took it out.

I couldn't sleep. I looked at the fire, at the watch, at my friend. In the pile of broken wood in the corner I noticed something that looked like a skeleton. Regular construction of a ribcage, dog's or a sheep's.

Chapter 3

"Live or die. If you want to die, die."

That's the kind of shit Bandurko was selling to us in a bar called Crossroads, late autumn of last year. It was evening. Down the concrete gutter of Łazienkowska thoroughfare foamed a colourful sewage of cars, a stream of glistening vomit flowing from east to west and from west to east, while we sat in what felt like a terrarium, among people with dead faces and slow-motion gestures. There were five of us and each drank his favourite.

Bandurko drank red wine, Shorty sipped vodka, Goosy was on beer because he was driving; Kostek also drank beer, while I savoured cheap brandy. It was raining. We sat by the glass wall. The glass was wet, and people in the street looked like black kites struck down from the sky and blown by the wind towards the gaping entry of the subway, or towards the iron banisters leading down to the bottom of the concrete ravine. Articulated buses packed to bursting crawled towards Ursynów, passing the returning half-empty ones. Everything shook. The earth and the glasses on the table. Only cigarette smoke seemed to withstand the tremor.

"Socialism or death. Socialism, Bandurko. That's what *Commendante* Castro said, and that's what we say." Kostek's face was motionless, as if it wasn't him who uttered these words. Black-haired, thin and swarthy, he looked like a Gypsy, or at least like someone who was there merely by accident. He always looked as if he was with us only because he'd just taken a spare seat at the table. He thought, jeered and got bored, all off his own bat. With his hands stuffed in pockets, legs stretched under the table, the collar of his jacket up and his eyes fixed on the label of the Okocim beer, he sat like a fan at a boring match. We – elbows firmly dug into the table, faces resting on hands holding smoking cigarettes, staring at the ashtray in the middle. Focused, one might say. Vasyl talked crap, but no one minded. Perhaps the crap was simply too great, too interesting in its crappiness, like an article in *Hello!*.

"You're talking crap, Bandurko, because you're a bourgeoisie."

"Typical class bias. I'm not a bourgeoisie: merely a receiver of private scholarship, and you're a tramp."

"Yes, I'm a tramp. That's why I demand you buy me another beer. And a round of what they like for the rest. I assume you do want us to hear you out."

"I got money," piped up Goosy.

"We all know that. Wait your turn, it'll come," muttered Kostek and straightened up in his chair to call the waitress. There was a break, like during a party meeting. Bandurko fell silent. He sat looking into his wine glass, probably offended by the silly jokes that interrupted his flow, unable to pick up the thread anew, or rather unable to muster the emotion that allowed him to be carried away and talk for half an hour at a stretch. It was a matter of inspiration. Bandurko was a man of vision. Everyone knew that. And a proselytiser. A keen but sensitive soul, easily wounded. Which is why we sat listening to him in silence until Kostek took out a pin and let some air out of Vasyl's balloon. So when the waitress arrived our circle broke and we started talking all at once, about what we did yesterday, what we should and what we'd rather do tomorrow, and who with. Goosy jabbered on about his latest business scheme, his car, his latest business scheme, his car, and he was getting excited just like Bandurko, except that in his case the excitement manifested itself through stammer and beads of sweat on his forehead.

"Shit! I forgot I'm driving." He'd push away his freshly started beer, take his glasses off and clean them with his jacket, ready to resume where he left off. But Shorty was already talking to Vasyl, trying to persuade him about something in a slow, measured voice, his hand cutting the air into thick juicy slices. Kostek sat quietly as before, sipping his beer, giving no sign that in a minute he'd put the empty glass on the table, say "See ya" and leave, which I would follow with "I'll be off too" and rush after him. I caught up with him in the cloakroom, looking at the glass box with various brands of cigarettes, finally asking the cloakroom granny for a packet of extra strong. I didn't stop him, he didn't look back. I waited for a bit and walked out on to the wet street to think about Vasyl Bandurko.

Chapter 4

And now I was looking at his still, quiet face and I swear I could see a smile lurking in the corner of his lips. It wasn't playing shadows or shimmering specks of golden red glow. It was a triumphant smile. It radiated even through the mask of sleep. For Bandurko triumphed, he convinced us that our lives were shit and so we should do something. He was the one to tell us what.

That speech he made in the bar, although it shocked us, was merely a beginning. After that he worked on us individually. He must have been spying too, for we tended to bump into him in the street, on buses, in bars. He never tried to catch us at home, as if he knew we would be more resistant there, that a more ordered world would protect us from madness.

So it was streets, bridges, laying traps. Once he dived after me into a taxi only to tumble out ten minutes later in some useless place, Industrial Służewiec or something. On a Sunday there was no living soul in sight. He must have wandered among the huge glass and steel cubes, halls and hangars perfecting the art of rhetoric, fasting in the desert, receiving visions and prophesying to the Jerusalem of corrugated iron.

I can't remember who it was he converted first. We continued our meetings, but every time he tried we invariably concluded Vasyl was still off his rocker.

Who was first, then? Shorty? Kostek? Goosy? Funny little game. I didn't have to play it but the night was long. So – Shorty? Or Goosy? Goosy certainly not. He had the most to lose and wouldn't have the balls. On the other hand he was sentimental and could, at the last moment, summon the courage to shout, "Guys, I'm coming with you!" Just as the guys were disappearing round the corner of a narrow street of wooden huts, similar to the station hut but never painted. "Guys! I'm coming with you!" – although he knew we were going for one of those dangerous excursions that usually ended in a crazy run with some mad bastard charging stark-naked behind us, courtesy of Ginger Grisha who, bored with open-air porn, was stepping out of the bushes with a line: "Excuse me, do you have the time?" or "Shut up, baby, fucking doesn't kill."

Shit, did we run. Not out of fear, for there are natural limits to the speed even the maddest bare-assed fucker can develop in pine wood undergrowth or a wild rose thicket. Normally they didn't bother. So we ran like the stealers of forbidden fruit, bewinged, cursed and free. The youngest didn't have a clue as to what really happened in paradise. They felt fear, the breeze of the unknown. The oldest, like Ginger Grisha, would spit with a special, masculine contempt, turning their eyes away in order to give their friends – and themselves – to understand that it was no hypnosis.

So, Goosy was probably the last. But then he could be just as well the first, caught in Vasyl's Machiavellian snares. Bandurko knew his weak spots well; we all knew: "Listen, Goosy, everyone has agreed, you are the last, we care about you, think about it. We can't wait for ever." And if it was like that, the order didn't matter. Each of us could be first or last, and all deceived.

The fire was going out. I picked up a few sticks from the pile and gently laid them on the coals. They began to crack. Sparks shot up but darkness was putting them out like water. The cold had gone, or I had got used to it. There was only hunger. My guts twisted themselves into a knot and ached. Even cigarette smoke couldn't untwist them. I thought of the Indians, who swallow the smoke. The thought made me burp.

The previous night, on the train, we had a hamburger and a beer, and that was it. Warsaw Central, Warsaw West, and then the black screen of the window with the blurred beads of the light of passing stations, cigarettes, and no vodka. It was supposed to be better that way. I fell asleep before Radom. We didn't feel like talking. We had talked ourselves out. I curled up in the corner and lost Vasyl from my sight. Some time after Sandomierz I was awakened by his voice.

"They nicked our rucksacks." He stood with his hand on the lightswitch, looking around the compartment as if that barren, empty cube of space could hide two massive canvas bags.

"They fucking nicked them . . ." as if it were something beyond human comprehension, something supernatural.

"They fucking did. I think it must have been thieves," I suggested helpfully from my corner. "We asked for it."

We had thrown them on the seats as if we didn't care, like they do in the movies, like old troopers, those who have nothing to lose. And on top of that it was so hot inside the carriage we had to sleep with the door open. Well, I couldn't care less. Sleeping-bags, long-johns, food, the stove, a bottle of meths.

"The map! We lost the fucking map!" moaned Vasyl. "Half a year of work. A tourist map but with lots of notes, corrections, every hole in the ground marked, bus timetables . . ."

"It's not Siberia. We'll manage."

"What do you know?"

"I do. I was there."

"Not there. You were more to the east. And it was summer."

"Money?"

"I got it on me."

"We'll buy the necessary stuff when we get there."

"We will – condoms in a bar. It's a Sunday."

I was pissed off but didn't want to crawl out of my corner into the middle of the brightly lit metal cage. Suddenly we felt naked without those shitty bags. Soon after, we arrived in Tarnobrzeg, and Bandurko stuck his head out of the window. But the guy who had stolen the bags wasn't stupid and had probably thrown them out into the bushes before the train got to the station, possibly even a few hours earlier. Good start, I thought. We've already had a theft; now it's time for murder, with a rape thrown in somewhere in between, say at Dębica.

But we saved our asses. When we got off in Grobów it was dawn. The street from the station was clean and quiet. Wooden villas with gardens, old-fashioned signs recommending home-cooked dinners, glass display cases with saints. Above the white roofs the sky was getting pinker. It was a terrible colour, bright and ice-hard. Even a stone would bounce off a sky like that, I thought. On the hill in front of us, a coal wagon loaded to the brim was coming down the road. A skinny white horse was practically sat on its rear while the bridle cut into its mouth so deep we could see its red tongue and gums.

"On a Sunday?"

"Maybe he's been going since Saturday, maybe Thursday?"

On a slanted, cobblestone town square we found the bus stop. The bus arrived not too long after. Seeing us, it skidded and stopped sideways. We hopped into the empty coach as the driver was sending everything to fucking hell – icy roads, sand-sprayers, capitalism and quite possibly us, but we hid right at the back.

"Do you remember when all the coaches were blue?" asked Vasyl.

"I do."

And then we travelled south-east. The sun was rising a bit to the left. On the right spread a wide, flat valley. Well-trodden paths and sleigh-tracks led off the main road to huts and sheds, barns and pigsties. Over the whole vista, a blue veil of morning chimney smoke hung on the black-green mountain line. The light was so bright, so translucent, as if we were heading not for the geographical but some mythical, ideal south-east.

The driver put on a pair of shades and switched on the radio. It crackled like hell, but he must have liked it for he turned it up. Through the electric storm came scraps of Warsaw news. Like a hue and cry, like a memento, or an exhortation.

After an hour we reached Gardlica. The sun had disappeared. There were no clouds; more like a whitewash. Warm, sticky currents flowed in the air, the sort that drives people to madness. We bought a bag of cigarettes, different sorts, and read the poster: "Katyń, Kozielsk, Ostaszków – by bus in two days."

"Cheap," I said. "Three hundred."

"Competition," explained Vasyl.

And then we got on another coach, together with a big family and three sober citizens. Half an hour into the journey Bandurko remarked: "So, to all intents and purposes we're in a different country now."

Chapter 5

When I woke up it was freezing and grey. Vasyl sat by the cold bonfire, putting on his army boots with gently ringing buckles. My boots were only barely dry.

"You can sleep."

"I was completely exhausted. The last few days I couldn't sleep a wink," he said.

We stepped out into the bluey twilight. Broken staves of the low fence and our tracks from the previous day were all we could see. The trail of irregular foot holes led up the slope, disappearing in the milky-blue suspension of snow and light.

"Let's get to the wood and wait for the day."

I didn't answer, couldn't be bothered to nod my head. After a few minutes I felt warm. I picked up a handful of hard, grainy snow and started nibbling it. It tasted like icicles, like fragile little swords. As kids we used to stage theatrical duels, but our weapons broke in our hands at the first thrust, changing into lollipops. Our priest in a black cassock would come out in front of a low building and call, "Class 3, in! Quick, or you'll get frostbite on your willies!" We would sit down behind wooden school desks with wooden tops glassy from the touch of thousands of hands and for the next forty-five minutes watch with hypnotic fascination as Father reduced a packet of twenty by half, while from behind the wreaths of blue incense there flowed theodicy embellished with bold examples involving God as bread but not – God forbid – as sausage, for "Hell, sausage one can live without, unless one is Malinowski, future atheist."

The sight of Father serving mass always unnerved me. He didn't smoke then, didn't gesticulate. He died of cigarettes, alcohol and temperament.

Suddenly I felt that my throat had gone numb. I threw the icy lump of snow away. We passed the junipers and reached the first trees. The valley was filled with clouds of mist. The wind tore them, chased them, pushed them up the stream ravines on the opposite slope.

"See? The road goes along the bottom of the valley. We'll have to cross it at some point and we'll look for tracks." After half an hour we ran down the steep slope, along the beech windbreak, all the way to the bottom of the valley, right on to the river bank, or to be more precise the bank of two merging rivers.

"The one on the left is Uhryński, the one on the right Black Stream. We have to go right. Along the river bed. We'll follow the Black. This valley is practically a cul-de-sac. Once a road ran here – more like a path really – but there was a landslide. There's no way we can avoid getting our feet wet."

We entered the stream. The pull was awesome. We waded thigh-high. One false step and the current would have dragged us away. Vasyl stopped on the other side.

"See? This is the ford and the way to the forester's lodge."

There were no tracks. Nothing. We turned right and continued along the stream, hopping stones, now and again forced back into the water. But it took ages, so we gave up on acrobatics and waded in: after all, we were nearly there. After some time Bandurko decided we could scramble back on to the bank. We proceeded down a flat, narrowing little valley, crossing the Black twice more as it flowed in zigzags. And then I caught a waft of smoke. Vasyl looked at me, smiled and nodded.

"About a kilometre."

The valley narrowed and finally closed. In its furthest nook, shielded by a copse of firs, practically invisible, stood a wooden shepherd's hut.

"Pretty spot," I said.

"Quiet. Pretty in summer."

The snow outside the door was trodden down.

"Couldn't they piss somewhere else?" remarked Bandurko, seeing yellow holes in the snow.

The interior was dim and smoky, and all we could see was the glow of a fire. Someone rose and approached us. It was Goosy. His eyelids were red, and his face looked grey, but he smiled with the same old cheeky scowl.

"We've been waiting since yesterday. What happened?"

"Nothing. The instruments were playing up. We had to spend the night some distance from here."

Behind Goosy's back stood Shorty, blocking the door frame.

"Hungry?"

"Fucked," answered Vasyl. "It was like crossing one huge swamp."

We sat around the stone hearth. In the red little pot hanging on a wire boiled water. The beech logs gave out so much heat it was hard to sit still.

"Coffee?"

Shorty poured boiling water into metal mugs and added instant coffee.

"No sugar. But we've got this." And he showed us a freshly started bottle of Royal, ninety-nine per cent proof spirit.

"This shit takes life out of petrol," opined Bandurko and shook his head.

Coffee in one hand, I undid my boots. They were steaming, getting very hot. Later, when the coffee cooled down a bit, I administered myself a measure of the Royal venom. Goosy handed out thick slices of bread and a knife and pointed at the slab of pork fat hanging in the smoke. I gorged myself and slurped to my heart's content, minding my bare feet by the fire, while Goosy reported: "The shepherds left quite a lot of firewood. All chopped and dry. Nights are bearable provided the fire is well stoked. There was even a bucket to draw water with. We could do with an axe. If we stop all the gaps we could have a snug palace here. I can bring some stones from the river, put them around the hearth and make a sort of stove. It would keep the warmth. By morning, the cold does get to you. I even found nails in the shed at the back. There was a shovel, a fork . . ."

"Has anyone seen you?"

"I don't think so. I mean, someone in the village might have. Only two of us got off the bus. It turned off to Niewierki, or whatever it's called, and we walked on. We could have been going anywhere, couldn't we? When we got to that abandoned farm, we turned into the wood. Just there the deer must have crossed the road. The snow was so well trodden it looked as if a whole herd had swept down the hill. At first we tried to mask our tracks with branches but later couldn't be bothered. We moved along the edge of the wood until we got here. About three hours . . ."

Vasyl kept asking more questions, but I gave up listening. I crawled into a black sleeping-bag, curled up and just before falling asleep realised I'd forgotten to have a smoke.

Chapter 6

"But Goosy, it had to stop, you told me so yourself. When you think about it, I wasn't trying to persuade you to do anything. Then, in the bar, Kostek laughed that I talked about death, and in that tone. But how was I supposed to talk to you lot to make you listen? We talk about death every day. Good morning, Mother, good morning, Father – and that means death. Every move of your toothbrush, every new bubble gets you closer to it. Would you rather hear this sort of crap? About the woodworm of our – your days? I don't want to despair and feel sorry for myself, Goosy. Let's say I want to die without the help of the toothbrush, let's say I want someone to see that, because I'm scared and I don't want to die of fear. Is this so bad when we're in danger of dying from disgust? Just look at you, you miserable yuppie of the new dawn. You'll die or go mad when you run out of things to do. Except that it's impossible, so you'll die or go mad way before the end, if only because you'll never see the end coming. There's only one end, but obviously the thought's too big to squeeze into your brain. I'm thirty-two, gay, I was a pianist, then I read books and wandered the streets, believing myself to be the image and the likeness. Especially when someone kicked my ass. I suffered a lot then, and no other likeness seemed to suit me better. And what did you tell the wife?"

Inside my sleeping-bag I was dark and warm. I lay enveloped in the scent of my own body. When my mother tucked me in and left my room, I used to give myself to the world of dreams and fancy. My bed would sail through the foulest weather, snow, rain, through icy waters of some northern seas, wind, freezing cold and darkness. And in the middle of it all there would be me, safe and warm in my burrow, invulnerable.

And that's how it was now. I was cocooned, curled up into the tightest ball possible. I farted to banish all evil and listened.

"Nothing particular. I told her I was tired and needed a few days away. In the mountains. We have friends in the mountains."

"Somewhere here?"

"Not quite. Near Przemyśl."

"Could you tell her the truth?"

"What truth? That I was going away to play guerrilla warfare? Be serious, Vasyl."

"And if you die?"

I wish I could see Goosy's face, but of course I couldn't even stir, let alone stick my head out. I had to imagine how he looks at Bandurko, how his shifty eyes grow still behind his glasses and search Vasyl's face for any indication it might be a joke, irony, something that would undermine the simple sense of the question.

"You mean here?"

"Anywhere, Goosy, anywhere."

"Oh, stop fucking me about. And stop drinking this firewater. You've lost me already."

"It's a serious business, death is."

They both fell silent. I heard a knock on a metal mug, the bubbling noise of 98% proof spirit being poured and a splash of added water. The burning wood slumped in the fire, and a stray gust of wind fell on our little hut. Goosy could no longer withstand the specially-prepared-for-him silence.

"Want one? No point waiting until it blends."

"Why not. And give me one of your Camels. All we got is some godawful shit."

I bet at that moment he sent Goosy one of his stiff smiles, in which only the upper lip participated, revealing a row of even yellow teeth. This kind of smile took some getting used to.

"You'll get lost in the woods and we'll find you. Or you will find yourself. Something like that."

"If only weather were better. A bit of sun. We could go for a little trek. You said we would."

"We will, Goosy, we will. Weather or no weather. But now beddy-byes."

I waited until the noise died down, until they settled in their beds and their breaths grew deep and slow. I stuck my head out and then got out to find the spirit and the Camels. Got back to the sleeping-bag, took a swig, which took my breath away, lit up, and rested my head on a beech log. Goosy slept curled up, and his hair looked like another big clump of cotton wool coming out of his old duvet. Bandurko and Shorty slept on the other side of the hearth, screened by the flames.

So, we were a guerrilla group, and our commander was Vasyl Bandurko. Guys in their thirties, with kids, some married. At this precise moment Goosy's wife would be sitting down in front of TV to catch up with the news from east and south – news about thirty-something guys with families. She would be watching them squat and crawl through the rubble as tiny puffs of dust, mark 7.62 bullets hit the wall and paving stones. From the sandbags trickled sand, from under the helmets sweat. Or she would be watching the same guys walk slowly among the rubble, stepping over fallen objects and bodies. Their kalashnikovs in one hand, barrels up. Practically all the guys would be dark-haired, as if murder and madness spared the blonds, as if the blond were some angelic race inhabiting those regions of earth's civilisation where dying happens beyond the screen, surrounded by silence, antiseptic cleanliness and shame. Goosy's wife is a thirty-something blond with medium-length legs. She is a sensitive soul and hatred terrifies her. After the soldiers left, when the serious guys in suits rolled up their sleeves and washed their hands, she will enter her light, pine wood kitchen full of colourful, plastic kitchen utensils – red, yellow, black – to make herself supper: wholemeal bread, milk, red pepper, perhaps fruit juice. Then she will take it back to the room, place the food on the low glass-topped table and sit in a comfy chair and pull her legs up. Her knees are white and round, her clasped thighs make a straight line that runs into the shade under the hems of her cherry-coloured dressing gown. But nothing of it tonight, only books – *Kentucky Clairvoyant, Organism and Orgasm, Healing Self-Massage, The Secrets of Tibetan Lamas* – each of which she will put away after flicking through a few pages. She will go back to the kitchen to fetch a packet of salted peanuts, then pick up the remote control again to see what is new with Ricky and Daisy, and when the episode is over she will go to the bathroom and then to bed, and slip under the duvet as on the radio a phone-in starts about broken hearts with the DJ the confessor who spills all the secrets, forgetting they belong to God.

So we were a guerrilla group led by Vasyl Bandurko, though I bet Goosy would rather it were his wife.

"Listen, it's no big deal. We'll disappear in the wild for a week or two. I know a place where even if someone tried he wouldn't find us. We'll go deep into the forest, into the mountains. It'll be dark, cold and empty. We'll have to struggle for food. The nearest shop is ten kilometers away, and we won't be able to go there."

He was walking right behind me and had to lean over to make sure his words reached my ears. It was five p.m., Marszalkowska Street at the height of the rush hour. Impossible to walk in pairs. So he ran behind me shouting out those great ideas. I'd got off on the Zbawiciela and saw him coming out of a shop and cutting through the crowds like a heat-seeking missile. He left me no time to be surprised.

"Don't laugh, there's nothing to laugh about. It's a matter of faith and instinct. I can't prove anything. I have no rational arguments. What can I afford now? And in a year's time? Two years? You live like a tramp and you keep telling yourself that's how the world is. You live like a tramp, you know it yourself, only the rubbish you live off and your hunger are slightly different. You are desperately trying to hold on to that newspaper where no one really wants you, you sell them scraps of news that a Russian bit a Chechen's ear off; that Miss Putacoy elected in a riotous beauty contest has the finest ass; that a shopkeeper punctures condoms because God told him to fight evil . . ."

He dodged, skipped and hopped, and he spoke. His long grey-green coat flapped about, sweeping over the passers-by.

". . . and how is that shit different from this?" And he looked down the Marszalkowska filled with stalls, tables, beds, its pavements covered with beggars and zombies with Aids. "My heart is big and it loves all those bastards. My heart is great, for in place of hatred it has contempt and love. And it weeps, for we too will stand with them in a line that has no end, for the end of the world and the Apocalypse are all a fucking lie, and even if they aren't these animals won't notice, even hunger won't make them, as they will be devouring each other until the last gobbles up the one before him . . . until the earth stops dead in its tracks and shakes this vermin off its back. Remember how we walked these streets ten years ago, drunk, tormented and lonely? Remember how I dragged you out of the Surprise Bar, which is no more, and carried you to a taxi rank and it was empty, dark and cold, so I carried you into the yard at the back of the cinema and waited with you until you sobered up? We were poor, grey, poisoned with cheap alcohol, but we could always find all those places, which are no more. And everyone around us was like we were, poisoned, poor, but we all could . . . I don't know . . . we could everything . . ." So I told him I was going to see Shorty and that we all should get drunk, but he only waved his hand and turned off towards the yawning mouth of the underground passage, head in shoulders, someone walking into him, but he probably didn't even notice.

Chapter 7

The wind stopped at night. When in the morning Goosy pushed the door open, his silhouette instantly dissolved in light.

"Come on, guys! Get up! Look at that!"

Behind the green of the surrounding spruce trees stood the blue of the sky. Between the tree trunks fell diagonal shafts of light, sending the dust inside our freezing hut into a whirling dance, just like on a summer afternoon. Shorty lay with his back to me. Against a wall of his black jumper, Vasyl, sitting and rubbing his eyes, looked small and strangely vulnerable. The wind, then the smoke and now the light – as if the world set out to make him bleary-eyed for ever.

"That's shepherds' gear too," cried Goosy, waving a dented, sooty frying pan. By the time we crawled out of our sleeping-bags the fire was on, pork fat sizzled in the frying pan and water in the pot began to boil.

"Coffee in five minutes!" Goosy was a Scout. Someone had to be. Vasyl squatted by the fire thoughtlessly, warming his hands. Shorty went outside and I followed him: the jolly camping routine rubbed me the wrong way.

It was warm, like in March. The trunks of the beech trees towering over us had a silvery sheen. On the slope beyond the river, rows of firs, dotted here and there with an odd spruce, rose one over the other towards the black, jagged skyline of naked tree-tops. The valley was flat, covered with copses of bushes and wild apple trees hirsute with moss. We walked around the hut, turned towards the river and then upstream until a gorge, several metres deep, barred our way. The stream washed away the soil and came to rest against a vertical wall of rock. From the cracks sprouted seedlings of hornbeam. A few metres downstream there were remnants of a path, a little shelf clinging to the wall. The water was a transparent deep green. Huge boulders that had fallen off the rock face created a waterfall. Jumping from one stone to the next, one could cross the river, which we did. The other bank was low and overgrown with alder. Shorty pointed at the thicket.

"Something's going on there," he said.

We moved in that direction, and after a while we saw among the black trees a fluttering flock of crows and ravens.

"Carrion," muttered Shorty.

As we approached, the birds flew up in the air, circling and cawing.

It was a deer. Or, to be more precise, the skeleton of one, jumbled white and pink. Scattered tufts of brown fur on the snow made the site look a terrible mess.

"She didn't die a natural death," said Shorty. "Something got her."

He put his boot under the carcass, trying to shift it.

"And it wasn't the birds that stripped the flesh. A bird couldn't have lifted an entire leg. See?"

Indeed, a hind leg was missing. And then we noticed that a front one was broken just below the knee.

"It was wolves. They must have chased her over that cliff. She leaped, broke her leg and they got her. No other animal can bite through bone like this."

We turned back. This was just what the birds waited for. They flew off the tree-tops and, cawing, returned to their feast. I turned round to throw something at them when I saw a bird as white as snow. It was big, the biggest of them all. A white raven. It was the last to join the flock, pushed its way in among the others and disappeared. Several birds flew up to make room. I could have sworn I saw its beak flash in the sun. I looked at Shorty. He was looking in the same direction, squinting.

"Did you see it? Did you see what I saw?"

"Hm . . . But I'm not sure what," answered Shorty slowly, his eyes fixed on something in the distance.

We turned back again. The birds fluttered off the ground amid hostile cawing and dispersed among the tree-tops like a black cloud.

"Shorty? And now?"

"Nothing."

"Were we seeing things?"

"If two people see a thing at the same time, and it's the same thing, it means the thing exists."

"Hallucinations aren't infectious. What did you see exactly?"

"A bird. It was white. But there are no white birds of that size around here. Yet it was completely white. Not a shade, not a smudge . . ."

"It had a shiny beak, perhaps it was the sun . . ." I interrupted him.

"That I didn't see. But the bird was as white as snow. And big. A raven. *Corvus corax*. Feeds on everything. Doesn't caw. Crows caw. It could just be an albino. But the others should have pecked it to death by now, or driven it away . . . unless it's stronger than the others. *Corvus corax albus*. Let's keep quiet about it, shall we?"

Sometimes he had weird ideas. Of late, we all had weird ideas. He pre-empted my question.

"You know, these days, Vasyl's mind seems to work like a super-stitious old woman's."

But Vasyl's mind did nothing of the sort. One could suspect him of anything but superstition. Shorty meant himself. After all, he was the only suicide attempt among us. Twice at that. And no wonder — how could such a huge body finish itself off? It was simply too big for that, and all the ways invented by ordinary mortals didn't apply. It's quite possible that it was that huge frame, its mass and surface, which allowed him to pick up all those signals the rest of us normally failed to register. Shorty was so big he could barely squeeze through even the biggest of holes, always catching on the edges. But like a spider he could mend the net, stitch it up and patch over the void through which others fell and crushed themselves, shocked and dismayed that the world had pulled such a nasty trick on them.

One day, Shorty gobbled up twenty luminals, washed them down with half a bottle of vodka, slept for three days and when, on the fourth day, he woke up for once in his life he felt rested.

"I simply didn't take enough of the stuff and later I couldn't be bothered. I felt so good, I looked out of the window – people were running around the same as before. I thought I'd saved myself a bit of time." As he told us during one of our all-night drinking sessions. We used to buy only one bottle and when it was finished we would go out to buy the next, and then the next, to get some fresh air, just to have a pretext for going somewhere. We would finish the last bottle at six in the morning, ready to go out again, this time on to the balcony, to see the Last Judgement and Resurrection, a spectacle on the grand scale of the biggest intersection in town. Below, just like in the paintings of medieval masters, little figures crept out from a void, flipping their little lids and hatches, an electric trumpet blaring in remote suburbs to raise them; the only thing missing was a pair of big scales balanced on the spire of the Joseph Stalin Palace of Science and Culture. Then, the FANTA and SUGAR IS GOOD FOR YOU trams would trundle along and the resurrected would board them, moving stiffly like true zombies on their way to meet their maker. Shorty would go back into the kitchen, make toast and a jug of disgusting coffee, and then, smiling, would ask whether we wanted to hear the story about how he tried to hang himself.

"It was in an old prewar building – high ceilings and all that. I fixed it up too high, and when the belt snapped I twisted my ankle. If the ceiling hadn't been that high I would've smashed my ass and tried again. But I was in such pain I forgot what I was doing. Who thinks of killing himself when his ankle is swelling up like a balloon? I'm telling you, nothing restores your vital energies like a fucked-up suicide."

So, for me, he was an expert on matters of life and death. I didn't know anyone better qualified. He would carry his heavy body from the kitchen to the bathroom and from the bathroom to the bedroom with quiet resignation. As if he no longer expected anything, as if reality would have already revealed to him all her traps and secrets.

Sometimes he lived on his own, but mostly with his girlfriend with whom he had a child. She was a quarrelsome creature. When he lost patience with her, he would pick her up and leave her out on the staircase, locking the door from the inside, for she would usually kick and scream for a while; he never tried to put her out of the window, as I suggested on a couple of occasions. She would come back in the morning, changed and silent. Shorty would slap her bum gently and ask how she'd been. Everything would go back to normal, because apart from her quarrelsome streak she had lots of good qualities. It's simply easier to be alone when you feel miserable.

That morning, when he finished his hanging story, alarmed by the prospect of an imminent hangover, we tried to find a better use for the flat that we had at our disposal. We rang a few girls, but they either didn't have time or they weren't in, or they knew us only too well to accept the invitation. Those who didn't have any money were dropped early on. Also, by way of a further selection, Shorty poured all kinds of filth into the receiver, and only when he got to the last number, an old friend of ours, he winked at me and asked her about the booze. We tried to kill the time drinking coffee, but nevertheless the doorbell announcing her arrival startled me out of a nap.

She had the face of Saint Teresa from a Cranach painting and a coat of the kind sold in the expensive shop downstairs. As she was squeezing her way through the long dirty passage, all that chic was sliding off her shoulders and we could see her pert tits under the grey dress.

"One day she'll kill herself," predicted Shorty, the suicide expert, a year or two previously. She entered with a shy, desperately determined smile, the same she had on whenever and wherever she entered. She put on the table two bottles of Kosher Vodka and I helped her out of the coat: it felt like getting a snail out of its shell. We drank in tiny glasses to give ourselves time before going to get the next couple of bottles. We drank in a gloomy yet jolly fashion. Shorty lay on the floor; we sat on the chairs. The trams rang and rattled on the street. From next door came the sound of the Polish Eagles. It must have been past midday, for the sun shone straight into the windows, bringing out dirty smudges on the panes. Then Shorty got up and said he had to go out for half an hour. When he got back we were sitting in the same positions as when he'd left us. Then I went out, but only to the toilet, with a cigarette, a glass and a book that I didn't bother to open. In the end no one bothered with going out. Sometimes one of us would fall asleep. Our faces were lifeless. Kaśka's eyes were empty. Shorty's eyes moved from object to object like a camera in some arty-farty film. Our bodies lived the lives of machines. Somewhere at the night's edge, when the street noise reached a carnival-like intensity, we finally lost the ability to feel anything. The skin and nerves grew thick, as if they were meant for some other huge bodies – whales, or rhinoceroses.

"I think I need to plug myself in to some power supply or something," I said from above Kaśka's back. Shorty didn't even take his eyes off the telly; there was a Mass on, or a blessing, and he liked that sort of thing. He only mumbled back:

"You'd better plug yourself in her."

"Mm," I said and returned to the activity that, I hoped, would in the end bring me to my goal. After all, one should have a goal in life, something that would let one stop to catch one's breath, or start again from the beginning.

Kaśka slipped out in the middle of the night. She abandoned our entwined bodies and left. Probably with the same apologetic smile with which she came in. The streets along which a taxi took her home were windswept, deserted and full of that peculiar nocturnal odour: the city trying to get rid of its daily toxins. The taxi felt the same; so did the staircase, letterbox, door lock, and the flat, filled with the scent of pointless cosmetics.

When she left, I'm sure one of us went out to buy another bottle: we had to get to sleep somehow.

Chapter 8

Who would have thought that the plump, baby-like Bandurko had so much strength in him? He would go ahead and then wait for us, until our short breaths caught up with his long and measured pant.

It was a strange mountain. Dead forest. Naked trunks of pine trees, branchless except for a rusty tuft at the top, stood in geometrical order, casting a regular net of shadows. Hard, glassy snow crunched under our feet, our steps stirring the echo, or so it seemed to us in that windless, sunny landscape. For the last two days it had been freezing and the sky had been clear blue. At night the temperature dropped into teens below zero. Water in the bucket froze solid even though Goosy had stopped all the gaps in the walls. We also built something like a stove or a fireplace. It looked like a heap of stones with a grotto inside which burned fire. Goosy got into a DIY mood and constructed a metre-long clay chimney. We missed the stolen sleeping-bags but, huddled together, we managed to survive until the morning, half-sleeping, half-dozing, and those of us more awake would stoke the fire through the night.

Pork fat with onions, bread, a clove of garlic – that's what I call a healthy diet. I thought fondly of the stolen sardines. They probably swam in some vodka lake in Tarnobrzeg.

By contrast, the days were warm. We would sit by the south wall in shirts. Cigarette smoke stood still in the air. In thistle tufts bustled robins, like little red flames dancing on dry leaves. The slope behind the hut was covered by an ancient beech wood. I saw a roe-deer passing among the trees. I could hear the iced snow crumble under her hooves. The stream murmured gently. The banks were covered with ice.

So, we sat on the south side smoking. The robins bustled some ten metres away. We heard a burst of rustling every time they tried to get to the thistle seed – or was it thorn apple? No, the birds were too frisky, their hopping too lively for the black, heavy seed of thorn apple.

At noon, when it got almost hot and we had to squint to protect our eyes from the snowy glare, Vasyl got up, put his jacket on and announced he had something to show us. We set off upstream, passed the craggy bank and climbed up the steep slope. We entered a dark tunnel formed by hornbeam and young spruce, the sun blocked by the mountain. The snow was firm, so hard our boots left hardly any prints. Bandurko turned away from the stream and started climbing the slope. We followed him on all fours. Suddenly the hornbeam ended, the slope broke and opened on to a big, flat top with old firs. Everything that might hinder our march across it was buried under the frozen snow, only here and there we were forced to jump over the trunks of felled trees. When the top turned back into a slope, the firs gave way to beech wood. The other side was just as steep, but the soles of our boots gripped the white rough snow and the heels dug little steps. Now and again we managed to catch up with Bandurko, only to fall behind him again. Reaching the bottom of the valley, we crossed a little green stream and entered the dead forest. Walking through its geometrical space, we tried to avoid the crossing shadow lines, just as when we were boys skipping on the flagstones.

I was following Vasyl, Shorty was following me and Goosy took up the rear. Just before the summit I stopped and turned to look back. The hills emerged from behind each other like a group of whales or some other, larger and even more peaceful creatures. First green, then blue and at the end pale blue, closing the horizon. And nothing else. No sign of roads or houses; simply nothing, only rows of gentle hills stretching out to the end of the world. The boys caught up with me and we stood, the three of us, without a word, panting, with crow's-feet at our eyes even though the sun was behind our backs.

"If one could fly. . ." said Shorty.

"If only one could sit down. One should sit more," answered Goosy.

But nothing came out of both. From behind our backs came a muffled whistle. We resumed the climb, and after a while we saw Vasyl standing in the bottom of a dale. Our mountain didn't have a usual bulge but a dent, more like the crater of a volcano or a meteor site. The oval, convex platter was the size of a football stadium. In the middle of it stood tiny Vasyl, waving. That's how we spotted him; had he stood still we'd have taken him for yet another juniper bush or a dwarf pine. When we got down to him he pointed at some stick lying nearby.

"Look what I've found."

We came closer, but it wasn't a stick. It was a straight, stiff snake. A dark brown, almost black zigzag ran through the length of its body, ending at the head adorned with a dark spot, silhouette of a man or a frog.

"It's dead. Well dead," pronounced Bandurko.

"And what did you expect?" said Shorty and kneeled down. He picked up the frozen body by the tail and examined it closely. He knocked on the hard skin.

"It's called Cain's ribbon, this zigzag," he said.

I took the reptile in my hand. Goosy winced when I put it to his nose.

"It's not for me. I've got too much of a Catholic in me."

"All Catholics are cowards, Goosy," said Shorty. "They're afraid that some iguanodon may have fucked their great-grandma. Maybe even a serpent, God forbid. Horror. Hence the idea of a personalised God. Makes you feel better, doesn't it? Your vanity will be your end."

"I'm not a Catholic," answered Goosy. "Just a few remnants knocking about in the head."

"It only seems like that. We are all Catholics. Accept that and you'll sleep better."

"Stop fucking about and let's go," Bandurko hurried us. "We shouldn't be here. It's not a good place to hang around in. Open and all that. Sometimes they hunt here."

"What do they hunt?" I asked stupidly.

"Here it's wolves and foxes. I'll show you. During summer they bring carrion here. A huge chunk of a cow, or half a horse. You can't see it now, but when there's no snow this little valley is covered with bones. Heads with horns, horses' hooves, masses of the stuff, and it stinks like that sausage factory in Żerań."

I wedged the stiff snake behind a small pine and we moved on. We reached the bottom of the amphitheatre and then the ridge on the other side. Just on the wood's end there stood a hunter's coign of vantage. It was difficult to spot. A big wooden box made of boards was hidden in the tree-crowns, and the four pine poles on which it sat were raw and unbarked. Only the ladder gave it away. On the ground underneath there were no clues either. I had an overwhelming fancy to start digging in the snow. Somewhere there should be a colourful cartridge-case. Red, blue, yellow with a black figure of a hare or a partridge, finished with a flange of brass, the poor cousin of gold.

A long time ago I used to go to my grandparents, on the river Narew. On the green marshes of the delta lived masses of birds: mallards, garganeys, grebes, little bitterns, herons. They all lived in the reed fields, endless rolls of osier. We used to track down Sunday hunters; the village boys barefoot, I in basketball shoes. We waited until they'd shot their fill, made enough holes in the sky and walked or rowed away. Then we would descend on a trodden bed of bulrush or osier and on all fours looked for colourful treasures smelling of gunpowder. I can't remember the colour of duck cartridges.

We would return from the marshes across a sandy flat. It had the vastness of a desert. Flat, dotted with tufts of sharp blade grass, practically treeless except for a handful of gigantic poplars growing far apart from each other, half-dead and lonely. We tried not to step into cowpats, already engaged in trading the cartridges. Of course, of highest value were those with a wild boar or a deer on them. Those were very rare. No one roundabouts had ever seen a wild boar or a deer, let alone shot that sort of game. Next down were hares and at the end birds. I was the poor relative. Barely a few worn-out old cartridges, exchanged for something completely different. My shy pride prevented me from going down on all fours to look for and fight for the cartridges. I was mightily tempted, but I never did.

Chapter 9

Vasyl said, "He'll come by coach at three p.m. from Kraków." But he didn't. I thought I should wait for the next one, at five-thirty. Everyone can miss a bus. So I waited, walked around the main square, checking out the place. In the sports shop under squat pillars I bought a red frameless rucksack and crammed into it two sleeping-bags – thin ones, but there was no choice. At the empty, green-tiled butcher's I got three kilos of bacon, a few tins and a bunch of smoked sausages for dessert, and because they were light. Inside the shop it felt like a swimming pool or a Turkish bath, with lumps of white and red meat hanging from silver hooks, the till and scales silver too. In the next shop with mannequins in the window I bought three pairs of very thick socks. In the axe shop I bought an axe and cigarettes. In the liquor store I bought two bottles of Polish 98% proof spirit. As I paid, my eye caught sight of miniature bottles of vodka. I lined my pockets with them.

Gardlica – no more than the main square. Four steep narrow streets exited in four directions of the world, leading down and into darkness. There, in the twilight, lived some people, presumably. Shadows leaned on each other as they descended down the murky shafts. Café Arabeska, located by the town hall with a tower lost in the darkness, now and again ejected elated citizens. Snow walls barred direct access to the empty and unfrequented road. The blessed ones fell on the snowy bulwark, rose, fell again, until caught by the slope of the pavement and carried away. I had nothing to do. I took to observing women's faces in the light of shop windows. They didn't strike me as any better or worse than all the others. The rucksack was heavy. I wanted to sit down somewhere, but I knew it shouldn't be in Café Arabeska.

Bathed in the blue streetlight, I walked slowly downhill towards the coach station. In the empty town square the wind reigned supreme, twisting cones out of dry snow. Gardlica was sinking into twilight. In the waiting-room, the passengers cuddled the radiators. A round black clock showed five-fifteen. I went behind the controller's office, found a cigarette and before lighting it downed one of the little vodkas. It did me good. So good, in fact, that before I knew it fifteen minutes flew past and in bay one there was a coach. The second and the last passenger standing on the coach step was Kostek with his canvas bag.

He stepped down and first looked at the sky as if making sure he'd arrived at the right place. The wind hit him in the face. He lifted the collar of his cloth jacket, pulled down a woolly hat with a bobble so that it covered his ears and then decided to look around. I felt I was spying on a lost, lonely person. I managed to hold back another minute and came out of the shadows. I intersected his path by the newspaper kiosk.

"I missed the express."

"The game's up anyway. No transport. We need to wait until tomorrow."

"Do they have a hotel here?"

"I don't know, Kostek. Maybe they do."

"Who cares anyway. Hotel . . ." He hesitated. "A stupid idea. A coach or railway station. We can survive until the morning."

"There's no railway. The coach station is shut for the night now. It's either Grobów, some thirty kilometres from here, or Orla, a bit closer. Shorty and Goosy came that way. They say it's a godforsaken hole, but the station has an all-night bar. With food and stuff."

And that's how we found ourselves catching one of the last buses to Orla. We got in and moved to the back. Kostek was silent. Downed the vodka in one, embraced his bag and fell asleep. Now and again, as we passed solitary roadlights, his face changed into a silver mask. He looked a bit like an angel, a bit like a metal fox. Kostek, the last person we expected to join our game. Always kept his distance, always present by accident or out of boredom. Did he choose us, or did we pick a stray? Hard to tell. No history. It was Shorty who found him; in the Remont Club or somewhere. "Wanted to touch him for a drink. He looked all right. He got up, went to the bar, and came back with two glasses, as if we'd been mates for ages."

If he was lonely, it was his choice. He appeared and disappeared as he pleased. He would come to Vasyl's flat, Shorty's noisy hovel or Goosy's neat and clean home, inveigled with a phone call or after bumping into him in the street. Always polite, well-mannered, until time allowed for greater familiarity, in which he partook to the extent that he was not one of us, that he was a guest who had to conform to certain ways and use words we could afford to do without.

"Sandpit friends," he called us. "Until you break up you'll always play in the sand. I'm from Łódź. I've grown out of it."

Of the four of us, only Bandurko visited his place. He had a weak spot for Vasyl. They bumped into each other in the Old Town, and Kostek took him to his tiny attic flat in Zakroczymska.

"From the window you could see the park and the mint. It was full of books and papers, no room to sit down. He's writing, probably; he wouldn't say. We drank tea with vodka. He lives on his own. You can tell. No sign of a woman."

So we carried on inviting him to our parties, which were less and less frequent and quieter, a pale reflection of the old, never-ending raves during which the world outside the window looked like a hallucination in grey.

These days, Goosy, filled with beer would say, "I must be going now," and leave in search of a taxi, even though he could ring for one. And if the party were taking place at his flat, Vasyl would get up from his bed to reminisce:

"Fucking hell, five years ago a trip from Mokotów to Żoliborz was a piece of cake, even in winter. Remember how we were woken up by the sexton at Popieluszko's church, then not Popieluszko's yet. God knows how we got inside. Six in the morning and someone's lighting the candles."

I remembered it well. I had a good memory. I remembered also how fifteen years before we all used to give Vasyl regular beatings on the football pitch by the railway tracks. He was fat, and it was easy to make him cry. We beat him up for the pure pleasure of it, not badly, just so that there was enough for everyone. The following day, his mother would come to see the headmaster and the shit would hit the fan. For Vasyl's mother belonged to the Party, and it all smacked of political persecution and counter-revolution, though none of us had any idea what that might mean. The Party meant the first of May, frankfurter stands, newspapers with red front pages brought home by fathers. Vasyl never gave anyone away. They couldn't send us en masse to another school or to Siberia. His mother guessed at the truth, but suspicions and torn clothes could not make for a clear indictment. Vasyl stubbornly kept his mouth shut. In the end he became one of us. Once, towards the end of high school, playing soccer on the same pitch by the tracks, Ginger Grisha was moving in on the goal with Vasyl on defence – for where else would he play – when Vasyl somehow got himself under Grisha's feet but failed to stop him, and so Grisha passed and scored. Only then we noticed Vasyl writhing on the ground, and it wasn't just gamesmanship: his leg had snapped in two places like a matchstick.

I can't remember whose idea it was, but we decided to visit him at home. He was supposed to lie in bed for at least two months. It was spring, the end of the school year, and he needed help with homework, that kind of shit.

We felt strange. None of us lived in a house like this. It stood on the outskirts of the estate, near the old pine wood. In fact it was more of a little manor house. It had a front with four white columns, a high red-tiled roof and wide steps, with silver firs in front. We found it hard to imagine that such houses were for living in. Vasyl's mother opened the door, and we were swept over by a whiff of floor polish and turpentine, like in a museum. She was a big, shapeless woman with grey hair, cut like a man's. There were three of us – Shorty, Goosy and me. Grisha didn't give a toss. He was repeating a year, drank cheap fruit wine and had probably already started stealing from drunks – "He didn't have to get under my feet, did he?"

Vasyl's mother looked at us with cold, unfriendly eyes, but just then he called from the other end of the house: "Come in! Come in!"

Kostek wasn't with us then. Nor was he for the next fifteen, seventeen years. Now he travelled next to me, sitting still, as if trying to catch up and cross that time in one half-hour dream.

Yes, Orla was a godforsaken place. The coach turned round on a small market square with two streetlamps and a handful of one-storey houses. We got out into the cold. Someone showed us the way to the station. It ran downhill. After ten minutes we saw icy lights on the platforms. The crash of freight wagons banging against each other made us feel trapped under a huge iron dome.

"It's a junction. The bar should be open," I said.

The light in the waiting-room was turbid yellow. A big tile stove stood in the corner, and probably nothing had changed much since the times of Franz Josef. From behind a green door flowed food smells, and the sign announced: "24-hour bar. Cleaning break 5.30–6 a.m."

The bar was like any other. A few railwaymen, a handful of old women and three men – the eternal sleeping ones, God knows whether travelling or merely drunk, probably both. Shelves in the glass display counter were full of *orange džuses, szewing gums, korn flakes* and *solt nutses*. But there was also tea and beans: the old gave room to the new with reluctance.

"OK," said Kostek, and we squeezed into a tight corner behind a tower of Pepsi crates. After ten minutes I felt that at long last, for the first time in a week, I was warm. Completely and unconditionally. Only the tips of my toes felt a little numb, but that was only a matter of a few minutes.

Chapter 10

"Large tea and one beans. We'll fortify the tea. The night is long."

"OK," I said. "Let it be tea. Tea makes for a good conversation. Coffee less so."

"You want to talk . . . we'll talk," Kostek answered slowly, as if considering a complex proposition. He stirred the black brew while I shared out another miniature; the barmaid disappeared behind the counter but for the tip of her white hat.

"I didn't know you were coming. Vasyl told us only yesterday evening. The guy likes secrets. You know what he showed us?"

"What?"

"A bunker. A real bunker. He took us for a walk. In the mountains. It was in a tiny, narrow valley, more like a canyon. The bushes were so thick we could hardly get through, thorns and stuff. In a rock, a cliff bank above the stream, there was a hole. It was overgrown, covered. We had to wade into the water to get there. A few metres down the steps and then a small room. Everything strengthened with wood, boarded walls; a bit scary, what with the rotten timber, but it held. The ceiling was propped up, all from the war days. Vasyl said no one has as much as looked in there since. There were crates with ammunition or something. With Russian and German writing. He said it might come in handy."

"The crates?"

"No, the bunker."

"Guerrillas have to have a hideout, don't they?"

"Kostek?"

"What?"

"Why have you come here? Seriously."

He looked at me and smiled awkwardly.

"Winter holidays. And you? Haven't you come for winter vacation?"

"And what about all that Vasyl's prattle? Prophetic visions? He's got some crazy idea up his sleeve."

"Rubbish. Visions? He's going through some early menopause. Or growing pains."

"Live or die – do you remember?"

Kostek rubbed his forehead, sipped some of our fortified tea and then, looking at the plate, began to talk.

"Listen . . . look around. Compared with all this, Vasyl's madness – if it can be called madness – is nothing strange, nothing out of the ordinary."

"Yeah, nothing out of the ordinary . . ." I repeated, trying to square the proposition that madness is ordinary.

"Guys our age, even older, go for games a hundred times more complicated than this. And Vasyl? He's got five guys hiding in the woods so that no one can find them. Seek and hide, nothing more."

"For me, it's kind of unreal."

In fact, everything connected with Bandurko seemed unreal. Then, when his mother finally let us in – with reluctance, for she had no doubt we were envoys of the world that persecuted her son – we stepped on the shiny, creaking parquet floor and hurriedly took off our shoes. We were sure we were dealing with some kind of unreality. We could see ourselves in a huge mirror with a carved frame. A huge black vase standing on the floor was full of dry grass, flowers and herbs. The doors in the corridor looked like dark oak. And the scent, that scent, a mixture of church, museum and of something else, perhaps silence. Our homes smelled of food and were full of noise. Always cabbage, burned fat and mothers scolding the children and nagging the fathers sitting in front of TVs.

"What is real, then?" Kostek looked at me with disdain. "Chechen Mafia? The Pope and the bishops? Or maybe our frocked-out peasant king? Well?"

"What do you want me to tell you? That we're two spectres, drinking spectre vodka? Give us a break. I don't have time for philosophy or poetry. I don't give a shit."

"No one gives a shit. Give us a cigarette."

"Let's go outside. It's no-smoking." Fearing for our rucksacks, I approached the barmaid, gave her a tenner and bundled them behind the counter.

The two platforms were empty. I'd never seen anything emptier in my life. Fine, dry snow fell, forming itself into miniature crescents. Not a soul in sight. We walked around the building and found a niche behind the timetable. We lit up on the third match. Beyond the two pools of light on the pavement reigned total darkness. The crash of rolling wagons sounded like war or a clash of giant robots.

"This is unreal," I said, half to Kostek, half to the empty space. "The darkness and the noise. But in the morning everything will become normal again."

"That tomorrow is another day may bring some consolation – to fools, and health-food enthusiasts – but not to serious people, those who smoke and drink and keep vigil at nights. They keep vigil against the received wisdom that there is nothing to wait for. Perhaps there isn't. But that's no reason not to keep vigil. Ye of meek hearts . . ." He didn't finish and smiled to me across the empty space. Then he put his arm around me, and we returned to the bar to repeat the tea and vodka trick. The black clock was showing nine-thirty-one.

A female voice announced the fast train to Kraków and before it finished we saw through the window a lighted train. A few moments later entered a group of people, five, maybe seven. Well-wrapped, grizzly figures, but vague, as if wrapped in darkness. They emanated freezing cold.

I sipped my tea and decided to attack Kostek head on. I was sure he knew more than he was letting on. I was sure Bandurko must have revealed to him a detailed plan. For us he had a talk, some inspired gibberish. It could be any old rubbish, for he was appealing to our shared childhood, which – consciously or not – we were trying to hold on to. But for Kostek he had to have something better, something more rational than all that pissing about the eternal return, Babylon and McDonaldism. Kostek was interested in reality, not in our sandpit dreams. He played somewhere else.

I stretched out in my chair, stretched out my legs and pushed my hands into my pockets. I waited until he looked at me, and then I laid into him: "Tell me all you know."

He looked at me for a while, his face like a mask. Then got on with all those things people trying to gain time normally do. He looked into the glass, raised it to his lips, put it down, clasped his hands together, unclasped them, scratched his head.

"And you? What do you know?"

"Nothing. Nothing more than what I've told you. Holidays, Scouts' adventure and all that fucking forest fairies crap."

"All right. Let's go for a smoke." So we went outside again, for it's easier to talk in darkness. The niche was waiting. We wasted some more matches. Kostek inhaled deeply.

"All right, I'll tell you. He wants to die. He wants to go deep into the mountains and stay there. He will vanish but will be active. He'll do something that'll make them look for him for real, something big. I don't know what. Maybe he'll rob a bank, maybe declare an independent state."

"Now? With us?"

"Maybe not yet. He said in spring. It's winter now. Snow, too many clues."

"So why the fuck has he brought us here? Winter manoeuvres?"

"I'll tell you why. He wants to find weapons."

"Jesus." I groaned and felt I was being taken back fifteen, twenty years, as if I were falling into the past, or watching some TV soap backwards. "To find weapons? Where? In the bushes?"

"You've just told me about a bunker yourself. He claims there are quite a few places like this and that he'll find them for sure . . ."

"Whose weapons? Hidden by whom?"

"Don't play stupid. The Ukrainian Independent Army withdrew in 1947. They were still fighting but already trying to figure out how to break to the West. They were leaving behind all kinds of scrap, just in case."

"Well, history gave them a nasty surprise. The independent Ukraine starts a good hundred kilometres from here. Hang on – and Bandurko says he knows where?"

"He doesn't know exactly. But he says it can be done, if we stick around for a week or two."

". . . or two," I muttered under my nose. "Jesus wept – Vasyl Fighterko, faggot and former pianist. It's crazy."

"Maybe crazy, maybe not. You asked, I told you. He's no Fighterko. It's not that. He doesn't care for all that. He just wants to be killed, doesn't matter how . . ."

"And get us killed with him? Sardanapalus's death, is it?"

"You can always go home. You can go right now. Get this train. Kraków, Warsaw and you're home."

It was then that it finally dawned on me that Kostek was mad. As mad as Vasyl was. He threw his cigarette end in the snow, and without looking back he started walking towards the platform lights. I followed him. What else was I supposed to do?

A double-decker train pulled by a steam engine rolled into the station. The bar emptied. We took another pot of tea for two. I dragged the rucksacks out from behind the counter and topped up our glasses with pure alcohol.

"Fuck, some celebration is in order. The occasion is unique. It all fits. Spirit and kalashnikov. Diamond and ashes. He had such a big TV at home. His mother wouldn't let him out. So he sat and watched TV. We had all those fucking movies figured back to front and inside out. But he sat in his room and had no one to figure them out with. TV – piano. Piano – TV . . ."

"Stop pissing about. Let's talk seriously. . ."

"What do you want to talk about? Let him throw himself under a train. Maybe someone will switch the signal. Let him throw himself from a bridge. Maybe someone will save him. People do this every day. And it's all right when they get bored with themselves."

"Vasyl doesn't want to commit suicide. He wants to die. There's a difference."

"Let him go to Albania, then. Or to Chechnya. They'll be issuing their own stamps pretty soon."

Kostek looked at me the way one looks on someone with whom discussion no longer makes any sense – a ticket inspector, or a Jehovah's Witness at the front door. The black clock gently knocked twenty-three past ten. Into the bar entered the Romanians and settled down for the night.

Chapter 11

It was raining that afternoon. On the carpet our grey, soaked basketball shoes looked like lumps of mud. Vasyl called to us from his room and his mother showed us the stairs. They creaked; we climbed two at a time. Not because we were in a hurry, more out of embarrassment, intimidated by the silence of that house. We found him in a room at the end of the corridor. The floor stopped creaking. Mercifully, it was covered with a red rug.

"It's great you've come, guys. Really great."

Our bashfulness evaporated. We again assumed our manly, scornful faces and came up to a large bed to give Vasyl's pink sweaty hand a nonchalant shake. A massive black carved desk didn't make any impression on us. Nor did hundreds of books lined in a bookcase, two cushioned armchairs, or the phone by the bed. We chose to ignore all that. Only two silver boxes standing on a low stand, a real Philips, a record player and an amplifier, and two huge, black speakers by the wall.

"Working and all?" asked Goosy casually.

" 'Course it's working. Do you want to listen to something? Records are on the shelf below. Sorry, I can't get up . . ."

Shorty squatted and began leafing through shiny covers as if they were second-hand albums, 3.50 apiece on a market stall.

"You listen to this stuff?" The derision in Shorty's voice was supposed to mask genuine surprise, but it didn't.

"Jesus, look at that. Beethoven, Bach, B . . . something, and so on to —" the collection, tipped to the other side, shook the stand "— Vivaldi."

Shorty got up and went to look at the books. Vasyl was quiet, lying like a little white mummy, silent and embarrassed. He had nothing to offer the barbarians. He was the mummy and we were the tomb-robbers in his pyramid, filled with his favourite things that gave a sense of security and peace.

"You play tennis, Vasyl? Come on, this racket's just for show."

"Look at this balcony! You can throw a fucking party on there!"

"Holy shit! A book on Lenin!"

"Let's have some music. Put the radio on. The FM top twenty's about to start."

"Vasyl, can we smoke here? Does your mother mind?"

His room was falling apart. Objects were losing their value, becoming hateful manifestations of some nasty sickness, like a smart dress among the street urchins, and I didn't know how it would end. We'd probably start throwing to each other those strange things – half-toys, half-bibelots, little deities, amulets, porcelain elephant, calculator, unused white running shoes with spikes – were it not for the mother who entered the room and asked if we would like some tea. In a split second order was restored. We were shown our places, and we stood in three corners of the room, mumbling no, thank you very much, shuffling feet. We came to fight, to mock, hands in pockets, and now this – the enemy offered tea.

"Of course, Mother. I'm sure they will. Won't you, guys?" And there was nothing left for us but to sit and wait for the bloody tea, which we suspected would be a trap, delicate little cups, spilled sugar and the ill-mannered ringing of teaspoons.

But the tea arrived in ordinary glasses with ordinary metal holders on an ordinary wooden tray, with biscuits that could be picked up and eaten by hand. So, probably out of gratitude, we started talking about ordinary things, about school, who beat up whom, that the last form was pure joy and power, for finally no one would dare to pick on us and it would be us who ruled supreme over the young ones, their lunchboxes, over their footballs during the big break, not to mention groping all the more bosomy girls from lower forms in the dressing rooms after classes.

And then Vasyl sat up in his bed and we sat around him, for the first time creating that circle that we thought unbreakable ever since.

The Romanians surrounded one of the tables. Three men and a woman sat on the chairs. The shadows caught in the lines of the woman's swarthy face made it nearly black. The younger women squatted on the pile of packs and bundles, with children forming the base of the pyramid. Their clothes, synthetic furs, shone with their own light. From behind the tightly wrapped kerchiefs that looked like yashmaks, the eyes of wives and daughters anxiously examined the surroundings. The men, in black hats and dark coats, sat still. Their brown, knotty hands lay on the table next to each other, leaving just enough room for a bottle. Their faces were empty. They were masks, part of a weatherproof travelling kit, protection against foreign climes, against the fear and traps of unknown lands. They looked like a little tribe, a chip off that huge tribe of nations which set out in search of food, land, freedom, pornography and hamburgers – depending on the times. They won't be stopped by hostile climates or oceans. Nothing can stop them.

The children were the first to judge the new terrain as safe. Dark-haired, big-eyed, they gathered by the counter and, talking in whispers, drew their fingers over the glass display, behind which were laid out all those Donald Ducks, Hollywoods and Spearmints, like colourful rubbish, like mosaic stones out of which no one can construe any coherent image.

"Look, these guys will be fucking our daughters," said Kostek.

"Who cares? Russians, Tartars, Swedes, Germans, half of Europe and a bit of Asia. They've all been doing it, and it hasn't done anyone any harm. Certain people in Łódź still claim there is such a thing as a Polish nation."

"I'd like to be their son," laughed out Kostek. "But I'd be more interested to see the Turks cross the Bosporus or Africans to arrive through Gibraltar to cover our daughters and granddaughters. Or maybe not. It'll come from the East. The Chinese. We will have slanted eyes but we'll be less dowdy. Better manners, less emotion. They are smart people, I think. Perhaps we'll elect an emperor? I'd like to live to see this new world, you see. We'll all speak one language again, our faces will again have universal features. Maybe even man and woman will fuse into one. Identical, bored with each other, people will lose their sexual instinct and gradually we'll die out. Cities will crumble to dust, and where they once stood there will be a forest of ferns, the second and the last paradise inhabited by the last man. I wonder what he will be talking about with God?"

He glanced at me ironically and continued.

"And when I think of Vasyl, I have a feeling that he wouldn't want to see it but he is certain it will come. The world without differences. But he's mad, which means he loves this world. And as true lovers always do, he wants to die for his love. Isn't it moving, such devotion?"

Before I could answer, a child approached our table, a boy or a girl, it was hard to say. The child fastened its big eyes on us in the manner developed by all televisions of the world and said:

"Frent, give tousent. Give, frent."

Frent Kostek looked at the swarthy innocence, took out his wallet and asked:

"How many 'frents' of you are there?"

But the little Gypsy didn't understand or didn't want to get into profitless conversation, so Kostek counted the group at the bar. Then he took out a handful of small change and divided some banknotes into five little piles.

"Well, my 'frent', it's one and a half each here. Share it out properly, won't you?"

The little one took the money and walked away, instantly and obviously losing any interest in us.

"I hope he'll share it out. Otherwise they'll never let go of us. They'll be coming one after the other, some twice over, like in a good queue. They know we can't tell them apart."

He put his elbows on the table and with his head hanging carried on.

"Yes, it moves me. That love of his. We're all born, we eat, our guts burst and we die. No one tries to become immortal. Just for the hell of it. No one. There is something dark about it, revolting, as if we all believed in that second paradise, which is not even 'The End' by the Doors in *Apocalypse Now*, but an ordinary physical phenomenon, like drying or evaporating. I take it for what it is. I'm no idiot. And that's why I like Vasyl. After all, one loves that which one never is or will be."

Chapter 12

And that's how it stayed. No matter where the afternoon took us –
a godforsaken high street with three shops, a railway station, a
terminus of a bus line, the box made of glass reinforced with wire
mesh, easily punched through with stones without crumbling into
bits – wherever we went we invariably ended up at Vasyl's. Even
though his house was on no one's route. It stood at the end of the
longest street, outside the estate, where the deer coming out of the
woods at dusk were a pretty common sight. After a while, Vasyl's
mother could tell us apart and called us by our names. We no
longer sneaked through the hall, while taking off our jackets and
shoes lost its awkwardness and embarrassment. She would greet us
with the few words grown-ups normally have for kids – full of
badly concealed superiority, pretending to be pals, which we
thought pathetic, resented even, for we wanted that grey-haired
monumental woman to be a mother, perhaps even the ideal of a
mother, which we all could miss a little, unable as we were to miss
our own. They were all too alike – pale in the morning, flushed in
the afternoon, a heavy bracelet with a black stone on a plump wrist.

"Come in, you few children of the Revolution. Vasyl has seen
you through the window."

Her eyes followed us to the top of the stairs. We were too busy
with ourselves to notice anxiety and sadness in them. We entered
Vasyl's room, throwing the casual "Howdy" and sprawling in the
armchairs. Goosy would ask questions.

"Eh, Vasyl, what's you mother's job?"

And Vasyl would answer, just as casually:

"She's an artist."

"Artist . . . ?" We'd never have guessed that an elderly woman,
and a mother, had anything to do with art as we knew it from
school, or Fryderyk Chopin. Besides, we knew she was a Party

member, something we had always felt to be a bit of a disappointment.

"What are you staring at? An artist."

"So what does she do, then?"

"Designs sets."

"Theatre sets?"

It was a theatre, except it didn't perform all the year round. When it played though, everyone had to see it. The first of May, Independence Day, October Revolution. The centre of Warsaw bathed in red – massive red rectangles with profiles of Lenin, Marx, the worker helmsman, or monumental geometries that composed themselves into digits and dates. She must have been influenced by Kandinsky, or maybe by Braque, except that it all seemed to have been done in a hurry, or maybe she was just lazy.

It always fascinated me to know how people lived in those rooms covered with stretches of red cloth. In the building of the Central Committee, the Palace, the Metropol. For a week or more they had to swim in a paranoiac, gory radiance. And all those portraits, gigantic puzzles – that's what really fascinated me; a Lenin of that size must have been painted from a helicopter. Perhaps somewhere out of town, or in a huge warehouse, they used a slide projector. I never plucked up the courage to ask her. Yes, it was she who adorned our town, thought out new symbols, scattered her puzzles all over it and put up new decorations. The draperies on the central rostrum were also her creation. Chairman Edward Gierek probably never knew with what precision and panache two massive pleated ribbons met at the height of his balls, creating a reverse canopy. I would march by with my father. Gierek had a dark green coat on, and the carnation in his hand was wine red. When he threw it into the crowd, people tore it to shreds, like a relic. I wanted to have a petal, a splinter off the stem.

In the second year of Edward's reign I was eleven years old. When I entered his aura, into the sphere of immediate physical presence, I experienced things I couldn't name at the time.

I didn't give a shit about politics, and for all I cared Gierek could be called Bierut or Chombe. In the world of streetlamps broken with stones for target practice, secretly smoked cigarettes and frogs puffed up through straws, secretaries – even the first ones – had no place. But then, seeing him a hat's throw away, I saw a pyramid of thirty-odd million people of which he was the very top. And that was something. Something in the vein of boys' boasting games that BMW is better than Mercedes and Lubański better than Deyna. But also something more, something that was pure feeling, almost a religious one. Despite hundreds of visits to the church, no one had ever showed me God. And there he stood, maybe not God exactly, but someone standing high, close to Him in the hierarchy of beings. Higher could be only Brezhnev; Johnson and Nixon were too distant. I was simply enchanted and felt weak in the knees. I even stopped dead in my tracks, but my father pulled and the crowds pushed me on.

And it was Vasyl's mother who designed the backdrop of those raptures. She had a studio somewhere in Saska Kępa with a view on the Vistula.

"Sometimes, when she's got a job to finish, she doesn't come home for days. And I've got the whole house to myself . . ." There was entreaty and hope in his voice.

"Listen, Kostek," I said. I felt I should have answered him somehow – but how? Where should I begin? I could not rewind the whole film and show it to him from the beginning. To him, Kostek the straggler, Kostek from Łódź, Kostek in love, while we were an old married couple. "Listen, Kostek. Don't exaggerate with that love of his . . ."

But at this point one of the Gypsies freed me from further elaborations. He pulled himself a chair, sat down with his back to the rest of the room and reached under his grizzly coat with a sheepskin collar. We heard a soft click and in his hand appeared a narrow spring-bladed knife.

"Not fear, not problem," he said, and to the shine of the blade was added that of his teeth. He was young, short, stocky, but he had a handsome face. To us, all Gypsies have handsome faces. He put the knife on the table. The green handle had a ball trigger.

"Fifty. Fifty tousen." He was glancing now at me, now at Kostek, smiling all the time. His black hat, pushed to the back of his head, gave him the air of good-natured jollity.

"C'mon, good knife. Buy, frent, cheap."

He picked it up from the table, closed the blade, then clicked it open again.

"Good knife, *khoroshy*. Take, frent."

He put the knife in Kostek's hand.

"What do I need a knife for, frent? I'm a man of peace."

"Ah, yes, but it good knife, cheap . . ."

Kostek stroked the handle with his thumb and sceptically examined the toy. His finger found the metal ball and pressed it. It was a pleasant sound. Soft, but at the same time determined, final. He wanted to fold it shut but didn't know how. The Gypsy showed him a tiny lever at the seat of the blade.

"Like so, frent, like so . . ."

The spring mechanism clicked softly. Kostek started playing. He kept clicking, mesmerised by the flash and the sound. The Gypsy sat without a word, well aware of the knife's seductive power. He sat waiting like an angler watching a fish nibbling on the bait. A shunter engine passed outside the window; from the kitchen flowed a stream of muffled clatter threaded with the cook's voice. A railwayman, black as a chimney sweep, stopped at the bar and knocked on the counter. Kostek folded the knife, put it in his pocket and took out his wallet. He found the right banknote and put it in front of the other man.

"Fifty."

The Gypsy took the money and stretched out his hand.

"Good buying, frent."

They shook hands, then the Gypsy nodded his head.

"Come. You come too."

We followed him not to his table as I expected but outside, to the same place we had been for a smoke. He rummaged in his coat and dug out a bottle with no label.

"What's that?" Kostek asked, uncertain.

"Not fear. Drink. Good vodka."

Kostek took a swig, and I could see it made quite an impression on him. For a few seconds he struggled to catch his breath like a fish on sand. Finally he coughed out:

"F . . . fuck me."

The Gypsy laughed in the dark and repeated with pride:

"Fuck *me*."

Then I took a drink from the bottle. Hundred per cent proof it was not, but at least seventy. It tasted like raki and was fucking good indeed. We sent the bottle on a couple of more rounds. Then the Gypsy rejoined his people, while we stayed behind for a smoke.

I looked into the darkness and heard Kostek playing with the knife in his pocket.

Then, in the middle of the night, when we had had enough of drinking and talking, we took our rucksacks from the bar, unrolled the sleeping-bags and stretched out on the benches in the waiting-room. We fell asleep, down a pitch-black abyss filled with clanging crashes and railwaymen's voices. Their hammers knocking on the brakepads had a dry, piercing pitch, as if the frozen metal had lost all its music.

Chapter 13

"Unlucky again," I said.

We stood under the yellow timetable in the empty coach station. It was morning, bloody cold. Black digits informed us that the departure time for Niewierki was six-thirty, while the clock showed past seven. The next coach was to depart before three.

"It's freezing." Kostek huddled himself under the heavy rucksack. "We could have checked that yesterday, that coach . . ."

"Yes, we could have done a lot of things."

The waiting-room was very small. A room without a view. In the corner by the electric heater slept an old man. The snow on the floor was thawing. Kostek sniffled and sat next to the granddad.

"Let's catch some sleep too, an hour or so. At this time of day we won't even get any food."

So we drifted back into a kind of lethargic suspension. The clock went on knocking gently, while the long hand peeled the skin off Kostek's hour. Then, we stepped out into the freezing fog only to see with our own eyes what a godforsaken hole Orla really was. It had its obligatory war gun, standing on a concrete plinth, aiming westwards, as it should, but its mouth blocked with a wooden log. Illogical, if anything. The rest of the town square consisted of one- or two-storey houses: shops with chains, horseshoes, rat poison, shops with colourful fluorescent video-TV-satellite signs. A beauty salon in a wooden hut with brown window shutters, Manhattan Music Salon in a wagon on wheels, throbbing to the rhythms of the Polish Eagles. By the monument to the gun stood a cart with a horse, its head half-buried in the nosebag, a big, furry plodder with hooves like dinnerplates. There was no driver; it looked as if it had harnessed itself and decided to visit just that spot. Inside the shops bearing signs – Meat, Bread, Poultry, Eggs – or none at all, women wearing kerchiefs and felt boots did their shopping. Two big blonds in black furs came out from under the sign Tutti-Frutti, but we couldn't be bothered to check what was inside. The women disappeared around the corner, leaving behind them little stiletto holes in the snow and a trail of the perfume mixed with the scent of horse sweat. A huge moustached peasant in a homespun overcoat walked by slowly, looking at the shops, searching for something that not so long ago was there but now was no longer, or was simply looking for a place to have a drink but the new Drink Bar Calypso in no way brought to his mind the idea of hot beer and a large vodka. We stepped into that bar for a moment. The three high stools were taken by thirty-something fat Apollos, one in brown leather, the other two clad in blue denim, each with a face like two Russian sinks. They quaffed brandy, jingling their car keys. The barmaid, high priestess of the new order, celebrated Mass before a Cin-cin altar. After that we ventured into one of the narrow streets. It wound uphill, gradually turning grey, until it turned into a field road with scattered houses, or rather huts. It was there that on one of the huts we found a rotting sign nailed just above a low door with peeling green paint. The sign said Inn and showed a painted mug of beer. Inside we found exactly what the sign had promised, so we stayed.

We were travelling for almost an hour when it started snowing. From the grey sky, which seamlessly blended with the bare hills on the horizon, fell big white flakes. The wind was southerly, and the driver had to slow down as the windscreen wipers couldn't cope. I unfolded the map on which Vasyl had marked for me the route and our hut in the woods. But what could I read off such a map, especially coming from the opposite direction? The coach passed through one village after another, string after string of ugly sepulchral dwellings. I kept staring out of the window, hoping to catch sight of a sign, a bus stop, a name. Goosy said they were travelling for a good two hours, so we still had time, but I'm one of those who like to know where they are. The coach stopped some-where called Plajsce. It was also marked on the map. A yellow ribbon with red rectangles clustering around it stretched for some twenty kilometres until it reached the foot of a big mountain, where it shook off the houses and started an arduous zigzag climb. On the other side of the Monastyr Pass the map road descended into green, while the houses again gathered around it like diamonds of ice on a twig. The yellow faded somewhere on the way, and now a white ribbon turned sharply east towards Niewierki, where it disappeared completely. At the turn it spawned a black thread that carried on, thin and lonely, for about seven kilometres. At its end dangled a single orange rectangle named Skwirt. After that there was only the border. Halfway between the crossing and Skwirt stood Uhrinski, and one could see there was a bridge there and the road Vasyl had showed me from the top of the mountain where we'd slept. On the map it all looked easy-peasy – just go and you'll get there.

Kostek slept, tired after our session at the inn, where into the hot beer we had poured Cassis, because it was there. Snow made the dusk practically impenetrable. At one of the stops the driver told the passengers to get to the back of the bus. That was the beginning of the mountain, and a drive in the fresh, soft snow might be a bit chancy. It was three to four kilometres of hairpin bends. I woke Kostek, and we took our rucksacks and joined the little crowd at the back door. The driver hurried along a couple of women busy with their gossip while Kostek blinked and kept asking: "What's up?"

"Uphill zigzagging in snow!"

The coach started off. After a minute it turned sharply right and began the climb. In the twilight, through the blizzard, I caught sight of the white roofs below. After that there was only unbroken expanse of white. I felt the wind strike the side of the coach, as if it wanted to push it down there, on to those roofs. The driver kept his cool. He kept to first gear and kept it steady.

"If it stops uphill it can only go down, and that's scary, man."

"We can push."

"You can push up your ass, man. Fifty tonnes? But she's all right. If she doesn't slip she'll dig herself out. Anything is better than going on foot."

The men debated in the dark. One, a bit nervous, lit a cigarette, breaking regulations.

As we entered a sharp left turn I felt the back of the bus slide away to the side, and it seemed we were stuck, but the driver pressed the accelerator a bit more and after a moment we moved on again in an interminably slow drag. Only the roar of the engine and the trembling of the floor were proof we were part of an ordinary journey rather than in a free fall through blizzard and darkness or swimming through black water. On the caked-up windscreen the wipers cut out two black fans.

"Now it should go. This last bend isn't so bad."

The passengers returned to their seats. We couldn't be bothered and sprawled on the long seat at the back.

"Beyond the seventh river, beyond the seventh mountain . . ." said Kostek. "I'm beginning to like it."

We were going through the forest. The torn patches of front lights picked out the snow-capped trees perched on the rocky roadside.

"That railway station, that night, was dreadful. Orla was dreadful. All that time I felt dreadful. Only in that inn did I feel better. How far do we have to walk?"

"About ten kilometres. I don't know the way very well. Truth to tell, I don't know the way at all."

"Brilliant. I like it better still. Have you got any more of those little helpers?"

I did. Four. I gave him one and took one myself. We drank to the darkness and the snow. The coach finally dragged itself through the pass and began its descent, just as painfully slow and careful as the ascent. Then a long, gentle ride down until we stopped under a lamppost in what looked like a big village. In a long, low building was an inn, out of which rolled out a few well-oiled customers. They got on, cigarettes in hands, and gathered around the driver, only to get off two kilometres later. That left only the two of us and three kerchiefed old women on board. I approached one of them. She jumped up at the sound of my "excuse me" but said she, too, would be getting off at the crossing. We carried on into the darkness and snow. We passed a few houses, or lights to be more accurate, then nothing for a long while, and then the woman got up and we followed. We got off the bus, trying to hide our faces from the driver. The woman was swallowed up by the dark. The red rear lights dissolved in the blizzard. The wind was warm. In fact it was much warmer than in Orla. I scooped up a handful of snow. It was heavy and sticky. We put on our rucksacks.

"Well? Which way now?"

"Straight ahead. The coach turned right, so we have to carry on straight."

We started off, following the bus tracks and straining our eyes for an opening on the left.

"Take out the torch from the left pocket." Kostek swung his back pack in front of my face. I felt for a flat metal box. The shaft of light penetrated the darkness only a few metres ahead, but eventually we saw that the bus tracks separated from two other, barely visible ruts made by a car or a sleigh, not yet covered by fresh snow. Underneath we felt slippery ice. After a while we were able to distinguish the white of the road from the woods on both sides.

"A few kilometres, three or four. There'll be a stream. We need to listen out for it," I said.

"Is it big?"

"How am I to know? I saw it during a thaw. It was big then."

We stood in the middle of that enigmatic road which seemed to have fallen from the sky. I threw the rucksack on the snow.

"What's up? We've only just started."

"Sit your ass on the rucksack, Kostek. It's warm. There's no hurry."

I handed him another little bottle. He held something out to me in return.

"Specially for the occasion. It is an occasion, isn't it?"

I felt a box and took out a thick cigarette.

"What's that?"

"Gitanes without filter."

"In that case I've got something extra too. Wait with the vodka."

I had to get up and pull out a sleeping-bag from one of the rucksacks, then from the bowels of the second I dug out a bottle of spirit.

"Watch out. It's like that Gypsy one but more so."

Kostek raised the bottle, sucked on his cigarette and in the glow read out the label.

"We're guerrillas after all, aren't we?"

"After all."

The black smoke of Gitanes and the white heat of spirit. Nice combination. We rinsed our mouths with the wind. Single snow-flakes cooled the tongue. We were ready to stay there. Somewhere in the middle of nowhere, in the middle of darkness, on a random spot on earth. It was like an acceptance of fate, of a dream, or of a hidden, secret sense of events. Here I wouldn't dream of asking the questions I had asked at the station. What else could I expect from Vasyl? He'd brought us here, put us on this magic road and the rest was our business.

We had another sip and set off south into the deepest darkness.

Chapter 14

"The stream, I can hear the stream." Kostek stopped and put his ear to the wind. I didn't hear anything, but it could be the place; we'd been marching for a good hour now. But I heard nothing.

"Listen."

But it was not the rumbling of water under ice. It was an engine. The road behind us turned in a gentle curve. At first we saw a shaft of light moving along the wall of the wood, then the headlights. The car moved slowly, as if deliberately giving us time to think.

"Leave it." Kostek shrugged his shoulders. "Let him go. Bratislava, Prague, even Vienna. What do we care?"

We wished. It was coming for us. It slowed down just behind our backs, and we turned, which was a mistake, as the blinding lights made us stop. It was a UAZ in a dark colour. And then everything became clear.

"Border guard. Please stop."

"But we have," answered Kostek.

The man was in a uniform, alone, a sergeant. The face, white-washed with light, bore no expression.

"Where are you going, gentlemen?"

"For a walk."

Kostek's tone was deliberately provocative.

"Where, exactly?"

"To Skwirt, sir." I tried to pacify the situation.

"But there's nothing in Skwirt. Just a few abandoned barns."

"We know. We want to spend the night there and then carry on."

"Carry on where? Further on there is only the border."

"That's correct. We're going abroad. United Europe . . ."

"Shut up, Kostek. We want to trek through the mountains to Gardlica, sir."

It did sound stupid. The sergeant looked at me as if I were a complete idiot.

"Sorry, guys, I have to ask you to show me your IDs. And your rucksacks too. It's a border zone, you understand."

Kostek said "Fine" and reached to his inside pocket. I had my papers in the rucksack, so I threw it off my back and began to rummage through it. Kostek, too, took his pack off and carefully placed it next to the sergeant, who, with the aid of the headlamps, was trying to pick something out from Kostek's wallet. From the corner of my eye I saw Kostek straighten up, step back, move out from the light and behind the man's back. At the same time the sergeant was falling on his face, his legs kicked from under him. Before his face hit the ground, Kostek caught him by the collar, and I heard a crashing bang against the car's body. And again, before the man's body slid off the mudguard, Kostek lifted it and swung it once more against the car. Then they both fell down. I heard moans and groans, but after a moment the shaft of light was cut through by a hand holding a gun. I closed my eyes, and maybe even screamed.

"Don't just stand there like a prick. We have to tie him up!" Kostek was struggling to his feet, white, panting, with a gun in his hand. He looked at it as if it was the first time he had ever seen it.

"I had to do him somehow."

But the sergeant was quiet, only panting. Kostek dived into the car, rummaged through it blindly and dug out a leather briefcase. He struggled with it and the strap, holding the gun and his new spring knife. In the end he put the gun on the bonnet, cut the strap and kneeled down by the body.

"Hold his hands. Cross them on his back."

I did everything as told but looked into the darkness. The hands were warm and wet. I felt the tugs as Kostek tightened the knots.

"Can you drive? I'm not that good. Load the stuff." He started picking up his papers. "Shall we take this?"

"No, Kostek, please . . ."

"Well, what's the point . . ." He walked out from the light. I saw him raise his arm and throw the gun in the bushes.

When we were in the car I realised I was shaking. Before I found reverse I stalled the car twice. When in the end I managed to get the car to go back a little, I turned the steering wheel, the wheels spun round and round. Then I remembered that the UAZ had four-wheel drive but it had to be switched on. Finally I reversed and we followed the tracks.

"Where do you want to go now, Kostek?"

"Back to Orla. Then to Gardlica. I don't know."

"In this car?"

"We have to get out of here. Fast. Even if it snows until the morning, the snow won't cover everything. In an hour or two the place will be green with uniforms. We must get out of here. Anywhere. We have to risk it. Drive on, for as long as you can. Even back to Orla. We have an hour or two before the shit hits the fan."

"What if they stop us? Say for a routine check?"

"Who will stop an army car? Have you ever seen a police car stopped? We've no other way."

In the light of the headlamps the wood looked like a huge Rorschach test. Not a trace of green, no branches, nothing but oval, drooping shapes, like symbols of anguish and hopelessness. The forest of lost hearts, one could call it. I was doing forty and kept to the tracks. I had no experience of driving in snow, or this kind of car. After a few kilometres I smelled a strange smell and realised I had my foot on the clutch. I accelerated and changed gear. The wailing of the engine stopped. I glanced at the round clocks. The tank was nearly full. I thanked God, for it meant we could run and run, and that was all I could think of, escaping, with an idiotic conviction that the car made us invisible, that as long as we were in the car we were as safe as in a mother's womb or under a duvet.

"What about the radio, Kostek? We've got a radio here. Someone will call us in a minute. That shit may hit us sooner than you think."

He looked at the grey metal box. It was silent, dead.

"He didn't have it on. Maybe they don't use it that often?"

We were approaching a crossroads. The lights revealed a well-trodden track turning off to Niewierki; old bus tracks covered with snow but still visible, and fresh ones, turning towards us.

"They must have a station in Niewierki. We must pray they don't have another car."

"Or that they are drunk or lazy. Or both," said Kostek.

Just before the crossroads I pressed the brake and the rear of the car swung across the road. I turned the wheel and the car slotted into the deep ruts of the bus.

"I bet someone tipped them off. The driver or one of those women. They've been sitting there fifty years, waiting for something to happen, an invasion or a massive cocaine shipment."

I didn't give a shit. I accelerated a bit and we hurtled along like on a toboggan. Softly and quietly. I hoped the snow would make the car white and invisible like a ghost. We passed a few lighted windows, then the road began to climb, which automatically made me accelerate, but I had to slow down before the summit; the car skidded a couple of times. As we rode down into the valley, I still hoped that we were invisible, a figment of our own imagination and nobody's business.

"Can you go faster?"

"No."

Kostek hung over the seat and started rummaging in the luggage. The commotion irritated me and I almost screamed.

"What the fuck are you looking for now?"

He didn't answer. After a while he slumped back into his seat with the bottle of spirit in his hand. He took a swig and passed the bottle to me. I raised it to my mouth, at the same time taking my foot off the accelerator. The car started dancing on the road. I dropped the bottle and grabbed the wheel, twisting and turning it all I could, but to no avail, and we smashed into a wall of snow on the left-hand side of the road. Kostek was crawling all over the floor looking for the bottle, while I tried to drive the car out of the snow. After the third attempt I managed to get the front wheels out and the car backed on to the middle of the road. I snatched the bottle out of Kostek's hands, took a massive swig and slowly moved off. Kostek lit up two cigarettes and started talking.

"We have to go to Orla. Are there any biggish towns on the way?"

"No. Just villages."

"Exactly. There's nowhere we can leave this banger. That is, there is – but what then? No coaches at this time of night. What can you do? Go to a peasant and ask him for a night? In the morning the place would be swarming with uniforms. Try and make it on foot? Where to? Through the woods? Take the road to Orla?"

I nodded like in a trance. The cigarette stuck to my lips, but I was afraid to take my hands off the wheel; we were going up another hill. From the top we saw some lights. We were descending to that godforsaken hole with an inn. Two lampposts, a fence and a sign: Orla 39. The same dirty yellow light of the inn's windows. Then the hairpins. I counted the turns. Then the pass and descent. I moved slowly, very slowly, first through the woods, then the lights hung suspended in black and white space. I knew I had a precipice, now on the left, now on the right, and the only protection was a wall of snow on the side of the road. At the last turn the village lights spread out before us again. Kostek said, "We're doing well", and I said "Yep", and at long last managed to spit out the chewed-up cigarette.

Chapter 15

It was easier than I thought, especially when we got on to a proper road, the one marked yellow on the map. Five, maybe seven cars crawled in the snow, all the way along the whole stretch. I managed to overtake one of them. Then not a soul in sight again, not even a dog's soul. I checked in the mirror but all I saw was the red glow of our own rear lights. And then the railway crossing in Orla. During those five minutes I began to tremble again. As long as we moved I was busy escaping, hands on the wheel, foot on the accelerator. But there, under the red barrier, I got the shakes like in a fever, and even a big swig of the spirit from the bottle didn't help to raise mine. When the last carriage of the interminably long freight train passed in front of the bonnet, the moment the barrier went up, I put my foot down and shot off like a madman, afraid the car might have stalled. In the bright light I felt everything was transparent. I drove with my head between my shoulders. Kostek was checking both sides of the road, but only backyards, warehouses and empty plots of land offered any shelter.

"There," he said, "on that estate."

On the left side of the road, through the veil of tiny, swirling snowflakes, we could see a dozen lights belonging to a miserable imitation of a modern estate. Three three-storey cubes and a flattened box of a shop specialising in everything and nothing. I turned into a narrow access road and on to the square in the middle, where a few cars were becoming mounds of snow.

"Move in between them. They won't find it before the morning."

I squeezed in with difficulty, switched the engine off and rested my head on the steering wheel.

"Lights. Switch the lights off. Let's make ourselves scarce. Fucking rucksacks . . . Can't we leave them somewhere?"

"We've got food for the boys."

"But they'll be looking for two guys with rucksacks."

"Let them. We can split."

"How? I don't know the way."

"So how is it, then? Now you want to go there? You said any train and get the fuck out . . . !"

"Well, it would be bad to walk away like that, now that it's started for real . . ."

So that was it, then. Someone, somewhere was trying to start a Fiat 126. We threw the rucksacks on our backs and timidly, heads down, made our way back to the street, under the glare of streetlights and then on, without asking anyone, to the railway station.

We went straight to the platform. The train to Grobów was leaving in half an hour, just before midnight. Later, on the train, in the middle of the night, on the top of a double-decker train, I looked at Kostek's face, and as he smiled, smoked and smiled, I was sure he was as surprised by the turn of events, by the ease with which we had crossed the border between craziness and madness.

"Someone had to do it," he said in the end. "Someone had to, so don't look at me like that. You wouldn't do it; neither would Goosy nor Shorty."

"Shorty would. If he wanted to. As for me, you may be right . . ."

"Look how well it all turned out. Vasyl wouldn't have thought it out better. Touched by fate at the end of the world."

"Leave fucking fate alone, will you? Do you think he's going to be all right?"

"Sure. He's probably sitting with a bandaged head, telling a story about Israeli paratroopers, having a great time."

"We won't get away with it. They'll have us in the sack before we can scratch our balls."

"But who will be looking for us? There?"

"Maybe we should have shot him, then? Eh? With his own gun. Torch the car and leg it across the snow? Wouldn't that be a real challenge to fate? Twice the fun in half the time? Eh?"

This time he was annoyed.

"Didn't you really know what you were getting yourself into when you decided to come to these fucking mountains? Are you really so stupid? Did you think that thirty-year-old men were going camping to be friends with nature and hunt wild animals? It's

absurd. Did you really think we would go hopping around the
fucking mountains, send postcards to our dearest and in the end
take a lovely picture of us all as happy Scouts? Did you? No matter
whether you think it mad or not, no matter how much you've been
deceiving yourself, the truth is they are already after us, and they
won't stop until they get us. Our job is to escape. And this is what
we're doing. OK, fine, it's all my doing, my fault, my triumph. But
I was afraid that Vasyl wouldn't do anything. That he would go on
dragging us up and down the mountains, showing us fucking holes
in the ground and making mysterious faces until the circumstances,
an accident or the stars, forced his hand. Because he's a coward, the
kind of a coward who'll defend himself to death but will never
attack. He's like a trapped animal. Only when someone grabs him
by the throat, when life is at stake. That's why he goes on about
death so much . . . that's why he goes on so much at all. Do you
understand? I had to do it. I'm interested in the sense of it all . . ."

"Sure," I said, and I looked at him almost playfully. "Sure. Very
well. Carry on, please."

"Oh, get off it, for fuck's sake. You know we've passed the joking
age. We've come here to stop joking, to stop joking at last, to clean
ourselves of that joking shit, of going home when the beer's finished
. . . I don't know. They'll go after us, and we'll be trying to escape,
even though we've done nothing, even I haven't done anything, for
it was just an empty gesture, a vacuous act, there's no guilt to it, no
profit, we don't want anything in return . . . Do you know anything
about disinterested acts, apart from smoking? Fuck, not even that."

Did I have to listen to it? Couldn't I just imagine it, the way I
imagined a big, black map of Poland and our train on it, a tiny point
of light moving north-west, and when I changed focus, when I
turned the zoom of my imagination, I saw us, two wrapped-up
figures, sitting in a toy-like glass box and leaning towards each
other. And when I looked even closer, I saw we were naked, barely
protected inside something transparent and fragile, while outside
raged the darkness and cold and we couldn't tell our story to anyone,
although by now there must have been many people quite keen to
hear it. And as if that was not enough, the train slowed down and
then ground to a halt in the middle of nowhere. Not a light, not a
trace of life outside the windows, only a rectangle of turbid light on

the snow. And silence. As if the train belonged only to us, as if it were given to us like a deliverance, or a trap, just like in a dream where everything has a dual nature, love changes into loathing and escape is never far from the chase. So in order to deal somehow with that silence and stillness, I turned the handle, opened the window and looked outside. The signals were green, remote and hazy. Then we heard steps on the lower deck, and a moment later on the stairs appeared a uniformed figure. I wanted to do something, immediately, to find a cigarette in my pocket or to say something to Kostek, something ordinary, casual, something that would show it was all taking place a year, five years earlier, or later, and we were going on holiday, or to work, on the night shift in a factory or something. But I did nothing. A skinny fellow with a crumpled and – I could swear – a soot-covered face, said:

"Another son of a bitch found an emergency brake and a short cut home."

The railwayman went on looking for a broken emergency brake and probably found it, for a few minutes later the train moved on. It was only then that I finally managed to find my cigarettes. Kostek sat as white as a sheet, looking out of the window. Words began to spill out of him like pebbles, like sawdust from a teddy bear.

I couldn't be bothered to listen to him. I knew all those fast, rattling monologues that run through our heads in moments of ecstasy or madness, when all the words seem to fit . . .

". . . and you're not listening. Don't miss this chance now, I'm telling you. They won't put us in the same cell. Have you ever been inside? Of course you haven't. I'm not asking if you sat in a cell for five hours sobering up. That's not inside, not real. It's just a nightmare, no metaphysics, just a hallucination. All right, we can leave it out, the cell I mean. At least for the next . . . how much of the journey have we left? Two, three hours? Now we can talk. Not like at the station, where we had to put our heads in the sand. Now everything's changed. Even if you laugh, your laughter won't do anything, neither to me nor to you. We'll miss it, this laughter, for one misses stupid things. Even if one is wise, or maybe especially then . . ."

"You want to say that this is some kind of wisdom trip?"

"Perhaps. Maybe even more than that. A blood-for-the-heart trip, or a die-to-live trip, as our chief Bandurko called it in a moment of inspiration. It's a trip, all right. There's no denying that. It's one of the most real trips you've ever had, isn't it? A real trip. It has real time and place. Poland, year 1993, please note, for on New Year's Eve you were probably too smashed to notice. Nineteen ninety-three. The sum total gives twenty-two, that is the first and at the same time the last card of the Tarot. In this case it must be the first: I can't believe the world has gone to seed so much it would be its crowning. So let's assume it's the beginning of a journey. These are esoteric reasons, my dear, the reasons of our metaphorical and real trip. Apart from the esoteric, there are many other reasons, physiological, for instance. We were sick, but now we are on the road to recovery. Remember. Poland, 1993. Yep . . . the twenty-second and at the same time the first card of the Tarot, that is the Fool or Antropos. We are searching for the Holy Grail. Well, the kind of Grail we can afford. That is, we'll die, out of our own free will, our only adversary. Free will, our last attribute, as the machine will soon master the art of self-destruction. Poland, 1993. Remember. Winter. We've chosen this place, full of un-Polish but pleasant names. No one is a prophet in his own country. To fast, one has to find a refuge. We have retreated as far as it was possible, without the risk of making an international incident. Poland, 1993. I'm thirty-three, as from three weeks ago. I heard a voice, though it wasn't the voice of our dear friend Vasyl. It was a totally inner voice. Thirty-three. Three and three makes six. In Tarot the sixth card is the card of Lovers. I was alone at the time, so it was a bit ironic. Then I realised I should become a lover of myself. Maybe I'm androgynous, for I had no problem with that. And what is love if not the realisation of a potential? Three times three makes nine. The ninth card of Tarot is the Hermit. I weighed all the reasons without listening to either wisdom or stupidity and followed the middle of the road to the very heart, where lives all that we fear, all that we never clad in words, even though it shapes our days, determines what we eat, who we fuck, that thing which makes our women Virgin Marys or Ulrike Meinhofs, and which makes us start smoking because we're too scared to throw ourselves under the train. Yep. That Hermit, the Eremite and his Lux Occulta, that afflicts young boys. Protected loneliness, nurtured, dark and the only one, as it's there where brood all loves, fears and desires. It's hard to be a young boy again. But I've worked hard at it. The last three years . . . OK, let's leave Tarot, it's rubbish. Arithmetic and psychological aberration. Gibberish, drivel for those to whom nothing ever happens. Listen, the last three years, I've done the work of a young man. How can I explain it? You remember those days when everything was obvious? No. OK, let's take geography. There, in Łódź, I was lonely. Then, when they died, that is my parents, I moved to Warsaw and was lonely again. I couldn't stay there. I sold their flat, their car and moved to Warsaw. A hundred and thirty kilometres on the yellow–blue train, three suitcases. Why? I could have moved anywhere. To America, in order to get lost. To Mexico, to die. To some poor country in the south, to Lisbon, for instance; you can't go further than that. I had a bit of money. But still I went to Warsaw. A hundred and thirty kilometres on a yellow–blue train, and three suitcases. *As of country, anus patria* . . . the hole in a concrete floor where drunkards piss. Bend over it with a magnifying glass and you will see all the diseases of the world. Sure, I could go to New York, sure I could, but I preferred Warsaw. It's closer, and the difference is merely that of quantity. Three years ago you didn't have to go to New York; Warsaw was cheaper and more interesting. In Łódź I would have to wait longer. Why am I telling you this? As if I believed I'm able to convey things, not through logical exposition but with every single message, because every little thing is a reflection of a bigger thing, and so on until the most important things. Three years ago I came to Warsaw to write a book. I'm a writer, you see. At the age of seventeen I had a poem published. Honest. But the moment I stepped out of the train at Warsaw Central, I knew I'd fucked it. A kind of premonition. Though it wasn't so bad to start with. Writer that I was, I began with buying a typewriter and a flat. A good start. Then the research, wandering around the streets and bars. I didn't know exactly what sort of thing I was looking for, so just to be safe I collected everything. Tired feet, that's all I got. I should have stayed home and watched TV. And one bar a week would have been enough. All right, and a tram ride on route 36, from terminal to terminal. But soon I realised it was beyond me. Too much competition. Everyone was inventing stories, and someone bigger was inventing stories about those who are inventing, and one level up there was someone bigger still, some kind of Moyra, like in Homer, and she is inventing the greatest story of all, which contains all others. I would have to invent something really monstrous to make it, for every lavatory lady used to tell stories Sheherazade wouldn't dream of when she finally hit the sack. Last summer I waited for the day when the wind was southerly, went on the Gdański Bridge and sent off my pages like kites. Three years work. Hundreds of pages. It was night, but the river turned white. I'm telling you, it was like broken ice flowing down to Gdańsk, that's what it looked like. In Gdańsk, writer Huelle could fish it out, dry it and use it. I couldn't. I ran out of enthusiasm to sling the typewriter. I should have taken it to some palace, the government, or the Seym, left it by the wall, or behind the toilet, and rung them to say there was a bomb. I must be some sort of a militant leftist, or a rightist. Imagine those bastards in black berets, each clad in iron like a medieval knight, throw themselves on those marble floors, pull their guns out and crawl towards my black box, my revenge, a caseful of shit, burps, farts and wheeze, for that was the only form my *oeuvre* could assume. Yeah . . . And then, in the autumn, Vasyl told me to drop in at the Crossroads."

Chapter 16

And the clank of the wheels. Sometimes Kostek's voice merged with that regular sound, it climbed over it like vine, wrapped itself around it like hop on a pole, somewhere near Pulawy, by that road overshadowed by old linden trees, from where one can see sometimes the rising scarp of the Vistula and the smooth mirror of water, stretching out and disappearing in the haze of the southern horizon. Summers were really hot in those days. We would arrive on the glowing-like-fish-scale town square, sweating, with bums sore from overtight jeans, half-dead. The drivers who had given us a lift must have regretted it, unless they were lorry drivers in cabins with the windows wide open. We were skinny, poor and hungry. That's why we set out on those mad hitchhiking races around Poland, going two, three days without sleep, leaving black marks on the signs outside towns. That's right, that was our reason: skinny, poor and hungry, pursued by our own dreams. We had a deep contempt for tents, and for anything that had weight. We would lie hidden at the top of a limestone cliff, a quarry beneath us, and on the other side of the river, perched on the skyline, the ruins of Janów Castle. We would leave our things among the white rocks and make it to town to find something to eat. The road ran along a deep, loess ravine. The crowns of trees growing on the edges formed a natural canopy. The shadow was thick and moist. Then there was a bridge, high and vaulted out of lime slabs. Spanning the ravine, it led to an overgrown old cemetery. We would stop under the bridge to hear our bouncing voices, hardened as if by a casing of a well. Shorty's footsteps pressed into the soft loess clay were huge and so wide I could fit into them only with great difficulty.

So Kostek's voice was like ivy, like vine, winding itself on to the hard core of the clang. He didn't look at me but through the window or at his hands, then again through the window, as if all the images and events emerged from there, as if it were the screen of his memory. And perhaps it was. The reflection of his face was blurred, murky, ghostlike. Perhaps with the help of words he was trying to redraw its contours, to find it anew in the midst of all that mess, the hurry, the panic. So he carried on and on and on, as if his words were to form into a new, heroic body, complex but resilient, composed of wounds and beatings, of mistakes, of all that makes up the heart of stories picked up in bars, inns, night buses, the yarns spun out by men, always by men, bloated, red-eyed, exuding a whiff of tiredness from under their suits, sobbing now and for ever, amen.

So I didn't interrupt him. Why? He wasn't talking to me. He was talking to himself, to his self in short trousers, to his self standing by the window on a warm, rainy day, when the puddles grow blue as the storm retreats, to himself from ten, fifteen years ago, to himself by the typewriter, to his characters making decisions, going left or right but leading him here, sitting on the cold green bench, to himself standing behind that soldier, to himself from half a minute ago.

How long did this journey last? Until dawn? No, it was a journey to the end of the night, when the darkness is still thick, undiluted, and human bodies like white worms crawl out of their stuffy, stinking sarcophagi and start burrowing tunnels with feeble light-bulbs, tunnels to kitchens, to lavatories, sometimes only two steps away, to the chair with a yesterday shirt or a cup of cold tea.

The train travelled along some hopelessly zigzagging track, slipping among the white hills and little valleys, rising and falling, or at least that was how it seemed to me, lots of hills, lots of valleys between us and the pursuit, like in a fairy tale where a thrown comb changes into a forest and something else into a river to slow down the dragon.

But in the end, after a few hours, I had a feeling we were being kidnapped, that this was a labyrinth and the locomotive was in cahoots with the pursuit and was dragging us into a blind canyon, blocked and surrounded by guns, dogs and justice.

Kostek remained oblivious to it all. He spoke, slowing down when turning and softening his voice at stops, while his cigarette packet slimmed down to the thickness of its paper wrapping. Words and smoke veiled the feeble light of two glow-lamps. Brilliant camouflage. Wrapped in gibberish like in a mosquito net, hazy, immersed in the royal waters of logorrhoea – who could possibly fish us out? Who? And with what?

Grobów. Two lampposts, a low platform and not a soul in sight, except for a railwayman's hat sticking out from the last carriage. Stepping across the tracks, we headed for a dark building. Through the half-open door seeped yellow light, a fire substitute, ersatz warmth.

"Eh, is this Kraków? Kraków?" A man burst through the door, almost knocking us to the ground.

"Grobów – not Kraków," I said.

"But the train! Is this the Kraków train?"

In reply Kostek pushed him hard and almost screamed.

"What the fuck do we care? May it go to hell!"

Then I realised it was the second time in a few days that I was in Grabów and that this time it was not me who was led but that I was leading, though it was not such a sure thing. The sure thing was that I was back here with a madman.

The ceiling in the waiting-room had the same colour that was seeping out through the door. The floor drowned in dusk. We hesitated for a moment and simultaneously made for a tiled stove. Naturally, the room was empty. Two freshly painted benches glistened with green paint. And rows of nail heads in the wooden floor, polished by thousands of feet. And peace. We propped up the stove and tried to doze off all that jazz, wipe it off with sleep like with a wet rug. But neither of us had the strength.

"And from here? Do you know how?"

"I do. At dawn. Don't worry, the worst is yet ahead of us."

And not a word more. Perhaps the surrounding silence pushed down our throats tufts of cotton wool, thick and hairy, breath-stopping. They entered through the mouth and spread out along the arteries. I woke up feeling unable to make a move, and if anyone wanted anything from me he would have to drag me like a bale, a corpse, like a dead animal. I worried they might crack my skull on the threshold.

When it got lighter, I experienced a weird *déjà vu*: those same houses, the same climbing street, everything like a week ago except there was no horse, and the sky, instead of pink, had the colour of frozen dirty water, the only proof of the passage of time.

The bus had just left. The next was in less than one hour. Sleepy lorry drivers didn't even blink at us. We stood at the bus stop. Van and lorry drivers didn't give a shit about us; nor did the few other drivers. At long last an unannounced bus stopped, took ten zlotys a head and said it would not stop until Gardlica. The last thing I saw was the stone viaduct. My head lolled on to my chest, a trickle of saliva set off from the corner of my mouth. I fell asleep, repeating to myself that we had an hour.

Chapter 17

That's where we decided to hide, on that big square of trodden snow and mud. We paid the granny who guarded the station lavatory and she assured us that there was no need to worry about the rucksacks – the worst that could happen to them was that they would stink of bleach. We had five hours to kill. First we checked out the station bar.

"Lukewarm piss," said Kostek and went off to buy another coffee. He drank it as if it were yesterday's, and then we left the bar.

"Let's go where there's a lot of people."

The "fayre" was about two kilometres away. That's how the locals called it – "the fayre". A square of trodden snow and mud, plus a half-thousand men and women. At least half of them had something to hide. And it was a perfect hiding place. Cars with Russian registration numbers were lined in rows. Like tents. Every other one had a carpet, rug, or kilim thrown over the bonnet. Eastern splendour – electric drills, lathes, super-glue and the local entrepreneurs who waddled about with a streetwise gait and Marlboros on portable displays.

"What a choice," said Kostek, pointing to bathroom taps, pipes, showers, none of them new but ripped out of a wall somewhere. Where? I wondered, but the infinite vastness of the empire paralysed my imagination. A woman with a bag collected the stall rent, accompanied by a muzzled dog. I put my wallet into my front trouser pocket and joined the slow procession along the stations of the Lord's Passion; it really felt like that. A seventy-year-old woman was selling squares of sandpaper, a thousand zlotys apiece, and pink fasteners for women's underwear – provocatively colourful against the greyness of her face, her clothes – her eyes fixed on something beyond the crowd, as if seeking consolation from the heavens above. She was selling nothing else: just brown gritty paper and flesh-coloured plastic.

Kostek kept moving, poking his head through gaps in the crowd, and probably forgot about me, immersed in this tale of 1001 nights, an Aladdin's cave of cardboard boxes – pale blue and red – out of which stuck the butts of American M16s, produced somewhere in Rostov or Moscow's suburbs. Their constant rat-tat-tat hung above the crowd. A fair-haired girl, her face scarred with a leprosy of purple make-up, sent round after round into the tree-tops. The crows didn't mind. Huddled, with beaks under wings, they sat on the branches like migrating flocks of black sheep. There were also grenades, brown incised eggs, not much bigger than the Easter ones also on display. Kostek walked up to the girl and without a word took the weapon out of her hands, turned and, when his eyes found mine, sent a round into my stomach.

"How much? How much do you want for it?"

"Fifty. It's elektreek," she said proudly.

Kostek handed it back, took me under my arm and said:

"Just the thing for Vasyl. Comes with spare batteries."

"Buy it."

"It won't fit into the rucksack."

"Carry it in your hand. You're not afraid, are you?"

"No. Calibre 5.56 makes little holes on entry but knocks out a kilo of meat on exit. The bullet goes somersaulting through the man's body. It's light but long. A kalashnikov is shorter but a bit heavier. I'd rather have an Uzi: the smallest, a micro-Uzi, weighs under two kilos."

A strange character wandered in between us. He opened a flap of his green nylon raincoat and showed three bottles capped with plastic stoppers:

"*Tovarishtchi*, vodka . . . Fifteen each . . ."

"Too cheap, *tovarishtch*."

"Good vodka, not cheap. Good . . ."

He was looking into our eyes, opening his coat wide, like a flasher, or perhaps a sick bird, or a master of levitation.

"No, *tovarishtch*, we don't drink this sort. In fact, we don't drink at all. We're Boy Scouts . . ."

His eyes examined our faces closely, looking for an escaping giggle, hoping our masks would crack.

"Boy Scouts . . ."

He nodded his head, coming to terms with his bad luck, then shut his shop and waddled off in his black, clapped-out brogues towards a large wooden hut, to dissolve in its shadow together with his mates who, knives in hands, ate fish out of tins, their forearms blue with tattoos.

"Armature and tincture," muttered Kostek under his nose and wandered off to look for his Uzi.

A Soviet grandma handed a Polish grandpa a little piece of sandpaper. He handed her the money. Paper for paper. There was no wind, no flutter. The girl stopped firing; despite her shapeless coat and awful make-up, she was quite a beauty. The Russian entrepreneurs finished their meal. The kicked tin rolled in among the manometers, circular saw blades and cartons of cigarettes with Peter the Great on horseback. Another machine-gun rattle – not a head turned. The sellers stood motionless like true people of the north, saving vital energy. Our people shuffled along, stooped, sleepy, with their noses stuck in the junk – touching, picking up, buying or putting back, now this, now that, and everything with the same contempt, for they never really wanted those hopelessly unheroic goods, those sad dolls, tired teabags, all that grey, pitiful rubbish marked by rain and frost, by the horror of that vastness which can fold on to itself but will never end, where everything gets lost like a man on foot. Gas meters, water meters, cutlery ornamented with universal folk patterns, pepper, dog collars, officers' boots, leather, string, scythes, sickles, enormous panzer-bras, ashtrays, timber, stones – as if they were dispossessing themselves, as if above the empire hung the spirit of a new religion – relinquishment – the ultimate form of mysticism which regards the immaterial as the only reality. They were sweeping their homes clean, awaiting a revelation that should come to fill their souls and their homes anew.

"*Eto kosmicheskiy pistoliet*," said a young man to Kostek. His laser gun with flashing yellow and red lights was emitting a weak buzz.

"To shoot the Martians, is it?"

"Maybe Martians." The youth smiled, unsure, and pulled his head back into the collar of his denim sheepskin, like a tortoise. "Maybe Russians."

"Who has anything against Russians today?"

"We, Ukrainians."

"So you've nothing against Poles any more?"

"There are no Poles in our country."

"Only Russians? Hold on to your cosmic gun, then. It may come in handy yet. The Russians used to hang out in space, so it may work on them."

The youth looked at him hard, but Kostek didn't give him a chance and walked on. I moved on too. I wanted to have a look at a huge Volga covered with rugs. In fact, the car itself was invisible but so big it could only be a Volga. The rugs were piled on the roof, flowing down on to the bonnet and over the boot. On the rugs stood crystal vases, bowls, goblets, decanters. Samovars from Tula. Carpets from Bukhara. Where had it all come from? Plunder, most likely. It was like a tent of a Mongol khan pitched in the middle of a grey desert of everyday junk. People would give those wonders a tap and listen to the high tone, which was soft and pure – the "fayre" had nothing purer. They were old people, old women, old men, grey-haired, wearing warm boots. They would put their ears to the crystal, listening, motionless, until the sound dissolved in the air like a shaft of light, and then they would tap it again, straining for this something remote, something beautiful and unattainable.

Keeping an eye on the shop was a tall fifty-year-old man, thin and straight. His was not a Russian potato-face. From under the broad black cape lined with karakul fur peered a grey Stalin tunic. Silver hair was shaved high up the back of his neck, and the salt-and-pepper moustache tapered into points just below the corners of his mouth. I came closer to sniff him. I was curious if he smelled of anything. He did. Eau de Cologne and pipe tobacco. I liked the man. Moreover, he had all his teeth. They were as white as porcelain. I thought they must give out the same sound as his crystals. The grey breeches disappeared into high black boots which wrinkled softly around the ankles.

Finally our eyes met. His were cold grey-blue. They hypnotised me. I got stuck on those icy needles. He nodded at me to come closer. I did. I made three, four steps and stopped in front of him. His eyes examined me from head to toe, as if he were trying to put a price on me, as if buying me, something like that, and I was afraid to make a move or ask what he wanted of me. Then he glanced quickly above my head, his eyes swept over the marketplace with lightning speed like the eyes of a bird of prey, like an eagle owl perched in a tree, and before it crossed my mind that he was being cautious or conspiratorial he raised a rug hanging over the back door, yanked at the handle and hissed – "Quick, quick." I fell in head first, folding up like a penknife, the doors clapped shut behind me and the darkness swallowed me up. Suddenly I remembered that Kostek wouldn't know where I was and would be looking for me.

The darkness was not complete. On the pillar between the doors glowed a small yellow light. The engine was running, but the thick layer of wool smothered all the noise. I felt the car vibrate, and it was warm.

The first thing I saw were her eyes. Two great shadowy puddles, and inside them, in the pupils, a golden glow from the feeble lightbulb. How did I know it was a she? The smell. A sickly smell of perfume, fragrant oils or herbs, God knows what, of something feminine anyway. The head, the face, the entire body was swathed in a blanket, a bedspread, a dark, patterned winding sheet. She must have moved a moment earlier, as the seat under my hand was still warm. The eyes and the arm: she held the drapes somewhere under her chin. Her arm was thin and small; it emerged from the folds naked to the elbow, the bangles of glimmering metal seemed enormous.

I felt hot. I reached for the zip of my jacket. The gesture made her burrow deeper into the corner of the seat. Her jewellery jingled softly; the folds slipped off her face and I saw she was still a child, twelve years old at the most.

She must have been naked underneath. I noticed her bony knees as she attempted to squat on her heels, trying to take up as little space as possible, to fold herself into a little ball, into something closed tight, something difficult to unfold. One foot dug into the black upholstery but then slipped off with a mournful screeching sound. She tried again, pulling her foot with the other hand, which was handcuffed to the elbow-rest.

I withdrew to my corner and put my hands in my pockets. She calmed down. The drapes slipped off her head. She had straight black hair. In five years' time she would be a beautiful woman.

From under the folds escaped an overpowering stench of unwashed body and cosmetics. It made me dizzy. I pushed at the door, felt it bang against something and got out, gasping for air; it tasted of coal dust. The man barred my way. He seemed to have lost some of his cool.

"A hundred," he said, almost whispered. "A hundred."

"You'd better give her a wash first," I said, charging past him, head down.

Chapter 18

This time there was no hut, no ruins, nothing but a hole in the ground padded with branches of fir. They must have been fir, for even though we broke them off in the dark they had a sweet perfume.

"The Czetwiertne dogs," I said, just as Bandurko had a week ago. I decided to take a different route. Bandurko said we could reach our hut going over the Czetwiertne. I saw on the map that this was right. I decided to go along the top of the valley, stick to the edge of the wood, keeping the dogs and the village lights on the left. We could even see the bloody place: five widely spread-out houses, pigsties and barns, sheds on the slope, meadows where they kept hay. The dogs didn't bark at us; they barked at the night, continuously. No one could see us. The bottom of the valley and the road lay a good kilometre away.

In the grim twilight the wood looked hopeless. Its edge was made up of alder, ivy, wild lilacs and pine growth, which kept falling, wave after wave, giving in to rot, stony ground and wind. Forest it was not. The bushes were cut with little ravines of mountain streams that, despite the cold, were barely frozen, making us fall ankle deep into mud as there was no time to look for a way round. And hazel, which grew everywhere, especially in the ravines: dry, fragile, naked roots hanging from the cliff landslips.

Kostek walked behind me. In the clearings the snow was deeper; we waded knee deep. He marched on, without a word, panting and whistling but pushing on like a little steam engine, for after all he had a good reason to be in a hurry. He swore loudly when the brambles caught at his feet.

"There's no need to rush. We won't get there today anyway."

We came to a strip of old wood, stretching down to the bottom of the valley like a huge tongue. We must have passed Czetwiertne, past meadows and pastures. We found a hole made by a fallen beech tree, practically fell into it and had only enough strength to take off our rucksacks, gather some branches and strew our lair. There was no wind in the hole. We had three sleeping-bags, and Kostek's was a down one. We had food and drink. Five minutes before the departure of the coach we'd stocked up on alcohol and stuffed our rucksacks with bottles. I even had the great idea of buying a torch with lots of spare batteries. So, smoked bacon and the two-thirds-empty bottle of spirit, into which Kostek dropped a few tea leaves to give it colour. He even made me switch the torch on to witness the metamorphosis. It wasn't too bad. Especially when the alcohol slipped into the bloodstream and we into the sleeping-bags, each into his own and then both into the down one. Only our feet, soaked through, frozen stiff, as if not ours, refused to warm up.

"Put the boots into the bag," I said. "In the morning they'll be rock hard."

"Morning? When's that, then?"

"Nearly twelve hours. It gets light after six."

Hats on, scarves on, gloves on, we lay on our sides, cuddling into each other, I into his back, pretending to be asleep. Perhaps we didn't want to sleep through that safe time, those twelve hours we knew we were in no danger, except from pneumonia. We had to appreciate it, to relish it, slowly, every crumb. The forest boomed above our heads. There was no other sound. We lay on the surface of the earth, two tiny figurines, stuck to the spinning shell. Who could possibly care about us, our existence? Mere pebbles, not worth spitting on. If the shell spun faster we would have floated off into space like two withered leaves, or fleas off the dog's back. Perhaps someone could spot us from a few hundred metres, maybe a kilometre. But from further away? From above? Decaying, rotting like litter on the forest floor, like white larvae under tree bark waiting for the winter to pass. I felt as we turned, as we sped into the black, icy space, cocooned in our own warmth, as we twisted under the earth's skin like a splinter or a crumb of quartz. It made me open my eyes from time to time and stare into the dark, at Kostek's neck, to get rid of that nauseating feeling.

In the coach, a few stops before the shelter the peasants talked about us.

A day was enough for the news to spread. Someone had a family in Niewierka, happened to be visiting, or maybe it all came out from the local border guards in Pietra? After all, it was only twenty kilometres and only us wandered about like two soldier Szweiks while they just phoned from one station to another. The peasants talked about it with indifference. Robbed? Killed? Who knows? Nobody knows. Some trouble in Niewierka, near that empty kolkhoz. Contraband or something. Fuck knows. "Eee, who goes with contraband in winter? What contraband?" "Well, people say they got a soldier, you know. But no one's been caught. Though in Pietra there are two carfuls of officers. From Kraków. That's what I heard."

We sat behind the peasants, one in a brown overcoat, the other in sheepskin, both wearing sheepskin earflap hats, both old, wrinkled, unfazed, even if death was involved, for of that they had seen a fair bit and now they were only interested in their own. Kostek, shrinking into his own coat like a turtle into its shell, didn't as much as glance at me, probably dying for me not to hear all that, desperate for the murmur of the conversation to remain in his head like a nightmare, a hallucination, God knows what, his private thing.

Was it really like that? I don't know. At any rate, he didn't look at me, saying, "Someone had to do it"; didn't bat an eyelid, just sat there staring out of his shell, his clothes, which somehow moved up, the collar as high as the top of his head. He looked on at the black and white village outside the window, a typical mountain chain of huts scattered along the bottom of the valley.

The houses were long, old, built of logs, painted blue or primed with oil, almost black with white joints. All stood below the level of the road, with their yards empty except for freeze-resistant ducks squatting on the snow waiting for a thaw. Not a soul in sight. Only sometimes a blurred face behind the nets curtains, the eyes following us from behind the row of geraniums. Two mongrels sniffed each other's legs. Overwhelming stillness. Except maybe for chimney smoke, capricious, winding, a transitory form between the whiteness of snow and the black of the rotting fences and hedges.

At last the peasants got off and we remained alone in the back of the bus.

"Did you hear?"

"I did. People here like a good natter."

"Yeah, they just talk. For the hell of it. Village gossip, like old women . . ."

And with that we closed the subject. The coach climbed up a long, easy, straight road. Now and again someone would approach the driver with a thousand zloty banknote and the coach would stop in front of a hut. Proper request stops. The passengers were trickling out, and I was afraid that soon there would be only us left, unshaven faces with eyes like holes pissed in snow, and that no one in his right mind would fall for the stupid tourists trick. But nothing happened. No one even looked at us as we scrambled out near the tourist shelter. The snowed-over rear of the coach disappeared in its own smoke and we started walking. Just like the last time with Vasyl, after an hour we turned west and so found ourselves in this hole.

In my head I was recounting everything that had happened to us in the last two days and two nights, going over it ten, twenty times, to bore myself with it and fall asleep while there was still some warmth in the body. I must have been finally falling asleep, for suddenly Gardlica's fayre changed into a church fair of twenty years ago, and February into August. The wooden church stood on a high river scarp. The other side was as far as the eye could see an empty, sandy plateau, flat as a table-top, dotted with herds of cows. The village bumpkins would point to the other side.

"It's the Bialystok side," they'd say with pride. There was an admiration and yearning in it, as if the capricious and green river Bug was a line dividing two continents. We sat hidden in the bushes, drinking cheap wine, Golden Apple Tree, Serenade or Harnaś, making fumbling attempts to grope the village girls. Behind our backs, the promenading public in their Sunday best and gorging themselves on lemon ice-cream were getting more and more into the swing of things. Shooting ranges, massive plaster hounds and glass palaces, colourful, multistoreyed constructions with steep roofs sprinkled with shimmering glassy powder. Opulence beyond description. Watches with motionless hands, pocket mirrors which instead of our own pimply faces offered smooth aspects of Brando or Captain Kloss, all framed in gold, blue or pink. Treasures of Ophir, fireworks, scarlet riches. Guns, myrrh and frankincense. Unheard-of wonders, squashed spheres on elastics, filled with sawdust. Dyed feathers composed Aztec-fashion into flowers, farting balloons made of red condoms, suction frogs, pneumatic devils and not a single angel, hair-thin jewellery, swans inside snowing orbs, nothing of use or value. Holy day. We sipped the wine, throwing up from the heat, waiting for the evening fun and games at the fire station. Cowboy belts with buckles the shape of cows' heads, penknives on silver chains, trumpets, whistles, ocarinas and green recorders. Drums, the scent of caramelised sugar, dusk and foraged orchards. And those tits and bums, which we were still afraid of. And huge colourful combs sticking out like knives from our back pockets.

It must have been a dream. Garlands, opulence, pageants of plaster figures: the Virgin Mary, the hounds, gamekeeper, Saint Joseph, a cat, all to be won in the raffle. Plenary indulgence. Remittance of sins.

Kostek was nestling his buttocks into me; I was breathing on the nape of his neck. We probably did sleep. I'm sure we did, for in the end we were woken up by a massive boom, as if everything around was falling on our heads. Kostek moaned, "Jesus, I'm freezing," and began to twist and turn. It was creeping from the feet up, a tingly cold cramp spreading across the back and shoulders. Up above, a roaring wind. I put my head out. It was snowing.

"It'll bury us," said Kostek.

"It'll be warmer, like in an igloo."

"Like in a grave."

Waste of breath. We pulled the sleeping-bag over our heads. I remembered the spirit, but to get to it we'd have to destroy our snowy shelter. So we lay, half-dead, like Lazarus, wrapped in tattered sheets of snow. Scraps of dreams tore at our souls, snatching them from our bodies, which bit by bit were becoming strange, dead, disgusting and painful. The gigantic beech wood boomed above our heads like a bridge swept by sheets of icy wind, banished from the black void to die high among the crowns of trees. The branches banged against each other. We could hear as one after the other the broken boughs fell down, withered, fragile, filled with ice. It was apparently the wind's job to sort out the woods, to rid it of all dead growth. The eagle owl that hooted us good night disappeared. Maybe the poor bird simply gave up with his feeble warning, laughable in comparison with the mighty rumble heading our way, as if the Great Bear herself was tearing through the forest to get us.

"I can't sleep." Kostek said that in a tone of voice as if we were on two separate beds in a hotel or in a Scout camp.

"Count something," I whispered to his ear.

"Count what? I'm shaking."

"Anything. Years. I'm shaking too."

And so we groaned and mumbled to each other. The space between the groans could be hours or minutes. Exhaustion was drawing us in like a suffocating deep trying to drown us, yet our bodies were still too light, floating up to the surface, choked, swollen, white corpses, while dreams and thoughts drilled through us like eels through carrion, like through a horse's head thrown for bait. Inside my head were all the fairs and bazaars I'd seen in my life. Inside Kostek's probably Uzi – what else would he be dreaming of in his situation? I was sure he already regretted leaving that Makarov behind in the snow. For at the "fayre" he had reeled from one pile of rubbish to another like a lunatic, pulling out those miserable replicas of death which clicked, rattled, farted and flashed in colour yet all refusing to turn in his hands into something more like a deadly threat: a bow and arrows with metal heads, a sabre with a plastic handle . . .

He forgot about me. He waded through this arsenal of nightmares, possessed by the thought. I got worried that I'd have to remove him by force, drag him away or kick him out from among those delusions, pack him into the bus, nurse him like an idiot or just keep slapping his face. After an hour everyone knew him. The Russians, Romanians, Poles and Tartars. They were all shoving in front of him green, blue, yellow and black offers, including water pistols with a Russian Bugs Bunny, while he shook his head, picking and choosing, making knowing faces until they, too, began to take him for an idiot.

"*Malchik*, come, *Katiusza*."

After I got away from my palace of delights I couldn't find him again for a long time. Then I spotted him with three jeans-clad loafers. They stood in a tight circle behind the kiosk with grilled sausages in the corner of the square. Stooped, heads together, whispering; one could tell from a hundred paces they were whispering. I headed in their direction but Kostek failed to notice me and only one of the others clocked me when I was two steps away. He turned to me his ugly face, marinated in fear and cunning, and

croaked: "What do you want?" Then Kostek said: "It's my friend."
And the pickle face: "You have bodyguards?" And to his mates:
"Let's split." Before we knew it, we stood alone in the stink of
burned fat. Kostek took out a cigarette.

"How much do you have?"

"Not much. Five, six hundred."

He shuffled sideways and, just as if I were one of those dawdlers,
he whispered from the corner of his mouth, "There's a kalash for
three melons. Plus sixty pieces of ammo."

"And you want to buy it? It won't fit into your rucksack."

"It will. It's one of those with a folding butt," he answered
completely straight-faced. "Trouble is, I have only two. If we added
your money, perhaps they would let us have it. They said they'll be
around until the evening.

He was looking at his feet. A great billow of smoke fell on us
from the chimney of the sausage kiosk. A girl in a dark blue overcoat
walked past with a rococo clock made of golden plastic. The three
bums stood by the carpeted Volga.

"It's not my money, Kostek. It's the guys', the kitty. I'm not
sure how badly they want this gun."

The argument was out of his mad world. But it worked. Kostek
withdrew, with contempt, but he did. Pearls before swine, that's
what he must have thought. The money was of course mine; I had
blown the kitty ages ago. He gave up on me but started scanning
the crowd for a possible source of help. Three cops appeared. I
nodded my head at them and took Kostek by the arm. He followed
me meekly. The uniforms reminded him who we were and why we
were there.

Now I was breathing the odour of his unwashed body. Despite
the chill in the air I could smell the stench of exhaustion and of
cold sweat. Or were they mine? Who could tell?

Chapter 19

First it was knee deep, then balls deep, and then when we managed to get out into the open even waist deep. Underneath the white, sloping surface hid treacherous snowdrifts, like traps. And zero visibility. The white blizzard blew straight into our faces. We marched on with closed eyes. It didn't matter. The direction was downhill. All other directions looked the same – they were invisible. After an hour I fantasised about seeing something black or grey; anything but white. The trench ploughed by us in the snow was disappearing in a matter of seconds. So, balls deep: I in front, Kostek behind me, with a burning fever. He said it was nothing, but when at dawn we dug ourselves up from under the snow his eyes were glowing like coals. Now and again I had to stop and wait, or go back and pull him out of the fluffy snow traps. I had never seen a blizzard like this. We were soaked through, with sweat and snow. We should have reached the bottom of the valley by now. Even if we moved only one kilometre per hour. We should have reached the stream, some wood, bushes, anything. I kept closing my eyes, or watched my knees. And kept pushing on. On and down. The one thing I was sure of.

I looked back. Kostek wasn't there. I shouted. I could shout until the end of the world. Even if he heard me, his answer would have been snatched from his mouth and blown the other way. What was his little voice against tonnes of whistling blizzard? I took off my rucksack, stood it upright and went back. I found him neither sitting nor kneeling, waist deep in the snow, leaning like an old statue. He'd got stuck in a snowdrift with not a drop of will left in him.

"I can't," he said. His face was dark red and his eyebrows white. "I really can't. I have to have a rest."

I felt like kicking him. He would have probably keeled over, like a statue, and just lain there. Instead, I kneeled down.

"You would make a pretty picture with your kalashnikov. You could stick it up your ass, like a snowman's broomstick."

He looked at me blankly, as if his eyes had frozen over. Or was it hatred? I, too, felt I didn't want to move, that I wanted to stay with him there, where the wind didn't seem to blow so hard.

"All right. Let's rest a little."

"Yes, let's. It's the twenty-fourth of February, ten-thirty a.m.," he said, scratching the snow off his wristwatch. "I really can't. Three days and three nights on the road. I'm so tired. I know I'm stupid, but I'm so sleepy. Hot or cold, I just want to lie down and have a bit of sleep. I know, I know . . ."

"Listen, it's not far now. An hour, maybe half." I said that without actually having a clue. "Just a few minutes more."

I got up with great difficulty and walked around Kostek to open his rucksack. From among the rags and loaves of bread I pulled out instant coffee and a bottle of vodka.

"Have you still got that knife?" He rummaged in his pockets and took it out. I punctured a hole in Café Prima, spilled some on to my hand, added some snow and began to chew. It wasn't too bad. I handed him the packet. He was putting in his mouth portion after portion but without enthusiasm, even choking on it.

"Take more snow. Make it into a paste."

He followed the instruction so closely that after a while he forgot about the coffee and started stuffing his face with handfuls of snow. I wanted to touch his forehead but thought he would take advantage of the gesture and let himself go to pieces.

After coffee, vodka. I took a good swig and waited for it to be distributed down the arteries. Kostek sipped a small mouthful.

"A smoke and we'll go." He nodded.

It soon became quite pleasant. We must have been sinking deeper and deeper into the snow for the wind barely touched our heads.

"A smoke and we'll go," he repeated after a while, as if to himself. "We're going and going, day, night, a week, a year, two, three, the wind blowing up the ass, now in the face. Perhaps something's changing. Don't worry, I'll get a grip on myself. I'll pull out. Fucking shivers. When I was little I liked shivers. You lay under the duvet and when you felt cold you knew it was an illusion, for how could you be cold under a duvet? I liked fever too. Cold lemon tea.

Sleeping and not sleeping. Kid's delirium. You know what I liked best? Sandwiches with pickled gherkins. A piece of bread, a little butter and sliced gherkin. I survived all my childhood illnesses on that. Look at that, let them look for us. In half an hour there'll no trace left. Just like in Kazakhstan. This kind of wind is called buran. It blows for two weeks and then sleighs trip up on chimneys. Or get stuck on the roofs. I read it somewhere. You wish it hadn't happened, don't you? Admit it. You wish you could turn back the clock, don't you? It won't. We'll get the others and carry on. Until they catch us. No one will go back home. Not you, or anyone else. This we can arrange. I need a rest. You say the hut is down there? I'll lie by the fire and dream and not dream. A gherkin? Up yours."

He raised the bottle and drank to gherkin's instant death. Or so it looked. The vodka trickled down his chin. He passed me the bottle.

"Drink and we'll push on. I'll tell you one thing, though. So you know. I've never liked you. Not you, not Shorty, not Goosy. Bandurko maybe. And now you'll have to nurse me. Especially now. You'll have to keep me and fatten me up, your very own scapegoat. If that man was found there, you know . . . No one will know for sure which one of us . . ."

"What the fuck are you drivelling on about?" My head was filled with the swishing wind. As if I had the whole valley resting on my head, an empty sphere with a blizzard inside.

"I'm not drivelling. I meant what I said. Now let's go."

He got up quickly as if he were no longer tired or didn't feel the weight of his rucksack. He sank into the snow but straightened, up, pushed past me and followed the barely visible trail. When we got to my rucksack, a snowy wound, he asked:

"Which way now?"

"Downhill. All the way."

After half an hour we could make out some black tree trunks. I dragged myself to the first copse, breathless, lungs on the verge of bursting wide open. Kostek recovered all right. He tore through the snow like an icebreaker. Then he stopped and waited for me.

"Well?"

"The stream should be somewhere here. It should flow to the right. We need to go downstream. It's the same stream we heard then."

Among the trees the snow was not so deep. We reached a little ravine. It looked like a river bed but covered with snowdrift as far as the eye could see. Kostek made a step and fell into snow up to his chest. He managed to push his way through to the middle of the clearing, the supposed river bed. For a while he dug the snow with his boots until he got to the ice.

"I think this is it."

We got there in the end. I recognised the loosened cliff. When running over the stone thresholds, the stream left behind the snow. Green water gushed from deep, icy gullies. We clambered up the cliff and there it was, the hut. I could smell the smoke. A barely visible path ran from the stream.

"Not a bad place," said Kostek and assumed his position behind my back.

I went first then. The door creaked, pushing away a pile of snow. Inside was filled with the stench of burning; the smoke made the eyes water. They sat around the fire, wrapped in sleeping-bags, crouched, shrivelled and still. Kostek slipped in and closed the door. The red glow made our friends look like a bunch of tramps, or rag dolls; and this smoky stench, as if they had just escaped fire. Singed, in tatters, filthy. Proper fugitives.

Kostek stood still. So it fell to me to tell the tale. I did it before anyone managed to open their traps, voice a question or complaint. I rolled out a trip report from hell, our lousy odyssey. It didn't take me long, but I still had to squat to keep the smoke out of my eyes; they'd run out of dry firewood. So I gave them facts and zero adjectives; didn't have the strength. I couldn't see their faces, but it must have hit them hard. None of them said a word. Bandurko hung his head and cradled it in his arms. Shorty didn't stir. Goosy, who sat leaning against the wall, rustled the rugs.

I lit up. Kostek, leaning against the door, I in the centre of the hut, squatting, and they, scattered around, allegories of surprise, stilled panic, of petrified emotions that at a stroke must have rendered them unconscious, even robbed them of their names, turned them into a huddled grey lump, a heap of rugs, a tangled mess of thought ground to a halt. It looked as if we came to punish them, to hand them the eviction notice of their lives, a telegram, notice of death.

At last Vasyl raised his face.

"What a fucking mess. Goosy's sick, with a fever." He groaned as if it mattered very much, or as if he meant to throw Goosy on the scales, to make them tilt a little, to outweigh – even if only by a hair's weight – the weight of our news.

Then he got up, stepped into the fire, sending red sparks up to the roof and started walking to and fro, at least making some noise that filled the numbed silence and erased his helpless cry.

I thought that we, Kostek and I, had done our job. I thought that now I'd earned my rest and it was their turn. I delivered and didn't give a shit what was going to happen next. I sat by the fire. A saucepan with water stood on the coals. The water was struggling to reach boiling point.

"We brought coffee," I said to Shorty, who got up without a word and started rummaging through the rucksacks.

Goosy turned his face towards me. Blackened, worn out, with hollowed cheeks etched with dark lines of dirt and shadow, his hair clammy with sweat.

"When did it get you?"

"The day before yesterday, in the evening. We've no medicine."

"We'll feed you up."

"My bones ache. I'm freezing. And shivering, all the time."

"We've got some alcohol."

"Tell me, is this all true? Did he really do it?"

"He did, Goosy, he did. Some seven kilometres from here. We managed it quite well."

I brought him a drop of vodka in a mug. He stretched out his black hand from under a filthy duvet and drank it. He rested his head against the wall and closed his eyes. After a while he opened them and, as if woken up, he fluttered his eyelids:

"Really? Go on, tell us. How could he, just like that . . . Why? For fuck's sake, why? Listen, it's not a hoax, is it? It all sounds so stupid. We have to get out of here. Man, if they find us here . . ."

He spoke faster and louder, even though he was trying to soften his voice to a whisper, but the words sprang out of him as if out of a compressor, as if he kept too much air in his lungs, like under water, or in fear. I took off my hat and wiped sweat from his face. The grey fringe stuck askew to his brow. He looked like a little boy with an old face.

"We have to run, get the fuck out of here, back to Warsaw, try to forget about it. How stupid . . . What have we got ourselves into, eh?"

The water finally boiled. Shorty poured in the coffee and busied himself with the food.

Fat was sizzling in the frying pan; the fire spat sparks, little miniature explosions. Goosy shook under the pile of rugs. From the cold, fever and alcohol, and from his own words which terrified him. I forced him to eat some fried bacon. He chomped on the food in his parched mouth and with coffee pushed it down into his stomach. "Help me. I need to go out," he said.

He disentangled himself from the layers of rugs, leaned on my shoulder and we went out. Past the threshold he threw up everything he had just eaten. I had to practically carry him back inside.

"Hot beer," he mumbled. "I want some hot beer. Jesus, I'm desperate."

"We haven't brought any beer. It's a miracle we managed to get here as it is. Do you want some coffee? With vodka?"

He shook his head.

"No. Beer. I have cravings like a pregnant woman. Don't worry about me."

Ten-fifty, I thought. Ten zlotys and fifty groshes, that was how much hot beer with sugar cost in those days. It could have been February too; it was cold. Inside that stone hut the size of a dog kennel there was enough room for a stainless-steel counter, a huge aluminium kettle and a fat lady. She swore and shouted at the drunks, all the while filling the beer mugs and counting the money – here's your change and move along, about turn and get out in the fresh air – into the concrete little square fenced with an iron balustrade to keep the boozers from spreading out. No one sat at the metal tables; everyone stood, shuffling and stamping their feet, in the mist of their own breaths and the steam of rapidly cooling beer. Hot with sugar for ten-fifty. They also sold beer with syrup, but no one drank that. What was the point of trudging across the town, of standing in the line with dirty grey men, in the gloomy shadow of leafless trees?

The shadow of the trees, and the bigger shadow of the Palace of Culture made it doubly cold. The wind never stopped whistling.

Depending on the season, it carried dead leaves, rubbish or handfuls of dry snow from the nearby park alleys. Half the town, a wide river and one-fifty for the bus fare – that's what it took to get there even though on the way there were at least ten or more certainly warmer bars. We pissed straight over the dark-grey maple trunks. We had no shame. No one had. At any one time every tree had someone standing by it with his todger out. In winter it was another steamy contribution to the local mist, a kind of hot springs. For some strange reason the trees never wilted.

So one word was enough, a signal to drop everything and go, stand in a queue, stamp and shuffle and smoke cheap cigarettes. We would gather in a circle, like knights of the round table. Shoulder into shoulder, collars up, it seemed that in this way we protected the little clouds of warmth escaping from the beer mugs. We had no King Arthur. So anarchy ruled OK. But then we were sure we were all cast in the same mould. Hence the circle. All the local soaks also stood in a circle. All boys form circles, like Indians, like Zulu warriors. Goosy was there, so was Shorty, and the rest.

Summer, winter, the time of year was of no consequence. Except that in summer we could make it there on foot, weaving our way through little squares, back yards, parks and cinemas, whatever we fancied in this city of wonders. What a pleasant democratic city! All faces equally grey. *Egalité! Fraternité! Liberté!* Those years, '77, '78, '79, '80 and '81 – how free were we then. Lost in the belly of that languid, listless beast, that monster, inside Leviathan's intestines, feeding on them like parasites, like tapeworms. Thousands of passages, hundreds of places, hours; love is a privilege of bums and loafers – only later does this become obvious. Years of back yards and benches, winters in smoky rooms filled to cracking point with our presence, so tight you couldn't stick a pin of doubt. Goosy stood drinks, for he had cash. I drank them because I had no cash. No trace of Hegelian triad. Pure synthesis a priori.

"Let's go watch hookers at the Polonia Hotel." But no one in the end felt like it, so we ordered another round, smoked another cigarette and continued spinning out those yarns, mythical exploits, heroic tales. How Bolo jerked off for a year, collecting it in a milk bottle which he kept in the fridge, telling his folk it was a herbal remedy for some ailment or other. How Gągol would come into his sister's room in the middle of the night and take her duvet off. As she slept naked and the room was on the ground floor he charged twenty zlotys. How Franek Żebro always warned before starting a drinking session that after half a litre he shat himself and how everyone forgave him for in the past he carried out the romantic job of a Customs Officer on the western border. How Gągal's grandpa filled condoms with gas, tied a fuse and blew them up in the blue sky of the suburbs. How Oscar Peterson was twice as good as Errol Garner, or the other way round. About Buźka's huge tits and Dziuba's small ones. About the white napkin hung over Krzysiek's prick as he opened the door, thereby letting you know he had new flesh in his bed. About Goosy's father, who once in a bar knocked out a fellow twice his size because the bastard wanted to dance to the Red Poppies. About how many murders Leadbelly had on his conscience. About how Uriasz left his balls on a fence as he was trying to escape some big nasty people, and how later he had to wear women's sanitary towels by way of a dressing. A hundred of other myths, equally frayed at the edges from overuse, but as good as those about the betrayal of Sir Maldred, or finding the Excalibur, about Sir Galahad's shield or about Lancelot and the Holy Grail.

"Well, if not at the Polonia, then where?"

"Why do you have to?" answered Majer, pissed off he had to interrupt his whistling of "Round Midnight". "Go and watch the hooks at the butcher's. At least those are naked."

If it were summer we would set off down the Świętokrzyska to look up in the East German record shop to see if they had Mulligan playing with Brookmayer, and then straight down the Tamka to the riverside and the Mermaid's, where we had our first stop and the first round, only to move on along the river to the Albatross for the next round and another spell among the tramps, bums, soldiers and professional leg breakers. Up on top of the high scarp, above our heads, there was a plot afoot. In St John's, in St Martin's, at St Jack's, at the Virgin Mary's there was a conspiracy, a coup being plotted against our égalité, our fraternité, our liberté. Who could have guessed? Who could have known that in the cellars, in the woodwork-ridden stalls, among the black confessionals and golden chasubles, among the fonts and mummies there were fleeting shadows that had nasty designs on us. Had we known we should have moved south, up Mostowa, and piss on all those proud portals. But being naive and unaware, we moved north instead, stopping for a rest on the massive embankment steps, built for the arrival of some river giant.

In the distance, etched against the darkening sky, stood Gdański Bridge. Through the thicket of its black trellis passed red trams. White terns skimmed the green water. On the other side, in the zoo-gulag, the animals sang their mournful songs. Vasyl Bandurko marched at the end. Dressed in US army issue, he looked at the red-brick steeples of St Florian's, feeling a bit lonely and heavy, what with all the beer we had drunk, which for him was a little too much. Out in front was Goosy in his black leather bike jacket playing on his blues harp some silly tunes of foreign shepherds or criminals. Shorty marched beside me, screening the sun, which in turn was hiding behind the buildings of the mint. And ahead of us, just like Bandurko at the back, marched Majer, whistling Thelonious Monk to spite Goosy.

Somehow we still managed to get "behind the pipe" as it was known locally, for the last round. The corrugated iron hut had no sign. We'd get there just as the remains of the morning shift were getting slaughtered. So, yes, we couldn't have foreseen the scheme plotted against our freedom. We lived in the world of real men, didn't we? Tough, stubborn to the point of boredom. It was they who filled that bar; the car factory on the other side fed on their bodies. The rest was spat out at two in the afternoon. This was where they stopped on their way home. Those who were going for the second shift snatched their last minutes here; the real men. Goosy's father, Shorty's father, mine; they never complained. They just put their jackets on and left. They always came back. And we never heard a word. Living with them, growing up in their shadows, we were sure the construction of the world was complete; they'd never betray us. They beat the shit out of us now and again, seeing as we slipped out of their control. But it was them who gave us real freedom, the freedom to escape. The betrayal came from another side. It came from those sad fucks who couldn't take their fate. From women; no surprise they were hiding in churches among the men in frocks; the thought would never enter our fathers' heads.

Then Mr Waldek would collect the tin cans full of cigarette-ends and that was it, the shop was closed. We would go under the bridge to watch floating condoms, listen to the rumble of trams and instead of fraternité of blood become piss brothers, joining streams of our urine in a solemn act.

By eight in the evening the second carriage of the number 6 tram was practically empty.

Chapter 20

Goosy, then and now: a hairless face, the worn face of a boy who never took care of his skin.

"We ought to make ourselves scarce before something happens."

"Nothing will happen, Goosy. It's more likely it will if we *do* move. We threw them off our scent with that car in Orla. That's where they are, looking for us, sniffing. Just think how much they have to sniff through. It's darkest under the lamppost . . ."

I was trying to cheer him up, and myself. He sat like a mummy, like a caricature of a woken-up mummy. A duvet corner hung over his head like a little roof.

"None of that was in the contract. We were supposed to come here and have fun . . ."

"There was no contract, Goosy. No one promised you anything."

"Now you'll tell me this is fun, that killing people is fun!"

He stopped suddenly, scared by his own shouting. He shut up, convinced that the wind snatched at his words and carried them out into the wide world. From inside the hut came Vasyl's voice.

"He's right. We have to make ourselves scarce."

"That's interesting. Who's going to carry him? I've got a heavy rucksack," said Shorty from above the frying pan. "He can't make even three steps. He's going for a piss and he's about to faint."

"Perhaps not today. Tomorrow, the day after tomorrow, when he gets better. But we have to get out of here."

"Where to?" I asked.

"Out of here."

"You want to get out of the forest, flag the coach down and you're off? You think you'll go as you've come? That easy? I think they've already sobered up and are keeping their eyes wide open. If they had some generals in Pietra already . . . This is heavy. Only two years ago they sent half a brigade if some rucksacked asshole put as much as one foot on the Czech side. Do you think things have changed that much? I doubt it. It's not some pissing-on-the-wall business they're dealing with now."

Quite a speech, mostly because I didn't feel like going anywhere. I wanted to hit the sack, stuff my face and go to sleep.

"Sure. But listen, this is how we'll do it." Vasyl was changing into a leader again. "Neither to Niewierki, nor the other way. We continue east, through the forest. Twenty, thirty kilometres. Not too close to the border, through the mountains, away from roads and villages. I know the area pretty well. There are two hostels on the way. We'll see. It will be difficult to start with. But if we stay in the woods we'll be all right. I think even this place is quite safe, but why tempt fate? Maybe they'll want to check the road by the bridge? Maybe they'll check the forester's lodge? In fact I'm sure they will. They'll check out Czetwertne; they'll be asking around. They will be asking, but they won't bother to go into the forest. They'll check out the hostels, the old kolkhoz, but not here. How much food have we got?"

Shorty was wiping the fat in the frying pan with a crust.

"Depends how much we eat. Three days. Four days. It depends."

By the time I had my bread and sausages I was half-asleep. I took out my new sleeping-bag, purple with yellow dots, and took off my trousers and long-johns. Shorty gave me his, dry and clean; he also gave me a second sleeping-bag. I curled up by the fire and could hear Vasyl say something about the axe and how he and Shorty should go out to get wood. They were going to pull down the other hut. I fell asleep staring at the red glow of shifting landscapes. But my sleep was as fragile as the fire landscapes. I heard everything. Somewhere near my feet Kostek was making himself a bed. From the outside came the crack of smashed boards and the intolerable screeching of rusty nails, the guys swearing, all immersed in the boom of the wind. It blew high, only occasionally hitting the hut with single gusts. It wasn't even proper sleep, even though I dreamed, short, fast films from which I woke up surprised that it was all untrue, that the fire still crackled, that I wasn't running waist deep through the snow but lay in warmth, even relaxed, and so re-entering the stream of decomposing plots. The beginning and the end of night, without the middle, without that black void that separates days. Kostek was in a deep sleep, snoring. Goosy was struggling. I was pleased. With every opening of the eyes, I knew that in a moment I would slip back into the chaos of images, not terrifying or hurtful, even though they were the images of the immediate past. But every awakening separated me from them by a vastness of space, snow and wind. And even when I saw men in uniforms, armed, I was pleased it wasn't me who waded through snow, with all that crap on my back, pursuing business that didn't really concern me all that much. It was them, for hours exposed to blizzard and stupid orders, who cursed their superiors and dreamed of what I was enjoying at that very moment – warmth and peace of mind. Fuck it all, I repeated to myself every time I came round. I curled up tight, to become a real me, squeeze out from the folds of my clothes any remnants of foreign space, all the air, every atom of anxiety and accident. Even my feet finally warmed up. I farted into the sleeping-bag and the odour of my very own sulphur helium was pleasing to me. I floated in farts like in foetal waters. I even covered my head. At times I heard steps, wailing engines, dogs barking.

But if dreams couldn't touch me, the reality could kiss my ass too; I was dreaming. I tried to imagine a woman, a bit of sex, but nothing turned me on. War films, Marshal Tito, horses belly deep in snow, wide-open valleys, and a serpent of people crawling through unrelenting, naked vastness. I saw it all from on high, like a pilot from a plane. They marched immersed in whiteness like in water, some of them holding weapons chest high, loaded with things the colour of military green, in perfect visibility, perfectly alone. They climbed towards a low pass behind which stretched another valley, and then another and another, to the infinitely distant and constantly shifting line of the horizon. A long human serpent. I saw their faces too: blackened, gaunt, unshaven, wrapped in rags, in woolly hats with earflaps. They looked like Paulus's soldiers after their defeat, though Tito was among them and nobody escorted them or took away their weapons. They were climbing towards the seat of the pass, leaving behind a deep snowy furrow, heading for the next pass and the next, in a slow, monotonous rhythm, like automatons, their faces showing no sign of suffering, pain or effort, masks of extreme weariness. I saw it from high above, but also from below. Sackcloth rucksack sashes, leather Sam Browne belts. Weird army. Not quite in retreat, or in march. Fuck knows. Maybe I was an angel? Suspended above them like a ghost? I didn't feel the cold or warmth, just like in dreams. Or maybe it was no Paulus, or Tito, but the Russians in 1914, heading for the Hungarian flatlands, for Vienna? It did happen. They marched through these valleys, in snow, smoke and blood; they marched towards the low Carpathian passes.

After all, their image could not disappear without a trace. Perhaps it had just returned, reflected off some star, galaxy, a nebula, there is so much of it out there, and found its way inside my eyelids. No big deal, weirder things happen. I felt sorry for them; soon they would be coming back. Seeing their pointless misery, feeling the warmth of my sleeping-bag, I was very pleased. Not with their misery, no. With the border, the thin line between the sleeping-bag and the vast white grave of the valley. I wanted to hold that line for as long as I could.

"Fuck that," said Shorty, throwing down a bunch of chopped boards. "Bandurko, you worry too much. After all, it's how you wanted it, isn't it? Why these hysterics? You're a leader, for fuck's sake. Now even a chief, like the Indians had for war. When they wake up we'll have a powwow. But now we can have a drink."

"I don't feel like it."

"I do. Up the snake's."

He meant the snake on the wall; he took it with him then. On our way back from that bunker Vasyl led us along a different route. But Shorty said no, that he would go back the way he had come, for he liked it on top of that mountain. Bandurko mumbled something under his breath. Though he was no chief then, he suggested various things to us, that was all, yet it looked like a breach of discipline, a quiet rebellion, or a plain kiss my ass. At any rate, when by dusk we got to the hut, Shorty was already there. He sat by the fire stretching the snakeskin on a board.

"*Vipera berus*," he said when I sat by his side. "Quite big. Female, I think. She never attacks first, *Vipera berus*; more inclined to run away. Unless you step on her. Compared with a grass snake, rather heavy and slow. Until she's got her back against the wall, that is. Then she's like lightning. But will always opt for escape. Haemorragina damages blood vessels, coagulum creates blood clots. Eats mice and shrews, occasionally goes for a frog, rarely though. One thing is certain – she shouldn't have gone out until April."

"It was a very warm day," I said.

"A snake is not a bear. It sits a metre under the ground and doesn't have a clue whether it's warm or cold. They often sleep with toads, the very same toads they will later gobble up."

"Civilised beast. A winter armistice, eh?"

"Right. Not like salamanders."

"What about salamanders?"

"They eat each other inside their mother's belly. One another. Larva eats larva. It's called adelofagia."

"Cool," I said. "Maybe I had a twin too."

"Bandurko did, for sure. But he did it out of love." Shorty got up and hung the board high above the fire. "It'll conserve itself. It'll go black a bit but won't rot."

"What do you need this shit for?"

"Moses doth a copper snake and put it on a long pole." And then he winked and added: "You never know what may come in handy, man."

And so the snake, gutted and flat, remained with us. Vasyl kept moaning that it stank. Goosy wasn't saying much, but you could see he was disgusted.

I couldn't sleep and in the end gave up the struggle. Shorty sat nearby, sipping from a tin mug, staring at his trophy. It had grown blacker, as he said. It acquired a matt sheen of smoky gold. Only the zigzag hadn't lost any of its deep black.

"A general wouldn't be ashamed to wear it," I said. "What elegance."

"Damned right. And Goosy doesn't even want to look at it. I'm telling him it keeps the sickness off. But he prefers to have fever."

He handed me his mug. Kostek dug himself out of his sleeping-bag. His swarthy face had turned deep brown, like baked clay. I took a swig and passed the mug to him. The powwow was assembling. Vasyl sat opposite us with his back to the wall.

"Give me something to drink, guys," said Goosy in a quiet, pained voice and immediately burst into a fit of coughing.

"I've got something for you, man. Just for you." Shorty removed from the fire a bruised saucepan and poured some awful brew into a cup. "Don't make stupid faces. Drink. Those who survived survived thanks to this."

"Who survived? Where?"

"In Siberia. It's a gulag tea. Green needles and boiling water. In other words, vitamin C. You don't have scurvy, but you could do with some Paracetamol. Drink, Goosy. Snake's health."

"Will you leave the fucking snake out of it?" Bandurko nearly screamed. "Poke in the eye, that's all it's good for, fucking reptile . . ."

I thought Vasyl's nerves had finally snapped. Or maybe he couldn't forgive Shorty that he went off on his own way. Goosy drank like a chicken. With tiny sips, he swallowed drop after drop, grimacing – medicine, for sure. Three of us sipped vodka; Vasyl didn't want to. We sipped and smoked, in silence. Everyone was waiting. Stoking the fire, poking the embers, snivelling, scratching, clearing throats, like a bunch of apes, like Neanderthals by the fire, no human voice. Shorty went out, brought some water, put the pan on the stones, the water began to steam and still no one broke the silence. We were halfway through a second cigarette when Goosy decided to step in.

"So, heroes of Bieszczady, will anyone open his gob and tell me what to do with this shit? I don't care, but I'm curious. To be honest I think you've really fucked up. We were supposed to have a holiday, mountains – come on, guys, let's go to the mountains! I put aside so many things . . . let people down . . . I practically ran away from home because my friends fancied going on a trip to the mountains. Together. So maybe now you'll tell me what you're going to do now? Eh? Kostek? And you? And you, Vasyl? I can see all your talking wasn't just shooting the breeze. God, had I known that we'd end up in this shit. Come on, tell me, you were in cahoots . . . ?"

The last word sounded like "khahoo–hoo–hue" – he was in another fit of coughing. He pressed his chin down to his chest and performed a sequence of funny jerks, stopping his mouth as if afraid something was about to spill out of him.

"Calm down, Goosy. What's done's done. We have to think how to get out of this shit."

Shorty was trying to keep cool, as if he was the only one with any reason left in him.

"Done indeed . . . The murderer and his accomplice . . ."

"They said they didn't know for sure."

"What's the difference who knows it? Eh . . . ?"

He turned to me, his eyes full of fear and resentment.

"And you let it happen? You? I don't care about this straggler – he always listened a lot and spoke little. I never trusted him. Or Bandurko, this one I know has his brains fucked up, a mythoman . . . But you? Did you just stand there like a prick?"

And then I was standing on that road. Two shafts of light were picking out in the darkness whirls of snowflakes. The engine purred. The world slowed down; the air grew heavy. Only the words sounded high, and Kostek's movements were unbelievably quick and decisive – I certainly didn't think to stop him. Every blow, every metallic knock cranked up the tension inside me. My muscles ached from the strain, and I was ready to leap and help him massacre an innocent man who didn't even have time to be surprised. I stood with my fist clenched, listening to the sound of thumps against the bonnet, while my imagination fed pictures of ripped skin and flesh with the glaring white of bone. Maybe I was afraid of that noise? Perhaps that death seemed too artificial to me now, not animalistic enough. Just a quick, clinical murder, effortless and automatic? But not then. I would have stepped in to help without hesitation, and we would have ripped the soldier limb from limb. When he fell, when Kostek pinned him down with the weight of his body, I saw a helpless naked head in the snow, and I knew I could crush it with my heavy boots like a cabbage. Had someone told me that half a minute earlier – as the whole thing didn't last more than that – I would have thought him off his rocker.

Again silence. Only the wet firewood let out prolonged whistles and spat handfuls of sparks at our feet. Bandurko sat slumped, hands stuffed under his jumper, elbows on his knees, his woolly hat pushed down on his forehead. Perhaps he felt his head was completely empty, or maybe he was waiting for his words to be the last. Then Kostek got up. He kicked a half-burned plank, which released a small umbrella of red sparks above the fire, stepped out of our ring and stopped in the middle of the shed. We had to turn our heads. In his brown cloth parka with a hood, he looked like a monk. In place of his face we saw a dark smudge, and his teeth when he started talking.

"Now listen to me. Vasyl's right. We have to leave. Tomorrow at the crack of dawn. I think he's sufficiently familiar with the terrain not to fuck up."

"Sure." Bandurko jumped to his feet. "Sure I know, if only I had my map."

"Don't worry. You'll do fine without it. So tomorrow morning . . ."

"Count me out." Goosy's voice was weak and shaky, either from the effort or from self-imposed determination. "Count me out. I'm going back."

Kostek made three steps. Slow, measured, thumping steps, like on a stage. He stopped at the foot of our Lazarus's bed and said:

"You're coming with us. With all of us. No one can go as he pleases. You will go as I tell you. He already knows that." Kostek nodded in my direction. "Now let me make it clear to you. That soldier is dead. It's a working assumption. If you want to make sure, feel free, but I don't advise it. So if he's dead he won't breathe a word. But I will. I will tell anyone who will ask. Do you think they will believe you that you came here to bury yourselves in the snow? Who? That soldier didn't. Moreover, who will believe that a professional, armed soldier was overwhelmed by a civilian? Even if they did, they wouldn't admit it. Pride wouldn't let them. God, honour and all that shit. At any rate, they will – in fact, they already have found both our fingerprints. And where there were two, there could be three, four or five. And what will you say to that? That you sat at home? Alibi? What alibi? I'm your alibi. You're in it as deep as I am. Only I can scrape it off you. If – and when – I feel like it. Am I right, Bandurko? You know well I am. From now on you are my political commissar. And you, Goosy, you can go if you want to. I'm not going to get into a fight with an old pal, am I? Go back to the capital. Maybe you'll slip through, though I doubt it. But go back and start thinking. Think and listen out for the doorbell, day and night. Every ring and you'll tiptoe to the door like a cat to look through your wide-angle peephole. And one day you'll see in it strange, slightly deformed faces – two or three; the others will be waiting downstairs – handsome, masculine, short cropped hair. Kafka you ain't – you won't write *The Trial* – so go. Go, if you manage to stand up, that is."

And then he fell silent. It must have been dusk outside, as inside the hut there was complete darkness. Irregular gusts of wind pumped the smoke back inside, mixed with isolated whirls of the blizzard. A small mound of snow had formed by the door and kept growing. Only standing close to the fire made it bearable. Shorty gave me a cigarette, while Kostek paced behind our backs like a guard. Thump, thump, thump, seven thumps in one direction, a short break and seven thumps back. I even started adding them all up, but the cigarette tripped my calculations. Goosy sat straight, still, with red shadows flickering across his profile. Now and again, a golden flame flared up in the corner of his eye. There was life still in him, but he looked like a corpse. The words must have hit a very sensitive point, some organ, a gland, which broke and flooded his insides with a catatonic enzyme.

Shorty's arm was touching mine. The cigarette in his hand looked like a match or a lolly stick. He was staring at the fire, his left hand pushing his Alcatraz hat from his forehead to the back of his head, and back again, keeping to the rhythm of the steps behind our backs. And Vasyl, who was sitting in front of us? He was following that pendulum, that hollow, thumping monotony like a tennis fan at a match, except that his eyes moved much more slowly than the forehands and backhands, seeing him out and back in again, stuck into him, linked to him, like on strings. It was a kind of reverse hypnosis, as the other never even glanced at him, only after some time, time unmeasurable by clocks, stifling, choking like the moments of awakening from a nightmare, he rummaged through his rucksack, came up to Goosy, squatted next to him and put on his lap several white pills.

"Here. Polopiryn and piramidon. You have to be all right by tomorrow."

Chapter 21

That sour taste in the mouth. It's a taste of effort, when the body wants to rid itself of all poison and is sweating through the mouth and tongue. That's what it felt like at two in the afternoon when we reached God knows where, a top of some mountain; third or fourth since the morning. Perhaps Bandurko knew, but no one bothered to ask him. He marched first, then Kostek, Shorty just behind Goosy, and me at the end. Flat top, no proper trees, only bushes, sallow and hazel. And a copse of frail young firs, just the spot for a nativity play. Everything else around was shaven clean, felled, rotten, though you couldn't see it under the snow. We just tripped over it. A bare mountain, you might say, like a pile of shit with matches stuck in it. The true wood was left on the slopes. Tall, thick firs broke the blizzard, and our trail in the snow was clearly visible.

"It'll be here until spring," Bandurko had said half an hour ago, but no one bothered to answer. No one had the strength, except Kostek. He was pushing ahead, breathing down Vasyl's neck.

That mountain had little snow on it, and we climbed it clutching at roots and bushes. Stones mixed with clay detached themselves from crags and overhangs and came tumbling down, and if you weren't careful you could catch them on the head. Over the years, wind and loose soil had uprooted trees, and the holes in the ground slowed us to a crawl. A true Carpathian forest.

Goosy wasn't getting any better. The fever did fall a bit, but he was still sweating like in summer, except with a cold, trembly kind of sweat. It was very hot but his teeth were chattering. We put him in the middle; he was constantly falling behind. Shorty would give him a lift, pushing his bum up out of the holes left by a century-old spruce, while Kostek would pull him by the hand, though with reluctance, disgust even, angry, for rather than set off at dawn we wanted to eat and drink first. Shorty got the fire going, made coffee, God knows if out of spite or need, the latter more likely since he wasn't spiteful by nature. So we ate, packed up and at the end Kostek got up on the hut's roof and tore off a few sheets of asphalt.

"When the snow gets inside no one will suspect anyone could have lived here."

And then I thought it looked like we had gone never to return anywhere.

On the mountain's top our stretched-out gang folded into a small group, a clump of green denim and dirty grey wool, a lump of colourful rucksacks. Our faces were red-grey, dirty, and Shorty again said something about coffee. Kostek turned to him. "Forget it."

Shorty deliberately put down his red-blue rucksack, came up to the copse of firs and began to break off dry twigs. Then he walked away a few steps and with his boot pushed off the snow and put down his handful of firewood.

"I said – forget it." Kostek's voice was quiet but hard.

"You don't have to drink. Melted snow isn't all that great," said Shorty, rummaging through his pockets for a piece of paper. He found an empty cigarette packet, a sheet of paper and bits of newspaper.

"Who wants to drink goes to fetch wood," he said and returned to his little pyre. His great body bent over a tiny flickering flame, which gave a little crack and a hiss and finally licked the rest of the twigs. Kostek walked up to the fire as if he wanted to stamp it out and walked straight into Shorty's back, which barred his way.

"We can't light fires when they're after us, man," he said in a conciliatory tone of voice, seeing that Goosy had already traipsed off for more twigs and Vasyl stood undecided, while I was simply waiting to see what was going to happen next.

"It's you they're after," answered Shorty, turning his face away from the fire. "And stop this crap about what we can or can't do. A bitch on heat wouldn't give a fuck. Three steps to heaven, miles from nowhere and he gives me Scouts' wisdom. I want coffee. And you can stuff your fucking gob with raw snow, I don't care." Shorty stretched to full height, but didn't need to, for Kostek had already backed off. He checked how far he could push and decided to wait for a better occasion.

It was lousy coffee. We put a lot in but it tasted of dust. The pleasure was in the sitting. Green trees protected us. The blizzard was coming in white choppy waves, with flashes of blue in between. Shorty took out his axe. The fire grew bigger. Soaked trousers steamed, sticking to the flesh like cataplasm. We each had a bit of browned bacon. Goosy winced but ate. With difficulty, slowly, the food grew inside his mouth, but he was swallowing, just the food then the coffee. Wind fanned the smoke, bringing tears to the eyes. Kostek sat to one side. Vasyl shared his coffee with him. We didn't talk. Each spun his own story, with its own beginning, middle and end, completely different stories. Amazing how quickly it all split us up. Though not Kostek; he wasn't in the race. His madness manifested itself as nurtured for a long time, in a premeditated and rational way, and our contempt was suddenly mixed with fear and shame. We couldn't bear to look at each other. Yesterday, none of us got up and kicked him in the balls to right the balance. Even Shorty, who feared very few things, was only able to defend his coffee and nothing more.

Now and again wind would whirl in among us, and it was a relief – we could rub our red eyes or turn up our collars. When the wind died down it became quiet, like in a grave, or in a waiting-room. We sat muffled up and dirty, just like our travelling citizens, or pieces of luggage, waiting to be taken away, transported, taken care of; sheep at least bleat.

Kostek Górka and Vasyl Bandurko. Górka. His surname cropped up in my mind for the first time there, by that fire. Górka and Bandurko. Rym cym cym. Paranoia's general staff. And three divisions of stragglers. Fucking tossers, as Regres would say. Regres used to go to demos to beat up the cops. And the patriots. He would leap in the middle of the fiercest fighting and start beating the shit out of anyone who happened to be near – cops and patriots alike.

"Justice has to be done. I go for the mathematical mean. Maths is the science of gods, ain't it? That's what they said at school."

I thought we could do with Regres. Five foot ten, eighty kilos, a lean body and a brain to match. He did have ideas that he liked putting into life. That was his hobby. Justice was one of them. He went to Stockholm and died. Of Absolut, the vodka. He wanted to go gold-digging in Lapland. Five foot ten, eighty kilos and no trace of fat. Neither cops nor patriots, not even local yobos from Brzeska Street could top him. Only the Swedish cold could. When they carried him to the police station, or mortuary, it must have been with the bench. When that kind of a body freezes to something it's for good.

Three against two. That's what it looked like. Or, to be more precise, two against each. In which case the maths made it three against six. No chance.

So we sat, almost leaning on each other, sipping coffee. Kostek had to have Vasyl. In these mountains he was blind and deaf, like a child in a fog. He could just as well dig a hole in the ground and bury himself under leaves. And Vasyl needed Kostek, for if he had a plan he was too weak to carry it out. That plan, which one spoke of and the other carried out without a word, was a kind of death. I was looking at their faces in the grey air. Against the backdrop of grey and black tree trunks they merged into one, a deformed one. Regres. He, too, danced his war dances, shook his trophies under our noses, truncheons, visors torn off police helmets, a single boot, a watch.

"Man, I'm telling you, I tore half of his ear off. But my hands were busy so I had to spit it out. Couldn't breathe." Dissatisfied, contemptuous of the one-, two-, even three-dimensional world – as if these dimensions were not enough for him.

"To be a cop, and a thief, it ain't enough. I wanna be one, then the other, then skulk both and crop up in some third place. So that some people shit on you, others love you, and then the other way, until I find a hole in the fence and get on the other side of both."

And those two, the twins, Stan and Laurel, the hybrid of will and ability, they figured they would pay off their death in instalments really quickly, maybe even in cash, provided there was enough courage and opportunity. And who were we in all this? Underwriters? Undertakers? Corporeal memory? A chorus in a grotesque tragedy?

Vasyl could have well thought it out during all those long hours in his empty house, when we didn't visit him or ring him. We had greater things on our minds as the world suddenly got too roomy to bump into each other every day. Vasyl's love was great. Each of us was an unwanted doggy taken in by the others, but he felt it the most. Double, triple love. It's not inconceivable we were ungrateful assholes not repaying him all that he had given us. Sometimes it made you want to puke. When we led him out of the Babylon of his family house, when his mother relented and finally let him out from under her wing, when he managed to hobble out past the front door, he behaved as if he was doing us a favour. Like some poor relation. It drove us fucking crazy, his asking could he come with us, or would we mind taking him, the incessant supplications and apologies for being alive.

I remember one day I wrote on the school wall, where we used to go for a smoke: VB IS A SMOKELESS CUNT. Marlboro were twenty-eight-zlotys then; dear. Vasyl gave us a packet but didn't want to come with us. Not out of fear. Out of embarrassment because he didn't smoke. Goosy said, "Leave it," and blotted out my statement with a piece of brick. Bandurko was younger than us by a whole generation. He was a newborn baby. Keen and shy, like a virgin on her wedding night.

Not far from where he lived there was some fantastic land overgrown with bulrushes, little ponds and rubbish dumps. This is where the local proletariat brought their rubbish. On carts, wheelbarrows, in broad daylight. It was we who showed it to him. He had no idea. He had his rubbish collected by a garbage truck. Incidentally, when the rubbish men had a migraine, or better things to do, they, too, would dump their trucks in the bulrushes. With that Eldorado round the corner he was wasting his time painting soldiers, a hundred and fifty zlotys a box.

Polish weeping willows stood knee deep in wonderful rubbish. Cans, paper, glass, wood, plaster, headless Virgin Marys, metal sweet boxes full of spiders, unsaleable empties, alarm clocks, newspapers sodden with rain and frogspawn, things whose origins and purpose were discussed for hours. After all, how were we to know what a stomach pump looked like? Koehler's typewriter – sheer poetry: golden, *fin de siècle* letters on a black metal plate. Or the physiology behind women's sanitary towels. Only toys found in that shite were no longer fun. We exercised our imagination as we picked up one trophy after another: the prewar glass "Baczewski's Vodkas and Meths", cans, brushes, green oil paint for fences, shit colour for floors, white for windows, rigid, set still for ever. Sometimes a broken cigarette holder, a porcelain elephant, trunkless and tailless.

We must have stunk like hell, when occasionally someone set the whole shit-heap on fire and we waded through the green smoke. The rags man, from before the war, used to chase us away. Saw us as competition to the rags and paper. Those willows – how did they cope? It's a miracle they didn't grow metal leaves. Proles knew no mercy.

"Let's go shite fishing" – it was our signal.

"What for?" Bandurko used to ask, and we had no good answer for him, but when in the end he joined us he caught the bug in half an hour. If only his mother could see him in his brand-new trainers, digging through piles of the slimiest shit to get to the bottom layer to pull out a rusty Remington – "They used to make guns and typewriters." Or as he separated mouldy pages of an aeroplane magazine, *Winged Poland*.

Autumn, wet and misty. We used to stay there until dusk, until the surrounding landscape began to ooze grey-sepia light, until our faces began to fade and blur, and further search was impractical.

Or late spring, on the other side of the railway tracks, in the birch wood shot through with sunshine. We used to go for a swim where a sandy tongue slipped deep into an old clay pond. A real peninsula. The bottom was muddy. We pulled out our feet smeared in bluey slime. The water was chest deep, no more. "Vasyl, and you?" He always stayed on the bank, on the peninsula, fully dressed, until one day Szmaja, Tojfel and two others, all of them older than us by at least a year, already in vocational schools, warmed up by cheap wine, grabbed him by his hands and feet and swung him – *splash*! – in the middle of the pond, complete with his Wrangler jeans and waterproof watch. We were as it happened in the water, afraid the bastards would pinch our clothes and blackmail us for another bottle. We didn't bat an eyelid. Later, as we were returning along the tracks through the shimmering heat, the conversation faltered. In the end Bandurko proclaimed: "It's my fault. If I swam with you, nothing would have happened."

Later, when imperceptibly he became one of us, though a little bit better dressed and better mannered, we took it for granted, with the indifference of creatures with no memory, without an ounce of admiration or gratitude for all that he had done for us, even lying to his mother became as easy for him as it was for us.

*

Vasyl Bandurko spoke out first. Shook the coffee grounds out of the mug and without addressing anyone in particular began: "We are sitting on top of Kiczora. When we descend on the other side, after half an hour's march we'll come to a narrow, overgrown ravine, and if we go left we'll come out above Huciska. It's a Polish village. Five houses short of a dozen. Destitution crossed with poverty. Cut off from the world: there's no motor transport, no buses, no tarmac. The tarmac road begins five kilometres out of the village."

"What if we go right?" asked Kostek.

"Nothing. Hills upon hills. In summer it takes a day to get to Gardlica."

"How far have we got from the hut?"

"About six, seven kilometres north, in a straight line. We're fourteen to fifteen kilometres away from the border now."

And so they chatted. No one else interfered. The fire was waning. It was getting cold. The wind was dying out, and more and more blue was freeing itself from the clouds. It meant a very cold night. Shorty nudged me and pointed with his head. Some twenty metres away, on a gnarled beech tree, sat a white raven. I spotted it only because the beech's branch was still swaying. The raven faced us. It was massive. It had a yellow beak. Feathers around its neck made a frayed-edged collar. Only two of us saw the bird. The leaders were in council while Goosy tried to warm up remnants of the coffee on the remnants of the fire. Then we heard that sound. Distant, faint, monotonous. Unlike any forest sounds. We sat motionless; the sound was drowning and resurfacing again – a muffled drone. Goosy heard it too.

"What's that?"

The other two stopped talking. It was a mechanical sound, like a tractor, an engine. But why here, on the top of a mountain? Perhaps it was somewhere down below. The sound kept cutting out, and then it began to get closer. Goosy leaped in the air. So did the raven.

"Guys, it's a chopper!"

It was like an electric shock that gets you in the water and goes through the whole body. Someone was kicking furiously, putting the fire out. We were fastening the rucksacks when Kostek screamed in a strange sort of whisper, "Down! Out of the open!" and rushed off first with his sack. The hard reverb was getting louder and louder, as if a great black machine – that was how I imagined it – was about to loom out from behind the trees on the hillside, which we had just climbed, and from where the drone was now coming. Before me ran Shorty with his axe. All I could see were the orange straps from his rucksack. Like coloured flags, just like flags, an ideal target, that's all I could think of. And before I began losing my breath I ran on to the slope.

I tumbled down. I still kept on my feet. The trees. I ran through them, hearing cracks and a deafening, weird swoosh of the snow, a sort of hiss as it gave in under my boots, under my bum, and silence as I flew through the air. This side was as steep as the other. I tumbled down a muddy scree, narrowly missing tree trunks of firs and beech, terrified of the noise I was making, as if those above could hear anything less than a nuclear explosion. Taking a desperate turn just before a huge dead tree, I lost the ground under my feet and landed in a hole amid tangled roots. The silence was immediate. I burrowed deeper into the hole. My heart fell silent, then my breathing. Nothing. No chopper, no drone. Only loose soil kept falling over my head. And then I heard, somewhere high up and far away, the scattered shards of noise.

I crawled out of my burrow even though it was the last thing I wanted to do. Here, in the wood, on the northern slope, the daylight had already begun to turn ink-blue. A sound of broken branches reached me from below. I followed the sound, and a moment later someone whistled behind my back. Stumbling down the slope was Goosy, wet and covered in clay. Propelled by the weight of his rucksack, he stopped with difficulty. He leaned on my arm and bent in half, panting and coughing. When he recovered a little he began to listen. I shook my head.

All three stood among the young spruces. We didn't see them. They had to call us. They, too, were listening. We stood like that for a very long time, maybe several minutes, until Shorty spoke.

"Shit, my coat was open." Carefully he pulled up his jumper. His shirt was soaked with blood. "I ran into something, I don't know what." He pulled up his underlayers and showed us. It was red and white. A long, lacerated wound, not so much deep as rent open; hard to tell where it began and where it ended.

"Aren't I heavy? A skinny fellow would be barely scratched. Give me some vodka."

Kostek took out a bottle. Shorty splashed some on the wound and drank the rest.

"That's against faintin' "

Bandurko stared at the blood and mumbled: "What a mess, what a fucking mess. We have to dress it somehow. I haven't got anything, everything was nicked."

Goosy unpacked a pink towel.

"It's practically clean. I haven't dried myself with it."

"And how am I to use it? Make a turban?"

We bandaged him somehow. We tore the towel into strips and it held up. He pulled down his jumper. And we helped him to put on his rucksack.

"Maybe it was just a coincidence with that chopper?" Vasyl was hoping against hope.

"Maybe it was, maybe it wasn't. What's the difference?" I answered.

"It's getting dark. I'm sure they didn't see us. They didn't even fly over this hill. If they had spotted us they would be hovering above, wouldn't they?"

"Don't worry, Vasyl, it would be too good – search parties, radios, parachuting. Sorry, I know you would like that. Foresters sometimes hire a chopper to count their herds. I read about it in a specialist magazine, *Polish Hunter*."

True, Shorty read a lot, all kinds of rubbish. Catalogues of aircraft, the lists of the most idiotic objects, comics and porn mags. He even bought a Danish–Polish dictionary "to find out what they talk about when they fuck". After two days he took the dictionary to a second-hand shop. "Nothing interesting."

And now, as if the loss of blood had given him more life, he started to hurry us, to move us on, and for fuck's sake get some-where, for it's getting dark, unless we wanted to spend the night in some hole in the ground. Nobody did. The sky was turning dark navy-blue and at the west, at the mouth of the valley, frayed little clouds were lighting it gold and red. The cold was beginning to pinch. Leader Kostek was silent, Vasyl too, so I said we should risk it and get ourselves into some warm place because of Goosy and this sort of crap. I felt we were all thinking the same, and Vasyl relaxed.

"Huciska . . . We can try it there. I passed through last year.

Houses spread out. It's a Polish village, as I told you. Spread out, not like Russian ones with houses crammed one into another. If we ask at the outskirts, no one will need to know."

"Except the farmer," said Kostek.

"Can't be too careful, can you?" hissed Goosy.

It was settled. We sorted our clothes on the march. Bandurko set the trail. The snow was dry and blue, our silhouettes black. Everything around us was becoming black, the spruces, dry thistle stems, the wooded ridges of the hills. Only the valley's mouth was ablaze in bright orange, as if something was burning there with hard, icy flame. Against such a backdrop the tree-tops looked flat and sharp-edged, like a paper cutout. The glowing clouds had a straight base, as if drawn with a ruler, and a frothy mane, like a crest of a wave. They burned out in a few minutes, rolled up and curled, charred like scraps of paper, and the sky glowed now with phosphorescent radiance. We reached the edge of a wood. The ravine opened on to a wide valley, treeless except for junipers that looked like frozen human figures with dark blue shadows. A kilometre further down, in the middle of a gentle slope, there was a black copse of trees, among which burned a little light, just like an ember crumb of the just-extinguished sky.

"Let's wait until it gets completely dark." After all, Kostek had to say something. We lit up.

Chapter 22

Everything was unsteady, wobbled every which way: stools, the bench, the table, from under whose leg someone kicked away a thin plank; even Our Lady of Częstochowa hung crooked. On the TV screen hopped blue images and shadows. And we sat still. Goosy sat in the only chair, sweating by the stove. His face was wet. We sat around a table covered with oilcloth, red roses on white; through the holes gaped patches of greasy wood. We were quite warm, whether from seeing the fire and boiling water, or vodka – the last from the bottom of my sack – it was hard to say. We drank from one glass, thick, angular, grey on a massive stem. The news was on. A fat runt kept saying that he feared nothing, for he cared only about justice. Runts never have enough justice. The capital spread out its supersonic waves, carrying runts and louts, fat ones and thin ones, who landed in that filthy room lit by a forty-watt bulb encased in a metal bowl turned upside down. Perhaps it was their very business – for they were gadding about like grasshoppers, like ants, like squirrels, fieldmice – which cast us sitting in such stillness.

We ate potatoes, his, old man's potatoes, buttered with our pork fat. We drank his tea in glasses with metal holders, which pleasantly burned our fingers – he drank our coffee. He let us in straight away. Possibly because he wanted to see Shorty's face, as he stood first in the doorway and the door was so low even Vasyl had to bend. He stepped back into his room, watching us come in, squeezing out the air and light, but his face remained still. Perhaps it could not change its expression, cast for ever in a kind of chipmunk grimace, as if the mouth and eye sockets had just begun to set, stretching the rest of the skin. We told him we were tourists, lost, only wanting somewhere to sleep or sit in a warm place. He sort of fell back on a low stool by the stove, took out a blackened cigarette holder, cheap cigarettes, broke one in half and lit it up from an ember. Gathered into a tight little herd, we stood by the door; the old yellowish sideboard, a pile of smoky pots above the stove, once white but now covered in patches of dry rot, the clay floor and a moaning that came from the black hole of the alcove – all that made us shy and bashful like debutantes at a grand ball. The gingery calf in the corner by the door: we noticed it only when it moved, when we heard a rustling of straw. It stood on its bendy legs, weeping pus, miserable, scared. Pressing its rump into the the pen, it was afraid of us, as if it had never seen people before.

Finally we broke out like a ball of mercury. We scattered around the room, sitting anywhere without invitation, but then it seemed the old man had accepted our presence. Perhaps he was a good Christian and at the same time a distrustful peasant and decided to wash his hands of the whole affair, leaving everything to fate and the course of events. He refused our cigarettes.

Vasyl started to say that the night was going to be cold, as the sky was starry, but didn't get anywhere. The old man remained silent, smoking and staring at the grinning beauties on television. Then he flicked his cigarette on the pile of ash under the stove, got up, rattled the pots on the range and took a heavy, prison-issue aluminium bowl to the calf.

From the black hole behind the stove came a moan, noises, hard to say whether human or animal, words deformed with pain or effort, simply devoid of presence of mind. The old man went out to the hallway, returned with a bucket and entered the black hole. Something groaned, rustled, the old man came back with the bucket and fell back on his stool by the stove. A long while passed before he could catch his breath enough to right up the other half of his cigarette. And again he gave himself up to the television. In between short and violent outbursts of wide and diagonal stripes on the screen some silly cow was showing her shaved legs.

Vasyl asked if we could fry some pork fat, that all we needed was a frying pan.

"Go ahead." We heard his voice, the same as his face and his wrinkled mouth. While Vasyl was going ahead, cutting bread, heating a black cast-iron pan that he had simply pulled out from the heap of other pans, I took out a bottle of vodka and put it on the table. It shone. It was the brightest point in the whole room. After some searching on the yellow, altar-like, utterly filthy side-

board, Bandurko found a glass. He poured a drop and made a toast
to our host, then poured a good half-glass and handed it to the old
man. Grandad downed it and gave the glass back. When we were
about to start eating, he said: "Potatoes in the big pot. Have some."

So we did. They went well with the pork fat. It was good grub.
Then we made tea. We found everything in the sideboard; didn't
ask for anything. After the second glass the old man expressed a
wish for some coffee and told us where to find sugar.

"We wandered off the track, looking for a short cut, you
understand, and just happened to come straight upon your house."

"I ain't asking." The old man slurped and stared at the TV.

"We wanted to get to Gardlica."

"A bus. Tomorrow."

"Where from?"

"Szklary."

"Is it far?"

"About five kilometres, maybe more. You have to get to the
village, go through the village, get to the tarmac road and then go
two kilometres along the road."

Bandurko poured the old man a glass, out of turn. The man
downed it, wiped his mouth with a sleeve of his blouse. He liked
vodka. For the first time he looked at us openly, a long, thoughtless
stare.

"And what's the point of wandering about in the cold like this,
eh?"

"The pleasures of tourism." Vasyl must have had a pleasure
quite of his own, making himself look a fool.

"Pleasure is when you stay in bed and scratch your balls."

"Well, there are different kinds of pleasure."

"Sure, some people like to have their balls scratched, others
frozen."

"We're students. We sit around a lot so we like the chance to get
out."

"Students, my ass. Students don't get out this time of year.
Christmas they do. Now the vacations are over."

The conversation didn't gel. Everyone could see it except
Bandurko. Kostek stretched his leg under the table but couldn't
reach him.

"But we've got it – special leave. And it's better now, no crowds."

"As if they ever come this way. Before the war, maybe."

"So you've been here since the war?"

Apparently the alcohol inside grandad must have burned out. He fell silent and again gave himself up to the blizzard of TV images. He leaned forward, rested his elbows on his knees and, like a downhill skier, dived into the whirl of commercials, news, on to the rutting ground of all those poor bastards who got their slice of electronic ambrosia, three seconds of vision, a crumb of immortality, no trace of decay, of decomposition of guts and heart. The old man watched them as they leaped into each other, groaned, it being the news, great mating season of the nation, the males framed from the chest or the waist, calling to each and every one; some squeaked, some bellowed, while the females let them take their turns. Autumnal calls at the end of winter. The rustling of paper, cameras and evening gowns like the rustling of leaves, until in the end entered the first stag. He, too, brayed and mumbled something, and I could not – despite the supernatural radiance – shake off the image of wrinkled Y-fronts the hue of cornflower, which blinded me once on a photo with a fishing rod.

Grandad regained his voice: "Here's a smart ass. Fucked everyone."

In his voice there was spiteful, bitter admiration. A moment later he added: "But the Virgin Mary – you can't beat that. The Pope himself blessed her for him."

Shorty was turning anxiously in his seat and whispered into my ear: "It's begun to hurt." Kostek and Vasyl found refuge in the TV world – you can say a lot of things about TV, but there are few better bringers of oblivion.

Who started that rocking game? Must have been the old man. Crossed his legs, loaded his cigarette holder with another half and set his torso in a monotonous rhythm of an orphan's malady. Bandurko poured grandad another vodka out of turn; maybe he was curious, or to spite us – after all, we needed a drink too. When the screen changed and there was something about Czechoslovakia, and the word Slovakia was repeated several times, the old man put his glass down next to his rubber boot and bellowed out a ditty, "Good Father Tiso, bless his heart, hang the Jews left and right" and then finished in prose, "I was ten during the war, but I remember the blind accordionist who used to sing that."

"And what else do you remember?"

"Everything. When the Germans, guns and all, rounded us up to clear the snow off the road. Mostly Poles, but the Russians too."

"Was there a lot of Russians here?" Bandurko switched on his interview mode again.

"There was. More than us. After the war they left for Russia; took the bell from the church, the flags, everything. They thought they were going to a Russian paradise." He wanted to laugh but only coughed up clouds of grey smoke.

"The rest was taken by our soldiers, west, in '47. Fuck 'em. Russian, Russkies, fuck 'em all. I don't miss them. Germans – they was smart. Pleasure to look at. Boots, uniforms, tailor-made. Russians, when they came, cooked chickens in the pot, feathers and all. Scum. What can you say?"

"And the Jews?" Bandurko was obviously leading grandad to temptation. But the old man had already sunk into his own thoughts; rocking forwards and backwards, he was gently falling to the bottom of memory.

"Oh, they was smart, they was masters, all right. Hitler was like a king, he was. Like Herod, the king who wasted half the Jews when he felt like it. Hitler wasted half the Jews, and if it weren't for the Russkies he would have wasted the other half, and then there would be peace unto people of goodwill on earth. I was ten years old, but I remember when they brought them all to the Parchacza mountain, rounded them up into the ravine where the devil used to show up, and buried them all in pits. From Szklary, Huciska, Tloki they came. We used to go there to pick up old cartridges. The devil used to show up there. We saw him. Black all over, black face. Once we saw him sitting in the bushes. We crossed ourselves, and he ran off into the hazel grove over the ravine. Old people used to say he was going there to dig the Jews up, dig 'em up and drag 'em about, for the Jews don't die after death but are left for the devil to torment them. We didn't bother to pick many cartridges. Maybe one each. Hard to find in them brambles. That's when he cropped up but got scared of the cross and ran. And we did too, down the ravine, hard to run, the clay fresh, barely covered with leaves, chucked every which way. Afterwards one said he saw a hand with a golden ring sticking out of that clay, and he wanted us to go back with him but we was all scared. Maybe one of us did, but not me. Those Jews don't die. They can dig themselves up, and if the devil let them slip through they can go back to the world to do more harm. Germans must have known it, for through the first week they left guards outside the ravine, with guns and everything, and we went there when they left. Maybe they struck a deal with the devil so he would keep watch for them. Black, black as tar, black as coal on the face, had a poker or some such rake in his hand, but he feared the sign of the holy cross and he ran. We heard him tear through the hazel, dry wood cracking, and we went down, across the clay that was catching us at the feet, or maybe it was them Jews, wanting to drag us under and drink our blood, as the old people used to tell us, that they drink blood, like bats, catch it and drink, they do, and if it weren't for the Russkies there would be peace once and for all. They even had Tartars under them. They passed through, on horses, puny beasts, ate raw meat, and each had five watches on each wrist. But they didn't stay long, a day, and on they went to Gardlica, didn't do any damage in the village, for the Russky officers kept their eyes on them. They wanted to go after the Germans, though great lords they were, those Germans, the world hadn't seen the like, the boots, the uniforms, tailor-made, black, silver . . ."

Then I saw Shorty get up, grimace with pain and make his way from behind the table. He pressed an elbow to his side, came up to the old man and – neither too hard nor too gently – slapped him twice on the face. Like a nurse, or as a man slaps a hysterical woman when she doesn't react to his words of comfort or succour.

Everything came to a halt and became still. Only the TV pretended that nothing had happened. It continued showing a svelte body smeared with something new. Shorty returned to his place. The old man was still rocking but less so, like a nodding dog in a car window when the car has stopped.

From the black hole, from a half-opened door, came a weak, nagging voice of an old woman speaking Ukrainian: "Hrycko, Hrycko, get me some water."

Chapter 23

"China, China, Chinaman, no! Don't take a Chinaman, he's got yellow balls!" came from behind the thin partition, second hour running: "Chinaman's got yellow balls!" It was a shitty partition, no partition in fact, letting through the light mixed with cigarette smoke. "Yellow balls!" We might as well have had no partition. We wanted to have a nap, but it just wasn't possible. It was cold and it stank. And that Chinaman! We tried to get the stove going, but the wood was wet and half-rotten, straight from under the snow, and the fat bastard with a moustache said that was all he had. There was more in the woods and if we wanted we could go and fetch it ourselves.

"Fifty a head," he'd finished. I wanted to spit on him but then thought we'd probably die outside, and he had the upper hand, so it was better to keep my mouth shut.

The rotting, heavy-as-stone pine logs smoked like hell, flickering with miserable little flames, and the stove was as cold as a corpse.

"Fifty a head. In advance." He'd put the notes together with some lewd exactness, stuck them in the back pocket and added: "Boiling water is in my room."

He'd then climbed off to his mezzanine, ducking his head under the low slanted ceiling with the sign ONLY ASSHOLES KEEP THEIR BOOTS ON.

"Nice place," muttered Goosy.

"What a place!" muttered Vasyl. "When I was here the last time it was run by a mad guy with a beard. He drank and carved figures of a sorrowful Jesus. He looked like one himself. Especially when he got pissed. Sad picture indeed."

"This one doesn't look like a holy figure to me. He stinks. Let's get out of this freezer."

Goosy had headed towards the end of the stone hall and had

pushed the door indicated by the fat bastard. Barren room, a few spongy mattresses and a stove.

". . . yellow balls, yellow balls, yellow balls!" It was now eight o'clock and they were only beginning. We'd seen them from the window. They came in a long line, ten, maybe more, all dressed in professional walking gear; some had anoraks and chimney rucksacks packed high, probably with bottles. The fat bastard welcomed them like old friends; there were a few girls. They ended in the room next door so we kept quiet, just in case. Only when we heard them get going properly did we start moving, to stretch old bones or look into that shitty stove, wrapped in our wet socks and boots; just as well it was cold or the stink might have brought in all the search parties from miles around.

And those behind the wall were settling in, throwing their rucksacks, laughing, clattering metal mugs, stomping boots. Someone struck a few chords on a guitar, some godawful box, which made Goosy sigh, "No sleep tonight". He was right, of course, but then he added: "We haven't seen any wildlife. A week in the woods and not a single deer."

But nobody cared. Shorty was lying in the middle with a fever caused by his wound, silent. He hadn't said a word since yesterday. Maybe he was thinking of the old man.

He was finally brought back to reality by the woman's voice. He got up, took her a mug of water, and when he returned he took his seat by the stove and, as if nothing had happened, downed another vodka. By then he was more cautious and refrained from reminiscing; nobody really wanted to hear it anyway. We stared at the TV; the news was over and the screen was flooded with wave after wave of horizontal and diagonal stripes. A film started, but we couldn't see anything; none of us bothered to do anything about it, and grandad was apparently used to it. He listened to the French words mixed with Polish translations without taking his eyes off the screen. The bottle was finished. When that happened the alcohol evaporated from our bodies in some instantaneous, supernatural way. Drowsiness mixed with the stuffy air in the room was slowly rendering us senseless. Shorty fell asleep sitting. Nobody thought to take care of him. One after another, we fumbled our way into our sleeping-bags and keeled over on the floor. Bandurko stretched out on the bench by the wall. Grandad was stepping over our bodies, pottering about, stoking the stove, rattling something; he probably went outside, for at some point a gust of icy wind swept into the room. I fell asleep with the light on.

In the morning we got up wrapped in the same silence, unrested, stiff as boards, aching, with the remnants of unhealthy sleep and fatigue in our eyes and mouth. The morning was barely grey. The fire was on, grandad was outside but soon came back with a little bucket sloshing with milk. He poured some into the bowl for the calf, the rest into a pot that he put on the stove. He went out two or three times more, but we didn't pay any attention to him; nor did he to us, treating us like a necessity or another element of nature.

In the end Bandurko collected himself, and then collected empty glasses from the table, rinsed them somewhere and made coffee, to which we sat still half-asleep and indifferent to everything around us. After a while we woke up enough to roll up the sleeping-bags and fry the same as yesterday, though this time no potatoes were on offer. The old man poured warm milk over the remains from last night and took it to the little room. Through the half-open door we could see a part of the bed and a heaped duvet, nothing else. They didn't speak. Perhaps the room was empty; no sound came out of there, and in the silence filling the room we could hear a fly breathe.

After coffee and food, after cigarettes, we had nothing else to do. The day arrived at last and bright sunshine poured in through the window. Every detail of the shabby room – rubbish on the floor, streaks of dirt on the windowpanes, a cracked and empty flowerpot on the windowsill, the gingery calf lying on the floor – was awash with golden light. The old man was sitting on his little stool smoking. The flood of light rendered him virtually invisible. We had to squint our eyes to catch him on the brink of dissolving into thin air. When his customary half cigarette burned out and sizzled in the blackened holder, he got up and said: "Come with me, one of you."

I and Bandurko followed him.

The farmyard was as poor as the house. In the middle stood a well covered with spruce branches, like a children's summer hut. A path ran to it, touched it and ran towards a wooden cowshed with a thatched roof patched up with rusty sheets of corrugated iron.

Next to it stood a tall shed with hay and some hovel, perhaps a pigsty.

Grandad went inside the cowshed and closed the door. We stood on a manure-trodden little patch, looking into the gap between the buildings. Several hundred metres further down, on the other side of the glaringly white expanse of snow, stood another farmstead, towards which ran a crisply cut trail of perfectly parallel sleigh-tracks. The cowshed filled with commotion and baying. The door opened, and grandad dragged out a sheep. He manoeuvred it on to a clean, virginal patch of snow, bent over it and as quick as lightning turned the animal on its side. The sheep writhed and kicked, but he held it down at the neck and the rump.

"The knife's above the door."

I fetched a long bit of steel, thin from years of whetting, set in a wooden handle.

"Hold the rump, one of you."

Bandurko looked at me with absent eyes, fell on his knees and sunk his hands in the dirty yellow fleece. Grandad took the knife from my hand, put his knee on the sheep's shoulders, pulled its head back and with his left hand slashed its throat with a sharp, quick cut.

We dragged the corpse across the snow to hang it on a hook fixed to the shed's beam. We had quite a job trying to lift the dead flesh, while the old man punctured the skin on a hind leg at the tendon and pulled the hole over an iron spike. We watched him as he cut along the belly and legs, on which he left furry socks, and pulled off the heavy, steaming skin in three sharp jerks. Vasyl's jacket was splashed with blood.

On our way back I noticed that the red patch on the snow had darkened. I carried a bucket with the liver, heart and kidneys; the old man brought the skin, which he dropped somewhere in the hall. The guys were sitting at the table. Kostek studied the map. Grandad came up to the sideboard and took out a bottle without a label. He raised a glass to Vasyl and nodded to give me a glass too. He put the rest back in the sideboard; just as well – the moonshine was vicious.

After midday, as Kostek and Vasyl whispered over the map, the old man spoke out. "The best way to the hostel is over the hill. You don't have to go down to the village."

*

So Shorty was silent, Goosy was mumbling about deer, Vasyl was poking in the stove and Kostek was sitting on the floor, legs in his sleeping-bag, smoking and probably making plans for the future.

By nine o'clock the party behind the wall was so pissed they sang two songs at the same time, while their steps grew heavier and stiffer, as if they were walking on stilts. I thought, "Fuck it, we need to organise some food or we'll die of starvation, cold or conspiracy." I told the others I was going to get that hot water from the fat bastard. I pulled on my wet socks and went out into the stone corridor. The walls of roughly hewn sandstone were lit by a dim lightbulb. On the mezzanine I found the door with a notice burned out in wood: DON'T BOTHER COMING IN IF YOU CAN'T BE BOTHERED TO KNOCK. I heard an inviting noise and went inside. It was much warmer there, three times. The fat bastard was sitting on a sofa covered with artificial bearskin, holding the breast of a big blond; well oiled too, I guess he was, for seeing me he awkwardly pulled away from her. On the table stood an almost empty bottle and a few nibbled sandwiches. Generally a good atmosphere, smelling of skansen village: a horse-collar on the wall, spurs and a bridle, and above the host's head deer antlers and a highlander's axe and hat.

"About that hot water."

The master of the house tried to collect his thoughts and, to gain time, pointed to the chair.

"Sit down, young man, and drink. I know I charge a lot, but winters are harsh. Have to make a living somehow, don't I?"

I thought I'd better sit down. He looked drunk and easily provoked. He poured the rest of the bottle into a glass and nodded.

"I'm not inviting every one. I don't like crowds. Jolka is just a representative. Aren't you?" He slapped the girl gently on the back.

Jolka nodded thoughtlessly. She wasn't bad, in fact. Big and gentle. There was something of an animal about her, a cow, a pretty cow, something like that. I downed my daily bread. From the corner of my eye I noticed they were not just sitting but watching television. The set stood by the door. The time was just after nine. The news should be on, but instead two blokes were maltreating a woman with big tits. The cassette was probably German; that's why there was no sound.

"Move your ass, Jolka. Put the kettle on."

Jolka heaved her big body. Her thighs hit the table as she manoeuvred herself from behind it amid a great racket. Her blue jeans were pleasantly stretched at the seams. Clutching at air, she made her way to the kitchen stove and started another racket. The host looked at me, sort of sharply, but his eyes were already a little glazed.

"Hard times. Fucking Commies. I know I charge a lot . . ."

But I was already focused on the screen. The images whirled, changed, reassembled, and I could almost hear the woman's "*Schnell, schnell . . .*"

"Water's ready."

I leaped to my feet and went to the kitchen. A massive aluminium kettle rattled its lid; Jolka swayed over the hot range. Quite a pretty little animal, thoughtless and dazed. Lifting the kettle, I rubbed against her bum. Immediate response. I was a guerrilla, after all.

I informed them I'd bring the kettle back in a minute and left. Goosy had the mugs ready with the coffee. I poured the water and thought of her ass. Of her ass and television. Of television and her ass. Of her swooning, empty looks. My trousers felt tight. I picked up my coffee and a piece of bread with a slice of pork fat and lit up a cigarette. I drank, ate and smoked; inside my head ran a video.

"Here goes a black man with a big one." The group behind the wall changed the tune with a continent.

"They were here," said Goosy.

"What for?"

"To invite us. To join them in the fun, as they said."

"And?"

Goosy looked me in the eye.

"I wouldn't mind sitting with those idiots, just so that I don't have to look at your mugs."

"Go on, then."

"I think I will."

Bandurko quickly analysed the data.

"Quite right. They've already seen us, so we can go and fraternise. Camouflage."

"They're getting through a sea of booze." Kostek said that like a warning. "I think we shouldn't make ourselves too conspicuous, but . . ."

"Well, Goosy," I said, "you don't have much luck, do you?"

"Aah, fuck you all . . . at least I'll play a few chords."

Only Shorty had no view. He lay with his arms crossed, looking somewhere beyond the wall.

I gave everyone a top-up and left with the kettle. I met her on the stairs. She was climbing down sideways, holding on to the banister with both hands. The stairs creaked. She managed to get down to the hall and leaned against the wall. Then she burped.

"Sssleepy litty sssleepers . . . Sssleepy squire sssleeeps . . . and you litty sssleepy . . . ?"

A hiccup shook me out from her field of vision. It took some time before she refocused. Her red lumberjack shirt was unbuttoned, showing a white bra.

"Lllook at 'im. Not a sssleepy sssleeper . . ." She bent like a penknife and swept the air with her hair. Some sort of ceremonial bow. "Jola'sss not sssleepy. Jola'sss going wee-weesss . . ." She pushed herself off the wall, and then again before she managed to stand upright unsupported. I put the kettle on the stairs and took her under the arm.

"I'll help Jola."

I managed to heave her onwards. She walked with her head down and belly pushed out, waddling in her undone trainers. We went out in front of the hostel. Down below, under the ice, murmured the stream; the stars shone above; the snow creaked. I was in my socks. I managed to lead her away from the entrance; she was fumbling at her flies but getting nowhere.

"I'll help Jola." Quite a useful phrase, that. I positioned myself behind her and pressed myself to her bum. I found the button. Boy, was it strong; I could hardly force it out of the buttonhole. Then I started to peel her trousers off, with great difficulty, together with knickers and tights, inch after inch. She was swaying forwards and back.

"Jola goes wee-wees. Will you help Jola?" And she got a fit of giggles. At last I pulled the pants off her buttocks. I wished she was dead, just a warm corpse, that's what I thought, massaging the two fleshy hemispheres. Now and again she raised her hand in a strange gesture, as if she wanted to stroke her cheek, but the hand fell down lifeless.

"Jola's doing weee-weees," she announced. She didn't fall into the snow only because I squatted with her. We made a lovely pair. I pulled my hand back at the last moment and we became engulfed in clouds of steam.

"Done," she announced again. I put my hands under her arms and stood her up. "Jola's done. And you done? You not doing wee-wees?" We were standing as before. I thought an outlaw on the run had to be quick. I pushed her against the wall. Instinctively she stretched out her hands and so she stayed, still, whiter than the snow.

When I managed to drag her back inside, only Shorty was in the room, just as I'd left him. With his arms crossed, like a romantic poet, horizontal version. I lowered the body on to the mattress next to him.

"She's a good girl," I said.

"So I see."

"The guys?"

"Can't you hear?"

Indeed. There were no more Chinamen or blacks. No coloured people whatsoever. Just silence. And in that silence Goosy's voice, singing in English "It's all over now, baby blue."

"I'll go. I haven't listened to him for a long time."

"Go."

I took out from the rucksack a bootle of moonshine that the old man had sold to us for fifty zlotys and put it next to Shorty.

"Switch the lights off?"

He made a downcast grimace and shook his head.

Those guys had it incomparably better. Furniture, benches, a low table – or a few planks resting on bricks, to be more precise – and heat. The shithead gave them coal; two shameless buckets of it in the corner. It wasn't such a high price for Jola. She was one of them; a bearded guy in specs asked me if I hadn't seen her.

"She's with the squire," I told him, and he only nodded. They sat Goosy in the place of honour, if in that mess there was a place of honour, in the centre at any rate, or the centre happened by itself, for everyone was looking at him. And he played, smiling to himself, as he always did when he played. He looked like some guru from twenty-odd years ago. His face smoothed out. He was sitting cross-legged, wearing a denim jacket and red socks. His right foot was moving to "It's all over now, baby blue". He was pulling chords on some wooden box without complaining it was not his favourite Martin, dreamed of for years and acquired only last year, when he had the money and no time to play it. Now he'd turn up his nose at any other guitar, even the best. You could give him a box made of Lebanese cedar and he wouldn't even fart into it. And now he played, his eyes half-closed like cat's in the sun, singing in his half-baritone just as he'd done years ago in Zakopane. Only the faces were younger and the people didn't stink as we did then.

The fellow with a beard and glasses slid towards me on his bum holding a bottle and a glass. He poured a shot, drank it and then poured one for me. He waited for me to swallow before asking: "Not bad, this guy. Friend of yours?" I don't think it was really what he wanted to talk about, for after a while he asked again.

"What are they doing up there?"

At first I wanted to tell him, but at the last moment I was overcome by Christian pity.

"Watching telly. There was news about the president." For a moment I wanted to go back to that other winter, when everything was cheaper, when we didn't even need anything, a bottle of vodka and cheap wine on a train so crowded the entire personnel must have been sitting on top of the engine driver, and even if the conductor bothered to show up, by the time he would have got to the first compartment he would be doing backward flips on the puke. Honest truth. The nineteen-thirty to Zakopane slaughter-house on wheels; past Kraków it was Golgotha without a drop left between us, but we were still proud and full of contempt for the world.

Now I was looking at his face, which was getting smoother by the minute. It was the smoke; people smoked like in a prison cell, and all fancy brands. The time of crumbly cigarettes had gone, gone with that winter when we begged for food, drink and a place to sleep in that crazy hellhole where the young came stuffed with cash, except us. Never mind. We were proud and full of contempt for the world. In fact it was me who was doing the begging; Goosy played. Among those halfwits from good homes he was the only one who could do anything, even though at that time he still couldn't play all that well. So they stared at him, just like these were staring now, pouring him round after round while I had to ingratiate myself, or stealthily drink his. And even though he was fatter, shorter and pimplier than I was, it was he who in the end pulled a bird who could visit you in a dream, and who put us up, that is him, while I slept on the floor trying to pull the knickers off her opposite number, and didn't. I should have; maybe then I would have gained the wisdom and like a true wise man I'd be pissing all over adolescent emotions that sit in your belly like a stadium full of football hooligans chanting. "Give us a fuck, give us a fuck!"

In the corner of the room there was a pile of colourful anoraks and rucksacks. Colourful sleeping-bags formed a frenzied, orgiastic lair, and everyone was swaying and rocking, each in a different way. No surprise; you couldn't do a wave to these numbers, though they tried. Goosy stopped, but only to light up, take a couple of drags and stick the cigarette under the strings at the head of the guitar. He must have learned it somewhere, maybe from Lee Hooker. The vertical ribbon of smoke rose slowly, steadily and picturesquely. The fans had something to look at too. He was fingerpicking, slamming an occasional chord just when least expected, and so everyone listened. A girl with dark short-cropped hair was slowly inching her way towards him, sliding on her bum; I was waiting for when she'd get stuck on a splinter and scream.

Goosy looked like a cat in the sun, with his eyes half-closed. Didn't even drink much. A glass of vodka stood next to his red sock. He was getting drunk with playing. He could get high on playing more than on any booze. "It doesn't give you a hangover," he used to say. He was capable of ripping through a night on a couple of beers.

Another girl started off towards him. Also dark but with longer hair. Baggy trousers with lots of pockets polished the floor so it was difficult to draw a conclusion about the ass. She had white fur-lined slippers and a turquoise polo neck. When after a while the third moved, a redhead in a green battledress, I thought we were all heading for a spot of trouble, as all the guys stayed put. Goosy sat in the middle; the first circle were the girls, and we guys made the outer circle. And yes, finally someone shouted: "Eh, don't you know any Polish stuff?" But then the short-cropped one turned and threw over the shoulder: "Shut it, Wiesiek!"

She had a pretty profile. Perhaps a little big but nicely shaped nose, and she looked a bit like one of those little wonders cut out by the short man in glasses, the only true artist operating in Warsaw's Old Town; cutting out people's faces practically out of thin air – that's art.

The girl's words had an effect of creating an awkward silence. After giving five public performances, Goosy knew what to do and he jumped into this silence. The last stanza of "Love minus zero, no limit" he sang in Polish, and only for the short-cropped one, although he had only looked at her twice in his life. But she knew the rules of engagement well, and so did the rest. People have normally few things on their minds, and when they get rat-assed together in mixed company there's only one.

Goosy finished the number and glanced at Wiesiek, third generation after land reform, with a metal badge of the tourist guide on his jumper, who may have even smiled in reply. If his face was anything to go by he was probably a decent and open-hearted fellow by nature, something that definitely could not be said about any of us.

Kostek sat behind the artist's back, and I could swear he was playing in his pocket with his knife. It was simple, enough to get among people and all that mess flowed away, receded into the realm of dreams, acquired the status of a figment of the imagination, or an insignificant accident. That was the thing on his mind. The stupid, mundane normality that, like a sponge, wiped all that madness clean. Even Vasyl Bandurko escaped for a moment. I saw him talking to a young boy with long wavy hair. Because of the hair I couldn't see his face, only his hand, slender, white, like a girl's.

It was all happening quite fast. The one with beard said: "I'm Maciek." We drank another round; he offered a cigarette. I took it, and for a short while we became good friends. It was short because he soon started asking: "What's she doing up there?" I began to feel sorry for him and our male friendship dissolved; I didn't answer. Instead I asked him if they were going anywhere else, and he said that they were but most likely they'd stay here until they'd drunk everything they'd brought with them, which should be next morning.

Then a short-cropped boy crawled up to us and asked if we had anything. He downed a round and stayed with us, the way people change boxes in the middle of an opera. He was just opening his mouth, probably to say how well this guy was playing, when the door crashed open and in the doorway stood the fat bastard, rested, swollen and wearing a hat. He closed the door and leaned against it, looking at us with a stupid smile, pleased, as if we had arranged all this specially for him, as if it were his birthday.

He must have caught sight of our bottle, for he abandoned his patriarchal pose, pushed himself off the door, shuffled towards us and sat down. Without asking, he poured himself a glass and drank it. Obviously everything belonged to him: asses, vodka and blessings. My new friend didn't even look at him. He sort of stiffened up, stooped and froze still, sending murderous flashes off his glasses. I thought I had better go back to our room, for sooner or later they would start talking and then search for that drunken bum.

Chapter 24

But there nothing had changed; nothing could, except that Jola was lying on her back, in a sleeping-bag up to her neck. She had her mouth open and she was snoring.

Shorty lay as before, his eyes peering at the ceiling or the walls, next to him the bottle, only a little bit emptier.

"Are they having a good time?" he asked.

"Very good. Can't you hear? Both groups. Goosy best of all."

"So he isn't that sick, then? Maybe the singing makes him better."

"He's getting better from sheer enthusiasm."

"Good. My wound reopened. I got soaked, so to speak. I wouldn't mind a fresh dressing. A clean, proper one."

He took out a cigarette and lit up as if the problem of dressing concerned someone else or was due to be settled the day after tomorrow. He smoked, and I pulled his jumper up and gently touched the dark patch on his blue shirt. It was hard, scabby, but underneath warm and moist.

"It doesn't hurt. It's just leaks."

"That fucking bastard should have a first-aid box somewhere, maybe bandages. This has to be washed clean and checked for any shit inside."

"I've got the snake."

"The fat bastard came downstairs and if I know him he'll get plastered. We'll find something then."

"Sure. Wounded partisan, aren't I?"

Bit by bit we got back on the vodka and listened as Goosy's repertoire began to change and his voice to weaken. Jola grunted innocently in her sleep. It was nearly ten o'clock; the night was young. Kostek was playing click-clack; Bandurko was looking deep into the hippie cherub's eyes. Everyone was busy. We rested, killing time by waiting for something to happen; something always does, no sweat. I looked as the smoke rose from Shorty's half-open mouth and settled in horizontal layers, mixed with the fumes from the stove and little clouds of half-digested alcohol. I had a runny nose, which I wiped with my sleeve. When I finally keeled over and covered up, it felt quite comfortable.

"Shorty, what if we just went? What if we just put our boots on and followed the tracks to the village? We could wait out until the morning, catch the bus and simply get the fuck out of here, drinking all the way; that we can still afford. We could even go through Wroclaw. Nice city. I went there once. They're busy having fun now, Goosy, Vasyl; Kostek is watching them and he's enjoying himself the best. What do you think?"

He was silent for a while, stubbed his cigarette on the floor and flicked it towards the stove. He said without looking at me: "I don't think so, for several reasons. First of all I just can't be bothered. That's probably the main reason. Secondly, I'm curious how it will all end. Plain curious. I want to see how they . . . how we're going to get out of this mess. I'm not scared, I don't think. It seems to me it's all a game, and that the rest of the world thinks that. So I'm tempted to see how this game changes into something which is no longer a game."

He took another cigarette, lit up and flicked the match into the air.

"In fact I don't think there's anything else in it for us but the game. So I'll stay to watch it."

He slipped his hand under Jola's sleeping-bag. "Pretending she's asleep. She was pretending then and she's pretending now."

"Leave her. There'll be two guys looking for her soon. Perhaps they've already started."

"You have to make her decent, then. I can't manage."

He pulled the sleeping-bag off the girl, and for the last time in my life I could feast my eyes on Jola in all her splendour. Putting on her knickers and trousers proved a more difficult task than taking them off. Shorty was right. She had to be pretending. There seemed to be no limits to the length women go to to preserve their innocence. Finally I pulled up the zip and fastened the button. Hard work, made me sweat. Though more from fear than anything else, that they'd come in and there would be trouble. But they didn't. I pulled the red winding sheet over the body and we both took a swig from the bottle. The moonshine stank like the vilest poison, but it worked as it should, annihilating contradictions.

"Prince Mishkin and Rogozhyn," laughed Shorty.

"Good morning, little schoolgirl. Taj Mahal," I laughed back.

And so we chatted away, flicking cigarette butts. The moonshine was working and not working at the same time. It exploded in the stomach in short bursts of narcotic enlightenment only to drop us into a state of euthanasia. From ecstasy to euthanasia in four minutes flat, and back again.

"Did you mean it? That we should make ourselves scarce?"

"I don't know."

For how should I know? Meaning had no sense, if it ever had any. We were like children going through one caprice after another, until the whole world begins to sway like a drunk, shouting, changing rules by the minute depending on a fancy, accident or whatever gets into his head. So what could I tell him? That I was in a state of weightlessness, that apart from tiredness and cold nothing seemed real and that it didn't matter any longer which way and with whom we would go? That time was up, the buzzer had been pressed, thank you very much; you had thirty seconds to come up with an answer, like on a TV quiz. And now we had reached zero gravity, zero meaning. I could stay, I could go – who cares? Held back by tiredness, hurried on by fear, which I had to imagine anyway because I didn't really feel it, not enough to run knee deep through the snow without sleep or food. In truth I could just as well go among the people and become one of them, get on the coach, eat some stinking cabbage at one of the coach stations and simply return to my old life, which had probably ground to a halt and now waited for me, for no one else would go near that pile of shit. Too complicated for words. I had only premonitions. And the time when we could sit all night and talk had long gone. We had learned enough and both more or less the same thing. Nothing interesting. Waste of time.

"What's the difference?" I said.

"There must be differences . . ." But he didn't finish, for the door opened and in it stood our friend Maciek. In fact he put his head in first, sent out a flash off his glasses and looked on as if getting his eyes used to the great and silent space of our room. The visibility was too good; not enough smoke and people. Too simple a configuration of bodies. Finally his eyes saw and, without looking at us, in three long strides he made it to Jola's bed and sort of swooned, or maybe just carefully – so as not to wake her up – lowered himself to his knees. The prince and the sleeping beauty. He probably wanted to sweep the hair off her forehead but only passed his hand over her face like an undecided hypnotiser.

"What's she doing here?"

A sort of silent scramble developed between me and Shorty, a kind of "you say it", "No, you say it", and I won – or was it him? Hard to tell, for in the end he grunted in this heavy and perfectly indifferent voice of his:

"Nothing. She's asleep."

"Here?"

"Here. Can't you see?" Then he took pity on the man. "She came in smashed and wanted to have a nap because it was quite impossible in your room. She got a sleeping-bag and here she is. Was I to kick her out? Let her sleep."

"I've been looking for her," said four eyes, as if it weren't quite obvious he had already found her. "I asked the squire. He said she was there, sat with him a while. She always writes our names in the book, pays for us. He said she sat a while, drank a coffee and left."

"It was more than a coffee, methinks," said Shorty. "There must have been something more."

"She always takes our names to the squire. He has his humours, doesn't like strange people wandering about his rooms. Sometimes he'll invite someone upstairs, but rarely. He comes downstairs if he wants to play."

"Mean bastard, isn't he, the squire? He took fifty zlotys each for some sperm-soaked mattresses and a litre of boiling water, the fucker. At least you got coal."

"He gave us two buckets. The room was still warm. Someone was there before us. I'm not all that fond of him myself, you know. He's . . . I don't know . . . like an animal, no contact. You never know what he's thinking."

"What can he think? You want to do Wittgenstein with him? Fat bastard. If we only had somewhere else to go he'd get a kick in the teeth, not money. It makes my blood boil when I think about it, fucking swine . . ."

Shorty became strangely talkative. As if he, too, wanted to become Maciek's friend. He handed him the bottle and offered a cigarette. For a while we ruminated on the revulsion the swine raised in us, and then Shorty picked up the thread again.

"I'd be careful with the bastard. He's got something bad in his eyes. Do you have to pump him all that booze?"

"It just happens. We've been coming here for the last three years. The previous manager was different. We got used to the place. It's great in the summer. Secluded, you can walk around all day without seeing anyone. In the evening the deer come to the window. You see all kinds of wildlife."

"In winter too," scoffed Shorty. "It's wild all right . . ."

I didn't feel like talking. It became quiet behind the wall. Goosy must have started singing Cohen. The only sound I heard was the click-clack of the knife, couldn't shake it off. Dry, mechanical, in a strange harmony with the expression on Kostek's face, which was changing imperceptibly from scorn to determination. That's how he was; I'd never seen him sad. It was neither a smile nor a grimace, put on only because a face needs an expression, so he chose one that required the least effort.

It was the same then, that face in the furthest corner of a room with a slanted ceiling, legs stretched out, still. He sat practically through the whole house-warming party, his eyes following us around the room, examining configurations and constellations of strange people. It was halfway through the party when I noticed he was observing us. Goosy was in seventh heaven.

He was showing us every nook and cranny of his new flat, its niches and passages, stamped his feet on the wooden steps leading to the mezzanine, where he could put up a whole Gypsy family with all their worldly belongings. He stamped his feet, and the squeaking of new pine floorboards sent him into raptures. God knows who brought Kostek. Someone did. There were a good thirty people. It wasn't really a house-warming party so much as a regular soirée. The furniture in its place, old and new, pretty and ugly, salads, wine, blah-blah, high life for five zlotys, free nosh and everyone listening to his own voice, shouting over atmospheric ballads blaring at full blast. Only Kostek Górka was silent. He didn't give a shit about his own voice. He sat in a rattan chair with a bottle of white Sophia and a pack of cigarettes and he looked as if he was there on business, a secret agent, a journalist, or a nurse at the ball in a loony bin. Four years ago last autumn; the party was swinging, no one threw up, there was not enough wine for that; half the party came with wives, some even with children. So civilised we soon found ourselves on the mezzanine, Shorty, Vasyl and I, with a big bottle of Wyborowa which Shorty simply took out of the fridge. That mezzanine was a bit like the choir in a church, a sort of gallery. Sitting on poufs and cushions, we had a good view of the public below, and when we all warmed up, they and us, Shorty began spitting over the banister, just like we used to do at the movies in school days. If someone was hit he didn't admit it, civilised party after all, and only Kostek noticed Shorty's game and raised his glass to us. Goosy came upstairs, made a face because the bottle turned out to be his, and asked us why we weren't having fun. To which Bandurko answered that as a matter of fact we were having tremendous fun; Shorty had just scored another hit with one who was just holding forth about healthy eating, mother earth, wheatgerms and Kora Jackowska, and why Goosy is not sitting with us, it's our celebration, dreams come true, own place where you can listen to the Rolling Stones at full blast. But Goosy didn't sit down. Instead he went off to put on some more salads, talk business, the life of foetuses and the signs of the zodiac.

By midnight all the guests had left. Goosy's wife found herself a corner to sleep in, and there were only four of us; the fifth was Kostek. When the door behind the last guest closed, he went to the hall and came back with a bottle of vodka.

He put it on a small table and returned to his seat. In the surrounding silence the rattan creaked ominously like an end, or a beginning.

"If I'm spare I can go home," he said quietly, loudly, brazenly, making sure we knew he wasn't going anywhere, daring us to throw him out. But we weren't up to it. It was going to be like in the old days, a peaceful piss-up with quiet music until we keeled over where we sat, in our daily packaging. Goosy stopped grinning and was smiling like a human being. We probably thought, Oh, let him stay, the bastard has no one to get pissed with in this shitty town. So he stayed. As a kind of fun; we soon forgot about him. Well, not quite, but we stopped paying any attention to him or he simply stopped drawing attention to himself. A discreet fellow.

God knows what we were talking about. It must have bored him, as it bored us, with that old familiar boredom induced by the well-rehearsed procedure of questions and answers which recharges the mind like sleep. We must have been reminiscing about the old world, the only real one because it was dead, completed and unchangeable. We had no other world and were to have none other. All we could expect were half- or quarter-worlds, events, coincidences, happenings, things without context, all that shit that happens to everyone and as such meaningless, accidental crumbs of someone else's life which we pick up and examine, and since they do not fit anything we throw them away just to find another piece of shit which takes the place of the previous one. But it was no longer this world in which we swam like fishes in the water – stupid, thoughtless, pleased-with-themselves carp in the pond, moths that luckily avoided the flame, convinced daylight didn't exist, that flying in circles was the perfect form of life, the cosmos, eternity, fuck knows what. So, stupidity and faith. So we must have been saints, like everyone else before they saw the light. It must have been this we talked about.

And what was Kostek hearing? We must have argued as usual who screwed Gzanka first, a big girl with big tits, who tormented us from the eighth form onwards, even though she was only in the sixth. Those tits just wouldn't let us go; they were the biggest in the school. So Gzanka it had to be. Bandurko couldn't bear to listen to this and shouted, banging his fist on the table, "I protest, as a poof!" but probably he really hated her. Their so-called estates were practically next-door neighbours, the same Commie elite that chewed our fathers' balls off, as we used to say in the days of political maturity. But Vasyl's hatred had sexual rather than political roots. It was some sort of mass infatuation. After all, she was just a bimbo with big tits, while the process of beatification was actually taking place inside our heads. It went on for several years, disappeared, reappeared, died and was resurrected again, galvanised into life by an accident or boredom. Shorty was desperately in love with her and vice versa, but she wouldn't give him, or maybe he didn't want to because he loved her too much, just as I did, though not reciprocally, so she didn't even think of giving me anything. Goosy claimed he didn't love her but that she did fuck with him, love him or not, just to spite the rest.

The question remained unresolved as we all refused to believe Goosy, and he had no witnesses. It bothered us still after all these years. Gzanka was probably too fat, resentful, all corseted and lacquered, while we were still banging our heads against that palaeolith of love and sexuality.

"Sure she gave you. Knickers to sniff." That's what we used to say to Goosy, and it really wound him up. He would relay the whole film, script and Technicolor, of her bourgeois residence, a modern semi which seemed the pinnacle of good taste and desirability, with pink bath and white carpet, Italian espresso, with only a life-size porcelain dog missing to complete the dream design.

"So what was her pussy like, then?"

That was my line, for although she never gave me I had seen her pussy and I had witnesses. It was a pussy like any other, but at this point Goosy was beginning to be careful and mumbled something about her being shy and doing it in the dark. And as always the game ended in deadlock. Goosy was getting really mad because he probably did hump her, catching her at a moment of vulnerability, or his superhuman abilities.

Yep, Gzanka it was. She scorned us and eventually gave herself to some smartass who on the German garbage found himself a Merc, cleaned it up and arrived under her balcony at a time when we were fare-dodging and proud of it. To each his deserts. She should have given us the clap, that grand love of ours, and all would be fair. At three in the morning Vasyl told us to get a detective, find her and settle the matter with witnesses and photographs, for that endless hot air made him want to puke.

And then we ran out of vodka. We had a swift rummage through the kitchen, but there was nothing there, unless well hidden. When the night began to grow grey, Goosy announced: "Let's go there!"

"Where?"

"Our place."

We started getting dressed. The hall filled with commotion. Everybody was putting finger to lips going pssst, choking with laughter, when Mrs Goosy came out from one of the rooms, sleepy and negligeed, stretched her hand and said, "Car keys". Silence fell. Goosy dug the keys out of his pocket and gave them to her without a word of protest. For a moment it seemed we were defeated. Then Kostek came out from behind our backs and said loudly, to cheer us up, "I'll pay for a taxi."

Shorty, who leaned against the wall and was beginning to nod off, muttered: "Fuck it. I'll pay for the second . . . And you, Bandurko, the third."

It was one of those cold dawns of late October. I walked across half of Mokotów before we found a taxi, a beetroot Volga with a grandad who didn't care where he was going or with whom, as any journey could easily be the last. At five to six we managed to get to the night shop near Shorty's. We replenished our stock with Bandurko pleading with us, "Not vodka, not vodka," and pulling out fists of banknotes that were falling on the floor and which I was picking up on all fours. There was enough for a heap of bottles and a battery of cans. The taxi driver didn't mind, the more so when Shorty handed him a bottle and said, "Please accept this in advance as our apologies for our loud behaviour," and he sat in the front and guided the driver. Except that there was no loud behaviour. As we drove, the silence was growing deeper, as if we were sinking in some sort of a deep. We went over the Gdański Bridge. Down below, instead of water lay white mist. St Florian's on the right; on the left, far in the distance, the smoke of the power station strung out in black plaits. From the opposite direction came one of the yellow-blue electric commuters, with men waiting in the open doors; that was the point when the train would often stop on the bridge and they could jump off, catch a bus and gain a good minute or two, or at least add some variety to life.

We went around a roundabout and the Żeran factory began, massive metal cubes on the right, lines of trams on the left and crowds, with our fathers in their midst. They probably crossed the road in the underground passage, too old for hopping over yellow barriers and doing slaloms in between the oncoming cars. So it was silence in our Volga. The driver stepped on the brakes sometimes to let pass those who could not wait to get to work. He didn't say a word, and what was he to say? His jacket was of the same hue as the those of the hoppers and runners, only the face was a bit older, but they would quickly catch up with him. Past the last factory gate, he accelerated. "It's no car. It's shit. I started on a Warsaw, that was a car . . ." Hard to say whether he was talking about his own cab or the red Passat that had just whizzed past on the left.

For the rest of the journey he remained silent. He didn't care that we told him to go fuck knows where, to stop in the middle of nowhere, on the edge of a wood and a bumpy gravel road. Someone who started on a Warsaw couldn't be a chicken. He waited until we all scrambled out of the car, took our money and muttered: "Have fun."

"What have they done?" whispered Vasyl and turned to us, as if expecting an explanation. El Dorado had disappeared. Instead there was a massive expanse of rabble, scrap and not a single willow. The concrete stretched as far as the line of old linden trees, behind which hid Bandurko's and Gzanka's houses. Heaps, dunes, mountainous ridges of industrial debris and no pond; the frogs must have gone ages ago. He stepped forward, climbed the first mound, stood on the top and looked ahead, like across the sea, like Captain Ahab who looked for his white whale, then turned round and abandoned the story, vanished, never to return. A westerly wind tugged at his coat tails; the sun rose from behind tall trees. We saw him against the background of a big red disc, a black silhouette. He finished the bottle he had started in the taxi and began cursing the sky, the sun and the rubbish.

"Fucking bastards!" he screamed. Like never before. It's a miracle his throat didn't burst. Then he flung the empty bottle ahead and vanished among the grey dunes, his curses growing ever more distant and fading.

We moved back to the edge of the wood. It grew on a sandy hillock that offered a view of that shitty lunar landscape in its full glory.

"When he gets over it, he'll get back," said Goosy and gathered some dry grass and twigs. The smoke smelled just like autumn always smelled there. We lay down around the fire. Everything had the smell of the smoke, the wine, the beer, the cigarettes. We could see Bandurko climbing the hills, falling into valleys and emerging again. He was heading for the trees, stumbling and falling like a windmill, like a whirlwind, a four-legged beast, half-crawling, half-running. His coat tails flapped like the wings of a wounded bird. It looked as if he was leaning on them, pushing, as if trying to take off. Finally he reached the edge of the dump, shrank and vanished.

"He went to see his house," said Goosy.

"His is more to the left. The man with a peacock lives there," said Shorty.

We slept, stretched out on the sand, waking up for a drink, only to fall asleep again. The smoke hung in the air. Goosy threw up in the bushes and switched to beer. Then I threw up but soldiered on. Kostek just sat; it seemed he was there to watch over us. He wasn't saying anything. I think he saw through us, if there was anything to be seen in shitty pukers like us. He was wiping Goosy's nose when by midday he switched back to wine and lost his marbles. He wanted to play his harmonica but snots blocked the instrument. He sat making a strange buzzing noise, repeating like a mantra, "I shagged her, I did, I shagged her, I did . . ."

Chapter 25

Jola turned on to her stomach. Her bum rolled under the sleeping-bag like a gentle wave. Maciek carefully tucked her in; she looked like a corncob wrapped in a red rag.

"You know what?" whispered Maciek to Shorty. "He really is a swine. When we were here at New Year's Eve he was trying to get into her knickers. He's always after someone's ass."

"Piss on the bastard. And don't worry." Shorty was trying to cheer him up as best he could. "We'd better finish this bottle. I can't bear to look at it."

Easier said than done. The closer to the bottom, the viler it got. Behind the wall a female chorus came on as Goosy graciously switched to a more popular touristy repertoire and let them torture refrains from the hiker's hymnbook, the kind of singsong he wouldn't touch with a bargepole when sober. I winked at Shorty and nodded towards the wall.

"Ladies and gentlemen, please welcome the great stage wizard! The toast of spotlights and his six-bullet – pardon! – six-string guitar! Here he is, singing for us tonight – the great Goosy!"

If he heard us screaming, his voice didn't waver. And even if it had, the chorus drowned everything. The girls had found some peculiar tempos in the song, and the guys apparently wanted to fall in with them, for a weird Gregorian drone started seeping through the log wall. Something of our screaming must have got through. Just as we were lighting up, the door swung open with a kick and in the doorway appeared the squire, a badly hit ship, but not sunk yet. He blinked at us with his little fat eyes, as if our presence in the room was an unwelcome surprise. Shorty was right, he did look like a hog, a moustached hog. He wasn't grunting, and that was the only difference.

"What's going on? Are you not enjoying yourselves? Individualists, are you?"

He wanted to provoke us. He didn't have to open his mouth. But, joined in the silent understanding formed over the previous hour, we didn't even look at him. Shorty was lying, me too. Maciek sat in between the beds, chin on knees, all of us puffing on cigarettes like there was no tomorrow. No one raised his eyes. We didn't give him as much as a blink. He must have sensed his own nonexistence and stepped forward, as if wanting to cover us with his shadow. He stood on his shoelaces like some fucked-up monument, pushed his fists down his trousers and swayed. "So? Not enjoying yourselves then, huh?"

Shorty took a long drag on his cigarette and slowly let the smoke out.

"We are in mourning."

The squire swayed again. A thought was trying to get through but couldn't. He repeated, "Mourning?"

"Yesterday died Bororo Nambikiwara, author of books popular and scientific, beekeeper and scholar. He was my mother's father."

Some thought must have finally got through, for the squire swayed once more.

"Eh, you smartass. Don't be such a smartass."

"I'm not a smartass. My grandad has died. I had a telegram yesterday."

"Where?"

"Delivered to my own hands."

He considered the possibility and apparently judged it plausible. He relaxed.

"At least keep your voices down. It's past ten; night-time at the hostel. And if you don't want to play, it's your problem. It's your problem, isn't it?"

He was about to leave, stretched his hand back to find the doorhandle – at that point a good two metres away – when his eyes fell on our bottle. His face contorted in a more human grimace. He let go of the doorhandle he'd never grasped and crashed heavily on his ass next to Maciek.

"Give us a drink, boys. They've only got wine left back there."

"We've got a wake here."

"Ah, fuck the wake. Wake or no wake, I've got the right to

drink." He grabbed the bottle and took a good swig. He went red in the face and gasped for breath.

"Moonshine," he growled out.

"Wake," answered Shorty in the same sepulchral voice. But the squire, with a contentment peculiar to thick skulls, let it pass and rubbed his hands.

"Not bad. Not bad at all." Suddenly he was full of joy and friendly feelings. "I can't drink wine, you know. Bad for my kidneys. Vodka's different. It makes me feel better straight away. You should have brought more." This last one was directed at Maciek. "It's winter, innit? And you bring wine. Waste of time, dragging this horse piss all the way."

He lifted himself on his hands, trying to plant his ass firmly on the mattress.

"Who's this?"

His hands found Jola. He lifted the sleeping-bag and his mug stretched in a smile.

"Well, well, well. I thought I'd lost her. There she was, upstairs. I nodded off and when I opened my eyes she was no more. Naughty girl, naughty."

A slap on the jeans-clad bum sounded like a smashed paper bag, and his snort like a snort. Then Maciek – and who would have thought he had it in him? – leaped to his feet and in a split second stood behind the squire.

"Leave her alone, you bastard! You swine! Leave her . . . !"

There must have been something in his face that made everyone think of a pig. Perhaps it was the slow expressiveness, the metamorphoses of the facial cast played out in slow motion, verging on suspended animation. Everything registered clearly: surprise, astonishment, opening mouth, widening eyes, which turned on Maciek then on us, then back on Maciek, as if he'd completely gone off his head. And then the frown, the eyes narrowing in an effort to comprehend, until finally the thin, arched line of the lips, clenched teeth and the slowly protruding lower lip, meaning the penny had finally dropped . . .

"You little shit . . . you little shit . . . against me . . . ?"

He didn't even hit him. He rose slowly to one knee – for a moment he looked like someone kneeling in church – swayed on widely spread out legs, raised his hand, grabbed Maciek by the chequered shirt and flung him across the room, just like they do in cartoons. It was a highly acoustic space, that room; like inside a piano. We thought the boy had broken, shattered into pieces. He hit the wall sideways with his shoulder and slumped to his knees. The squire stepped over Jola and moved towards him like a wrestler. In an unconditioned response of a myopic, the boy managed to take his glasses off and squeezed them tight in his hand when a paw fell on his shoulder. This time the effect was not so spectacular. The body was just gaining speed when the shirt ripped, leaving the body behind.

"You little shit . . . You against me . . ."

Now he grabbed him by the neck. He pushed him down to the floor and sent him across the room like a toy car. Reeling, Maciek tripped on Shorty's feet, which was good luck for it saved him from smashing his head against the wall. He fell on Jola, who decided to pretend to the very last; she groaned and shook her bum as if trying to get rid of the weight. The squire gave her a helping hand. He grabbed the boy by the neck and, shaking him, hissed that "little shit" into his face and again threw him against the wall. That was his technique; apparently he didn't like beating. Maciek was stunned. We heard the thud and the boy froze still in a strange position, sort of squatting, sort of kneeling, like a marionette with cut strings. The squire came closer to have a better look at his handiwork. He stood over the heap of limbs, fists on hips.

"You want to know what I did with her? You do? You stupid little shit. Every time you were here . . . You blind shithead . . ."

He was spitting out filth, working himself up, getting high and carried away on it, forgetting he was in the middle of a small demolition job. He was simply tripping out of his mind and didn't even register as Maciek straightened what had got bent and twisted, pushed himself slowly up the wall as if on caterpillars, and slowly turned his head away, then his whole body; I can't remember from which hand came the flash. Squire threw himself forward, trying to squash the boy with his weight, but the pain finally reached his brain. His processing of sense data was really slow, but he eventually covered his face, and the second stab with cracked glasses landed on his fingers; the blood flowed like wine.

Behind the wall, behind the door that closed by itself, fifteen voices roared that they would build themselves a hut on a prairie among the herbs. Shorty sat more than he'd been lying earlier.

"It's an iodine and bandages job for sure," he said.

The squire stood rooted to the floor, moaning under the mask of his hands, swaying.

"I can't see. Guys, I can't see. I can't see . . ."

I pulled his hands away from his face. His forehead had deep cuts, and his left eye was covered with blood. I took him under his arm.

"Let's go upstairs, come on, let's go. Do you have first-aid stuff?"

"I do, I do . . . I'll kill him . . ."

But obviously it was a plan for the future, for without any opposition he let me push him out into the corridor. Stumbling, groaning and lamenting, he staggered to his door. Inside his room the light was on. I sat him on the artificial fur. He told me where the first aid was. First I wiped his mug with a wet towel and had a look at him. The cut finished just above the eyebrow. Just. I took from the box whatever there was, some gentian, gauze, bandage, stuffed some of it into my pockets when he again covered his face, and began to dress the wound. I splashed half his visage in purple, the gentian mixing freely with blood and dripping in picturesque rills. I covered the eye with three squares of gauze and bandaged the head, making him practically blind. He looked like a complete asshole.

"I can't tell you what's happened with the eye because I don't know anything about these things. At any rate, it doesn't look too good. With this sort of thing you're better off lying down."

I kept telling him this kind of stuff. I didn't want to see any more of him that night. I didn't want to see him, period. He was moaning and whimpering and meek as a lamb.

"I'll send you a nurse."

And nobody noticed anything. On our room descended the stillness peculiar to the aftermath of a battle. Maciek remained in a stupor, sitting next to Jola, who continued to pretend she knew nothing. She slept, the princess. So I played the doctor again. From the kettle I brought with me from upstairs I poured some water over Shorty's towel dressing to soften it up. We ran out of conversation. Shorty was silent, as if I was dealing with someone else. I told him to sit up. I unpicked the knots and ties and unwound the sheet. Shorty lay down, and I poured more water on the wound. Was it festering? Who could tell? It bled a little, festered a little; the edges were a little red. Nasty-looking mess. I smelled it. It didn't stink, at least not too much, but then I'd never smelled Shorty's interior; maybe it was his normal smell. I felt the edges.

"Does it hurt?"

He made a face as if he didn't really give a damn one way or the other. He shrugged his shoulders. I poured more purple stuff over it. He drew a complicated pattern around his bellybutton.

"Kalium hypermanganicum," he said.

I waited until the stuff dried up and told him to sit up again. He held the gauze while I strapped it with two rolls of bandage and fastened the lot with a safety pin.

"Not too tight?"

He looked beautiful. Like in clean underwear, like after a heroic struggle, like in a bride's corset. Only that sweaty grey face didn't fit the picture. He pulled down his clothes, lay down, apparently determined to continue in his silence. I left them, the whole threesome.

Things had changed here. The concert was over. Unstructured recreation in subgroups. The flat amphitheatre fell apart and now it looked like a café. Three, four people, drinking face to face, swigged some Azerbaijani port. But vodka was there too. They'd probably hidden it from the squire. Goosy sat in the corner cutting away fingering exercises, sort of for himself, but the black crew-cut sat in front of him, staring into the guitar's black hole, hand under chin, looking like a pop version of the Thinker. The atmosphere was quiet, cosy, drivelly. Bandurko sat by the wall and his long-haired friend next to him, like on a bus. I saw a thin, sensitive face, from which alcohol was slowly wiping all the charm. He was staring ahead; Vasyl was saying something under his nose, also staring into the void. They both looked like a pair of loonies lost in their own worlds, like a picture from a college party, when the guys, battered by alcohol, cigarettes and lack of sleep, go on churning with their tongues in the hope that the effort will finally pay off and they will produce some revelation, the truth, that for a short, fleeting moment they will burst into the all-consuming flame of mutual understanding, that in some inexplicable, miraculous way the night will change them into incorporeal angels, pure energy, pure living thought, before they keel over.

Only Kostek looked normal. He sat with Wiesiek, a glass between his legs, cigarette between his fingers. They talked. There were a few bodies already on the floor, a few bums stuck out of sleeping-bags, but on the whole the majority was trying to stay the course, steeped in memories, maybe even plans. I stood like that for a while. No one paid any attention to me; in that smoke they wouldn't notice Archangel Gabriel with a fiery sword. I was grey-black, inconspicuous, and didn't know what to do with my presence, which centre of intimacy I should attach myself to; outside was freezing, the other room smelled of blood, failure and silence, and I was desperate for a drink. I had no choice. Fuck it, I thought, I'll go there and have a sip from his glass. Being mad isn't contagious. And that's what I did. I came up to Kostek, sat down, drank all they had – and they had quite a drop – and so as not to appear churlish I kept them company, not too close, in fact more behind their backs, by the wall. Willy-Nilly, I started to eavesdrop, but they had nothing to hide.

"Peasant stock, I am, of course," Wiesiek was saying, "but it doesn't bother me. These days there are no real peasants just as there are no real workers. My father was a peasant worker, and I will be a virtual worker. My grandfather? Oh, yes, he was a real man. He would make wicker baskets in the evenings, but I have no craft . . . I used to visit him, had my scrambled country eggs, watched him work, stuffed my face and left. Flat fields, willows, people by the road, staring, on my way to the station; got the train and buggered off. One has to do something with this life. Pass the time, save energy, for a big and well-planned leap . . . Tsargorod, Ukraine, Stockholm – old, well-trodden tracks, if a bit forgotten. He who buys dear has to sell dear. Who said that? Old saying. Am I talking too much?"

He turned his face towards Kostek. I saw his profile. But he didn't get any answer and hung his head again.

"Grandad made baskets, great-grandad probably mended clogs. I'm talking gibberish, but so what? Tomorrow we shall part for ever. Who said that? An old tango. From before the war. Those were the days, eh? The war, must have been great, from what I've heard. Enough to direct a bit of courage not where the brave did and you had the world at your feet. Wouldn't think twice, signed the *volkslist* and watch which way the wind's blowing. Maybe I could even become a Gerry, if they let me. We missed everything. We're a lost generation. You can strangle your own mother and no one will care. All you'll get is an expression of society's reproach. But why strangle? All you need to do is wait. Unless you have no patience. Impatience. Who said that? Yuri Trofimov. Dead. Just like Zhelabov. Jesus! We've missed everything! You know, they really didn't need any money. They just didn't give a shit. Hryniewicki, black and scruffy. What was he thinking of? Like Samson shaking the column, except it was no ceiling that came down but the entire firmament. Jeeesus . . ."

Now Kostek looked at him, turned towards him and stayed like that, facing the poor windbag, and even if he wasn't looking into his eyes he certainly watched his nervous lips.

". . . in rugs, Alexander next to him, saying he was cold. We missed everything. Lost generation, fate, inscrutable, impenetrable . . . Fucking stinkers! And we believed them! Scratch a Yankee and you'll see a stinky. Who said that? I did. Zimmerman the prophet! Look at his face. What a mug! Yet people followed him like pigs off a cliff. Honey-eared smartass. My grandad was a basket-weaver . . . Magic Johnson from Rawa Mazowiecka . . . They cooked a chicken for my visit, I ate it and went back, and that was good, the mist over the river. In the mist stood a man with a fishing rod. I was at that time getting on the train, going to see Ginsberg. Sat on his ass, knocking on the floor with a stick, and the rabble gawked at him as if he was reading a new Genesis, the snothead . . . What am I saying? What am I on about?"

"Talk on, don't worry, talk on. You can even sing, for tomorrow we shall part." Kostek egged him on.

"Ginsberg was singing. Blake. Both muddy waters, fuck 'em. Why didn't he sing Donne, or something entirely different? The air was full of deodorant. I could hardly stand, the crowd groaned, or maybe that's how it seemed to me. Everything only seems to me, so don't look at me like that. One has to . . . you know . . ."

He got up, reeled, stepped over several bodies and, after a brief argument somewhere in the middle of that tangled heap of bodies, returned with a half-empty bottle.

"You have a drink too, or your ears will dry out," he said to me and handed me the glass. By now the stuff had no taste. I looked into his eyes. In that face like a field stone, his eyes glowed like two little embers, sunken deep and still, like a teddy bear's button eyes, hard and shiny, as if a different person looked out from that rough-hewn visage.

"Staring like a bluebird at cunt, huh?" I didn't answer, as I wasn't sure who was the bluebird.

"Only a drop for me," protested Kostek.

"Why, are you on duty?"

"I sleep badly after drink."

"That's 'cause you don't drink enough. You are one of those control freaks, I can tell. I just don't know what you like to control, yourself or others. Probably both, eh?"

"I sleep badly," repeated Kostek.

"But who asks you to sleep? It's carnival! Lent's miles away! Sleep it off during Lent, my dark-faced beauty. You remind me of Our Lady of Częstochowa, Queen of Poland. You suffer just like her. If they made me king of such a fucking mess I'd suffer too. But as it is I suffer only as a fellow subject. Barely an echo of a torment, but better that than nothing. One shouldn't ask too much. Don't reach out beyond the reach of eyes. Who said that? I did. I, the perfect incarnation of the nation's bard, the fusion of tradition and the here and now. It had to incarnate in something. It chose me. Could have been worse. It could have chosen the poet Zagajewski, or the other one, the poet's son, you know. As it is – it's me, Wiesiek Cz., son of a peasant from Rawa Mazowiecka, grandson of a peasant from the same Rawa, son of poor soil, with poverty, endogamy and alcoholism flowing through my veins, unable to resist the world's temptations because everything is temptation these days, and since everything is temptation it's like nothing is, even the devil is no more, the nineteenth century was the last . . . Willows by the river, tough fucking tithes for the poor devil, for all of us . . ."

He stopped, and his head dropped even lower. It looked as if he had fallen asleep, but it only seemed so, for a moment later he straightened up, clicked his fingers and shouted: "Eh, you, Mr

Player, why don't you play?" He shouted as if indeed it was a bar, and perhaps it was, perhaps it was about to become one, for everyone was kaput, still, leaning, losing strength, like in the Toruńska before dawn a few years before, though no one ever saw a musician there.

"What's up with you? No need to be civilised. We can hardly hear you. Or maybe you scorn the audience that accepted you so kindly? Play! Play, you . . ."

He was not aggressive. He just spoke loudly. He was throwing words that sank in the grey-blue smoky light. No one answered.

"Sing! Sing, I say! And not some false-coloured Zimmerman with a face like a Tartar's ass! Not that rotter who sold us down the line, wiped his ass with us and made us watch as he bargained with God, American-fashion, a hundred thousand dollars per half-hour. Sing in Russian for us! Sing Black Raven, the favourite song of Joseph Stalin, who was sentimental, stupid and tragic! Come on, sing!"

At that point the black crew-cut came back on the scene. Maybe she was experienced in taming him, or maybe she felt for Goosy as his hands grew sweaty and she saw him swallowing nervously.

"What's got into you again? Can't you enjoy yourself like a human being?"

"What human being?" he shouted back at her. "We're all human beings. Look at yourselves!" He jumped to his feet, walked in among the sitting and grabbed one after the other by the arm, looking into their faces.

"Human being! I swear! And this one, and that one too! There are only human beings in this shithouse. I'll check this one too." He pulled someone up to the light, close to his face, the better to see. Then let go, obviously disappointed, letting the boy slump like an empty sack.

"A human, all too human. Kazik, no angel." He tripped, turned round and moved towards the musical corner.

"Wiesiek, go to bed. Sleep it off. You won't invent the wheel."

"I'm sorry, but, as the prophet said, I wish to speak with human beings and not bags of shit."

"Boys, don't just sit there. Do something with this idiot."

But that night there were no real boys. No one moved his ass. They were only turning their heads away like some asphyxiated heliotropes, their eyes following the staggering figure until it fell down on its knees next to the black crew-cut and Goosy.

Chapter 26

"Don't get involved," whispered Kostek. I wasn't going to. The vodka pushed me against the wall. I succumbed gladly. Why should I get involved? We were a temporarily deformed detail, like during a landing operation, where everyone has to take care of himself. Even the artist and his audience.

It was just like during that lousy festival in the tomb-like social club. When Goosy for the first – and last – time stood under the point of light and announced that he'd forgotten the words and had to sing from a piece of paper, and the hundred or so people in the audience couldn't decide whether to cry or laugh. They really couldn't. It was a provincial hole where the streetlamps switched off at eight in the evening, and of the hundred people in the audience half were the local lowlife and the other trudged from far away to listen to folk music. Folk, which meant that Goosy's stinking trainers fitted there like Woody Guthrie's music, like the stark neglect and poverty which we cultivated so carefully in the belief that everything important had to be hidden, that the meaningful could not speak directly. I could be wrong, perhaps we were plain fools, perhaps it was only a fluke we didn't become Scouts, perhaps it was only fear that kept us together, or love, that tomfoolery of the cardiovascular system, the exaltation of blood cells – as if we were the only human beings under the sun. The rest was just a scene set specially for our coming. Yes, sirrie. Drunk and with eyes watery from gaping at the red lights of the overtaking cars, in a tiny, rusty can of a car, the guitar sticking out of the window, we made a hundred kilometres with Goosy, our *wunderwaffe*, in the back, who was to show the world we were great, great and invincible in celebrating our sweet souls. The cinema hall, full of creaking chairs, the audience expecting electric guitars and drums, or at least a stand-up comedian – and what a cruel disappointment. I think they wanted to lynch us when they realised that it was going to be an old box guitar and ditties in a foreign language. And Goosy, a grey sparrow in clapped-out trainers, trapped in a circle of light, with a crumpled piece of paper, and that voice, a stretched octave . . . But the noise died out, the audience grew silent, perhaps out of malevolent expectation, perhaps out of boredom or simply out of sheer amazement, and we drank that silence like a song of songs. He kept tripping up, hitting false notes, trembled and failed to play even half of what he could. But we were getting high with exhilaration, watching that bewildered Fuzzy the bear. At the end he whispered in English: "Tomorrow is a long time", took a bow and left the stage; the clapping of his unstuck rubber soles hanging in the air. Those days will never come back.

"No Black Raven? At least give us a romance, you artist. Pour it like balsam on our Slav souls." The guy wasn't giving up. He shouted between nodding off. Maybe he wasn't nodding off, maybe he was telling Goosy and the black crew-cut yet another story, of which he knew so many. After all, he was the incarnation of a poet and couldn't tell the difference between the imagined and the manifest.

"C'mon, young man, give us something in Russian! You blue-jeans king of the ballad. They have betrayed us. Instead of sending us jackets soaked through with the sweat of blacks and apostles, they've built factories of jackets. You got what you wanted. The factories churn out soulless rags that have as much in common with blue sky as . . . Oh, words fail me. Play 'Bradiaga'! You don't know 'Bradiaga'? Oh, yes, you do. I can see it in your eyes, you . . . spawn of the famous blue raincoat, you collapsible model sixty-two . . ."

But Goosy had no mind for playing. I watched as their heads, his and crew-cut's, swayed in a kind of a dance, communicating secret messages and promises, innocent and lustful vows. Like two ants in the middle of the forest, just these two, the chosen ones, brought together by a miracle of nature, their feelers performed their delicate ritual of touching up, pinching, not literally yet, but it all seemed heading that way. Good mother night will give them shelter in her belly, where for a moment it's possible to believe in destiny and all revelations seen in the middle of crazy parties when chaos and general demotion assume the form of ultimate harmony and a cosmic blessing – "That's why we've been wandering the world so long! We've met! Like two ants in a huge forest!" I could easily guess Goosy's thoughts. No sweat there.

"The soldiers are having fun," I said to Kostek.

He didn't answer; didn't even as much as prick up his ears. I could see his left temple and the tip of his nose. He was staring ahead. Kept vigil. Only he couldn't take time off.

"The soldiers are having fun," I repeated.

"They are not having fun. They are scared," he answered this time from the corner of his mouth.

"Rubbish, chief. You simply don't know them."

That's what I thought. Because for all those years we never knew fear. Not a dot. Like idiots. Like sheep that now and again panic but always return to graze and only when broken up into individuals raise their lonely bleat to the skies.

"You know fuck all, chief. You slept in the legs and covered yourself with socks. In the city of Łódź."

I'm not sure if it sounded as offensive as I intended; I couldn't see his face. I realised that I'd never seen the bastard offended. Never. As if he didn't have weak points. As if he were empty inside, or had a thick armour.

"He could live everywhere," said Shorty about him once. It was when we were coming back from the station. Regres got on the train and buggered off to Świnoujście, to get a ferry and die in Stockholm. But Shorty didn't mean Regres. Kostek said his goodbyes in the stinking purgatory of an underground passage. All the way he was laughing at our long faces.

"Well, you Baltic Penelopes, you are now going to drink and reminisce about yet another one who wanted to change his life? And in this way change your lives too, huh? In this tearless vale you need a good solid reason to cry."

From the shit-coloured ceiling dripped water, people rushed past; only besuited Arabs wearing turbans carried their stately bellies, as if it were the cool patio of some palace in the desert.

"And why did he have to go? Mirrors are everywhere. Everywhere in the world. Don't be such fools."

He ran upstairs to catch a tram whose hollow rumbling filled the passage. And we marched off to that beer garden by the Penguin, ruminating on his words, which had somehow hurt us. In those days each of us wanted to chuck it all, it was high time. We admired Regres for being so brave, going off with a small rucksack and a fistful of dollars, throwing from the window: "You can all kiss my ass!" Like a conquistador, or a hobo, just to press on, the further the better, to sustain that aura of fanciful sorrow, that nostalgia that gets you drunk like the subtlest of wines. We thought that running away we were untouchable, invisible, without possessions, bearing just a crumb of memory.

So, his words – that he can live anywhere – were filled with contempt. They meant that he could have gone to rot anywhere, here or there, no difference, no regrets, while we were so tempted by "nowhere", which was one and the same thing, except we were too stupid to understand.

From that hole by the Penguin we moved to the Gong, or the Amphora, or maybe to the Tokai or even the Surprise, just to feel old: play out those tired movements when lighting up, sticky sweat on our foreheads and in the palms of our hands, as the cheap white wine was coming out of us quicker than we were pouring it in. The August afternoon, when the streets are full of human dregs, those who couldn't afford to get away, those who had no idea what to do with themselves, those who simply didn't have the strength, stuck together, kneaded into a formless mass full of spilled spoons of sugar and bad but effective alcohol. So it was probably the Surprise, where old prostitutes were known to have left their teeth, walking-sticks and artificial limbs. Late afternoon. The barmaid had a measure at her wrist but didn't bother much with precision; we watched the ash fall by the ashtrays, drunks put their money into the jukebox and walk back out on the street.

"Let's go to Vasyl's," suggested Shorty in the end. "It's cooler there." Truth to tell we were running out of money while the evening had barely begun; even cars hadn't switched their lights on. We went down Koszykowa Street, that peculiar stretch, as if dead, going towards Rozdroże, the forgotten, practically abandoned part in the middle of Warsaw which was always silent. Then we turned right, along the Botanic Garden and on, past the guards at the Belvedere and the Russian embassy, dying of boredom and everlasting world peace. The narrow street was filled with the shadows of maple trees, gathering there throughout the long, scorching day. There was a cool breeze pulling from Łazienki Park.

His mother, Vasyl's that is, began to fall ill, and when she didn't have the strength to look after the big house any more they gave her a flat there. He was the first to get out of that suburban hellhole. Even before he finished his high school. Three massive rooms with windows to the east and west, plus a squeaking old parquet floor and brass doorhandles. Perhaps it would all end as these things do, us drifting apart, drowning in different worlds. There was nothing material to keep us together, no street cruising, no bus rides to school, now vocational and technical. Shorty was to become a technician, while Goosy and I, being working class, none of this. Sure, we met now and again; he would drop in to see us, we would go see him, but there was a whole big city to cross. And one day, as it happened on the bus ride to school, Goosy said, "I got a letter from Bandurko."

None of us had ever received a letter, so we looked at Goosy like at someone who told a bad joke. But he took out from his pocket a postcard which said, "Hi guys, look me up. My mother died."

In fact, Vasyl was all alone in this world. Well, he had an aunt in Kraków but she was completely loopy. She cursed her own sister for romancing with the Commies all the way back in Bierut's days and stuck to it, refusing to come even to the funeral. She appeared later only to state that she would never enter among the red spiders but that she would try to take care of her nephew from afar, for after all he was her blood.

So we decided to give school a miss that day, like many others before, and go straight to his place, correctly assuming that if someone is in deep mourning he is not likely to bother with maths and history either.

The stillness in that flat. Because of its space – the few sounds distinct and clear – the place always had a degree of inertia about it. But that day we seemed to have entered a mist, some sort of suspension, moving from room to room like fishes in an aquarium. Vasyl's face was chalk-white, no sign of his usual rosiness. And then, as we were leaving, stopping by the huge door upholstered with black sky, he made some gigantic effort and said with a weird lopsided grin: "Cool place for parties, eh?"

We were entering the cool silence of the hall, mixture of smells – most of which were of our own making – walls, furniture, floor, all were saturated with odours, each of which we could name and place in time of day or night. The same with stains on the red carpet, scratches and cracked plaster on the walls, as we often liked to party like tsar's officers or the bums from Brzeska Street.

"Regres has gone to sea," I said, and Bandurko replied: "Any excuse would do."

He sat in red pyjama bottoms, playing on a black Shredër with one finger a very slow, very banal melody, boring like a day imperceptibly changing into night.

"I don't know why I still haven't got rid of it."

We didn't either. When his mother was no longer, he stopped practising. Sometimes he would rock a little boogie on it, to please Goosy, but more often than not we kept empty bottles in it.

"Got any money?"

"There's white wine in the fridge."

And then we, too, took our shirts off, to feel the sweat trickling down our backs and chests, while Vasyl played incompetent bits of Jarrett, or maybe they were competent, maybe it was supposed to sound like that, maybe he didn't want to play anything else. Somehow, there was enough wine and we didn't have to go out, and fried eggs on bacon were just fine; nothing too crazy. The heat poured in with the darkness, and we felt like old and very tired heroes in a crap movie. We were flicking cigarette-ends through the open window, and the bursting crumbs of glow looked like red stars, which in this part of town was nothing unusual.

"You know fuck all, hobo." I said that in a deliberate tone of voice, but more to myself than to his profile, still and vigilant as before. Goosy stood up and the crew-cut stood up with him. They were probably going for a walk under the stars, twenty Celsius below zero, so I wished them my warmest. Someone moved out of their way; they had to step over some other bodies, and I was wondering how it all came to be if people remain in that state of inertia, like those people around me, like we used to be, like we always had been. Kostek didn't let himself be provoked. He smoked, looked on at the pile of bodies, wondering, too, how this static mess could be given a more dynamic form, how to convert this element to his own, as well as some abstract aims, how to fill the static world of ideas with almost static human flesh.

Of course they rolled now and again, like single waves on a

peaceful sea. Someone came in and sat down. Vasyl's friend got up and started rummaging through the pile of rucksacks. He came back with a little paper packet. I didn't have to guess what it was.

I left Kostek, who was too sober, too cold for this night which wrapped itself around us like a cocoon. In fact, I didn't give a fuck about him, or the others, but the alcohol began to sneak through the secret passages around my body, magnetising them in such a way that I had to seek company. Kostek – I could see it clearly now – through all these years never descended into a numbing, prenatal gibberish. I didn't dwell on it, though, and got up quite nimbly and, tripping over someone's boots hard as stones, I entered the very centre of soul communion, where the bottle had already been started upon. Bandurko looked at me like at someone who chooses to sit next to you in an empty cinema. His mate didn't even raise his head. Two bands of dark hair hung to his knees. He was sitting with his legs crossed, head down, looking like an ad for Nirvana from 1969. There is a glow in this hair, I thought. But it was only freshly washed and the lightbulb lit in it single golden threads. He didn't fit with this pack of loud, unshaven young males in chequered shirts. The tip of his nose peeking from under the dark, gold-threaded curtain was thin and delicate, and in stronger light could well be transparent.

"I can't sit it out with this one there." I shook my head towards Kostek. "He never gets drunk. The more he drinks, the soberer he gets."

Bandurko didn't answer. He handed me the bottle, without any warning that it was a cherry vodka. I didn't mind, though. It was past midnight, the next day began and there was still no change, as if time was an illusion, not a redemption, as if for ever we were to remain inside our bodies, suddenly so heavy and unwieldy.

"Having fun?" Something made me ask this stupid and obscene question, perhaps sheer jealousy, as I already had my five minutes and could only circle like a moth from one flame to another, or like a freezing tramp moving from one stove to another, rubbing hands, except I didn't know any story worth telling.

"We should get a move on at dawn. Ought to get a good night's sleep."

"Go ahead, sleep. Who's stopping you?"

He took back the bottle and took a good swig out of it, as if he wanted to drain it and thus remove the reason for my sitting with him.

"We've got a hard trek ahead of us. What did you say? Where are we heading for tomorrow?"

"Don't you worry your little head about it. Wherever we're going we'll get there."

"It's not my head I'm worried about but Shorty's wound."

He glanced fleetingly at me and then looked again as if I'd woken him up. He tried to focus on me as if on some ghostly apparition, so I helped him.

"Wound, remember? I've just changed the dressing. God knows what's inside."

The long-haired friend perked up too. Wounds and bandages seemed the only thing that still got people's interest.

"Who's wounded?" OK, he wasn't too bad, with this slightly too long face, which was still not horsy, and even if it was it would have been an Arab. The light was glowing now in his eyes.

"A friend of ours. A knife wound."

"Knife?" As if I'd said something in a foreign tongue.

"Knife. Ukrainian nationalists. Have you heard of Stepan Bandura?"

"Bandera, more like it."

"His name was Bandura. A slight error. Historians' fault. Bandera – Bandura. A flag or a lute, what's the difference? Both are good. The lute even better. After all, he wasn't a Communist."

"A Communist? Why Communist?"

"Don't you know the song? *Avanti, popolo*, something something, *bandiera rossa, bandiera rossa*." I must have sung it aloud, for several heads turned. "So you can see yourself he could not be Bandera. His name was Bandura. Though fuck knows, maybe he was a crypto-Communist. Those bloody Cossacks played on those banduras of theirs, making Communist plots like there was no tomorrow. Sicz, this sort of thing, you know. Everything into one pot, primordial and happy state of anarchy. You do support anarchy, don't you?"

He thought for a while about an answer, as if he were choosing a dress, a bandanna, or a suitable facial expression. He touched his nose, clasped his hands and looking somewhere past my eyes, somewhere into my temple, said: "I don't care, really. I'm not interested in politics."

"I'm asking about anarchy, young man. Anarchy is above politics. Anarchy is metapolitics, it's metaphysics, isn't it?"

"Maybe it isn't . . ."

"What do you mean – maybe it isn't? There's no maybe about it. Where do you live? It's either or. Who isn't with us is against us."

Vasyl, who had woken up completely, leaned forward as if trying to move in between us. I didn't give him a chance.

"Wait a minute, wait a minute. We need to enlighten your new friend. A bit lost, isn't he? Artistic soul or something?"

I saw in Bandurko's eyes a pleading light, a soft tearful gleam, which, if you are not exactly full of love for your fellow human beings, makes you want to play the most cruel games.

"This is what we need to do, so stop interfering. I would like to hear from you, young man, what's your political preference, political and ontological to be precise. No maybes. Go on, declare yourself, before we declare you."

The boy, glancing now at me, now at Vasyl, unsure of himself, sensing a stupid joke but too afraid to make a fool of himself, kept silent, just in case, hiding behind the silence in the same way he was hiding behind the mask of his face, which must have saved him from trouble before.

"You're not doing well. My friend could explain it all very nicely, but let me do the job for him. You will let me, Basil, won't you? Of course you will. So, about those Cossacks. Let's leave Greek democracy; it may be good for women, but not for us men, high on freedom, sweat and animal stench. So the Cossacks. They smoked long pipes, drank vodka like there's no tomorrow, living from one brawl to the next. Just as they should, on the islands, isolated, to keep the blood racing, on the boil. They ate from one pot, slept under one cloak. A true commune. And because true ideals require simplicity, they decided to rid their lives of further complications and guess what they did? Well? Come on, who will guess? You, Basil, can't play because you will win. I'll tell you, young man, anyway. The first and in truth the only important thing they did was to rid their lives of women. It was a male state. Where the males, surrounded on all sides by the river Dnepr, worked in their watchtowers towards a classless and unisex society. To get rid of the devil is to get rid of the detail. And just such irritating, superfluous detail in the masculine is the feminine. Now, young man, we have arrived at a model, and we can take up positions. What I mean is we can start a discussion which, God willing, will help us to polarise our positions. Or vice versa . . . Go on, young . . ."

He sat as before, motionless and beautiful, taking advantage of my verbal diarrhoea, rubbing the tip of his nose, folding his unbelievably long fingers. I was sure the only thing that concerned him was the position of his own body, the composition of its lines and surface in space. He was simply in a perpetual state of self-perception, continually checking for his presence in mirrors, in the air, in the eyes of other people, as well as his own.

As I opened my mouth again and spoke out my stupid hustling, "Go on, young . . ." Bandurko interrupted me softly:

"Stop it, please . . ."

Chapter 27

So how did it happen? How and when?

In fact, never, for it was happening slowly, imperceptibly; the circle crumbled as we drifted out from our interrelated system of orbits, undertaking lonely sorties into that other, parallel mode of existence, only to return like prodigal sons, defeated, disappointed, puzzled by its incomprehensible rules of engagement.

Gzanka's big tits fascinated us, tempted us to abandon our safe, familiar world. Maybe that was the beginning? Our churlish raids on the female body? The screams, the shrieks, the artificial scram in the school cloakroom or on the playground, where the girls strayed unawares, in twos and threes, babbling away, already grown up in their perfect imitations of their mothers' stately strolls. We would get Gzanka from behind, to close in our hands for a few seconds two chunks of that strange, yielding matter, invariably surprised by their unnatural softness, so different from the toughness and springiness of our boyish bodies. We must have been driven by curiosity and contempt, which we always felt about objects of our aggression – the smashed streetlights, stolen and abandoned bicycles, kids sent flying with a kick outside the staked territory. Desire and disappointment in one. We would walk away as if nothing had happened, hands in pockets, spitting nonchalantly, satisfied by the violence and victorious. Only Vasyl didn't take part in those grope raids. Nor did many others, but they were restrained by fear and good manners, which comes to the same thing. As we got Gzanka somewhere in the crowd, often just the two of us, me and Shorty, we saw around us a circle of grinning mugs, Goosy rubbing his hands, practically jogging on the spot with excitement, all those poor bastards torn between shame and desire – but Vasyl was never among them. As if he possessed an ability of reading our filthy minds, as if he knew in advance when we were going to launch into one of our lewd diversions. He would disappear, evaporate into thin air. He, who was normally inseparable from us.

But then it lasted only for as long as it did. We would return to our world clean, innocent, our curiosity satisfied, nothing to write home about.

Maybe that was the beginning, except for those weird dreams or visions which descended upon us in the middle of the day, caught us in a lonely moment, and for those porno pics with old women whose faces we scanned for similarities to the women we knew, our aunts, neighbours, teachers. We had to find them. What was going on in those pics was far too unreal, too incomprehensible, like lives of insects or anthropomorphic minerals. Those were really crappy pics, photos of photos from Scandinavian porn mags, made somewhere in a basement and sold on to soldiers and God knows where else. We were still unable to fit them into real life, connect them with Gzanka's soft balloons, with the girls seen on the bus, in fact with nothing, for it was beyond our comprehension that everyday life could be so interesting, so dirty and exciting. "And what do you think your old folks do?" Shorty asked Goosy one day. Goosy didn't argue the point, but his face sort of shrank and we could see it was going to bother him for a long time to come, at night, in a middle of Sunday dinner, on the way to church, the same it bothered us until we came to grips with it or erased it from our memories, relegated once and for all among the things better left unthought.

That is why our first loves were remote strangers, so remote we could not possibly get anywhere near them. The faces on the bus, those half-girls, half-women, distant strangers, fenced off by their age gap, unapproachable and safe, just like the one whose name I will never know, who used to get on the bus five stops after mine, with a slightly protruding upper lip which gave her an air of mocking cheekiness. She disappeared down the underground passage towards the trams, and I never attempted to follow her. Or another one, a tall blond with a horsy face. I nearly fainted once brushing against her in the street, the other trysts taking place in the church where every Sunday I spied from afar her green hat and scarf, or blue scarf and hat, for she had two sets which she changed regularly, no surprises there, her face showing no sign of adventure anyway.

They were all separated by a void, inside which no action was possible. They were holy, like saints from holy pictures. That space between us remained untouched by a single dirty thought, nothing that could make those sacred adorations any more real. Those loves were unnatural, I can see it now. The thoughts we did send out in order to reconstruct their still images suspended in darkness or in void gave us purely spiritual pleasure, which is not unlike the physical one but far superior to it in that it lies in yearning which can never be satisfied.

That is why we didn't care much for the girls from our class, those within reach. Groped, pushed, fat-legged, lunch-munching creatures, giggling in the safety of the teachers' room, they were merely trivial incarnations, too heavy, too corporeal. They came towards our thoughts, crushing them, destroying them, bringing chaos into the sublime kingdom of imagination. Yes, we had to fear them. We must have known instinctively that getting together with them would mean fall, a sin, while the imagination would be replaced by necessity and desire, which we would strive to satisfy, prepared to pay any, even unfair price.

How quickly it all passed. Or maybe it didn't pass at all?

The hookers from the porn pics reminded us of our teachers, whom we desired and who in turn changed into younger and younger girls, for how long was one supposed to wank to a vision of flabby breasts, fat thighs and buttocks deformed by years of sitting and farting into school furniture. Perhaps those mature and overripe women were only a skeletal construction that we dressed with young and delicate flesh. Their resemblance to the hookers in the porn pics was so evident that our sexual initiation could not have happened in any other way.

But Shorty did surprise us. It was an August twilight, boredom and hopelessness of ending summer holidays. We were returning from our rubbish El Dorado, where we found nothing interesting, for on such days nothing of interest ever happened. The next day, or the day after, we were to supposed to pull our socks up, start the second year of higher education and follow into our fathers' footsteps in gaining technical schooling. The shit-coloured wainscot of the interminable corridors, the monotony of the red bus leaving the terminus at seven-fifteen. The cold mist of September was already lying in wait in roadside ditches, and there was no sign of deliverance, no change on the horizon when Shorty said: "Hey, guys, I think I caught something."

The statement was so strange nobody even asked what it was. We walked on, partly on the pavement, partly on the street, in the shadow of a tall hedge; the streetlamps were just being lit. We were overtaken by a yellow Syrenka; the cloud of its exhaust hung in the still evening air.

"A sock's better than nothing," answered Goosy finally.

Shorty waited a bit. "But, guys, I really have caught something."

Only after a dozen or so steps did it hit us. It was a subject totally unknown to us, so Goosy, carefully, unsure if he wasn't being set up in some stupid joke, asked: "Come on. Where?"

Shorty stopped under a streetlamp, took out his dick and showed us what he'd supposedly caught.

"There's nothing there," I said, using the word "there" as if it referred to something unconnected with Shorty.

"There is. A spot, or a pustule, something like that." He started twisting and turning his stuff, as it was supposed to be somewhere underneath.

We still didn't see anything. Behind our backs we heard the click of high heels. Shorty started packing up in such a hurry he probably caught himself with the zip, and we resumed our march, in silence, not knowing what to do with this kind of surprise. We waited and waited until finally Shorty spoke again.

" 'Cause, you know . . . I've . . . you know . . . done it."

But we didn't throw ourselves at him with questions. None of those "Come on, tell us" and "How was it?", oh no. Only Goosy slowed down, and I saw an uncertain grin spreading on his silly face.

"Nah . . . You did . . . ?"

And that was how it stayed for some time. Nobody asked any questions and even Shorty, when he finally decided to tell us everything himself – for he had to; after all he did have something to tell – even he couldn't find the right words. He was unable to use words to describe to us what had actually taken place. It turned out that at the beginning was experience; the word came after. And it was not the problem of intimacy or bashfulness. She was an ordinary hooker, bored senseless with sitting it out at the Polonia or some other Metropol, who went out to find some fresh meat and picked Shorty off the street the way clients picked her. That's all. But we circled around it completely powerless, desperate to give it a name but rendered mute. Words were too unwieldy, they refused to obey, slipped like cats' claws on glass. It took us months of picking over crumbs to piece together a whole picture, some kind of mosaic. Shorty was really trying. But it was coming out of him very slowly, and our imaginations were equally slow in absorbing it. After all, it was our common property; nobody ever questioned that. The accidental, mechanical nature of the act made it impersonal and therefore universal. Somebody had to do it for us, and it happened to be Shorty. He did it on our behalf, to tame all those demons which by then tortured us night and day. We saw him as someone who survived and possessed knowledge. Yes, we did keep him at arm's length, but not because of what he was supposed to have caught – that was never mentioned again. He raised our admiration, and disgust.

The story was finally put together with bits and pieces, forced remarks, heroic and tragic, a miserable story. Flat, devoid of form or contrasts, without flavour, just a scent of some perfumes to which Shorty obsessively returned but still failed to describe. He was looking for it later in other women's cosmetics, in people's bathrooms, undoing the little bottles, sniffing, but never finding it.

But that was merely a story. It barely touched us. It merely encouraged us, it proved we could return from there alive, at worst with some enigmatic spot on the dick. The rest we had to do ourselves and follow down the trodden path. Me, a year later. Goosy? God knows when, as he changed his story several times, each more colourful than the last one. So, I followed a year later. It was June, coarse carpet at the foot of a wall unit the size of a skyscraper, the cars on the congested street hooted like mad and the trams rang as if they were at each others' throats. A hell of heat and stink. Three floors above the ground, open windows, we must have looked like a pair of white earthworms, as yet untouched by the sun. The black domes of the Russian orthodox church across the street shone as if they were sweating. The cops at the police station, which leaned on the house of God, flicked the switches of their fans, waiting for the night to go out hunting, like the rest of that thieving neighbourhood. I was falling into space. I saw my pale body as it sank deeper and deeper. At the time it seemed to me it was burrowing in that other body, but now I know that I slipped right through it like a bullet through innards and disappeared, vanished somewhere in the planes of solitude, drifting away on its own interminable journey. She was moving under me, black-haired, content, confident that our embraces were sewing up eternity, that desire was being fulfilled and that fulfilment was to remain solid, tangible, like a framed photo or a scar.

I always left at the same time to avoid her mother, a strict and austere woman who knew life and could tell us a lot about it if only we cared to listen and she let go of the contempt she felt for what she suspected we were at. It was a time of evasions and escapes, and life was one continuous conspiracy. "Why don't you drop in tonight? Shorty said he would be too." I would try to get rid of Goosy on the lamest of excuses. When they bumped into me somewhere, or when I went to see them with the best of intentions, they greeted me with derision, united, doubly strong and dis-affected. "Why, you have some free time? Have you got an evening off?"

It's as if they knew that story was outside the rules of shared experience, that it could not be sold or exchanged. It's as if they knew they had no right to it. We were all rejected.

They would spend the evenings at Vasyl's. I would drop in like a guest. Two completely worn-out records of Muddy Waters would be played round and round. His mother stayed in her room, with every month growing more and more immobile, object-like, in the end existing only in rare remarks, we hardly ever saw her. I think those were Bandurko's happiest days. They spent every spare moment with him. To their old folks they would say: "We're going to study with Vasyl. What's your problem? He goes to college."

Their parents were happy that they still bothered to invent some excuses. I was just visiting, sitting in with them for five minutes at the bar, feeling like a good citizen among bums, all the time trying to figure out how to leave them without losing face.

"You'll miss your bus," Shorty would say, as he took out from behind the curtain a bottle of cheap Polish wine and poured it into glasses that might still have had a smell of whisky about them. "I'm not giving you any or you'll stink like a bum."

Cigarettes in the damp twilight of late autumn. I was winding my way along a narrow pavement, hopping on to a bus, then a tram. I thought I could do this route with my eyes closed. The yellow light of bar windows. From half-open doors emanated the scent of love.

Bandurko must have been very happy then. When Shorty showed us his dick, Vasyl didn't say a word. He didn't take his place in the circle, didn't take part in our council. He stood in the middle of the road, his silhouette absorbed by the black of tarmac. What were his thoughts then? In what kind of fluttering panic? Our silhouettes must have merged into one many-headed trunk, Siamese triplets joined by sex, by the same desire, by the same curse. He didn't make a move towards us. I don't know if he was looking at us; perhaps he was looking into darkness, hoping that what goes unnoticed does not exist, just like our club of filthy gentlemen behind the school's dustbins where we smoked and passed around black and white photos, softened and marked by sweaty hands; just like our hunting for Gzanka's tits or crawling on the classroom floor to take a peek between the thighs of our geography teacher, or like our raids on the girls' loo, which for some reason gave out a completely different scent from our own craphouse. Then his reluctance and absence could be put down to good manners. Which is what we probably did.

"Vasyl's a girlie," we used to say, and after a while these words contained less and less contempt and became more a statement of fact, which helped us move around the real world. Girlie Vasyl, coward Goosy, Gzanka's tits, slow Shorty. In that world there was still room for everyone. Anyway, he rid himself of all those manners and habits of good upbringing and empty childhood pretty quickly, God knows how and when. He, whose weekly allowance equalled our monthly ones – if we could squeeze it out from our folks – he would run with us through parks and quiet back yards, places paved with thousands of bottle-tops, looking for the empties, and then, as our needs grew, he would even run with us through the pockets of those naughty public sleepers in brown jackets, looking for the remnants of their monthly wages. Shorty would first gently kick, then turn the body, and, if it passed the trial, proceeded with a methodical examination. He always left something to wipe the tears with, and a ticket, but pocketed the rest, calming our uneasy conscience: "What's the problem? Let's say we are here on behalf of all the under-age sons and daughters of these social deviants. Besides, they could be robbed by some thieves, God forbid . . ."

Goosy usually stood on watch, hissing, "Quick, hurry up", which in conjunction with Shorty's slow and methodical examination sounded hilarious. Bandurko looked on fascinated. One day he wanted to pull off a wristwatch but Shorty stopped him. "Nope. Let the bastard know how late he got home."

Small money, great loot – those were the keys to the world. From our shitty suburbs it took a good hour to get to the centre. Autumn, early dusk, only then streets can be so overwhelmingly hopeless, as if from all the cemeteries around the town the wind had borne the black smoke of burning candles, as early as October, September.

Dark streets glistening with neon lights. Communism was far from falling. Palaces of light, the deeps of shop windows full of white glare were like grottoes leading into the great body of the night. We got lost in it, like provincial visitors in a great city. And never was the city more enticing and more beautiful. That festival of strange faces, women in high-heeled boots, all remote like a promise of ravishing satisfaction . . . We took long zigzagging excursions into the streets like dark canals or long aquariums, swimming through the exhaust-filled air, feeling its exhilarating, electric touch. We felt we were entering the belly of a massive woman lying on her back. The lazy, warm body, its hands and feet already feeling the cold of the suburbs while we were right at the centre, at the entry into the interior where we could wander, brushing against the soft, warm and slippery innards, where the darkness gave way under the touch like the silky lining of a coat. The drunks' money bought us entry into the movies. People inside the Palladium, Atlantic or Śląsk were farting, noisily squeezing their bags of sweets, as well as themselves. With the same money we also bought – at first shyly but with growing confidence – bottles of sweet wine which were quaffed straight from the bottle in the park behind the War Museum. We didn't have to do it. We were off our heads as it was. Including Vasyl. Straddling the chaos of our lives, one foot with the snoring drunks, the other on the islands of études and preludes. Oh, yes, he still played, but never in our presence. Sometimes we did catch a couple of notes floating from the window on the ground floor, but the doorbell cut the music dead. For a long time we didn't even see that piano, as if it were some sort of an embarrassing family secret, a schizophrenic grandad, or an aunty with a beard.

We would press him from time to time – "What are you playing?" – but he would give vague answers with an apologetic smile.

"It's nothing, just fucking about. Mother wants me to practise."

With his mother he practised Brahms and Chopin and with us all those other numbers which in the end turned out to be more important, as Brahms remained locked for ever in that room on the ground floor and Vasyl eventually stopped looking him up, giving us all his time, all his love – the two things that are really inseparable, unless you are a cold bastard, or over twenty.

All those serious records were languishing under a layer of dust. We pushed them to the side to make more room for our scruffy and worn-out records of SBB and Niemen, which on Vasyl's top hi-fi sounded like a massive egg frying. We spared him the sound of our ancient record postcards. We happened to have an odd Hendrix, which Shorty picked up fuck knows where and put on "Hey, Joe". All that guitar went right above our heads; we didn't get it. Only Bandurko caught on to it, shaking his head over it, now with admiration, now with surprise. We, we were just happy to know it was Hendrix, the man who lived fast, died young and looked like the devil incarnate, though Goosy's father said more like an ape.

So perhaps there was no beginning. Everything had been cast in a never-ending metamorphosis since always, a mixture of death, love, women, the city, everything in motion, a blizzard of events and objects, which only a moment ago we were braving with wide-open coats, bare-headed, in soaked-through boots, lashed by desire, with guts out and an all-consuming hunger burning in our bellies, hunger that could never be satisfied.

It all ran through us like a film, wound and unwound in a split second, and for a mad moment of intuitive enlightenment that belonged somewhere outside time I saw his face: smooth, childlike, in clean light, the face of a boy left behind as we departed off the pitch into an early afternoon while he, the goalie, guarding an empty goal against the sky, kneels to lace up his boots.

I stretched my hand, wanted to touch his arm, but at that very moment the door opened. Goosy stood hesitating for a moment, then moved towards Kostek, squatted next to him, told him something and Kostek sprang to his feet.

Chapter 28

We jumped out one by one. Like parachuting off a plane. The air cracked under my weight like water covered by thin ice. It must have been well below minus twenty. I felt a fiery lick on my face. I put on the other strap of the rucksack in full run. High up in the sky hung the white plate of the moon. The shaggy willows by the stream threw an intricate lace pattern of shadows on the snow. It felt like crushing through a *Fata Morgana* of vegetation. The cracking noise was in fact the sound of crunching snow, but I could not shake off the impression that I was crashing delicate twigs. The sound made me petrified. My shadow moved at my left heel like a massive black hound, like a nightmare hanging on to my body, a mourning pennon that gave me away in the middle of the white, silent valley. I could even hear its flutter. I ran to the left, following Vasyl's instructions, and on to a trodden trail, uneven, full of holes, left by the young ones with rucksacks. Falling into deep holes, tripping up, I could hear some weird rumbling noise, echoes of every breath, of the slightest rustle. The trail ran along the stream, through the moonshadows of naked trees, and on the left a flat slope with a dark crest of the forest at the top. "Run to the left, keep to the left, all the time." I had to repeat Bandurko's instructions to myself almost aloud, being tempted by the black wall of trees on the other side of the stream. The moonlight was cruel. Everything except me seemed to be still and quiet. I wanted to cross the stream and dive into the darkness of the first trees and grow still myself, to crawl into a crack of this petrified landscape and hold my breath. I felt that in the clear, hard air I was stirring vibrations, making the sonorous particles collide with each other, and now the whole sky, the entire glass dome vibrated with my presence, betraying it to the furthest corners of the world. But maybe everything was made of cellophane? The sky, the earth, trees and snow, and myself? That crashing noise was petrifying, and all I wanted to do was to go deaf and stick my head into something soft, thick and still.

Then the stream cut across my path. I fell down on to the windswept ice. Suddenly everything went dead quiet. Pain in my knee and elbow brought me back to reality. I got myself on all fours and looked back: the dark mass of the hostel winked with three yellow windows. I listened, but the only sound I finally homed in on was the pounding of my own heart coming out of my half-open mouth. There was no other sound, neither from one side nor the other. And yet ahead of me should be Vasyl and Goosy, with Kostek and Shorty running up behind me. Not a sound, except for a distant crack of a tree in the vice of freezing cold. I moved on down the hazy path. Now I had the stream on my left, while the forest came closer to the path, running just above it, as the valley narrowed between two wooded hills rising on both sides. Then the trail split. The trodden one carried on ahead, with a deep irregular trough ploughed in the fresh snow leading off to the right. It ran up the naked slope for about fifty metres and disappeared in the wood. A whistle came from there.

Vasyl waited, hunched behind a bush on the very edge of the wood, from where he commanded an excellent view of the path, including the place where I fell, the moonshine picking out from the blue snow a little silver shine of ice.

"Where are Kostek and Shorty?" he whispered, panting, as if it was him who had just finished that mad run.

"I don't know. Haven't a clue. When I was leaving he was ready but waited for Shorty."

Below, far on the left between the branches, flickered the golden light of the hostel windows. We looked in that direction, particularly at the spot where the path, freed from the shadow, ran across the white plain towards the ford. Not a stir. Not a sound. To stop watching and avoid talking I started lacing up my boots which hadn't dried. I felt under my toes as they stiffened in the cold. I fastened my rucksack, a sleeping-bag spilling out of it like entrails from a wounded belly. I zipped up my jacket to save what was left of the warmth mixed with sweat. Everything was already going cold, wrapping me in an icy sheet.

"We've been here for five minutes," said Vasyl. I was sure he was dividing his attention between the path and his watch, and I was sure he felt the weight of every dripping second, one after the other, until the weight of time became unbearable and he turned his face to me. "Six," he said, and added a bit louder: "We have to . . . Listen, we have to. We have no choice . . ."

He waited for me to say something, but I just put my rucksack on and marched off, following the trail among the junipers and wide, stunted pine trees. Under one of them I found Goosy, wrapped up and kitted out, ready, as if waiting for my "Let's get the fuck out of here", for he joined me without a word. We entered the first trees, leaving Bandurko to his fate, though he soon overtook us and took the lead.

That wood felt like a park. We walked along wide alleys flanked by rows of columns, passing through open spaces flooded by light so bright it made me squint. It was like a dream. Vasyl's body was as limpid as it was unreal. The still, crystallised scenery steered our hurried march towards the nightmare. I looked over my shoulder. Goosy was right behind me, his black, at places silvery face emanating unsettled, commingled light. A zombie, someone not quite dead, who is just slipping out of the realm of life, walking the shadowline between day and night, between the mundane and madness. But he was making sounds. I could hear him panting, and the rustle of his rucksack rubbing against his back.

The march felt good. At times Vasyl geared it up; we practically ran, then waited for Goosy. Nobody spoke. Patches of light, patches of shadow, one after the other. We could see the slightest obstacle, of which there were not that many, as obviously someone had tidied up the place, smoothed the ground, not a single felled tree, no catching blackberries, everything was flat, even, smooth. In that hypnotic state I took slanted shadows for felled trunks. They would make my heart miss a beat, but my feet would carry me through and the march continued. I kept my eyes on Bandurko's tracks, for although I often took him for a mirage, that narrow trough in the snow was real enough.

I never suspected the moon could give off so much light, and so dense, almost material. That light was like metal, like tin, like mercury. It filled every crevice, but it shone only with half its power; its true power was to give form to things invisible.

"Stop. Guys, stop. I can't . . ."

But it was not being out of breath that forced Goosy to speak out. He had to return, even for a moment, into a normal human dimension. Vasyl stopped dead in his tracks, as if suddenly someone had woken him up. He stood with his back to us, then turned very slowly and came up to us.

"We can't stop. We're running away."

"Where to? Our tracks are visible, even now, at night." Goosy was prepared to pay any price, even the process of losing his illusions, to haggle out a few minutes. "It feels really heavy."

"The rucksack," said Bandurko. We repacked Goosy's gear into our sacks and handed him back his limp bag.

"We've got to. We have an hour, maybe, until morning. Maybe they'll be satisfied . . ." Vasyl stopped, but I finished for him.

"Sure they'll be satisfied. But it's not really up to them. That depends what our leader will tell them."

"There were only two of them." Goosy sat on the scaffold of his rucksack. His eyes shone, God knows whether with fever or with reflected light.

"Only two of them. They came on foot. They would have got rid of the car. Just two . . ."

"It'll take a while. They've got a radio in their cars. They'll find ten, twenty. They get the cops from the whole district on their feet. And the army." Vasyl was speaking slowly, as if surprised by his own words. In fact, one could put a question mark at the end of each sentence.

"There's nothing we can do. Let's go," he finished with a sort of helpless determination. Perhaps he realised that now he had become our leader.

We moved on, at first briskly, then fatigue got to us and we simply traipsed on, tripping up on an even road, feeling our muscles harden as if the cold and effort of the last few days was a real, nasty substance that had now begun to seep into our veins, solidify, and was about to turn us into squeaking figurines frozen still in the middle of the forest, halfway through their pointless journey.

After a while strange things began to happen. That moment when Kostek had crawled up to me and Bandurko and told us to go with him and in our room informed us the cops were in the hostel, that moment seemed to me as distant as the beginning of our trip, like a trivial episode, like all those accidental and superfluous incidents that make up life. I walked. I didn't care if we were to get anywhere. We would. One always does. I didn't ask Vasyl. I didn't want to make him uncomfortable. I knew that those two in the hostel could not possibly save us, even if they wanted to. All the young ones had seen us, the five of us. It was a matter of hours, maybe dawn, maybe noon. Goosy knew it, and Bandurko knew it. I was grateful to them that they were not saying anything but doing the only thing possible in the circumstances – getting the fuck out of there before they caught us. An animal reaction; it must be right.

Our route turned downhill, a kind of a pass, and then uphill again; the road was still good but we were getting worse. Goosy had now fallen behind for good, and we had to stop and wait until he caught up with us, panting and wheezing. We would resume the march without a word, and after two hundred metres the same thing again; sometimes we couldn't even see if he was still actually going. A minute's rest and we could feel the cold finding gaps in our clothing, sneaking up our sleeves, crawling up our backs, numbing even the skin under our hats. The moon continued to sprinkle down her metallic dust in total silence. The pass was so well lit we could see two long valleys to the left and to the right, trees, copses of bushes, black and white patches of landscape stretching way up to the horizon – and not a single light, a complete desert. We were alone in the world. Strange feeling. But as soon as we marched back into the woods the emptiness condensed, wrapped itself around us and the dizziness passed away. It was nearly three o'clock. The moon had long reached its zenith and begun to roll to the west. All that time I had a feeling that through some absurd analogy the cold should let up now, that it was the silver, polished opposite of the sun which was spreading out that all-penetrating cold and now that it was about to disappear behind the mountains we would breathe more easily, not through those blinding billows of steam settling on our eyebrows.

Vasyl stopped and waited. But when I caught up with him it turned out he was waiting for Goosy, of whose existence I'd forgotten. We watched as the interminably slow, black silhouette climbed the gentle slope. He was still out in open space. Perhaps he was not climbing; perhaps he was standing still.

We didn't feel like going down and climb back up again. So we waited; that, too, was a charitable act. But I only had enough charity for one person; I turned to Vasyl: "Where are we going?"

He remained silent for a while then answered slowly and distinctly: "By now it's nowhere."

"Nice place."

"Yep."

We waited a bit longer. Goosy was not moving. His silhouette was stuck in the same spot. He looked like a lonely bush.

"We should go to him, shouldn't we?"

"I guess we should," answered Vasyl, but I felt he wasn't quite sure.

Goosy was kneeling in the snow. As we approached him we slowed down, practically stealing on him. His eyes were closed. Vasyl squatted and started shaking him by the arm.

"Goosy. Eh, Goosy, come on."

Goosy's eyelids rose very, very slowly. His pupilless eyes gave us a white, disgusting stare. The frost on his hat and scarf enclosed his face in a playful frame of white fluff, just as if it were a furry hat and he was a ten-year-old girl. Vasyl shook him once more. "Goosy!"

The pupils reappeared. They floated out from under his eyelids but were focused only by their own inertia.

"Get up or you'll freeze."

I started to shake him from my side, trying to raise him to his feet, but he was a dead weight. It all flowed somewhere down and froze solid in his knees stuck in the snow.

"Get up, you fuck!" Bandurko was shouting now. Then he slapped him. Goosy's head bounced back and slumped on his chest. He raised it, and his eyes looked for us.

"No, guys . . . no . . ." he said with a sleepy, begging tone of voice. "Why . . . ?"

Vasyl slapped him some more.

"All right, all right . . . Leave me, just stop beating me . . ."

"What a dickhead!"

"Leave him." I tried to calm Vasyl down, but at that moment something must have clicked inside him and the previous hesitation evaporated without a trace.

"Listen," he spoke feverishly, "we have to take this zombie on our backs or something. See there? — " He pointed to the valley on the right "— There's an old village there, burned down soon after the war. There's practically nothing left, except for an old hut and the ruins of a Russian church. When I was there last summer both still stood. We have to put him somewhere and warm him up. It shouldn't be more than a couple of kilometres, downhill all the way."

When we threw his arms over our necks he was mumbling something but didn't resist. Somehow we managed. It was downhill. Sometimes he walked, sometimes we simply dragged him along, stopping every fifty metres. We didn't dare let go of him; no one would be able to shift the bastard up again. We made our way diagonally across the slope, aiming to reach the bottom of the valley somewhere in the middle, where the village was supposed to be. We were hot again. Vasyl fell once, I twice. A real cross-bearing, except the cross was too much of a limp dick. The moon hung just above the wood's edge. It was a real miracle Bandurko managed to spy out the dark, leaning form of the church's tower before it got completely dark. We headed straight down, just in time to spot the shapes of the crosses in the church cemetery. We dragged our burden through sloe bushes; something slashed me across the face. There was nothing, just a gaping hole and then the pitch dark of the hall. We tripped over some junk, and Vasyl lit his lighter to find a way into the nave. One wing of the door was still in place. We hauled our mate over the threshold and dragged him inside by the arms until we felt hard ground under our feet. Vasyl asked me if I had any paper. I took out from my rucksack's side pocket the map acquired in Gardlica and offered it to him. Instead, lighter in hand, he went back to the hall, where for some time he made a lot of noise then returned, probably with some wood, for he crashed it and broke it up with his boots, then his hands. In the end he took the map from my hand, crumpled it and lit it. In the flickering light I saw him kneeling, placing small splinters on the flame. Finally the rotten wood gave in.

Goosy sat with his legs splayed out in front of him, rubbing his eyes. When the fire was established, Vasyl went back to the hall to fetch more wood. He carried in a big armful of boards that he then broke with his hands and set in a little pyre. He worked in silence. The construction was symmetrical and precise. When he finished he knelt next to Goosy.

"How are you feeling?"

"I don't know. I'm hot, cold. I don't know. I'm weak."

"Move your feet. Can you feel your toes?"

"I think I can. I don't know. My feet ache."

Vasyl untied his boots and moved his feet close to the fire. He pulled out the sleeping-bags, wrapped up the patient and stuffed a pack of long-johns and jumpers under his bum. We huddled around the fire. I could feel its warmth on my face, though it still felt like brushes of freezing cold. The darkness was retreating. Red tongues of flame licked the walls, revealing here and there holes in the plaster with wide beams underneath. Along the walls stretched the remnants of the rotten floor. There remained only the platform surrounded by the skeleton of the iconostasis. A few columns still had traces of gold paint on them; the woodcarving was crumbling like a cookie. The rectangles left after torn-out icons gaped like windows in burned-out houses. But the two proper windows, a good two metres above the ground, still had most of their little square panes. High on the ceiling, right above our heads, wrapped in smoke and darkness, loomed some figures.

I searched my pockets but couldn't find any cigarettes. Vasyl gave me a packet. I picked out a cigarette. It was damp. I put it close to the fire and rolled it in my fingers until it regained its hard, rustling consistency.

It had a pleasant, sharp taste. Dark tobacco without filter. I inhaled a few times and passed it to Goosy. He took it and smoked, staring at the fire. His face was red. He smoked until the cigarette-end burned his fingers. He wrapped himself tight and put his chin on his knees. Vasyl went back into the vestibule.

"I think I have a torch," I said, but he wasn't interested. He started hurling into the middle of the church broken boards that he pulled off somewhere with ease, one after the other, throwing them on a pile that grew into a big mound. Then he came back, stoked the fire, pulled out a long, wide board and made it into a bench. I unzipped my coat. My scarf was gone; must have lost it or left it behind. Goosy leaned on to one side. His eyes were closed.

"Give us that torch," said Vasyl. He went back to this El Dorado of his and returned with two broad boards. They were blue, with a yellow strip on the crumbling edges.

"He has to get some sleep." He put the boards near the fire, and then we forced Goosy into two sleeping-bags and put a pair of boots and long-johns under his head. Vasyl found a jumper and put it on. Under his coat he only had a shirt.

"So, we're keeping guard," he said.

"Are we, then? So that they won't get us in our sleep."

"Oh, come on. Someone has to feed the fire. You go to sleep if you want. I'm not sleepy."

"Nor am I. I'll sit with you." We both laughed quietly.

"You sure will."

"Life or death, *commendante*, isn't it?"

"*Si, señor. Vida o muerte.*"

We burst out laughing. I looked into his eyes.

"Are you scared?"

He gave me a cigarette.

"Not any more. I don't think I am." He picked up a glowing splinter. "Not now. There, on the mountain I was. I was afraid I would still have to do something. But now . . . All we need to do is to feed the fire. In two hours it will be dawn. I have some coffee in my rucksack."

Chapter 29

I took my watch off and put it in my trousers pocket. Let it tick in my body, I thought. Let it tick together with that other vengeful watch, that mean gift from Somebody, so that we don't get ahead of ourselves. I didn't want to keep glancing at its face, those miserable crumbs, slivers of the circle that link stupid accidental events into a semblance of a sensible chain, which does chain us and before we know it we are just chained dogs. Could Vasyl have discovered it first? Earlier, a long time ago, when we still wasted our time on trivial and tiresome diversions? And now summed it up with "I was afraid I would still have to do something"?

He had time to ponder all those mysteries during his long strolls around his flat, from the green, gentle chaos of the park on the east to the distant line of the town centre, where the few skyscrapers looked like chimneys rising from smouldering rubble – that was the view from the west. Regular squeaks from the parquet stopped on the stretches covered by carpet or some exotic rugs. He had more and more time, while we had less and less. Perhaps that enormous number of seconds amassed in that flat, in its cubic containers, aroused his interest so much that he started studying their nature – or did he do it out of boredom? Maybe disgust? After all, it rubbed against his body, it touched his hands; there was no way he could get rid of it. It was in the kitchen, in the bathroom; the billows of steam rising from the bath could not swallow it up nor annihilate it, at best mixing with it and making it even more tangible. The mass of time. Neither the steam nor the sound from the silver Philips in the eastern room could do away with the matter of hours, days, and then years.

Room, hall, the other room, to and fro, passing the kitchen, bathroom, entrance to yet another room. "I can do it for hours," he told me once. "I like it. Those two views are so different. It's almost like a journey."

We sat in the park room: that is, I was sitting and he was standing, barefoot, in a white, knee-long shirt, his bum resting on the windowsill. A record was still turning, long finished, but the automatic switch was broken. We smoked cigarettes, the smoke drifting out of the window, and we were both thirty. It was early evening. The phone in the hall rang. Vasyl went to answer it. I heard him taking it to the other, western room and close the door. When he came back it was almost dark.

"Let's go somewhere," I said. "I've got a few bucks."

He was silent for a while, as if hesitating or inventing some excuse. In the end he said simply that no, not today. That was how he protected his world created in the vacuum left by us. He protected it gently, to have something of his own, the protection aimed to bring it to life. A soap bubble with which he was shielding his chest.

I had a bad day and needed company.

"Can't you put it off?"

"No." And then, after a long break, when the rapidly materialised, heavy silence of that "no" rang out, he added: "I've been putting things off long enough. Maybe you would put something off for a change."

I was slowly going down the stairs. Step after step. At the bottom, downstairs, by the heavy iron front door I brushed against a young boy. He looked at me, lowered his eyes and ran up the stairs with light, mincing steps. I started walking down a narrow, empty street. It struck me then that time was a void but it was also a kind of material. The city was a different version of Vasyl's flat. No better and no worse.

I cut through a crossing and moved down Belwederska Street. In the bar at the foot of Morskie Oko I had a cheap brandy, and with its flavour still washing around my mouth I started climbing uphill into the dark park. I didn't have any place in mind, or so it seemed to me. A drunk was coming towards me. He wanted to say something, but the incline carried him relentlessly down the path. The Heineken bar shone in the bushes like the *Titanic* in seaweed. I came out on to the Pulawska. I barely brushed against the crowds and dived straight into Madalinskiego. So, walking without any place in mind I suddenly stood at the foot of Goosy's house. The windows in the attic were dark. Goosy and his wife were in Sweden. They didn't go for the gold of Laponia like Regres did; they were earning their money in a more sensible and effective way. I didn't even know which. I hadn't seen them for a very long time. I, too, was earning money, unable to find something better to do. I thought that just as aimlessly I could have got on a bus or in a taxi, get on the other side of the river and look at my own windows. They would be lit, but so what? I could have had a cigarette, there, too, and walk the pavement five steps here and back. But I didn't do it. I knew I was down for it anyway.

Aimlessly, I turned into Aleje Niepodległości and as aimlessly into Rakowiecka to get to Pulawska and slip into Marszalkowska, where the crowds never bothered me. In the MDM bar I treated myself to a large Starka and walked on. Shorty's windows shone bright. But I didn't enter the vandalised staircase, or the lift that went up and down but never stopped. I didn't feel like it. I didn't like smoking in the bathroom or sitting through silent, nervous crossings of the room with throwaway remarks: "You know you have to get up in the morning." Besides, I didn't even know if Shorty was in, and to phone someone with a cut-off phone didn't make sense.

People around me were constantly buying and selling. In the underground passage some were dying, some were hurrying home. I resurfaced by the hotel. The taxi drivers waited, leaning against their motors, nervously looking round. I continued deep into the Aleje Jerozolimskie. Past Krucza, the crowds were thinning out, and beyond Nowy Świat it was positively empty. The Central Committee was blindingly white, like the rearguard of light behind which there was only night, as there was, all the way to the other side of the river. The row of streetlamps on the Poniatowski Bridge looked like a zip fastening the dark-blue sky. Entering the bridge I passed a square tower. The narrow pavement was perfectly straight. The water had the colour of black oil. Cars were speeding by like mad. I remembered a song – "Not for me the string of cars and their colourful starry lights" – the only one I heard from my mother's mouth when she was young. Or maybe it was only the radio? I stopped in the middle of the river. Looking south, I felt the trembling of the steel barrier. The screeching of cars and the rumbling of the trams mixed with darkness and the mercury-like light formed into a massive geometrical dome whose highest point was exactly above my head, up in the sky. I looked left and right, not a soul in sight. The grey pavement was getting narrower and narrower until it changed into a thin line and vanished at the end of the bridge. I took my hands off the barrier and resumed my walk. The first people I saw on the roundabout. I couldn't decide if I should go through the park or down the Waszyngtona. In the end I followed the road. A little further or there was a little bar where I could get a glass of something on the hoof. I had a quick Romanian brandy with a weird, herbal flavour. I cut across the street diagonally and ventured into the end of the park, its outskirts, an appendix with young trees and big stretches of lawn. I found a gangplank over the little canal and came out on Stanislaw August and right on the car park by Grochowska. Guests were coming out of the Kobra. I let them pass and slipped inside, called to a nice blond barmaid and asked for Stolichnaya.

Grochowska was practically empty. The number 6 tram was heading for Goclawek. The whole street was flooded with sickly pink light. The tram's sparks shot through the air like flares. At the Malutka Bar two drunks were having a conference; eventually they went to the corner shop, where they could always count on Polish wine. I turned into Podskarbińska. The cinema stood abandoned and dark, like the square on the other side of the street. I slowed down. On the second floor, behind green curtains, the lights were on. I took out a cigarette. The matchbox was empty. I stood for a while turning the last burned match in my hands. I turned back to Grochowska. At the bus stop a scared woman looked long for a lighter in her handbag. Just then a bus came, and I barely managed to catch the flame with the tip of my cigarette. I moved towards Wiatraczna. In the arcade I found a phone. It worked. I got a phone token from a grandad who had just finished talking. I dialled Vasyl's number. It was not answered for a long time.

"Can I drop in now?"

"Now?"

"Yes, now. I could be there in an hour. I'll get something on the way." Someone was passing. A little dog threw itself at me, yapping like crazy. The leash yanked him back.

"Say it again. I couldn't hear you. Some fucking dog . . ."

"I'm sorry, not today. Sorry."

I waited until he put down the phone. It took a long time; he was probably waiting too.

So time was a vacuum, and a kind of matter at the same time.

I don't think the lesson he gave me that evening was planned or deliberate. He never acted with premeditation, and the idea of hurting someone on purpose was completely foreign to him. It was he who was always hurt, and his refusal must have pained him more than my shit-empty evening hurt me. He was sitting in that world hurriedly assembled from crumbs, knowing how fragile and false it was, being merely an answer, a pale reflection of our worlds, the hopeless constructions of fear and abandonment.

My several hours of wandering about – what weight did it have against the unending journey through the empty rooms, when no one was dropping in and the phone repeated the reverse of our evening conversation. Hours, offered from occasion to occasion, moments, when our minds were somewhere else anyway, in that multiplicity of worlds which appears always in the course of doing things boring and accepted as necessary, to life, even to redemption. How soft was that shield with which he was trying to protect himself. Soft and at the same time noble in comparison with our trivial shells, inside which we swarmed like flies. Against the concrete toughness of our lives he was pitching his fragile attempts. Those boys appearing at dusk and disappearing at dawn to give him a double emptiness: full ashtray, empty bottles, record player with a broken switch and the click of a record stuck in the last groove, a replay of the sound of silence.

"Vasyl, why have you stopped playing?" I asked him once.

"I no longer can," he replied indifferently. A moment later I regretted asking the question. I knew that he had stopped playing ever since we came into his house, down the path between silver spruces. After that, every appearance was like gatecrashing a ball.

It grew quiet, distant. The piano was becoming a ridiculous piece of furniture, totally useless; even putting a stupid glass on it would leave marks on the French polish. With time even that stopped bothering us, especially after his mother died. "Plenty of room for parties, isn't it?" He managed to tie everything together once again. In fact, everything started all over again; time had turned back a little. Our games were a bit more murderous, but somehow we managed to enter that house for the first time – second time. Only it was a bit further away. But then we were growing bigger, so the town was getting smaller: a tram or a bus – no problem.

How on earth did we manage to pull it off? How did we manage not to die from alcohol, cigarettes, sleepless nights when after having finished all our shitty schools we struck camp in those three rooms for weeks, months on end? Our bodies were taking it in and cried for more. Vasyl was strolling around that trashland like a benevolent ruler, looking with delight on our helplessness, the inertia that kept us close to him. We came and went. Sometimes someone tried to make contact with reality, gave in to motherly despair and started looking for a job, found it and left it. Yep, it was the only workers' hotel with a piano in it. Goosy was pasting posters, Shorty was cleaning windows, I was a courier, all very romantic occupations, and none of us thought of following in our fathers' footsteps. I don't know, maybe I was a window cleaner and Goosy was a courier? Who cares? We also cleaned train compartments, read meters in people's homes, worked on building sites, churches as well as private ones, drove around delivering rice and sugar, each for a month or two, doing rounds between our homes, Vasyl's and the rest of the world, always on the move, impossible to track down, invisible and unstoppable, hungry souls in indestructible bodies. Now and again one of us would disappear, as the world was full of Gzankas, serious and less serious, some of whom we even managed to entice into our lair, though on the whole they found the atmosphere not to their liking, or maybe were put off by the fact that they were in a minority, one against the rest of us. For we used go out hunting individually, taking turns, never three of us at the same time. When one dropped out, the rest united in a pact of contempt and jealousy.

It was like weaving a cloth of a hundred colours, a warp and a weft, an accident and chaos. It seemed only he, Vasyl, was the constant factor, an immovable linchpin in the middle of that spinning mess, keeping it in balance. Without him we would have scattered and disappeared without a trace in the alien and hostile chaos. He simply was. He was home virtually all the time. If he left home it was with great reluctance, as if weary of all the world's tricks and traps. He finished his high school and crossed out reality; he erased it. It's incredible, but he didn't seem to have any business. Really. From time to time he would travel to Kraków to see his aunt and extract some cash that he didn't really need, as his mother had taken care of that. He was bringing back money and stories about a mad woman who talked to a portrait of Marshal Pilsudski and on 1 May and 22 July rolled down black curtains on all her windows.

Sometimes we managed to drag him outside, on the town, into the night, into the racket and chaos which, while it lasted, had the power of a drug. He resisted as if he were afraid of space occupied by others. The same happened when we brought along some old mates of ours. Majer, Regres, whoever, he immediately stiffened up like a cat sniffed by a dog, saying things like: "What will they have, coffee or tea?" When we were leaving, Uriasz would say: "The flat's OK, but this Vasyl needs to chill out a bit more." We didn't know what to say, and it was turning out that we were just occupying the place with all the benefits of the inventory.

He stayed behind, waiting for us, until we returned, that day, next day, in three days, never.

The water in the mug pushed into the hot embers steamed but refused to boil. I poured in some coffee and started stirring it, waiting for it to fall to the bottom. Goosy was asleep – at least, some groaning and mumbling was coming out of the sleeping-bags. Now and again I had to turn my back to the fire to warm it up. It felt like turning on a spit. If it weren't for the doors taken out it might have been a bit warmer. Like in that Siberian joke when a man wakes up and rubs his hands with joy for the thermometer shows only minus twenty-five. Or maybe it wasn't a joke? Well, I couldn't remember the punchline anyway. At least the smoke wasn't a problem under a high roof. On the ceiling that looked like the inside of a pyramid I could make out human shapes. Our father Adam rested leaning on his elbow, the other hand pointing high into the darkness, which one presumed was both heaven and the Lord. In the flickering, capricious flashes of light, the body came to life; the hand was now rising now falling, as if Adam was trying to push away the weight of the heavens, asking, "What have I done unto thee that you have created me?", as if immediately after drawing his first breath he took up the issue with God, suspecting it might all end in tears. His naked body kept changing from dark, indeterminate colour to fluid, flickering red, live, hot, bloody. The clay was burning out in the fire but instead of hardening it the fire was bringing out all that was soft and vulnerable.

When I felt my back thawed a bit I turned my face to the fire. Now, when I turned my head up I could see Cain and Abel. Between them stood a hazy form, probably a column of smoke rising towards heaven. In the dark there was no difference between them. One could think the whole story might have taken a different turn.

Vasyl was stoking the fire. He was doing it slowly, choosing a place for every little stick, every splinter of wood. He was laying the wood according to some very complicated plan. When something slipped, he would put it back in its place, rebuilding the order, sticking to the plan. Stick by stick, then across, then again one by one, until he had a kind of tower, or a well. Then he picked longer pieces, leaning them against the top so that the construction formed a tent or a pyramid. It lasted a few minutes. The flames nibbled at it from all sides until in the end it collapsed in a heap of red and black embers. Then he would start all over again. He levelled the embers, flattened the centre and started building afresh this crazy Tower of Babel, though perhaps it was more like a fiery hourglass, the senselessness of which was supposed to do away with time, destroy it, fool it.

"Do you remember *Wolves' Echoes*?" I asked.

He raised his eyes. They reflected red flames; the lower lids, where the tears gather, glistened.

"What did you say?"

"I asked if you remembered *Wolves' Echoes*, the film."

"Sure I do."

"And do you remember when Bruno O'ya is sitting with Karelova in the ruins of the Russian church?

"Sure I do." Then he thought. "But it was in the summer. Yep, summer."

"And, as the title suggests, the wolves howled."

"Nonsense. Wolves are supposed to howl in the winter. In the summer, howling doesn't have that effect."

"No, it doesn't," I agreed. "And do you remember what gun O'ya alias Slotwina had?"

He frowned, slipped the hat at the back of his head to the front, crumpled it at the top in his hand and clicked his tongue.

"Wait a minute, wait a minute . . . the same as Janek the Tankist – a Mauser. Very revolutionary weapon. In the Russian 'easterns' every commissar had a leather jacket and a Mauser."

"What was Perepeczko's name? Quick."

"Aldek Piwko."

"And what nationality was Ryszard Pietrasiński? Three seconds . . ."

"A Ukrainian, naturally. Cruel, evil and on top of that a coward."

"Three points. Why did they want to get to Szczecin? Ha?"

"Because it was the furthest point on the Polish map."

"And what was really, really terrible? You have time to think on this one."

"What could possibly be terrible in that film? It's a comedy. But all right, wait, wait . . . Do you remember when O'ya and that baddy run around the bunker? Smoke, everything's in flames and his mate, or what's left of him, lies at the bottom of the shaft?"

"Yes?"

"Well, you couldn't see anything in that shaft and it made it . . . you know – brrrr . . . and then that mug in the gas mask. I remember it well. And that character in the stripy shirt – he had a face."

"And I like best when they flogged O'ya with a hose. Nice sound."

The coffee boiled in no time. I put a stick through the handle and pulled the mug out of the embers. It was full of ash and crumbs of charcoal from Vasyl's construction. Goosy moved on his bier and curled up.

"Maybe we should move him," I said. "The sleeping-bag will burn."

"Leave him. Let him sleep." Bandurko got up, found a broken board and started to sweep away the embers from the yellow-purple cocoon. "Let him sleep. Let him at least rest."

"Do you play on?" I asked.

"It's bloody cold if you move away from the fire."

"It's because of the door. If we still had it it would keep the warmth in."

"The smoke is getting through it."

I tried to drink the coffee. It was fucking awful. All it needed was a rusty nail. But at least it burned fingers and lips. I chewed on the tiny crumbs of ash. They had a soft, slippery taste.

"I wonder where in the world is beginning to dawn now. Which side is it coming from? From the east, isn't it? It must be grey in Moscow by now."

"I haven't got a clue, Vasyl."

Chapter 30

Yes, that world was moving towards us. Slowly. I could see a huge map or a globe on which the edge of darkness moved like a cutthroat razor shaving a cheek. It revealed meridians, towns, villages and people busy with their naughty businesses, making love or simply wandering in the dark, catching them halfway through their motions, suddenly, without any warning. Some are pleased, others run into their burrows or desperately follow the line of darkness, hoping to hide in it for a while longer. Our geography teacher illustrated it to us with a globe and a lamp on a bendy arm. We even drew the curtains. I didn't think I would see this experiment again in such lucid detail. The day seemed indeed a thin, blade-like line slowly moving towards us. That blade was to raze us clean of everything that we had been. Just like a razor, to the seventh skin. I could not free myself of all those small towns and villages swept with the broom of light. Thieves were stuffing their bags, murderers were walking away from warm bodies. I could see millions of undulating duvets, feel the flutter of hearts of people rising early to work, furious or just determined, deceiving themselves with the same hope that this time it won't happen, that the night will last for ever, that something in the heavenly clock will break. The horror of the blue darkness, the stigmata of lucidity, repetitiveness and general madness. The shuffle of Father's slippers, the noises in the bathroom, unbelievably cold, inhuman and white as the windows wash themselves of the darkness, getting dressed in blue, the iciest colour of them all.

But then, it could not be just monotony and repetitiveness, for in fact it was not a string of days, it was one and the same day, the same blade ceaselessly peeling the earth's skin, the same earth under the same sun. Like peeling an apple. Yes, some invisible layers must have been continually removed and cast into the void. Continuous layers of the same day and the same night. So we, too, hadn't changed from the beginning of the world? So the cock's crow beyond this hill was the same as the one heard by Peter? And what about my fear? Was it not a cousin of that fear and reluctance to get up, to enter the bathroom, inside which still hangs the scent of Father's shaving cream and on the sink's walls splattered bubbles of white foam mixed with specks of black stubble, to enter that cold space and then the icy reality of the morning, repeating all the other realities past and future?

It was merely a reluctance to live. To death, served on a spoonful of sugar to a resisting child. Just an inconvenience, that's all. And a mild disgust.

A little, nauseating feeling. It must have been dawn over Kazan. Spoonful of sugar. Yuck.

Vasyl returned to his fiery Lego. Perhaps he preferred to tackle the question of space? That is always more tangible and so more controllable. You can jump off high buildings. You can stick a grenade up your ass and spread through space. I, too, was trying to return to something. The zigzaggy imprint of the boot's sole in the snow left very close to the fire. I kept glancing at it. It wasn't diminishing; it wasn't melting. I drew consolation from it, like from a broken watch. Perhaps something did stop. Perhaps the cold was so strong it froze the air, clamping the earth in a vice of solid atmosphere that through its connections with the rest of the cosmic clock brought the whole universe to a standstill. Everything's frozen still. Or else it goes through the same motions time and time again. But I'm sitting still. Vasyl plays with his construction, and people who are after us are still making the same step, like in the replay trick on *Match of the Day*. And when the temperature drops even lower they give up even on that one step and wait like ice figures for warmer days. I couldn't bear to think the crap going through my head.

"Let's talk, Vasyl."

"About films?" He didn't interrupt his building game. Only his hand holding a bit of wood stopped for minute while he looked at me.

"Anything. Films are fine."

"I can't think of any. I can't think of anything. Weird feeling. I'm not thinking."

"I don't want you to think. I want to talk."

"Bored, are you?" He placed the stick on a spot chosen according to the rules only he could understand. He took out cigarettes and threw me one. "Have one. It always helps. Kills time." He smiled with contempt, but the smile slipped off his face, leaving a grimace, half-confused, half-apologetic.

"Time," I repeated automatically. "Killing time, saving time. Is it possible? What if it doesn't exist?"

"What?"

"Time."

He caught the wrong piece of his construction and the whole thing suddenly collapsed, like a roof on a burning building.

"Time?"

"Yep. What if there's no time?"

He abandoned his game, fixed his eyes somewhere past my head and said: "In that case there's nothing. Nothing happened. All events are lined at the starting point . . ."

"And you were never born . . ."

"And Ginger Grisha never broke his leg?"

"Nope."

"And that night, you remember, Goosy brought that girl who threw up in the bathroom and then I lost my money? Do you remember? I didn't want to play, and she wanted to dance on the piano, naked."

"I remember. That didn't happen either, and nor did Goosy bring anyone. The money . . ."

"Oh, fuck it. I probably lost it or stuck it somewhere. It wasn't much, though we were skint."

"We always were, Vasyl. As far as I remember."

"And do you remember that morning, the dawn when we decided to make a trip to that power station? The bus going through the village, spring, behind fences trees in bloom. It was so early that when we got to the river the tower blocks in the centre were still black. And then the sun rose, somewhere over Praga. We still couldn't see it, and the tower blocks were set ablaze, like in real flames. Did that not happen either?"

"Nope."

"Shame. That was great. All around us dark green, dark water, while up there in the sky such a brilliance. For a few minutes only.

And then we, too, were in the sun. Everything disappeared, and Shorty showed us where the last river dredger lived. He had two small boats and a fucking big scow moored on the river. That house of his, total ruin. Shacks, little shacks, everything overgrown, and cocks were crowing."

"It was a ruin because the river flooded the place several times, but he refused to move beyond the dyke."

"Yeah, so many things in vain. You know, my memory seems to be gliding, everything it touches . . . it really feels as if nothing happened . . . Not even when we jumped on the freight train stopped at the signals. We wanted to go to Gdańsk . . ."

"But ended up somewhere in Nasielsk. It stood there for hours. Maybe it wasn't going any further."

"The controller caught us on the electric. It was night. The train was practically empty. We were too scared to run. Shorty wanted to, though."

"That too?"

"That too, Vasyl. It didn't happen either."

He placed his face in his hands and rubbed it, as if it itched, or as if he was trying to wake up. His voice coming from under his hands was muffled, deformed.

"It's terrifying when you think about it like that. Everything in vain, and it all might have not happened. It's true we didn't care, but maybe it did have some sense . . . was trying to have. My head's cracking up. It doesn't hurt, but it's cracking wide open with all this. Tell me, what were we doing in 1980?"

"The usual stuff. Nothing."

"And '81?"

"Same shit."

"Eighty-two?"

"Again."

"In '83 Goosy was in hospital. We jumped the fence to talk to him. He was on the second floor. Not much chance for a private conversation. The janitor used to chase us away."

"But then he stopped, when we gave him a glug from the bottle."

"Yeah, but then he stopped recognising us again, and we had to keep watering the bastard."

"Until in the dark we happened on a different one. He wanted to call the cops. A teetotal, or sewn up."

"Goosy said he was sewn up."

"Hm. And we didn't believe in those coppers. Until Goosy shouted from the window that he could see a police van. I twisted my ankle on that fucking fence."

He took his hands away from his face and looked at me with squinted eyes. He frowned and chewed on his lower lip. He looked like someone who was forcing himself to think. "So where did it all take place if we didn't participate? Where?"

"Perhaps in our heads? Otherwise we would've bored ourselves to death."

"In that case we could have also planned it differently. Swap things, or exchange them. That pal of yours . . . Majer?"

"Yea, Majer."

"Him. He wouldn't have gone mad, would he?"

"It's possible he'd never have gone mad, only had other things to do. Maybe he's grown into a decent man. Has kids, a car."

"And we haven't. Only Goosy has. Well, no more. Look at him. He looks as if he's about to be born again."

Or die. He lay so still we forgot about him. He looked like a huge coiled caterpillar. Fat and colourful. Vasyl leaned towards me. The fire lit his face from underneath, changing it into a red mask with black eye sockets. He was whispering.

"Listen, listen carefully. If it's all true, all that crap about time, it means we can actually leave here. Simply get up and go. Do you understand? Nothing will happen. We'll walk down the valley, all the way to the point where the two streams join, then left along the stream, three hours and we should get to the road. Any first car should give us a lift. Listen . . ."

He was talking feverishly, faster and faster. He was leaning so far into the fire that the flames were practically licking his face, but he didn't feel anything, as if his own words anaesthetised him, created an armour reflecting everything around him as irrelevant and untrue.

"It's only three, four hours. You're right. Everything up to now is unreal, and from now on, too, for why should it change all of a sudden? Everything is an illusion. We had to think about something through all those years or we would've died of boredom. No one can live in a vacuum, it's not possible, or so we thought. Time fills the vacuum, puts sense into events. Without time we are merely animals which are born and die the same. Since there's no time we can go, nothing will happen, no one will stop us. Three, maybe four hours and we're on the road. Why sit here? We need to make a move, move on, no point sitting here, we'll only get cold, freeze our asses off waiting for nothing because nothing happens. What's the point? We'd better get the fuck out of here, I'm telling you, to the stream crossing, and left, it's easy, all the way along the valley, nothing to climb, no bushes, flat as a table. You know, you've seen yourself, the snow isn't deep, ankle deep, frozen underneath. Shuffle, shuffle and we're there. I know the way. It's a coach route too. Three, four hours and God knows where we might be in the evening. I have some money left. What's the difference, here or there? You're right with this business of time. I couldn't understand it; it's been bothering me for a long time. Like in a dream – you're walking and not getting any nearer, everything's marching with you. Listen . . ."

His whisper changed into a hiss. The air was coming out of him, carrying the words, something like a prayer, a quick Hail Mary tripped out for peace of mind, or when dying, to fit it in before death comes.

"Vasyl!"

"What?"

"Stop it! Goosy won't make even ten steps!"

He straightened up. The red mask disappeared. He was looking at me from the half-shadow, suddenly distant and more real.

"Goosy? Why Goosy? Without Goosy. I know he won't make it. Without Goosy. He's asleep. He's not here. Why torture him?"

He sounded surprised, as if I suggested we do something stupid.

"Let him sleep. Let him sleep. I know he won't make it. Three, four hours of forced marching. We'll leave Goosy. We'll stoke up the fire, make it big so that he won't freeze. It doesn't matter whether he comes with us or not, you know that. Just as all this doesn't matter. We can do anything we want. For if what you've said is true, and it surely is, it means we're free, free and no use to anyone. Neither to Goosy, nor to them, nor to anyone. Now I understand. That's why I came here, to learn that. I wasn't sure, honest. I was thinking about it and thinking and I couldn't figure out. But now I know and I'm telling you – let's get out of here and you'll see that nothing will happen. A limping dog won't turn its head. Let's go, while we can. You're right, nothing happened, nothing will happen. It's all been brewing in our heads, a figment of our imagination . . ."

"Go, then," I interrupted him. "Go on your own. You're right, so go. You're right, it doesn't matter what we'll do. So go. I simply don't feel like it. You go, Vasyl . . ."

His figure grew dark. The fire was reduced to a heap of red embers, but Vasyl's silhouette wasn't swallowed by darkness. On the contrary, it became sharper, almost black. I looked up; the window was growing blue. It was still dark, deep aquamarine blue, but inside the church began to turn grey, as if in the black air someone diffused ash. The night still permeated objects and our bodies, but space was slowly working itself free.

He noticed it too. His head turned towards the window, but he didn't say anything. He sat staring at the windowpanes growing lighter by the minute, silent, as if that slow invasion of light pushed the words back down his throat, or maybe because he could not form those words with transparent matter, which was making our bodies more real. Perhaps it was a wrong medium for words, which were too heavy to fly in something so intangible and totally insubstantial. I got up and went out to the vestibule. In the milky light, thinner than in the nave, I easily found the place where he had pulled the boards from. On the ground, among the massive joists that used to hold up the floor, there was plenty of wooden rubbish. I didn't have to break anything up. I gathered an armful of light, rotten pieces, found a dry, hard log and took it back to the fire. Then went back again.

Just outside lay the remnants of the church's dome. The huge metal bulb, like a bathyscaph, was half-drowned in snow. There must have been a fence as there were two gateposts with rotting shingle roofs. Sloes and the grey-green trunks of young ash trees formed a natural hedge. I decided to take a walk and look round. The temple stood on the hill. The bottom of the valley was still flooded with darkness; the black tree trunks were still vague, swathed in blue. Our tracks ran uphill, along the cemetery. The frosted stone crosses looked ethereal, like lacework. I passed them by and walked out into an open space. In the east, beyond the long, flat hill, the sky was growing pale. It was not quite a warm golden haze yet, but the blue was growing, almost white, like molten silver.

But it was still too cold for walks. I went back to the gate. A barely detectable stream of warm air was escaping from inside. I stood in the vestibule, watching as the landscape gained in depth, the tree-crowns regaining sharp contours, one after the other, all the way up to the white slope and the dark line of wood on top of it.

Vasyl slipped past me and leaned against the remnants of the doorframe. He took out a packet of cigarettes. I took one and lit it off his.

"Is he asleep?"

"Yes. He should be warm."

"He was worn out."

The cigarette smoke mixed with steam and had no smell.

"There was a village here," said Bandurko. "Hence all that empty space. It used to be fields and meadows."

"Are you going?" I asked.

"Yes. I should be going soon. The sun will rise soon. Earlier up here. Down below it will still be dark. Can you see those five trees in a row? That's where the road is. Now smooth and white, no tracks. In summer after rain it's barely passable. Just mud and ruts. Sometimes it's used for hauling timber. But not now. Blocked between autumn and spring. A tourist on skis will pass through, but that's about all. You know, when I was here in the summer I, too, slept in this church. Some sort of a bird lived in the spire. At night I heard a flutter of wings, a terrifying voice, like a squeal. I was a bit scared. There, next to the dome I had my fire, but I slept inside. I wanted to see what it was like. At night, in an empty church. It was June, a short night, luckily. I fell asleep at dawn. At night that space was far too big. I felt like . . . I don't know, as if I was trying to sleep somewhere up in the air, in the black sky."

I was listening to him but at the same time I couldn't free my thoughts from the vision of his tiny diminishing figure. I could see him as he descends the hundred metres to the line of trees he had just pointed to, finds that enigmatic road, the white ribbon existing only in his imagination, then turns left, east, and wades straight into the dry, shallow snow, the ice below creaking gently under his feet without giving in. He should be growing smaller like a vanishing point, to the size of a pinhead, black, lonely, heading towards the world's edge, waving his arms, puffing, in those funny stubborn mincing steps of his, convinced he had at last and irrevocably managed to escape his own life. I fluttered my eyelids, but the vision was still there. He was moving through the landscape, which was trying to keep up with him, slipping back, catching up and finally overtaking him. A little brown-green bird with a bloody stain where the heart is, flying towards the end of air, towards the void, in which its wings will find no support. I could see him as he disappears in the dark wood just when the sun is spilling over the mountain-tops, marches on, full of hope that this time he is going to succeed, that at last he will cut all the strings and break out of the snares, even if he were to lose everything, memory included. I could see him as he finds the crossing of streams and roads, looks anxiously at the sky to check if the sun's rays are going to set new snares for him, looks back, panics at the sight of his own tracks and quickens his pace, making little fountains of snow which in a moment, in the full glare of the morning light, will glisten coldly, revealing his presence in the frozen landscape. And then he will catch this green lorry of his, or a coach, then a train going in some nonsensical, roundabout way to Poznań, Lublin or Jelenia Góra, where he will alight and, believing in his invisibility, stop with his head turned up under a great yellow timetable, find something fast and safe, and following his own rules of conspiracy will travel first class or locked up in a lavatory, only to get out at Warsaw Central to realise that spring's over and his funny clothes cause giggles among the thirteen-year-old waifs in breezy summer dresses, and the white soda trolleys have new prices painted on them. He will rummage through his pockets looking for money, catch a taxi and will be home in ten minutes. He will run up the stairs and, as usual, forgetting the bell, pound on the door, which will be opened by an old woman with silver hair. She will look at him and then say: "Thank God. I've been worried sick." And then everything will follow the well-trodden, familiar path until the day when we stood by the garden gate behind which stood a row of silver spruce and one of us will say, "All right, guys, it doesn't make sense. Let's go", while he, standing in the window, will watch us disappear slowly in a long perspective of linden trees, hands stuck in pockets, collars up; it will be raining, and our thoughts will flow in a completely new, unknown direction.

"Go," I said. "I'll try to slow them down, somehow."

He ignored me.

"It was a warm night. Maybe that's why I couldn't sleep. I was tossing and turning. And that bird. I heard its wings flutter against the bell beam. Yes, it was warm. I was lying in my sleeping-bag in my trunks and when going out for a smoke I would put just a shirt on. And the silence. I could hear a little stream murmur half a kilometre away. Maybe it had rained earlier and it was a little swollen. I can't remember. But that summer it didn't rain much. I had this small tent with me, you know, it was practically weightless. And I hardly ever bothered to pitch it; my sleeping-bag was enough. I was wandering around here for almost two months. Last summer. And the previous one too. Sorry, no. It was autumn then. How could I forget? The deer were troating. And the frost at dawn: white everywhere, and only when the sun rose was it bearable. Autumn. Very few people. It was my plan, to get away from people. I used short cuts. When I saw a path or a trail I ran away. I left at the end of October, I think. It was beginning to get wet, and the leaves began to fall. My stuff in the rucksack was getting wet; it was impossible to dry things properly, and they were growing mouldy inside. Yeah, it was the end of October. The weather gets really horrible then; everything looks the same. Wherever you look it's all grey. You can't tell east from north, and not a spot of sunshine all day. I'd like to come here in spring, you know? End of April, when the days grow longer and warmer. Back home everything is green by then, but here it's only beginning. I like spring. It must be beautiful here, flowers in the meadows . . . We should have come here in spring . . ."

"Vasyl." I turned towards him, and only this move stopped the story he was telling just to himself. He must have forgotten about me completely or treated me as part of his own memory, and only now that I moved he turned his gaze on me, looking as if he'd just woken up.

"You ought to make a move."

He sighed deeply, as if he wanted to exhale the remaining words, get rid of that stupid story, like a drunk who believes a few deep breaths of fresh air are going to sober him up. He nodded.

"Yes."

He moved back inside, and I walked a few steps and made it through the bushes into the open space. The sky in the east was getting paler. The distant, flat and long, long hill was dividing the world into two. On this side the blue light of dawn had already picked out thousands of shapes, single trees, shrubs, crests of vegetation running along the water clefts on the opposite slope. Everything had the right shape but looked flat, crammed and floating in a transparent dusk. There, on the other side – just air, air filled with a pale golden glow. The breath of light was so overwhelming it seemed to stretch for ever. Nothing but light, light and light, in which even air becomes immaterial, all those particles of matter, all those hydrogens, oxygens and nitrogens annihilated by a luminosity so complete it looked hard.

I heard the screeching of the snow. He stopped a step behind me, with a limp rucksack hanging off his shoulder and a woolly hat pushed to the back of his head.

"Listen," he started.

I grabbed him by the shoulders, turned him downhill in the direction of the five trees, just like one turns a little boy and gives him a push saying, "Go on, give aunty a kiss".

"Get the fuck out of here. Fuck off. And don't think about a thing. Just don't think."

I pushed him, he made a few long awkward steps, looked back at me but didn't wave. He adjusted the strap of the empty sack and headed off diagonally down across the hill. I waited until the contours of his silhouette blurred.

I turned uphill and walked past the church to the cemetery. Our trail was clearly visible. It climbed across the white plain, dissolving in the turbid light of dawn. I thought that when the sun rose the trail would be a hundred times more visible, glistening and storing the remnants of shadow, the only ones on that great and immaculate expanse.

We were naked. We had no chance. It was amazing how long it takes for such a thought to get through. Perhaps it never gets through properly. After all, we never die of fear, we never die of bad news, we never die of the certainty that we will die.

I was not afraid. I was too cold. I returned to Goosy. He was lying on the floor as before. I added to the fire and started blowing on the cooling embers.

Chapter 31

Time. All we ever did was fulfil its orders. We were getting old. There was no other way. It kept us in its care. It nestled softly in all the nooks and crannies of our lives; there were tremors. It was enough to succumb to its will. The eternally white-haired old man, containing all other eternities, every single white hair from the beginning of time. Everything happened inside him, and that is where the rest will. And there is no escape. Vasyl must have been coming to that path crossing, trying to find among the trees the road he had walked in the summer. It was then yellow, dusty, with protruding stones that looked like embedded skulls. It was hard, too hard to be marked by a footprint. Now he had a one in a thousand chance. Good odds, when one is trying to escape one's destination.

A flame broke through. Pale, transparent, devoid of nocturnal viscosity. The sun rose. Horizontal rays flowed in through the little barred windows in the presbytery. The flames became virtually invisible. In the cold light the streaks of smoke hung in the air like grey veils, one above the other, all the way to the ceiling. The mess around the fire. The clothes strewn around, debris of the floor-boards, Goosy's body in a bright cocoon – hard to tell if dead or alive, one fucking rubbish heap, like after a banquet of ghosts or vampires. Everything frozen, stripped of the nervous glimmer that would not let the eyes rest through the night. Like the end of a dream. A slow awakening as we open the eyes and in the room there is no trace left of the spectre that only a moment ago was making the body bathe in sweat. The delicate crackling of the fire was the only sound. The darkness had gone, no cover that could conceal the sound of a breath or a sniffle. Goosy was not dead yet. He moved. First he groaned, then curled up even tighter until in the end he stretched out and stuck his head out. Horrible sight. A big brightly coloured worm with a little grey head. He untangled one hand and sat up with difficulty. His face was like a mask. He looked at me with glassy eyes and then around. His lips, white with crusted saliva, parted and he whispered to himself, and to what he saw.

"What will I tell them at home?"

Both humour and cruelty were slowly losing their meaning, so I gave no answer. I moved the mug with the ashy coffee closer to the fire and waited until it warmed up. Goosy's eyes swept around the walls, the ceiling, the floor; his neck seemed like a muscle without bones. It looked like a slow gymnastic exercise, or an attack of fluid catatonia.

"What's this?"

"A Russian church. How are you feeling?"

"I'm thirsty."

I handed him the warm mug. He drank it straight away.

"I remember you were dragging me somewhere."

"You wanted to freeze to death."

"And I remember a fire."

"You fell asleep straight away."

"I dreamed of something."

"You have a fever. Are you cold?"

"Yes and no. Shivers. I'm soaked. If I'm cold it's from those sweaty rags. I would like more drink."

I walked out in front of the temple and shook the dregs out. The snow was blindingly white. I squashed a handful of snow into the mug, put it on the threshold and headed above the cemetery. I could not hold myself back. Our trail in the snow was sparkling and empty. The brash green of the wood reminded me of the army uniform.

"Where's Vasyl?"

Goosy had freed himself from his sleeping-bag down to his waist and was warming his hands at the fire. I was trying to find the best place for the mug. By the wall lay a few flat stones. I carried them over, put one on top of the other and pushed them into the red embers. On the plinth I put the mug and covered it with a thin piece of slate.

"He left. At dawn."

"Where?"

"Ahead."

"Alone?"

"Who else?"

"What a bastard," he said, a little surprised. "What a bastard, to run away like this . . ."

"I told him to."

He was silent for a moment and then said in a colourless voice, "They'll catch him, anyway. They'll catch everyone."

"It's not certain yet."

"Oh, yes, it is. Everything is certain."

He peeled himself out of the sleeping-bag and began to put his boots on. He was lacing them up tight, threading the laces all the way up through each set of holes. He ran the laces a few times just above the ankles and tied them up. He got up and reeled.

"I feel dizzy." He made few steps. "Not good. But we can try."

"What do you want to try?"

"The same thing – get the hell out of here."

I felt as if a great weight had fallen on my shoulders. I felt that nothing in the world would make me move, that my hands and legs were totally paralysed, that I was like a rag doll stuffed with wet sand.

"Goosy, you won't make a kilometre."

"I'll try. Everyone can try."

He got into some kind of nervous trance. He started picking all the stuff strewn around and stuffing it into his rucksack. Long-johns, his sleeping-bag, my torch. Looking around for more things to pack, he kicked a piece of wood to see there was only a scrap of greasy paper underneath.

"Have you seen the axe? Who had the axe?"

"Shorty. He always carried it. What do you need an axe for?"

"And the bayonet?"

"I haven't the foggiest. Last time I saw it, it was in the hut. Maybe Shorty . . ."

"Give me your watch."

"What the fuck do you want a watch for?"

"I have to know the time, don't I? I can't find mine. My boots are still wet."

He was strapping the rucksack with strong, fast pulls. I heard the rough whir of the plastic straps slipping through the buckles.

"Why didn't you wake me up? Why is everything arranged behind my back?"

He was turning round like a spinning top, doing up his jacket and looking for his gloves at the same time. He had put on one when he realised that his head was uncovered.

"Hat. Where's my hat?"

"We put you in the sleeping-bag with your hat on. Must have slipped off your head."

He threw off the rucksack and began to rummage through my sleeping-bag. He found nothing. He went back to his rucksack. Again he struggled with the straps, and when they gave in he shook everything out on the floor. He started digging through the pile, among which glistened a forgotten tin, but he ignored it. He picked up his sleeping-bag by two corners, raised it high and began to shake it. A little green bundle fell to his feet. He immediately put it on and started packing the rucksack again, stuffing everything in with his fist. In the end he stood up like a soldier, to attention, beads of sweat rolling down his face, his eyes darting in all directions as if he expected something bad to spring at him from the walls.

"I'm off. Nobody's woken me . . ."

"Where to? You don't know the terrain, you won't get very far . . ."

"One has to try. I'll follow his tracks. He knows the terrain."

"You were thirsty."

From under the slate cover escaped ribbons of steam. I picked up the mug through my sleeve.

"You were thirsty. You sweated all the water out of your system. You can't eat snow, can you?"

He stood undecided. At last he kneeled with his rucksack over one shoulder.

"Hot."

"It'll do you good."

He picked up the mug and tried to slurp the liquid together with air, but the handle was too hot even through his glove.

"I'll bring some snow," I said.

When I got back he was kneeling with his hands on his thighs, staring at the mug. I dropped in a small white ball. It dissolved instantly.

"Try now."

He slurped carefully.

"Have you got any cigarettes?"

He put the mug down and began to search his pockets, and he had about ten of those.

"I forgot to ask Vasyl to leave me a few."

"I have, I think I have. Wait a moment . . ."

"Maybe in your rucksack."

"No, should be on me." He stood up and started going through his trousers pockets. Finally, from one of the big, bulging side pockets he took out a crunched-up packet.

"It's still about half-full. I'll leave you a couple." He took out four and put them on the board.

"Have a smoke. You won't have time once you're on the move."

"I don't have time now," he answered, but in a strange absent-minded way put a cigarette in his mouth and sat with it hanging off his lip, as if he didn't know what to do with it next.

"I need to go for a leak," I said.

I went outside. I couldn't contain myself and practically ran up the hill. On top it was as empty as before, only lighter. I was sure that if I were to stare at our trail a while longer I would have seen there anything I fancied and more.

He was in the same position as I'd left him. His eyes were half-closed. Maybe he was asleep.

I picked a stick with a red glowing end and put it to his face. The cigarette was trembling in his mouth. He had to steady it with his hand, which was not much steadier. He inhaled deeply, then raised the mug, drank it bottoms up and put it down. Then he inhaled again and threw the cigarette into the fire.

"I'm off," he said. "You?"

"I'm staying. I can't be bothered. Even if I tried I won't succeed. You know what I mean?"

He wasn't listening. He was heading for the door. He tripped on the threshold and stopped in the doorway.

"Which way did he go?" he shouted over his shoulder.

"Left. And down."

I followed him out. He was already on Vasyl's trail. He was stumbling, waving his arms, reeling. He wasn't doing well.

I went back to my observation point and took up a position in the shadow of the bushes surrounding the cemetery, and just stood there, watching. My eyes were gliding, slipping off the undulating, white glassy surface. I tried to guess at the path of our tracks in the snow. It trailed off on the cusp of a gentle mound, behind which rose the next snowy expanse stretching all the way to the black line of the wood on the pass. I looked down. Goosy was wading through snow towards the sparse line of trees signposting the road. I thought the fire might go out and that I ought to go back. I couldn't resist one last glance. And then I saw them. It could have been anything. Tiny specks breaking away from the black line, just at the point where we, too, hurled ourselves downhill. Perhaps I didn't see any specks, just a pure motion in an absolutely still landscape. Goosy had just reached the trees and was about to disappear from my sight. I wanted to shout, but no sound came out of my mouth. I withdrew into the thicket. I thought of binoculars, a sudden flash when the sun hits the lenses, and that I watched too many films. Twenty minutes? Half an hour? The place suddenly came to life. One tree, another, tombstones, stone and iron crosses and the withered colossus sticking high above the line of the horizon on the opposite slope, all that whirled with me as I turned round and round, as if I was looking for something, a hole, a gap, a crack in the landscape, a rent in the cloth of the stage scenery.

Twenty minutes, half an hour? Three kilometres? Maybe only two? Four? I fixed my eyes on the distance again. The black dot rolled down and disappeared behind the trough between the mounds. I waited but saw nothing more. The last dot of a dotted line. Twenty minutes, half an hour. For the first time in a very long time I felt warm. Across the cemetery, leaping from one patch of shadow to the next, I got to the door. I was packing everything I laid my hands on, gathering sleeping-bags with sand and bits of wood, very quickly, even though my body felt like lead and put up resistance at every move. I could hardly lift the rucksack. It, too, was filled with wet sand. Twenty minutes, maybe half an hour. The fire had already turned into a pile of charcoal. It crossed my mind that if I ran I should catch up with them, catch up with Goosy and then with Vasyl, and then the three of us would run like ghosts and as long as we were running we would be beyond reach, sort of invisible. The others must be tired too, marching since dawn. They are only human, doing some wretched duty, fulfilling some shitty orders, so we in this race are certainly ahead and we will get to some place where the ground is barren and hard; it maybe even has a frozen stream. We will run down it, down below where there is less snow, plenty of towns, tarmac roads and crowds, which are better hideouts than the thickest forests, and if we run fast enough we will get to this place where people leave no trace. That chain had to break somewhere, the stitch on the snow should snap at some point, all we needed to do was run, run, run and not look back, just like in fairy tales.

It all ran through my head, but the fear of open spaces kept me inside the church. In the vestibule I realised I was tiptoeing. I wanted to get to the door from the side, brushing against the wall lookout and only then leap out and run. Twenty, maybe fifteen minutes. I was sneaking up along the wall ripped apart by Vasyl, slower and slower, more and more scared. Suddenly it hit me that the demolished wall wasn't letting through any light. One of the boards hung loose. I pushed it aside. Inside ran a narrow corridor. I could see that between the outer and the inner wall there was enough room to hide a man. Apparently the corridor ran around the plan of the church. I threw in the rucksack, ran outside, took off my jacket and started gathering snow. I carried the bundle inside to the fire. I stopped thinking by then, but I knew the fire had to be put out and the embers cold; otherwise they might want to stop and snoop around. I had to keep them on the move. There was a big hiss, and steam rose in a big cloud. The snow disappeared. I ran out to get another portion. Now I was throwing it by the handful, so as not to leave any white clues. I shook out my jacket outside and dived into the dark hole. Twenty, maybe fifteen minutes. No, this corridor wasn't going round. Only the vestibule allowed enough space between the walls; the nave was wider and closed the passage up. I looked up. Three metres above my head opened up the inside of the bell tower. The empty space was filled by an entanglement of wooden beams. High up towards the top I could see light coming through. I put my rucksack on and felt for the diagonal beams making up the skeleton of the vestibule's wall. I tried to climb up them, but the rucksack pulled me off. I extricated myself from it and on the second attempt managed to throw the damned thing over on the vestibule's roof. Now I could scramble to a point where I could get a good hold of the top edge and lift myself to where the rucksack was. I found myself between the ceiling and the roof, in the attic of the church. I made a step when suddenly a rotten board broke and my leg fell knee deep through the hole. Resting on the beams, I managed to pull myself out of the trap. I put on my rucksack. My aim was to escape as far up as possible, but I was afraid of going deep into the dark. The tower's four thick posts were tied together by a thicket of smaller, diagonal joists. The construction struck me as not dissimilar to a ladder inside a well. With a bit of luck I might get to the top and become invisible. Ten, fifteen metres.

I stood on the first joist. I could reach for the next one, but it was too high for me to step on it. The nearest point between the two joists was in the middle of the tower. I let go of the post and made a few careful steps. Now the higher joist was level with my chest. I jumped, hoisted my body weight over and sat on it astride. The next one was far too high. I could touch it standing up, but I'm no Schwarzenegger. It got close to mine only near the post. I slid to it on my ass, embraced the angular column and climbed the next metre and a half monkey-fashion. I was making progress. All I had to make sure was that I had a secure hold and that my rucksack didn't pull me down. The closer to the top, the lighter it got.

A tiny window at the top, the size of four cigarette packets, was already in my sight. I was clambering towards it like a moth towards light, holding on to the timber like a spider to its web, and clambered on. Three metres, maybe five minutes. Now and again I froze as still as a bird on a twig and listened. The silence was total. The only sound inside the tower seemed to be the pounding of my heart. And the tower was getting narrower. In fact, if I stretched my arms I could have touched both sides. On the last but one joist I lost my balance. I felt I was falling. I flapped my arms and instead of falling back I fell forward. Miraculously, I caught hold of a board holding up the rafters. I was hanging in the air. My right hand was ripped on a nail, but the left was OK. Ten, fifteen metres. Maybe five minutes. The joist I fell off was only a metre away, at the level of my waist. I tried to throw my leg over it but didn't have enough strength and only banged it on the shin. I tried to find a rest for my feet. There was none. The slanted roof was slipping away. My boots were barely touching the rafters. The next board was either higher or lower. I felt my fingers straightening up. Slowly, inch by inch, I moved away from the joist. Left hand, right hand. I thought I had nothing to lose and swung my body. At the second attempt I managed to throw my leg over. The last stretch felt like in a slow-motion film. Each move seemed to have consisted of a dozen smaller ones. I sat up on the horizontal joist, gripped the edge of the window and breathed deeply.

Under me spread out a wide, sun-flooded valley. The tower was higher than all the surrounding trees. I could see Vasyl's and Goosy's tracks in the snow. They ran through the white expanse, cutting through a copse of black, stunted trees, and disappeared among fir and spruce trees. I felt a lick of cold air on my face. The other side had no window; neither did the other two. Not a crack among the roof rafters. Beneath me a well of turbid grey. Carefully, I took my rucksack off and hung it over my neck. I dug out a white vest and stuffed it into the little window. I was enveloped by darkness. I took the vest out, wanting to look out a bit longer. I felt emotionally drained and had to keep myself busy, block out the pounding of my heart. My mind was blank anyway. I couldn't think, except that I would miss them coming but would see them follow the trail.

I hoped Goosy managed to get quite far. I hoped he would keep quiet or talk gibberish when they found him. Maybe they wouldn't have to return this way? Vasyl said there was a road further down. Maybe that would be the road they'd take Goosy and call for transport from there. At any rate, Vasyl seemed to have a good chance still. And then it occurred to me that once they got three, catching the other two would be just a piece of cake and I would be stuck in the tower until the end of my life, just like Vasyl would have to travel on lorries, trains and buses for the rest of his days. At least my situation seemed a bit simpler. I took out my gloves. "I'll try to slow them down." That's what I'd told Bandurko. Goosy should slow them down a bit. What's the difference? Shorty and Kostek also must have slowed them down. Shitty minutes, scraps of time. Now it would be a real test of time: does it crack, does it break, can one crush it like a wafer? In fact, the question was becoming interesting. Even on that fucking tower. Vasyl was right: the place was inhabited by a bird. There were plenty of crusty reminders everywhere around me. They were pinching my ass, crumbled in the hands. I was curious which lord would we serve now? The old one, whom we had served until now, or would something change and our memory would start from zero? Something like being born

again. And yet we were to return to the first birth, quite independently of what one thought of this winter trip of ours. I fancied a
cigarette, wanted to feel the taste of smoke mixed with the valley's
frosty, floating, high, laced-with-sunshine air. Nice thought. But I
was too much of a coward, even though the valley was as beautiful
as a dream. Barred by a long, flat hill, it split at the end, and the
right leg ran straight south, where the hill gave way to the next hill,
beyond which the eyes could not reach so one had to imagine the
next ones. And the hill opposite was not bad either. Green and
brown, and in the sun the almost red colour of the naked birch
trees. Their tangled crowns created patterns more delicate than the
most intricate lacework. Single trees strewn around the white
meadows looked like black cutouts, their shadows only a grade
lighter. And not a puff of wind. The cold froze the air the way it
turns water into ice. The view was rapturous. Except I was desperate
for a leak.

I didn't hear them. I simply felt them. The wooden construction
carried the slightest vibration. I felt them when they entered the
vestibule. A delicate shiver ran through the whole church. Only a
while later I heard their voices. Unclear, muffled by the distance
and the mass of timber. I bunged my hole on to the world. I was
hot. I could see their faces. Indifferent, clean-shaven, pink from
the cold. They were searching the place, kicking their way through
the piles of broken wood. Someone kneeled, must have been an
officer who put his hand out to the fire, maybe even picked out a
few coals to make sure they were as dead as the rest of the place. No
doubt they wore Siberian earflapped hats and high boots.

A few privates, held back by the command, crowded around the
entrance, kalashnikovs in hand. The professional soldiers went in
first. The rest were kept at a safe distance. They probably hadn't
found that pistol thrown into the snow, but they had a reason to be
cautious. They circled round the black hearth, disappointed that
they would have to keep going. Maybe even pissed off. They must
have been lighting up by now. Someone was going round the
church, too, looking for the trail and finding only one, the obvious
one. It's quite possible they hated us, the way one hates fools who
mindlessly destroy a well-established order. They must have been a
bit disappointed that no one was trying to shoot them from behind
a corner, thus depriving them of the possibility of a quick wrap-up.

They didn't talk much, or very quietly. There were moments I thought I was a victim of an illusion, that there was nobody down there, that they still had not come or had just gone. In the darkness and silence anything seemed possible. The tense grip made my hands go numb. My right glove was full of blood. It still hadn't gelled, so I took the glove off with my teeth and started licking the wound between my fingers. The nail went through the skin, tearing it. I could feel on my tongue the hanging shreds.

But it didn't hurt. The taste of blood made me feel hungry. And I was really desperate for a leak.

The sounds downstairs were weak and rare. There was nothing to focus the mind on. I made a little chink in the window. The light was blinding. I felt a ray of light pierce through the ball of my eye and scratch the back of my skull. It took me a long time to get used to the light. The tiny, irregular hole showed a few metres of Vasyl's trail and a naked bush. A tiny piece of the world, but still. At least one eye had something to do. I was cursing those downstairs. "Do something, for fuck's sake! Do something!" I thought. The dripping of single drops of sound was simply a torture. Trying to catch any of them made my head spin. I had my watch in a pocket. I was afraid to take it out. I could see it as it was falling, bouncing off the joists, getting bigger and bigger and finally crashing through the ceiling and exploding like a bomb. I was trying to count to ten, to a hundred, but the slightest rustle, real or imagined, would trip me up. I caught myself repeating – sixty-twelve, sixty-twelve – repeating and being unable to stop, just as in a fever one cannot stop one's teeth chattering. So I fixed my eyes on that sliver of landscape. I glued them to the shadow of the little bush, and I could swear I saw it moving like a sundial. I was so desperate for an event. I felt my body becoming unbelievably heavy, my seat groaning and about to break, that the skeleton of my prison made a loud cracking noise and I was unable to stop it. But it was only my bladder, getting as hard and heavy as a stone. I jammed my arm against the wall. Carefully, I took the rucksack off my neck and slowly lowered it between my thighs. With my free hand I unfastened two straps and opened the top. The flies were relatively easy. I huddled to the bag and freed my body of the pain and weight.

Soon after I smelled smoke.

Chapter 32

"We need events." Sentences that had no sense can suddenly return from the past with a power that equals the indifference with which we heard them the first time.

"Isn't there enough going on?" I asked.

"In reality nothing's going on," answered Kostek Górka a year earlier, as we walked down Francuska Street towards the Rondo, blessed with a morning beer in the Paris Bar after a party with accidental, basically strange people, though in a big house so we had managed to catch some sleep. We stepped in for one more and we were standing undecided – catch a bus or walk?

"There are no events." Kostek kept pressing his point, but I didn't feel like taking it up, for the morning was bright, sunny and frosty. A jet was glowing gold in the sun. It was flying south. In fact, I wished I could be alone. I fancied being alone in an empty park with two bottles of beer, to experience that pleasant explosion of alcohol in the arteries, which happens only in the morning after a night of persistent drinking.

"Look at them." He pointed at the crowds surging up the wide approach to the stadium.

"So what?" I wanted to put him off, but he was really talking to himself. He was walking with hands in his pockets, raised head, eyes fixed on the human mass on the march to buying and selling. I had to hold him back by the elbow or he would have stepped out at red lights. We were heading for the park, but he stopped on the pavement and started rummaging through his pocket for cigarettes, which he didn't have, so I gave him one and lit up myself.

"Nothing. But I was always struck by the accidental nature of most of human behaviour. When I think that five billion people may one day do something no one expects of them, something unpredictable . . ."

"Leave those billions alone. I don't know what I'm going to do tomorrow, and neither do you."

"Exactly. Everything wears out to zero."

"And what do you want? That they should go and win Constantinople for Christendom? They want to eat. It's no accident."

"They have enough to eat. They could be somewhere else altogether, and they haven't got a clue."

He flicked his half-burned cigarette into the dry grass and glanced at me.

"Shall we go?" he nodded towards the stadium.

I didn't feel like rubbing against strangers or looking at the ocean of objects, those shoals of wonderful rubbish. Unbelievable what people may think of as useful. I wanted to got through the park, buy two beers, have a bath, catch an hour of sleep or drink two coffees. At noon I had to be at work.

He only shrugged his shoulders and cut across the street, ignoring the cars and trams. Someone even hooted a horn, but he was already disappearing, blending in with the grey stream flowing uphill, just as grey but more nimble, quicker. I could still see him as he overtook people, almost running, to stop on the top of the stadium and look at the flow and ebb of the human sea at his feet.

My only reaction then could be a shrug, which I did. Pleased I'd got rid of him, I returned to the Rondo Bar, bought what I needed and submerged myself in the naked park. I reached the pond and on the bench I drank the first beer, feeling inside a growing sense of anxious light-heartedness. The factory on the side pumped the scent of chocolate and billows of steam. Ducks waddled on the bank ice, but I didn't have anything to give them. A very nice morning. Behind my back, thousands of people were fulfilling their dreams. Life was not bad, that's what I thought to myself. Hopelessness found some strange mobile forms for itself; even my life seemed to have agreed with itself. I had an hour of peace, didn't have to do anything, though I should have done many things. For instance, now I know it, I should have followed Kostek and spy on him, catch his eye, slyly tempt him to say words, sentences, thoughts which had just begun to form in his precise and mad mind. But the beauty of the morning was too tempting, making me accept any trap or danger. The still park was filled with clear-cut contours, bright, separate colours, light and shadow sharply divided. A sculpture of a naked woman glistened with a greenish gleam. The stillness of the air made one think of the world as complete. No threats, no omens. But I should have followed him and got out of him, delicately and skilfully, all those premonitions, ideas, which must have kept him awake at night, even though they may have not had a definite form, being just feelings, awkward nuisance, something vague and anxious, something that demanded fleshing out, or else we would never know it. I should have followed him and watch him buy cigarettes, open the packet and shuffle sideways through the crowd, delighted they had no idea of his existence, but he could apprehend them all with his thought, all those people on the stadium, all the people from the beginning of the world. And just as they are busy with their own lives, he is busy with theirs, trying to fathom all those laws of motion and inertia, thanks to which we can exist, stuck to a spinning orb, humble, unassuming, docile. He had to reason it all out with the help of images; he had to look at life real close to figure out that it needs correction. Kostek Górka, writer for whom paper turned out to be too light and too smooth – the hand glides on it and the soul leaves no trace, for there is no trace to be left, the moment something ends something has to begin. So, he must have been slipping through the crowd, looking into people's faces, practically feeling people's backs with his eyes, inhaling the body smells, fascinated by the material mode of existence, by the abundance of its unnecessary and chaotic manifestations, probably devising a new creation of the world, inventing new laws, leaving for himself a modest role of rational fate. I should have held on to him, I should have listened to all those seemingly random and fortuitous statements, and most important of all I should have started believing in all that in which he had already begun to believe. The world is full of madmen, so that faith would be most difficult, but if I had succeeded, if any one of us had succeeded, it all would have ended differently. As it was, we became Kostek Górka's private world within which he rearranged us like chess pieces, fucking demiurge of Łódź. But if every human being is a world, or even half a world to himself, then he succeeded totally, so that life and death were a question of a single gesture. His.

And if we were of a more philosophical bend of mind we should have been grateful to him for straightening up our paths and leading us bang on target, and we didn't have to choose, or worry that we might have chosen wrongly.

No wonder, then, I nearly fell off my perch with joy when in the little square window I saw him. No wonder my heart leaped to my throat. He was about to disappear just at the point where Vasyl and Goosy disappeared before him. He was following their tracks. For a moment I thought it was a hallucination, that the blinding light of day picked from the back of my mind a forgotten image, but a few seconds later I saw Shorty. After a minute he disappeared too. I wanted to shout, but fear had by then taken control of my body so completely that it became numb and unresponsive. I managed only to open my mouth. My skin crackled and my jaw crunched. I sighed, or rather groaned, only to freeze again and with bated breath listen to total silence.

At last I got rid of the rucksack. It was falling down, bouncing off the joists, went through the ceiling, thus letting in some light from below. Getting down was a matter of less than a minute.

The church was light and empty. A ribbon of smoke rose from the dying fire. I found one of those four cigarettes. I lit up. I had to do something, something simple, to return to life. They would not escape me, not walking the way they did. Or maybe I was just afraid to run after them and ask them what happened. I took out my watch. It was nearly eleven. I was smoking, squatting by the fire, warming one hand then the other. It took a long time, that cigarette. To give them a lot of time to get away. All of them. The circle broke and changed into a chain of single figures. To stretch it even further meant to weaken it and ultimately break it. I got up, picked up the rucksack from the vestibule and went out into the sun. It took a while for my eyes to get used to the light. I was looking at the trail we had all made getting here. Absent-mindedly, I moved on to my old vantage point, and then on, until I found myself in the middle of the empty, dazzling plain. The world was still as far as the eye could see. The air was still and warm. I gathered a handful of snow. It was slightly viscous. I made a small ball and put it in my mouth. But I didn't take that road. I didn't turn back. I followed them. All the way down.

*

My whistle stopped them dead in their tracks. A long, shadowy lane ran through the spruce wood. It was narrow, twisting, and they often disappeared from sight. They abandoned all precautions. I was twenty metres away and they still didn't hear me. I had to whistle. Their faces became one, the same on top of different bodies.

"What happened?" I asked.

"Nothing," answered Kostek. "We're following you."

"What happened there?" I looked at Shorty, who immediately took advantage of it, dropped his rucksack and sat on it.

"There? Nothing." He smiled oddly, as if he was about to say some stupid joke. "They didn't come for us. Surprise, you know what I mean. They came for our friend. There must have been a phone or a radio in the shelter. When the hog sobered up he bayed for revenge. They took him in our presence. We were ready, about to march out of the room. The hog pointed at the boy as a dangerous criminal. They slapped him, handcuffed him and took him away. End of story. Jola slept on. There was no point in running after you in the middle of the night. We waited until dawn. That is, he did. I slept."

"Where's the rest?" Kostek's voice was quiet but strained.

"There," I pointed with my head ahead.

"Why did you split?"

"And what the fuck do you care?" I almost shouted.

He looked at me from behind narrowed eyes and answered calmly: "I simply want to know where we stand."

"Who's 'we'? There's no more 'we'. As for 'stand', you can do that on your own dick, you . . ."

But I couldn't find a name that would be filthy enough. I also needed to make up for the hours of cowardice, to erase them with some niggardly gesture. I moved at him with my hands stretched out as I wanted to grab him by the throat but Shorty simply stepped in between us. And thank God for that, for I saw from a corner of my eye that he was about to swing his foot.

That was all. We moved on. The spruce alley narrowed then spread out, something like a chain of smaller and bigger meadows flooded with sunshine. And it was almost like the previous night. Moving from shadow to light. We were marching along the bottom of a steep-sided valley. It was warm. Now and again white cushions slipped off the branches. And that was the only sound except for the crunch of snow under our feet. The spoors of deer crisscrossed our path. Nothing much happened. Only once I spotted a deep, round hole off the track; I was sure Goosy was getting weak. But I kept my mouth shut. I didn't want to give any advice to this Moses of ours who first pushed us into this shit and now was leading us out of it. I thought I'd give him more time. Shorty was marching in front of me, and I had a problem following in his giant footsteps. It must have been noon. Even the narrowest of passages showed no shadow. Kostek was not hurrying us. When he asked where were the rest he really meant Vasyl. Without him he was blind. Without him he was getting dangerously close to slipping into the accidental, the unforeseen, into the trap of his own unawareness. It dawned on me that he must have been very sure that none of us would contemplate abandoning the others. And of Vasyl he must have been as sure as he was of himself; after all, he had no other ears or eyes. It dawned on me too that this setup was beginning to break down, and I was becoming scared. Kostek Górka was losing control of our fate. He was beginning to share our fate. And that might turn out to be the worst of all bad options.

I should not have left him that winter morning. I should have become his Sancho Panza and stolen his madness. We all should have become his pages.

We should have kissed his ass the moment he turned up the first time. But we treated him like one of us – "Sit down, have a drink." And it had not even crossed our minds that Kostek might not drink just to get drunk, or bummed around with us for any other reason than bumming about, or wasted time not for the pleasure derived from boredom and sense of security. We were too stupid for that. We should have kissed his ass or kicked it out at the first opportunity – "Fuck off, dickhead. Don't come to a round table with a square mug."

I was the last in the line, making my lousy discoveries five hundred kilometres away from home and a few years too late. I spotted another snow cast of Goosy's ass. Two hundred metres down, another one, but not as clean, as if he'd had a problem getting up. There was also something like a drop of blood. I knew we would catch up with him soon. My watch was showing quarter to one. I didn't say a word. There was no need. He was lying on his side across the path. He was trying to sit up. He looked just like on the sofa in his home when watching television. His legs were drawn in, thighs together. His nose bled. He wiped the blood off when he saw us. Shorty squatted next to him.

"Haven't got far, have you?" I said quietly.

"No, haven't." He was speaking calmly, no sign of the paranoia from a few hours before.

"There was no need, Goosy. No one's after us."

"Shame." He tried to smile. "We'll have to think of something else to do."

"We will," said Shorty. "Wipe your nose. Can you walk?"

"Not quite. My feet get tangled up and I fall."

"Just as well it's not me."

"Why?"

"Why? Would you like to carry me?"

The three of us laughed. Goosy immediately stopped his nose and our giggles died out, sounding odd and inappropriate in the absolute silence of the forest. Kostek stood several steps away, looking at the map. He stuffed it behind his jacket, took his rucksack off and said: "Wait here. I'll be back."

He followed Vasyl's single track and disappeared among the trees.

We sat Goosy up. He asked for a cigarette. We all had one.

"Where has he got the map from?" I asked.

"He took it from the shelter," answered Shorty.

"Any idea what he's up to?"

"Haven't a clue. He's not given to baring his soul. And what about Bandurko?"

"He chose freedom. I persuaded him myself. Left the church at dawn."

Shorty nodded and looked at me askance.

"Shame I failed to be persuaded by anybody."

"You fell in with the wrong escape party."

"I couldn't go any faster. I could barely move."

And so we chatted away. I told him how for more than twenty-four hours he played a part of the chasing party.

". . . so we're sitting down to a coffee and you're pissing into your rucksack. Wait, how did the grandad put it? Pleasures are many . . ."

"And you say Jola was asleep . . ."

"She probably still is. She's like a bear."

"Shame about Maciek."

"It's love. I wouldn't worry about him. If by some miracle he won't discover the truth about the object of his desire, he'll sit it out with his heart ablaze and feel a hero. Lady's honour, that sort of crap. Schlissenburg won't break him."

"Did they kick his ass very badly?"

"While we were there he caught it only once. But I'm sure they took him for a good merry-go-round. The squire was chummy with the cops."

"And how did you know where to turn?"

"You snothead, you left your scarf the colour of a rainbow five paces away from the path, like the true Sioux that you are. I have it in my rucksack."

Goosy turned his face to the sun, putting snow to his nose. It was beginning to feel like a picnic.

"I'm hungry," I said.

"We even had breakfast. There isn't much left, though. Some bread, maybe a bit of pork fat. I don't even know what I've got."

"Goosy has a tin of something."

But we didn't get to eat anything. Kostek returned. He walked to us, hesitated for a moment, squatted and looked at our faces one by one. He lowered his eyes and began to speak.

"Listen, guys, you have to tell me what's happened to Vasyl. Perhaps it's not my business, but the situation has changed." He nodded his head at Goosy. "We have to do something with him."

"Best to shoot him, *commendante*. Russian paras do it."

Shorty's joke didn't raise much laughter. Not even from him. But then I'm not sure if it was meant to be a joke. He said it in a quiet voice, with a strange tone, as if threatening.

"I need to know what's happened with Vasyl, where he's gone." I waved all that aside. By now Vasyl was far away, beyond our reach.

"He went this way seven hours ago. He's probably sitting on some train. He went home. He no longer gives a shit. Finished, *commendante*."

He swallowed. Didn't raise his eyes. His hand in a black glove was kneading a small ball of snow.

"This way you have to walk five kilometres to get to the road. At this crossing there is nothing, just an empty space. A good few kilometres either way to the nearest village. But after a kilometre there's a road to the left. An ordinary road through the wood. It's on the map. It leads to a quarry. All in all about three kilometres. I got to the point where it turns off the main road. There are no tracks. There's a barrier and a no-entry sign. I bet the quarry is closed in winter. We should go there. It's a place, not middle-of-nowhere. We should be able to carry him that far. But we won't make the ten kilometres with him."

We didn't look at Kostek. We looked at Goosy.

"Show me the map," he said. He spread it out on his lap and asked Kostek to show him the quarry. Three black squares stacked into a little pyramid stood in the middle of green. From there went out a faint black thread connected to another.

"We're here," said Kostek, taking his glove off and putting his finger in the middle of nowhere. "The church is here and the shelter here."

Our church was a little red mark with an orthodox cross. I was looking for houses, but the nearest was the shelter and only past that a handful of orange dots scattered like chuffs in the wind.

"I don't know. We'll see." He got up. Shorty picked up his rucksack. He made two steps, three, four, ten, with growing difficulty, until in the end he clutched at air and had to stop to start all over again.

"Just as if I was pissed," he said hopelessly. "I'm dizzy." From under his hat trickled rills of sweat. He was looking at us apologetically. "When I'm sitting I don't feel it. But the moment I get up I know I've got a fever. I'm soaked. I have a blizzard before my eyes."

Shorty handed Goosy's rucksack to Kostek and clasped his hand around Goosy's waist.

"You take him from the other side."

I felt pain in my wounded hand so we had to swap sides.

And so we shuffled along. We were not as quick as at night, going downhill, but we were making progress. We were making stops. We got to the place described by Kostek. A crooked barrier painted in red and white stripes barred our way. The road ran ahead up a steep hill, cutting simply straight into the slope covered by a dense spruce wood. No turns. Now we knew why the quarry was closed in winter. One could smash a kid's toboggan into smithereens coming down, let alone a lorry with five tonnes on the back.

The worst was the first hundred metres. After that the terrain flattened out. Goosy was doing what he could, but he was knocking between us like a drunk. When the toes of his boots began to plough the snow it was a signal for us to stop. We took Kostek's wide police belt and fastened it around Goosy so that there was something to grab hold of him by. Finally, the road levelled out. It was dead straight, and we could see that further ahead it was climbing up like crazy. The builders of the road must have been in a great hurry.

After an hour Kostek announced we were halfway there. We let go of our burden and he just sank to his knees, breathing even heavier than we were. He was gathering snow and stuffing it in his face. That snow was immediately coming out on his forehead and flowing down in streams. The sky was blue, the air still, and we were dead tired.

But it was neither the steep road nor winter that made the quarry empty. After some unbearably long time, which was painfully hacking its way through our bodies, we finally reached the top. The wood on the right simply disappeared; it fell away, together with a part of the road. At our feet opened up a fifty-metre-deep precipice, a sheer abyss. Massive blocks of rock were mixed with barren, white tree trunks. Like stones and bones, bones and stones, that's what it looked like. I felt dizzy. Only Kostek went up to the edge. Down at the bottom, in a yard the size of a handkerchief, stood a rusty skeleton of a machine, the brown wreck of another and a grey barracks whose roof had caved in under snow. It was very bright. We saw the quarry like a model in the science museum. The sun fell on the opposite wall. It was pale yellow. The whole thing looked like a canyon in the midst of gentle mountains.

The missing part of the road we negotiated through the woods. It was soon downhill. Then the road turned sharply right. The bottom of the quarry was already covered in shadow.

Chapter 33

"Like a dredger, isn't it?"

"What dredger?"

"Like those on the canal."

There were always two. Dirty, knocked about, painted in what was once marine grey. We had to get through a thicket of purple willow growing on the flat, sandy bank. The hot air was soaked with a bitter, leather-like smell, the kind given off by newly woven baskets in provincial markets. If the breeze came from the water, the nose would be hit by the odour of fish, though in the entire canal there must have been three of those at the most. Perhaps it's the fish smell of water, not the other way round. First appeared the conveyor belt transporter, looming high against the sky. Then the rest of the smudged hull and, rusted into stillness, the huge dredging wheel.

It stood ten metres from the fascine-strengthened bank. There was no mooring so it must have been anchored. If someone was on board, a small boat would be rocking by its side. Or maybe it was manned permanently? Such a mass of scrap metal should not be left unattended while the green thicket on the shore was teeming with drunks and bums not yet immune to flashes of inspiration. But we never saw it at work. Nor the other one, moored closer to the docks, among the barges and tugs. Both were equally dead. I think it was only once that we heard the engine on our one, a hollow thud and a little stream of water sploshing in the side gutter.

So we never saw the big wheel turn or a barge put its back under the conveyor belt. We never saw it work, for we always saw it on Sundays. It was enough not to get off the bus at the church stop and to go three more. "Goosy, don't worry, your mother goes for the nine o'clock." "The neighbour will grass on me." "Don't worry,

I'm telling you. Mothers are supposed to believe their sons, aren't they?" We used to go to Mass at eleven. Or rather used to go rarer and rarer. The godless cunt Shorty suggested we might just as well spend the time by the canal. An hour of quiet and back on the bus. It smelled of baskets full of fish. The power station behind the concrete viaduct looked so huge, as if it had fallen from the sky. There was nothing like it on earth. So we sat it out looking at the dredgers, on the bank sinkers plonked by the old anglers whom, just like the dredgers, we never saw pull anything out of the water except for their shiny fishhooks. In those days Sundays were always cloudless, and blue sky stretched over the sandy bank opposite, leaning against the railway side track crammed with grey-brown wagons.

White birds, gulls, maybe terns, glided on gentle green waves. Their beaks remained always empty, just like the fishhooks. In that pastel,smoky landscape the wine bottles once filled with local produce looked bright and surreal, like an arranged composition: Malwina, Leliwa, Rajskie, Serenada.

Sometimes we would go up the canal, reading out those names, which in the pre-noon stillness sounded like pure sounds devoid of any meaning. One day we ventured so far that no sound reached the barely visible viaduct. On the other bank the willows were spreading down to the water. And then Goosy said:

"You hear that?"

"What?"

"Bells. The bells are tolling for Mass."

A remote, muffled hum bowled over the immaculate blue dome of the sky. Like an invisible flock of geese.

"Let them," said Shorty and took out from his breast pocket a cigarette.

Indeed, the rusty beast did look like a dredger on caterpillars. The conveyor belt arm was stretching out over our heads, its rubber long gone to rot. All that remained was a metal scaffold, flat and sharp like a technical drawing against the luminous sky. We passed the massive corpse towards the fallen-off slope. A few huge boulders lay on the ground, past which the wall rose steeply, filled with torn and rotting tree trunks, and then shot up vertically to fold into an overhang at the top.

"Good thirty metres or more," said Shorty. "Are we going?"

"Are you crazy?" I said. "It's all hanging on a thread. It's too scary even to fart."

"It must have come down when they were blowing the other wall. The lorries added their bit. Say what you want, but Communists did it in big style."

We returned to the barracks. It looked like a train wagon, except the compartments were on both sides of the corridor. Everything was built of wood, sawmill leftovers. In one of those boxrooms we found a complete window. In the corner stood a barrel with a pipe. The metal had turned into rust, but we lit a fire in it. There was plenty of firewood. It was enough to go next door and take a bit of a wall. So it wasn't too bad. There was even a bed. A military-penitentiary kind, with a bare spring frame on which we threw an armful of spruce branches. And on that armful Goosy was raving feverishly. Lying under two sleeping-bags, changed beyond recognition, he was talking in short bursts, like an automaton learning to speak. We weren't listening. Kostek sat on some rotting stool, staring at the map, as if still believing we existed in a world that could be described or drawn. We were doing the rest. Kept the fire going in the barrel, giving Goosy warm water to drink and from time to time nipping outside so as not to think about those last cigarettes.

"Once he's had some sleep in a warm place he'll be all right," Kostek was telling us as we lay the raving Goosy on the bed. None of us answered him. "Cold, cold . . . just like then . . . Find some lemons in the fridge," muttered Goosy.

The rocky crater full of scrap and rotting wood was filled with watery twilight and covered by a luminous golden lid. Red, stretched-out quill-like clouds pointed to the west. Perhaps the reason we were going out was to steep ourselves in that weird half-light, incomplete darkness, just to feel we were ghosts. There was so much light high above while down below we gave not a slither of shadow.

We made a tour of the whole enterprise, which seemed in a state of clinical death. A few telegraph poles with remnants of cables marked the way towards a narrow strip of wood, which seemed to be the extension of the road. The relics of a massive, huge-as-a-house machine rose from the snow near our dredger.

"It's a stone grinder," said Shorty, who had seen many grinders in his life. What interesting things must have been hidden under the snowy carapace. We should be thirteen and stay here for longer. Hands in pockets, we wandered up and down, and I imagined that from above our silhouettes looked like exclamation marks. We stopped behind the hut and lit one cigarette to share. Despite the clear sky it was not all that cold.

"Just the place for this mole," said Shorty. "He's like a mole, like a rat. Did you notice how he laughs? He always bares his teeth."

"I did, Shorty. Many times."

Two blackbirds appeared, flying first across the thickening blue, silvery green then the gold before melting away in the red of the sunset. They left no scratches on the sky. They flew quite high, but we heard the whispering, dry swoosh of their wings. Somewhere from there came the bark of a goat – or was it a fox? – or something.

"I'd rather be sitting somewhere higher," said Shorty.

"Me too," I answered.

He handed me a cigarette. The sun was disappearing behind the first mountain, then the next and the next, slipping off the earth's edge, lower and lower, shining somewhere beneath us, deeper and deeper, forcing new and new people to life, leaving us in peace.

I couldn't think. I was trying, but in vain. We stood in a luminous soup that sharpened the contours and washed away colours. We were our own and mutual hallucinations. Hallucinations don't think. The sleepiness was natural too. We wanted to return to where we came from.

I was about to flick the cigarette-end into the snow but Shorty stopped me. He put it out and dropped it into his pocket. We returned to the hut. Goosy was moaning. Kostek was staring into the darkening window. Shorty dug out a piece of hard bread and a slither of pork fat. I took my share. The sleeping-bag pulled out of my rucksack was wet and stank to high heaven.

My perfume wasn't better. I took the rucksack as a pillow and crashed out by the barrel stove. The fire was blazing away. It was quite warm. Goosy was talking to some woman; the others were silent. I was staring at the barrel. Here and there the rust ate through and I could see tiny red flashes. I was worried that the stove would crack, the embers spill on the floor and we all would blossom in this godforsaken hole in the ground like some huge stinking orange flower. But the worry didn't keep me awake. I plunged into a dark abyss, tumbling, spinning and somersaulting. The darkness tried to spit me out, but my lethargy was heavier than a stone and so I came to rest on the bottom, in the slime of all past events. They floated around, gently rubbing against me, but their sheer size, number and complexity were so overwhelming it was not sleep but a cold, sweaty nightmare. I was soaked through. In such depths it's only natural. Just like you can't jump higher than your own ass. And even if they were silent, I was hearing hundreds of conversations. And if they sat still, I could not disentangle myself from the snarl of gestures.

Yet it must have been a dream, for from time to time I woke up and saw Kostek's face, a silver mask in the moonlight flooding through the window. As if it had been there through the centuries, a statue, or something like that. A hollow statue – strike it and it will ring out.

"Is this night? Is it yet another night?"

"Sleep, Goosy, sleep. It's night. Night's for sleeping."

Shorty's voice was coming from somewhere by the door, but even that was too far for Goosy to hear it from the bottom of his nightmare.

"Night, night, all the time night. When will it end?"

He gave up on lemons in exchange for the light. Whims and fancies. He moaned for a while before being swamped by another wave of fever, and all that was coming out of him were short, whistling geysers.

Shorty stepped over me and stoked the fire. I turned on my side to warm my back. I felt the warmth crawling up my spine and fell asleep.

It was their voices that woke me up. It was the wind. It was high and plunged down all the way to the bottom of our burrow. I smelled smoke. The gale was rough and spasmodic. It rolled a ball of air, dropped it on the roof and went back for the next one. Cold, vicious whistlers swept the floor. In my mouth I had a taste of old dust and in my feet I felt a creeping frost. Shorty was talking to Kostek:

"Check properly. I don't believe you."

"I told you I haven't got it."

"Check again." Shorty's voice was calm. In fact, it sounded more like a plea.

"I have."

"Try again. Find it."

Slowly, I rolled on my back and sat up, leaning against the wall. Kostek was sitting as before. Moonlight flooded and ebbed away from his face. Clouds ran across the sky in waves, so the light was unstable, shifty, time and time again blotted up by shadow and then all I could see was a dark, indeterminate shape, barely reminiscent of human form. It could be clay; it could be rags.

It bent forward, picking something from the floor. Shorty spoke again.

"Don't pack it yet. Find it."

"I can't see a thing here anyway."

"Open up the stove."

Kostek slowly straightened up. The moonlight picked out his tangled hair. He was looking right at Shorty. Then, when he was almost completely engulfed by the inky darkness, he said in a high-pitched tone:

"Will you get off my fucking back?"

Shorty's bulk disconnected from the wall.

"OK, I'll find it myself," and he moved towards the window, which lit up for a moment and then was blocked again. I heard Kostek's "Leave it" and a groan. Shorty bent down, a bit of a scuffle and Kostek flew across the room, hit the door and fell out into the corridor. I got up, sort of automatically, and closed the door, holding on to the doorhandle.

Shorty opened up the stove, and the room turned red. He shook Kostek's rucksack, holding it upside down, and squatted amid the rags and rubbish. I felt a pull on the handle. It was a weak try, just to make sure. Shorty undid the pockets one by one, rummaged through them and finally found what he was looking for.

"Fucking bastard. Let him in."

I opened the door. The darkness was icy, full of draughts. I waited a while. In the end I had to call him. He rubbed against me, cold and scentless. He knelt down and started pushing stuff back into the rucksack. Then he sat down in his old place and in a wooden, throaty voice said:

"Sorry, guys, I'm going off my platter."

Shorty shut the stove and was pottering blindly in the dark. I heard a clink of the mug. He was warming up water, sat next to Goosy and tried to bring him back from his ravings. I heard the rustling of plastic packing.

"Goosy, you have to swallow this, d'you hear me?"

Goosy mumbled and groaned but presumably let Shorty push the medicine into his mouth and, resting on his shoulder, sipped some water. Then he collapsed back on his lair without a sound.

The hut took another blow. The stove sighed. From behind its closed door shot a string of sparks.

"It's a bit pissy," I warned Shorty.

I pulled Vasyl's sleeping-bag from the rucksack. Shorty lay down on his back next to me. He took out a cigarette, rolled it in his fingers and then crawled towards the stove. He lit it up.

We smoked, taking turns every few puffs. When there was hardly anything left, he said to Kostek:

"Finish it. Wake me in two hours."

Kostek took the cigarette-end and said he would wake him even in three hours as he didn't feel like sleeping. I heard him open the stove door and struggle with an awkward plank.

I didn't dream. Goosy moaned on his bed, and the wind outside tore scraps of clouds and flung them at the moon. A restless night. The darkness wailed and whistled, stopped and started again. Too many noises. I sped through the black air. Momentary awakenings had a taste of sickness, or something nasty, like hang-overed nights, when the ceilings come crashing down on one's head, covering the body with a repulsive weight of concrete. I was trying to curl up and become a whirl of muscle and thought, and a tiny point vanishing in the vastness of an empty sky. It worked. But not for long. I would return, back at the stove, and had to open my eyes to check where I was. Maybe I was hoping for something, the way one hopes after some nasty deed to wake up somewhere else with the world tidied up, perhaps even younger, like a record played from the beginning. All the broken bits swept away, the puke wiped up, vodka back in the bottles and the whole episode returned to the mind, stored in its most secret compartments.

Shorty lay on his back and snored. Sometimes I thought it was me who snored, that it was me who was asleep. From time to time Kostek opened the stove and fed the fire. His formless shadow was a massive red hue. I had no idea what time it was. The night had no end. It spilled in every direction, rising from its banks, it was too scary to think how far it reached. It was as if we were to remain inside it for ever. It was hard to imagine there were other things going on in the world, that other people moved, walked down the brightly lit streets, wanting to eat, to drink, to fuck. Unbelievable. It was too much for my poor little head; the laws that governed this show were too complex. The stove door made a high-pitched jarring noise. The hut creaked. No trace of that nervous music suitable for this entertaining time of night.

Midnight, maybe past midnight. God knows what day of the week. Maybe Saturday. All the dodgy bars in the land were full of wall-pissers in suits and shaking tits and bums while we were stuck with one corpse, one crazed fucker and a not-so-bright future. I could do nothing. All I could think about was the rest of the world. My head span. It made me sleep, and it woke me.

We were too inert in that sarcophagus. If there is a Judgement Day all the resurrectees will have gone mad with waiting.

I asked Shorty if he was asleep.

"Sure I am. What else is there to do?"

"Me too. I fancy a smoke, though."

"There are two left."

"We can have one then."

"We can. We'll run out soon anyway."

He twisted inside his sleeping-bag and struck a match, his half-clenched hand emerging from the darkness pink, like a body-lamp, a lantern made of skin. He let out the smoke and fell on his back.

"Hey, you. What have you done with that cigarette-end?"

After a long while Kostek realised the question was for him.

"Me? Chucked it out. What else?"

"Find it and put it somewhere safe."

The cigarette was burning fast. We were heading back towards inertia.

"Give him some," said Shorty.

I stretched my hand into the darkness. His was cold and sweaty. He stumbled on something returning to his place. His presence became strangely suffocating. I felt he was growing scared. I should have gone after him and killed him. If he needed events he certainly wouldn't have anything against that. He shouldn't have. We would be somewhere else now, all in good health and excellent moods, thinking about something silly and useful, and the memory of him would have vanished as radically as he turned up among us. "Kostek? I've no idea. He must have gone to this Portugal of his." That's what I would be telling everyone, and everyone would have believed me. Or not, but it's all the same.

"I think it's snowing," he said from his seat under the window.

"Fun for kids," answered Shorty.

I lay for a bit and then got up.

"I'll go and see."

The blizzard wrapped itself around me like a cold, wet rug. The corridor was white with snow. Coming back into the room, my hand led me along the wall.

"It *is* snowing," I said. "Snowing like hell."

"It'll cover our tracks," said Kostek.

I took my boots off and got back into my sleeping-bag.

"You can sleep now," said Shorty to Kostek.

They swapped places. The window was now as dark as the wall, and Shorty's silhouette dissolved without trace. Crumbs of light spilled from the stove. Bed springs squeaked under Goosy. His breathing sounded like a drunken wheeze. He slept the second night running. Back at home he never had enough sleep. He was getting up early, going to bed late. There were no phones here, all the wires cut.

We continued our journey while asleep. One could believe things were sorting themselves out. And when we were far away, when the white darkness overwhelmed us from all sides and her hand slipped under the hut and flung it over the mountain-tops, when we finally felt safe, there was a crash in the corridor, the door swung open and in the doorway appeared a man, his figure barely lighter than the twilight, which made him look like a spectre.

"Just as I thought," he said and shook the snow off like a dog. "Managed just in time. Half an hour and everything will be covered. The snow's almost knee deep now."

He stepped over our bodies, squatted by the stove and undid his jacket. We didn't say a word. One gets used to things. A bit of snow, some freezing cold, night, and a ghost by your bedside is no surprise.

Shorty told him our story in five words and asked about

cigarettes. When we all got a whole one each, Vasyl Bandurko told us his. How he got to that road, which was white, smooth and slippery, and how in the middle of nowhere he stopped a long-nosed lorry loaded up to the sky with fir trunks. They took him in without asking; among the three hobos the atmosphere reeked of carnival, God knows if that included the driver. They dragged themselves through villages and hairpin bends until they got where they said they were going and no further, only to the side track, and to the normal station was four kilometres. So he got off, they laughed when he offered them money, and he found himself in the middle of a human settlement of five houses and a kiosk. First he went to the bar to stuff his face. He had proper food, washed it down with beer and vodka, and he felt that was really what he was after. Deeply satisfied, smiling, sleepy despite two coffees, he strolled to the coach stop to check when something would take him back. The rest of the time he spent with the beer. The coach didn't take him all the way, but he made the rest of it on foot, through the night, and even when it started snowing he could still see. He spotted our tracks, turned off the road and there he was with cigarettes, a massive loaf of bread, three tins, coffee bought out of habit and vodka bought for courage – after all, he was scared shitless.

That's how he told us his story, and we didn't ask questions. We were quite happy with the cigarettes. And the corned beef, cold and greasy, in thick slabs on soft bread. Anyway, there was no one to ask. He sat by the stove, hugged his knees and fell asleep like a fagged-out embryo in the belly of the night.

Chapter 34

"Hot, very hot," repeated Vasyl while Shorty broke, one by one, boards lined up against the wall. He dozed off at dawn, and the fire died. The light was grey. Outside, the snow moved in horizontal lines, nothing like the waltzing snowflakes in kids' cartoons. I stood by the window trying to see something. In vain. Within the first ten metres there was nothing worth seeing, and beyond there was just nothing.

Kostek lay on the floor. Maybe asleep, maybe not. His eyes were closed. The fire boomed inside the metal barrel. Shorty went outside to bring in some snow. Bandurko stood over Goosy, looking now at his forehead, now at his own hand, probably surprised he didn't burn himself.

"He's in a bad way," he said.

"This we know, chief," I said, pissed off he was souring my mood over morning coffee. "And we ain't in peak condition either."

Shorty returned with full buckets, put them on the stove and said:

"Fucking boot's come unstuck. Must be from the heat. I kept my feet by the stove. I didn't feel a thing."

He was getting a bit verbose, I thought. He swung his foot, and the sole flapped sadly. Not a great start to a day. And Goosy was beginning to wake up. He simply threw his cover off and dropped his feet off the bed. His eyes were sealed with fever. He was rubbing his face, white, dirty with tufts of hair. Then, staring at the stove, he asked: "What's this?"

"A quarry. Closed," answered Shorty.

"The church was closed too. Give us something to drink."

He got a mug of warm water, downed it and fell back on the bed. He was lying and panting.

Yep, we were all slowly growing alike. I looked at their faces.

They could belong to any of the wineskins from Warsaw East, swollen, dough-like, with a greasy sheen, lips drawn with a cadaverous tint. Their eyes reflected only snow and grey light, murky like the water we drank. Day wasn't much different from night. We were making breakfast. Each of us took a slice, then a bite, swallowed it and waited for a swill of coffee, mouth twisting and hot. It didn't even boil; we sipped it, sieving grinds through our teeth. Goosy didn't want anything. Not even a cigarette, while we puffed on one after the other, as if trying to hide in the smoke, wrap ourselves in it or fill our mouths with it, so we didn't have to talk. I drank my share and went out. The mountains were invisible. We could be anywhere. The blizzard veiled the whole world; the snow attacked my face, blinding me. I hid behind the wall. If there was a sky above, its swollen belly burst open, releasing that barely tactile, tremulous chaos with which it was filled. The blue sky is an illusion. Up above roared and boomed. It was all those trees bent to the ground by the wind, strained and patient. It was impossible to say which way the wind blew. At the bottom of our funnel the air just whirled, chased its own tail, struck at the walls, looking for a way out. At times it seemed to me I was seeing black tree trunks, a palisade surrounding the cliff's edge, but the wind kept covering it, dragging and scattering those bandages, lint, nappies and sheets, all torn. I couldn't think of it in any other way. The air stank of carbolic acid and Lysol; the freezing cold made me think of cleaning infinitely long, stony corridors. I flicked my cigarette butt; the tiny red crumb exploded and vanished.

I came back into the middle of silence. Their movements were slow and heavy. Shorty raised a bottle to his mouth as if it contained mercury. Carefully, his lower lip extended forward, waiting for the thickened liquid to roll on to it; perhaps he was afraid it may be too hot. Kostek sat. The red stain of the sleeping-bag spilled all over the floor, cooling down. Bandurko crouched at the edge of the bed, rocking lightly. Shorty stretched out towards him, his hand holding the bottle. He shook his head, so I took over. I didn't feel like drinking either but was worried that Shorty's arm would weaken, or maybe wanted inertia to reign supreme again. Unfinished gestures disturbed the indifference that protected body and soul from the rough passage of time. I took a swig. It tasted like rain with wind in November. It rolled down the gullet cold and stayed cold.

"Give us the top," I said to Shorty. He threw it to me. It bent in my hand as I caught it. I stood the bottle next to my rucksack. It was true: I didn't feel like drinking.

"What a fucking mess," mumbled Vasyl rocking to and fro. "We should have put him on our backs and carried him somewhere."

"I've already carried him," said Shorty. "It's your turn now. That is, yours and our friend's there. You've had a holiday. You're rested."

Vasyl got up, walked to the stove, turned back, stumbled on the bed and looked at his watch.

"Twenty-past eight. Kostek, listen, we have to make a decision. He can't just lie like this. We'll be snowed under in a minute, it's window-high now . . ."

"It's only a snowdrift, Bandurko. Stop panicking. It's blowing from round the corner," said Shorty.

"Same shit. We have to do something."

"Who are you talking to? Him? He isn't that outgoing now. He's trying to break loose himself." Shorty spoke with a cigarette in his mouth, legs stretched in front of him. Vodka must have washed over his hardware, cleaned the contacts, and sparks began to hop all over the wiring. "But he won't," he finished, stone-faced.

Bandurko stooped over Goosy.

"Can you move? Can you get up?"

"Leave him alone. We brought him here. Brought him – do you understand?"

"Goosy, can you?" He was shaking him by the shoulder, but all he gained was that the corpse turned his back on him.

"I want to sleep . . . let me. I'm OK like this . . ."

"Hot and sweaty . . ."

"But certainly a kilo or two lighter since yesterday. He has to be carried, I'm telling you."

Bandurko walked in tight circles, knocking about like a pinball. Then he went out and after a while returned, white and red-cheeked.

"It's hard going even empty-handed." He stopped by Kostek. "What shall we do?"

The other one sat motionless, back pressed against the wall, hadn't moved an inch since he woke up, and the stood-up collar made his face look even thinner. He didn't even raise his eyes. "We have to wait until it stops."

"And?"

"And nothing. Just wait."

"How long? A day? Two, three? It'll be too late, man . . ."

"Our friend plays for time, but he doesn't know how much of the stuff he's got. Vasyl, since you're there, pass the bottle."

Bandurko picked up the bottle, took a swig, shook like a cat and brought the vodka to the window.

"To springtime," toasted Shorty. "Let's just stay here. We'll sit and talk, tell stories, and when the spring comes we shall go among the people and be merry. Maypole's practically ready."

It was actually fun to watch this fucking mess grow. Yes, our faces began to look the same. I sat by the door, and I couldn't find a place for myself, couldn't think and couldn't be bothered. I was happy we had cigarettes. Slowly, the room got warmer, the window-panes grew misty. On the barrel stove danced a mug. We were a submarine crew, and as long as we had air I didn't give a toss if we ever surfaced. I only hoped that a great white sea would eventually throw us ashore somewhere in a foreign country. We'd change our names, and the rest would take care of itself. Naturally. That was what I could think and that was good. To stay still, like a nail in the wall until the house and its walls come down, stay still and do nothing. Just like sitting on a park bench, or on the bus going round from terminal to terminal and watching the world unroll like some carpet panorama, no need to do anything, everything happens by itself, barely brushing against the skin, the blood slowly grows old and the images barely touch the eye, passing by, like bus stops, line H, Zieleniecka Street, Francuska, the bridge, the War Museum, Marszalkowska and all the way up to Okęcie, where planes take off, leaving behind them a hollow rumble cascading over the green fields, the sky swallows them up and nobody knows what happens to them next. We should have stayed on our buses so that we didn't have to miss them now, travelling in some cold phantoms of transport. Line H, C, bus number 133, bridges and flyovers, each with its own panorama rolling out in the distance, detailed, miniaturised, with tiny flags pinned into them like on army maps, tiny pennons the colour of blood, in all the colours seen by the human eye, faith, hope, love the colourful ludo pieces moved along the grey canyons of streets, across the boards of parks, playing a game with built-in second chance. We should not have got off that bus or torn down the paper decorations. It was just a child's curiosity. The other side showed nothing. Total zero. Like the belly of a teddy bear – sawdust.

"I'm going," said Vasyl.

"Where?" Shorty licked his lips as if he liked it. I took the bottle from him.

"Wherever. To a village somewhere, I don't know. If we can't carry him, we have to transport him. To a village . . ."

"And have you heard about Potemkin? Not about the battleship, the man?"

"It shouldn't be more than ten kilometres. The main thing's to get to the road and then either left or right. There are villages. I know, I passed that way yesterday. Going the other way, just before the border, there's something too. The map . . . I'll take someone with horses. If you pay a peasant he'll come. Nine o'clock. I should be done by three."

The words were falling out of him like dry peas out of a pod. They were bouncing on the floor, rolling off and dying out when he stopped speaking, growing still, each stuck in some gap. A light hysteria against our melancholy. Kostek moved and unstuck his back from the wall. All gestures were broken off, all conversations unfinished, tongues mixed, in depots rain washed over buses, for I could swear it was raining down there, and people looked like wet cutouts or old fifty zlotys notes. Featuring whom? The miner was on five hundred, woman on a twenty. Maybe steelworker, maybe fisherman, in a big hood, just right for the rain.

"Yep, that's the only way. Ten kilometres, seventy kilos. We can hardly stand up as it is. I've got the money, a peasant will come if we pay him, I know peasants . . ."

"Hey, Bandurko. I see you fancy a troika, eh? Or a sleigh ride? Fun in the snow? How about some music? Have we been through all that fucking conspiracy only to go marching with an orchestra now? One peasant with a sleigh comes here while the other goes to the nearest law-enforcing agency, right? Both cash in half a grand each and drink our health for three days. Vasyl . . ."

He got to Shorty in two bounds and snatched the bottle from his hand.

"Stop drinking. We have to talk."

"I see no conflict of interest here . . ."

Bandurko sat on the edge of the bed, the bottle hanging forgotten in his hand, like in a park when waiting until the alley empties of intruders.

"As for myself, you can go, poor soul, wherever your eyes take you. I'll stay here and keep warm, making my mind up if I have business or time to wait for you. And please give me back the magic vessel if you're not partaking of its content . . ."

A massive rumble rolled over our heads. The wind stripped the roof of the loose sheets of eternit roofing. The ceiling was raining dust. The hut wailed and whistled like something live. We were by ourselves and yet we weren't. Perhaps that flutter and motion protected us from madness? In silence, we would have been at each others' throats, just to break it.

"All right," said Bandurko and got up. God knows what it was supposed to mean, for the bottle remained on the floor. He started pottering about the room, doing up his jacket, finding things – hat, scarf, gloves – pulling out his wallet, looking inside. Then he took out a brand-new packet of Marlboro and threw it on the bed, checked if everything was laced up, fastened, if something didn't hang loose, shirt out of his trousers or flesh out of his clothes. I would do my best to delay going out too. None of the rest moved. We were busy with our thoughts. Shorty thought about the bottle, I about cigarettes, Goosy about being left in peace.

"All right," said Bandurko. "I should be back by afternoon. You do what you want."

He smoothed his jacket. I expected a click of heels, but he simply turned round and moved towards the door, head hung low. When he was a step away and stretched his hand for the handle, Kostek leaped to his feet, so fast, as if all that time he was gathering strength for it. He stood in the doorway, hands fastened on the doorframe.

"You're not going anywhere. Shorty was right about . . . that orchestra. And about the rest too. They'll be here in a flash. We have to lie low for two, three days . . ."

Vasyl grabbed Kostek's hand, trying to pull it away from the doorframe. They struggled for a while. Finally Bandurko, pushed on the chest, reeled back.

"Eh, you!" Shorty headed for the door. He moved Vasyl out of his way, as if he were drawing a curtain.

"You! You've manhandled my school friend. If need be I can slap him myself, but you keep your hands to yourself."

Kostek still stood by the door.

"He'll go nowhere. You know yourself he can't. It's mad."

"But it isn't you who'll stop him. Get the fuck out of my way. By the window."

He spoke slowly, sort of pleadingly; in fact, he might as well have been joking. Kostek didn't budge, so Shorty took him by the lapels, turned his big body and sent the rag doll across the room. Vasyl just managed to get out of harm's way, and the stove wobbled as Kostek Górka crashed against the wall and slid down to one knee.

"And you'd better stay put," said Shorty and squatted by the stove's door. He put in a few pieces of wood. Vasyl bolted for the door. Shorty didn't even turn his head.

"Go and bring something. The fire's dying."

I took the axe and stepped into the cold of the corridor. At the exit I saw Bandurko's track through a small snowdrift. The next-door room had hardly anything left in it. I moved on to find something fireworthy.

The axed boards cracked lengthways and all it took was a precise knock and they split along the nails. They fell off by themselves. Through the broken half of the window the snow came in. I collected an armful and went back. Shorty lay on the floor face down, trying to get up. He looked like a slow-motion swimmer. I let go of the wood but didn't really know what to do next. Shorty got up on all fours and turned his head as if shaking off a weight.

I helped him to his feet and sat him on the edge of the bed. He moaned and touched the back of his head. His fingers had blood on them.

"With this . . . I'll put it aside, to dry it for kindling later."

It was not thick; after all, it snapped in half. It lay on the floor, together with the other planks ready for burning. I examined his skull. Nothing serious. Cut skin and a growing bump.

I left him and went outside. He must have been running, for the holes in the snow were big and spaced. They were quickly filling up. Shorty joined me, leaned on my shoulder and stared into the white madness. It was leaping up and floating down, the moving, effervescent wall. It seemed it would repulse anyone who'd dare enter it.

"We have to go after them," he said. He let go of me and felt for the wall. I nodded.

The trail kept disappearing. I walked practically blind. After a while the ground tilted up, we entered the wood and visibility cleared a little. Where the trees grew sparsely the snow formed around them in crescent snowdrifts, resembling blades of some exotic weapon. I was trying to see something – there was nothing. The sky was coming down on earth, crashing the tree-tops. I couldn't hear myself breathe. I felt the air entering my lungs and leaving them hot and hard but couldn't hear it. I wanted to move fast. How much advantage did they have? Five, ten minutes? Three, four hundred metres? But so what? I couldn't see further than a couple of paces. I walked with my eyes glued to their trail. Up and down. I had a feeling I was going round in circles, as if in complete darkness when the hands grope for a wall or a piece of furniture. The ground levelled out. I felt the pain in legs and lungs subside. I stopped. Into my head wandered in a thought about that packet of cigarettes. Just sit down and have a smoke. I moved on. The trail was giving no clues. It simply was leading further into the white deeps. I could try to move faster. So could they. I thought I might catch up with them on a slope. It turned out I didn't. On my left the trees disappeared. The snow was coming now from under the ground. The whirl threw up white billows like thick steam from under the lid. The trail came right to the edge, the snow was disturbed, heavily trampled. No one in sight. I circled the spot, didn't find anything. I returned to the edge. I was too scared to get too close. It was difficult to tell firm ground from white illusion.

I went back. I told Shorty. We stopped at the foot of the overhang.

"We have to climb up there," he said.

It was steep, but the boulders and felled tree trunks gave support. Spaced apart, we scrambled up in zigzags, checking everything with our eyes, from time to time looking at each other through the blizzard, reading our silent gestures. When I lost sight of our point of departure, I heard Shorty's whistle, way to the left and higher up. Soft scree was giving in under my feet as, splayed like a toad, I crawled towards the spot.

It was Bandurko's green jacket. He was lying on his stomach, head down. His legs, trying to catch up with him, curled up under him in a funny way. We turned him gently on his back. He was soft and heavy. His face was covered by a mask of earth and blood. We took him under the arms and began a controlled slide. It wasn't too bad; the weight did the job. All we had to watch out for were boulders. At the foot, Shorty took Bandurko's top end and I carried his legs.

We laid him by the stove. I washed his face. A trickle of blood flowed from under his scalp.

"He's breathing," said Shorty. "Faintly, but he is."

He started undoing Vasyl's jacket to check his heart. He brought his hand in front of my face. The fingers were red. He took the bayonet and cut through all the stuff Vasyl was wearing. There was a wound, a long, narrow wound ceaselessly pumping blood. The whole of his chest and stomach were red. We covered him with clothes and a sleeping-bag. His eyes were half-closed, still. I bent over him and called his name. His breath became wheezy. Maybe he heard me, maybe not, but he wanted to say something, for his lips moved. I put my ear to his mouth. Hissing and whistling, he kept repeating, "I told him . . . I told him . . ." My ear tickled. On his lips appeared red, transparent bubbles, just like soap bubbles. For a moment I expected them to take off and float majestically towards the open window only to vanish, to be killed by the pricks of the sun's rays.

"I told him . . ."

Once more we moved uphill, past the scree, clay, tree trunks and boulders. Higher up, there was one wall of rocky slabs, cut through with vertical gaps, and higher still, way up, stuck out the tongue of the overhang, like a crest of a frozen wave. We passed grey slabs of sandstone, holding on to them, looking into every crevice like into windows in a huge wall. We found him but couldn't reach him. We needed to traverse to the other side of the wall, into the shadow of the overhang. There, between the slope that had come off and the hanging trap, there was a kind of corridor – long, cold and treacherous. But we made it.

Bad luck. He had fallen head first. Knocked himself into the crack like a well-fitted wedge. We pulled out his lifeless body with great difficulty. Shorty knelt down, searched his pockets and took all his papers. Then we dragged him to the very foot of the wall, right under the overhang.

"In spring the whole fucking thing will come down," said Shorty, and we started walking downhill.

Goosy lay on his bed, twitching and muttering. We dragged Vasyl out into the corridor. Shorty performed the same ritual as with the other one – took all the documents and threw the lot into the stove. He stood waiting for them to burn. We spread out Kostek's sleeping-bag: red, well made, with good metal zip; exactly what was needed.

God knows how long it took us, but eventually we got Vasyl Bandurko up on to the hill. They lay next to each other, almost touching. Shorty picked up a handful from the ground and cast it. But it was only snow. His face was still and black and his eyes practically unseeing from exhaustion.

"Let's bury them a bit," I said, unconvinced. Shorty shook his head and pointed up.

"We'd better get out of here quick."

Apart from the wind there was only a rattle of pebbles rolling off the slope.

Down at the hut we searched their stuff once more. The map, train tickets, newspaper cutouts, a notebook – all went into the stove. The rest was packed into the rucksacks.

"I don't want to go back there," I said.

"OK," said Shorty. He threw both rucksacks over his shoulder and went out.

We left at about two. Goosy travelled in comfort. Our stove stood on a sheet of thin metal. We bent the corners, cut the front edge with the axe and tied both with a piece of rusty wire. And we had a toboggan. Shorty had to climb up there for the last time to cut the straps off the sacks. Goosy moaned a bit, but in the end let us wrap him in together with the sleeping-bags. We harnessed ourselves like huskies and moved off. Shorty's boot got completely unstuck. He rummaged his pockets for a piece of string, but he only found the snakeskin, but enough to tie the sole twice over and make a knot. We made stops every twenty paces. We shared the rest of the vodka, eating snow. At the spot where I had fancied a smoke earlier I had one. We didn't talk. Goosy did. We circumvented the edge of the precipice through the bushes. Our toboggan tipped over. We put it right and wiped the snow off Goosy's face. He didn't like it, so we told him to shut his gob. Shorty pointed out the snow whirl rising from beyond the edge. "See that?" I did, but told him I didn't and to leave me in peace.

Then we got on to the slope and the going was easier. We had plenty of time. I was desperately trying to remember a story, a trifle from the past, something I could use as a relief, a lump of snow under the tongue. But my memory was empty, windswept, and the place where all those things one is supposed to treasure and remember was white, turbid and cold. A symmetrical, monotone whirl kept sucking up people, years, things, and carried them somewhere into the nonexistent, ripped-up heavens from where rough, irregular crumbs rained on our footprints, which were to disappear any moment now.